Kathryn ... ...acist but soon re... ...dwriting wasn't for her. In 2011, backed by her family, she left the world of pharmaceutical science to begin life as a self-employed writer.

She lives with two teenage boys and a husband who asks every Valentine's Day whether he has to bother buying a card again this year (yes, he does) so the romance in her life is all in her head.

kathrynfreeman.co.uk

twitter.com/KathrynFreeman1
facebook.com/kathrynfreeman

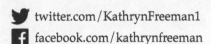

THE BEACH READS BOOK CLUB

KATHRYN FREEMAN

One More Chapter
a division of HarperCollins*Publishers*
1 London Bridge Street
London SE1 9GF
www.harpercollins.co.uk
HarperCollins*Publishers*
1st Floor, Watermarque Building, Ringsend Road
Dublin 4, Ireland

This paperback edition 2021
First published in Great Britain in ebook format
by HarperCollins*Publishers* 2021

A catalogue record of this book is available from the British Library

ISBN: 978-0-00-846228-4

Printed and bound in the UK using 100% Renewable Electricity
by CPI Group (UK) Ltd

This is one for all bookworms (and butterflies), book clubs and book club members, book bloggers and book readers.

And it's also for all fans of romcoms, chicklit, romance and happy ever afters. Life would be a duller place without them.

Chapter One

The moment Lottie carefully opened the door of the library reading room and slipped inside, she had a flashback to her school days. Once again she was sneaking in late, hoping the teacher wouldn't notice. Once again, she hadn't done her flipping homework. Eve's gaze zeroed in on her, and Lottie sighed.

Yep, and once again, the teacher had it in for her.

'Sorry.' Lottie shot Eve, who ran the book club with military precision, an apologetic smile. 'What did I miss?'

'The first fifteen minutes of discussion.' Eve gave her a frosty look. 'Perhaps you'd like to tell the group what your favourite part of the book was?'

'Err, that's a good question.' Shit. Blagging was hard when she couldn't even remember the title of the bloody thing.

Eve raised a dark eyebrow. 'It's the same question we ask every month.'

Okay, she wasn't at school. She was a twenty-seven-year-old trained electrician who ran her own business. She was here not because she had to be but because she'd chosen to be. Yet since joining Eve's book club, the fun had slowly been sucked out of the idea. Now when Eve asked a question, she felt the same creeping dread she had when the teacher had started picking on her.

As Lottie parked her bum on the spare seat and struggled with how to reply, Gira leant across and whispered, 'Tell her the best bit was the humour.'

'Err, wasn't it about a serial killer?'

Eve cleared her throat. 'Are you answering the question, or is Gira?'

Oh, bugger it. This was the second month on the trot she'd failed to pick up the nominated book. Sure, it said something about how busy she was, how knackered when she got home, but it also said something about the choice of book. 'Confession time, I haven't read it. Whatever it was.'

Eve narrowed her eyes. 'You haven't read *My Sister, The Serial Killer*? Like you didn't read *Big Sky* last month?'

'No. I'm really sorry, but no.' Lottie felt all the eyes of the book club members turn to face her. 'The thing is, the books that are selected, brilliant though I know they must be, judging from the reviews, they're quite … heavy. They take time and a fair bit of concentration to read them.'

'I can see how concentrating might be difficult for you.'

Laughter echoed around the room. Usually Lottie was up for having the piss taken out of her, but Eve had touched a nerve still raw from the endless prodding and rubbing her teachers had given it during her school years. 'Why do you say that?'

'Come on, Lottie.' Eve gave her a small smile. 'You're always talking. It must be hard to focus when so much of your brain power is used for speech.'

Lottie's temper, rarely seen, started to wriggle out of its burrow. 'Isn't that what being in a club is supposed to be about? Talking to each other?'

'About the books, yes.'

Lottie drew in a breath, her gaze bouncing round the room. All faces she knew, yet behind them, people she had no clue about. This felt less like the club she'd hoped for and more like a stuffy meeting. 'Shouldn't we be able to talk about things outside books, too? Get to know each other a bit rather than stick to a rigid set of questions? And hey, maybe sometimes we could throw in a suggestion of a book to read, rather than following a regimented list? Include a few lighter, fun reads, like a bit of Jilly Cooper?'

Silence. If a pin had dropped, Lottie would definitely have heard it.

Feeling awkward, she tried to smile. 'Okay, judging by your expressions, maybe not. In fact, maybe the best thing for all of us is if I stop interfering with your meeting and leave you guys to it.'

It might have been a cool exit, if she'd not tripped over the chair in her desperation to get out.

She was halfway down the corridor when she heard her name being called. She turned to see Gira and ... God, how bad was it that she couldn't even remember the other woman's name?

'What you said.' Gira gave her a hesitant smile. 'Heidi and I, we totally agree with you.'

'Jilly Cooper's one of my favourites.' The woman Lottie now realised was Heidi started to laugh. 'You've got no idea how many times I wanted to suggest we read a big, sexy rom com for a change. I used to read them all the time, but then Eve set up the book club. Don't get me wrong, it's been great, I've read authors I've not come across before and books I'd never have tried, but…'

When she trailed off, Lottie smiled. 'But you miss the rom coms.'

Heidi groaned. 'I miss the fun. And the sexy bits. And God, the love story. That feeling of your heart being twisted, but then everything working out in the end. It's such a high. Like I imagine you can get from cocaine, only this is cheaper and without the damage.' Clearly horrified by what she'd just said, she placed a hand over her mouth. 'This is why my daughters say I shouldn't be allowed out on my own. Sorry, we'll let you go. We just wanted you to know you weren't the only one wishing the next book was a Jilly Cooper.'

But why shouldn't it be?

The thought pinged into Lottie's head as she made her way back across the car park. Just because Eve's book club wasn't right for her, didn't mean she should give up on the idea of a book club. She'd seen how they were meant to work,

4

how good they could be. In fact, seeing one in action was the whole reason she'd got into reading. She'd hated it when she'd been at school, much as she'd hated school itself. But then, working as a waitress in a coffee shop while she figured out what to do with her life, she'd witnessed her first book club meeting. Seeing the look on their faces, the excitement, the delight when they'd only been talking about books … it had made her wonder if she'd been missing out. Then she'd read one of their recommendations. After that, she'd been hooked, going on to devour all the books she could get her hands on: the book club reads, those lent to her by friends, borrowed from the library, or just sat on the bookshelf at home. She'd especially loved her mum's rom coms.

'Real guys don't walk around with roses between their teeth,' her brother had mocked. 'And life isn't full of sappy endings.'

'If you think that's what romance books are all about, you've clearly never read one,' her mum had countered. 'They're about hope, about joy. About handling adversity and coming through the other side stronger. Yes, they're also about love, the most powerful emotion you'll ever experience.'

It had shut her brother up. And Lottie had kept on reading. She'd also kept up with the book club, wangling permission to sit down with them for those precious two hours a month. The other members had been older, but sharing that common interest had made it easy to talk to them, and not just about books. It kept her going through

5

days when she'd doubted herself. Lifted her when the path ahead had seemed so uncertain.

Sadly, the lady who ran the club had moved away a few years later and the group disbanded. Lottie missed the connection, but by then her life had picked up and she was busy learning a trade. And falling in love.

Fast forward a few years and she'd seen the flyer for Eve's book club. Keen to get back into reading again, to rediscover that joy, she'd joined.

Yet as the months had passed, Eve's schoolmistress manner had chipped away at any joy she'd found, and the serious, heavy nature of the chosen books had made reading feel like a chore again.

She wasn't going to give up on it again though, no way.

Nor was she going to give up on sharing the love of books, of reading, with other like-minded souls.

She just needed to find another book club, one that included books more aligned to her own taste.

And if she couldn't, well, maybe she'd set up her own.

———————

A few days later, Lottie parked up outside Books by the Bay, a dream of an old shop whose every nook and cranny was filled with books, new and second-hand. The large premises also boasted a café, nestled in one of the large bay windows that overlooked the beach. A place to sit and ponder your next purchase, or get stuck into your newest acquisition. Or maybe to sneakily retrieve the book you'd started the day before, and carry on reading it while enjoying a cheeky cappuccino. Yep, she'd done that a few times when money had been tight.

All in all, it was a magical place for bookworms, only slightly marred by the presence of a new owner. Larry had been genial, always greeting his customers with a broad smile, happy to talk about anything and everything.

Matthew Steele, whom she'd admittedly only met briefly when she'd bought *My Sister, The Serial Killer*, seemed a lot more reserved. One hell of a lot better looking though, which was a bonus on rainy days when the usually spectacular view across the Solent was more on the grim side, as it was today. February wasn't the best time of year to be by the coast.

As she was early, instead of heading straight for the café, Lottie strode up to the counter, clutching the book she'd bought but never opened. Matthew, busy looking through some file, immediately looked up. Once again he was wearing a dark suit – this time charcoal grey, with a white shirt and spotted blue and red tie. Smart, definitely, the way it hugged his broad shoulders suggesting it wasn't run of the mill M&S. And wow, the race of her pulse was proof he looked good in it. Yet there was something about the formality of it that didn't sit right with her.

He sold books, for goodness' sake. Not office equipment/cars/double glazing but *books*. Items that could fascinate, thrill or comfort. Could scare you to death or make you laugh out loud. None of that said suit, even if the wearer looked hot in it.

'Hi.'

He gave her the same polite smile he had last time. 'Can I help?'

And yep, just like last time, the smooth, deep timbre of his voice caused a weird flutter in her stomach. Ignoring it, she placed the book on the counter. 'I'd like to return this. I bought it a few weeks ago to read for a book club, but I didn't get round to opening it, and now I've left the club, so … well, I no longer need it.'

'I see.'

He picked up the book; long fingers, neat nails. Kind of a sexy hand, really. And that watch. It wasn't like the fake Rolexes she'd seen, the ones sold from the side of the road near city tourist attractions.

'You have no desire to read about a Nigerian woman whose sister has an unfortunate habit of killing her boyfriends?'

At his dry tone, she dragged her gaze away from the eye-wateringly expensive watch. 'It's more that there are other books I'd like to read instead. Happier books.'

His deep brown eyes finally met hers, and Lottie felt that flutter again. God, they really were eyes to get lost in. Eyes that surely had the power to envelop, warm the recipient of their dark gaze to the core, if only the owner allowed them. 'Books you might buy from this shop?'

Lottie searched his face. Was he teasing, or trying to make a point? 'I might, if the shop had a decent refund policy.'

'And by decent, you mean…?'

Lottie flashed her most charming smile. 'If the policy gave a full refund on an unread book that was definitely purchased from you, though the owner can't actually prove it because she's lost her receipt. She'd say the dog ate it, if it didn't sound so lame, though in this case there is a dog and he's not always the best behaved, so it could very well be the truth.'

Was that a twitch of his lips? She couldn't be sure and staring at them any longer wasn't a good idea, not if she didn't want to get tongue-tied, because they had one heck of a sensuous curve to them. Together with the high cheekbones, the deep-set eyes, the short cropped dark hair … yep, it was quite a face.

She watched as he pushed some buttons on the till. Then swore and pushed some more. 'You look like me on a pinball machine. Next you'll be kicking it.'

He gave her a mild look. 'I'm aiming for a less aggressive approach.'

'Well, as long as you know the right buttons to press…'

He shook his head, emitting a sharp laugh. 'Not always a strong point.' Finally the till drawer opened and he'd just plucked a ten-pound note out with those long, tapered fingers when he hesitated. 'Are you about to tell me you wanted the refund on your card?'

She was in serious danger of laughing. 'I wouldn't dare.'

He carefully placed the note and some coins onto the counter. 'That's how I like my customers, scared.'

Lottie couldn't tell whether he was joking or not. 'Well, thanks for, you know, the decent refund policy.' The bell on the door jingled and she turned to find Heidi strolling in, Gira a few paces behind her. She waved and pointed to the café before turning back to the owner. 'You'll be pleased to know I'm now going to spend the money on a mug of tea and a giant slice of cake.'

He nodded, and though he didn't say anything further, she wondered if the brown in his eyes had warmed, just a fraction.

———————————————

Matt watched the blonde with the vivid turquoise top and incredible pale eyes walk over to join her friends. He remembered her from when she'd come into the shop to buy the book, though he hadn't admitted it for fear of sounding either a) creepy or b) like he had so few customers he remembered them all. He liked to think he wasn't the former, and business was steady enough that he only remembered customers who were distinctive. Like blondes with curly hair and cool grey eyes that were a stunning contrast to her warm, vibrant smile.

From his pew at the cash desk, he saw her speak to Amy. Whatever she said, presumably an order for the tea and cake, his sister responded with a shy smile. Amy was about as far removed from a serial killer as it was possible to get. If he was clever enough to write a book longlisted for the Booker prize, he'd have to call it *My Sister, Who Won't Kill a Fly.*

Behind him he heard a crash, followed by his father's dulcet Midland tones. 'Which twit put that box there?'

With a sigh, Matt rose to his feet and walked round the corner to find the site of the latest disaster.

'The twit would be me.' He glanced at the books now spread across the floor, upended from their apparently unsafe perch in a box on the footstool.

'Don't know why you bother with all these damn books. Nobody's going to read them.'

'Possibly not.' Matt crouched down and started to pick them up, slotting them back into the box. 'But a bookshop isn't much of a shop without them.'

'Except then this would be a decent-sized café. Bloody sight more sensible use of a place on the beach.'

Matt had heard the argument before. In fact he'd been hearing nothing but that argument from his dad ever since he'd broached the idea of moving to the south coast and buying a bookshop. *Never make money from selling books. Nobody buys books now, it's all electronic. You're more of a fossil than I am.*

In the end he'd stopped arguing, but he hadn't stopped looking for the right place. Not just for himself, but for his dad and his sister, too. A fresh start for them all.

Except a fresh start didn't necessarily need a new place, it needed a new mindset. Something they were all still working on. Meanwhile, the shop, and the sprawling house with stunning Solent views he'd bought only a short walk away from it, would hopefully help.

The bell jingled again and Matt looked up at his dad. 'Do you want to serve while I clear up here?'

His father grunted. 'I told you when you bought the place. Do what you want, it's your money, but don't expect me to help.'

'I don't expect it.' Hoped for it, yeah, he did that most days. 'Just thought you might enjoy it now and again. Meet some of the locals.'

'I can do that down the pub.'

'And how many times have you gone there since we moved?'

His dad snorted. 'How many times have *you*?'

The retort stung. He could put the blame on being busy with the shop, but the fact was, in the evenings he'd chosen the easy route and stayed in, just like his dad had.

'Maybe we should all go out. Amy too.' He made a mental note to suggest it when they got home. Part of that new mindset. Rising to his feet, Matt unconsciously bent his back a little when he realised he was towering over his dad. Somehow over the last thirty-three years he'd grown to be well over six foot, and his dad had shrunk a little. 'I'll go and see to the customer. Don't worry about this lot, I'll sort them out later.'

He walked towards the front of the shop, knowing full well his dad would be crouching down and picking up the rest of the books. The old dad, the happily married one who'd smiled a lot, had disappeared a year ago when his mum had died. This recently widowed version was, understandably, quieter, angrier, the sadness he always carried around with him painful to watch. He was, at core though, still Matt's dad.

Once he'd sorted the customer out – *See, Dad,* he wanted to yell, *this woman has bought an actual book, for actual money* – Matt's eyes strayed once again to the curly-haired blonde. She was chatting with two ladies who looked at least twenty years older than her. He wondered what they had to talk about that elicited so much … passion, he supposed, was the word. The blonde in particular, with her hand movements, the animated expression, frequent bursts of laughter, looked so happy, like she was really enjoying herself. Matt suddenly found he was envious. When was the last time he'd felt joy?

Chapter Two

Lottie pushed aside her empty plate – the cake had been a bit of a disappointment, too dry, but not dry enough that she'd left any. 'Do you really think I should do this? Form a new book club?'

The thought sent a tingle down her spine – nerves? Excitement? Probably a bit of both. She wanted to do it, no doubt, but *could* she do it? *You've set up a business, you can manage a book club.* The thought settled her, though it didn't stop the damn insecurities and their incessant poking.

'Definitely,' Gira answered.

'Absolutely. And you've already got two members.' Heidi leant across the table. 'I've started reading the Jilly Cooper you mentioned, just in case.'

'Then let's do this.' Lottie clapped her hands together, the excitement winning, pushing past the nerves. 'God, I can't wait to stick my nose into a rom com again. I missed all that passion with a giggle sooooo much. It's been ages since I last read one.'

Gira looked at her questioningly. 'Because you've been focused on Eve's choices?'

'Partly, but even before I joined her book club I'd stopped reading them.' Memories flooded back, and Lottie felt the familiar ache in her chest. Less sharp now, it still hurt. 'I was in love with this guy, Henry, but then he got a job in California. We decided it was better to split, agreeing the distance and time difference would make it impossible.' Had Henry been The One, the love of her life, and she'd given up on him too easily? 'Straight after he left, I found I couldn't pick up a romance book without bursting into tears. It didn't take long before I missed reading, though. That's when I saw the advert for the library book club. I figured, what better way to help me forget my heart was broken than to meet up with like-minded book lovers and dive back into an imaginary world?'

Heidi smiled sympathetically. 'When I got divorced, I had a phase when I threw all my romance books out. I didn't want to read about happy ever afters. I told myself it was all sentimental poppycock and for a while I read nothing but thrillers.'

'Only thrillers?' Gira shuddered. 'I'd have been a basket case. I love to read in bed, just before I go to sleep.' Briefly a shadow crossed her face but then she seemed to shake it off. 'I can't do that with a thriller. Last time I tried, I had to drink chamomile tea, spray the room with lavender and check the doors were locked three times before I could relax enough to fall asleep.'

'Weirdly, my thriller fixation actually got kind of boring,' Heidi admitted. 'I found I was reading about a gruesome murder and turning the page not to see who'd done it, but whether the cute detective and the hot lawyer got it together.'

'Once a romance lover, always a romance lover.' Lottie put down the mug she'd been drinking from. Decorated with two rows of pretty coloured books, she wondered if it was the choice of the shy girl running the café or the serious new owner. 'Eve's book club was really good at the start. I did meet new people,' she grinned. 'Like you guys. And it helped me forget how miserable I was for a while. I also got to try authors I would never have thought of reading. Even the discipline of having to read was good for me, like an enforced down time. But as the months rolled on, work became busier and my down time more precious. I found I didn't want to spend the little free time I did have reading one of Eve's chosen books. And then having questions fired at me afterwards. I know this sounds awful, but it started to feel like homework, and God knows I was never good at that.'

Heidi hooted with laughter. 'Eve does have a headmistress vibe about her.'

While Heidi and Gira began to discuss what it was about the librarian that gave this vibe – her buttoned-up-to-the-collar blouses, the single strand of pearls – Lottie found herself glancing over Heidi's shoulder to the till area, and

Matthew. Her heart jumped when she caught him staring at them, his expression unreadable. She expected him to quickly look away but he surprised her by inclining his head in a brief nod. It could have said anything: *Yep, you caught me staring... Sorry...* Or it could even have been a dismissive gesture. Still, Lottie had a strange feeling he was silently applauding her for some reason.

The young dark-haired waitress came back to their table.

'Is there anything else I can get you?'

Lottie looked at her name badge. 'No, I think we're good, thanks, Amy. Just the bill when you're ready.' As she turned to walk away, some instinct had Lottie asking, 'Were the mugs your idea?'

The waitress shrugged, a slight flush to her cheeks. 'Kind of.'

Sensing she felt as if she'd been put on the spot, Lottie smiled. 'It's just we think they're lovely. Perfect for this place, and for bookworms like us.' She considered the young woman in front of her. 'We're going to start a book club and we're looking for members. Are you into books?'

'Not really. I mean, I read some at school.'

'Ah, okay. I just thought as you worked here, you might be.'

Amy's eyes darted towards Matthew, who appeared to be tidying up around the already very tidy till area. 'Books are more my brother's thing. He owns the shop.'

'Oh.' Lottie felt her jaw drop. It was hard to see any familial connection between the tall, broad-shouldered, brooding owner and this slight, shy, much younger woman.

'That sounds pretty brave, working for your brother. I love mine to death, but no way would I want to work for him, which is probably a good thing, considering he lives in Australia now.'

A small smile tugged at Amy's mouth. 'Matt's okay.'

Lottie glanced at the brother, who was now straightening the bookmarks. 'I'm sensing he's a bit of a neat freak?' Amy let out an unexpected giggle that changed her face from quietly pretty to full-on attractive. The sound caused Matthew to look over at them. 'Oops, I hope I haven't got you in trouble.'

She shook her head. 'Nah, he doesn't shout.' She flashed Lottie a smile. 'He just sorts everything out the way he wants it after I go home.'

When Amy left, Heidi gave Lottie an appraising look, one that had Lottie hoping desperately she wasn't blushing. Thankfully, instead of asking the question that was written across her face – *Why the interest in the new owner?* – Heidi simply smiled. 'I wish I had a brother.'

Gira also looked amused. 'Me too.'

Okay, she needed to get the conversation back on track. 'Yes, I know I'm lucky. I just … well, I wish mine was closer, obviously. But not so close that I was working in the same shop as him.' Crap, now she was rambling. 'Anyway, back to our new book club. I thought the focus should be books that uplift, yes?'

'And that can be easily picked up and put down,' Gira added. 'I usually only get to read at night, when I'm tired.'

'Books that don't take themselves too seriously, where

the sun shines,' Heidi waggled her eyebrows, 'and the sex sizzles.'

'God, yes.' Lottie felt a ripple of forgotten desire. When was the last time she'd even thought about sex, never mind had it?

'Beach reads,' Heidi added excitedly. 'That's what we're describing, isn't it? Books we'd want to take on holiday with us.'

'And books that take us on holiday.' Gira, the quieter of the two women, looked at them both. 'I don't mean they have to be about beaches, but they take you out of your head. Transport you to another world for a while.'

Once again Lottie saw the shadow cross Gira's features. She had an awful feeling Gira's own world wasn't a happy place right now. 'Okay, so we're all agreed? Beach reads.' She felt a buzz of anticipation, a shiver of excitement. Grabbing her mug, she raised it aloft. 'Here's to the Beach Reads Book Club.'

Matt went about his usual end-of-day routine: straightening books on the shelves, sweeping the floor, sorting the cash register. Cleaning the loo.

Yes, he now spent a good part of every evening (except Sunday, when the shop was closed) wearing rubber gloves and wielding a toilet brush. There were people in his former life who would pay good money to see it.

Once everything had been done to his liking, he went to

help Amy clean up the café. 'We'll need to get some help soon,' he told her as he loaded the dishwasher, surreptitiously rearranging it as he went. Amy was bright and hard-working, but she had no clue how to stack a dishwasher efficiently. 'I'm aware I'm working you too hard. I'll stick another ad in the paper.'

The last ad for help in both the shop and the café had elicited a lukewarm response. A handful of potential candidates on paper had, on interview, translated into zero people he'd wanted working for him.

Of course, if he could persuade his dad to help out more, cover a regular morning or afternoon so he could catch up on paperwork – even better, a whole day so he could have a life outside the shop … Hell, maybe in the future a whole week so he could go mad and go on holiday. Assuming he could work up the enthusiasm for a solo adventure.

Turning on the dishwasher, Matt sighed. Right now, days off were a thing of fantasies.

'I don't mind working here.' Amy shoved the clean mugs onto the shelf behind her. 'There's nothing else to do.'

'I'm sure you can find something besides making tea and coffee.'

Amy just shrugged, a silent answer he was becoming increasingly familiar with. He and Amy had always got on, though the nine-year age gap meant they were never really close. As she'd started becoming interesting, a girl he could have a conversation with, he'd gone off to uni, and then to work and live in London. Trips home to Nottingham had been rare and fleeting. Now he, Amy and his dad were finding their way around one another. Not easy in a new town where they knew no one else.

'I saw you chatting to that group of women today.' The words were out before he could wonder why he'd noticed. And then been interested enough to mention it.

Amy looked nonplussed. 'Isn't that what I'm supposed to do? You said to smile and be friendly.'

Damn, he was desperately bad at this, actually communicating with someone beyond the surface pleasantries. 'Both of which you always do.' He dragged a hand through his hair and tried to order his thoughts. 'What I meant was, it was the first time I'd seen you giggle.' He smiled, hoping she'd see he was trying to break down the reserve between them. 'I enjoyed it. I wish I could see you do it more.'

'Yeah, well, maybe you would, if you'd not forced me down here, away from my mates.' She slammed the last mug onto the shelf, causing a clatter as they all rattled into each other. 'I'll see you back at the house.'

Bugger it. Matt cursed as he watched Amy storm off through the shop. For the millionth time, he asked himself whether he'd done the right thing, dragging his dad and sister down to the coast with him to follow *his* dream.

Figuring he needed to give Amy some space, Matt stayed in the café. First, he turned the remaining mugs on the shelf so they all faced the same way. They'd scoured the internet for them. He'd insisted he wanted mugs appropriate for a bookshop. Amy had told him he was being ridiculous, it didn't matter what they looked like.

Then surprised him by leaping up in excitement when she'd found them. Next, he straightened the cutlery in their respective caddies and refilled the napkins. He knew it was all fine as it was, yet the actions helped to calm him. Gave his brain something else to focus on besides the perpetual, torturous guilt trip.

Ten minutes later, he walked through the front door of the house they'd moved into the month before. From the hallway he could see his dad pottering around in the kitchen making a mug of tea, and Amy sat on the sofa in the adjoining open-plan snug area, flicking through her phone.

'I thought we should go out for dinner tonight,' he announced, loud enough that they could both hear.

Amy didn't respond, her attention still on her phone. His dad came out of the kitchen and stared at him. 'It's a miserable rainy Thursday and you want to go out?'

Actually, he didn't. All Matt wanted to do was take a shower and curl up on his bed with the book he'd just brought home; yep, *My Sister, the Serial Killer* was in his pocket. He'd been meaning to read it for months now, and the refund had jolted his memory. Maybe a tiny part of him had also wanted to tell the blonde she'd missed out on a great book. If she ever returned to the shop. And if he could get it into the conversation without sounding like a prick.

His dad was still looking at him. Right, they were talking about going out. 'I thought it was time we tried the pub down the road.'

'Well, if you're paying.' With that less than promising

response, his dad turned back into the kitchen. Biting back a sigh, Matt followed him in.

'Amy?' She glanced up briefly, her hazel eyes shuttered. 'Are you up for going to the pub to eat?'

'Whatever.'

Maybe he should just forget it. No point forcing the issue. But then, before he knew it, another month would have gone by and he'd have achieved what, exactly, by bringing them here? 'Right then, that's decided. Let's go.'

Amy's head snapped up. 'Now?'

'Why not? I'm hungry and I could murder a pint.'

'So what, we all have to do as you say?'

Matt briefly closed his eyes and counted to ten. 'No, you don't.' Wearily he rubbed at the back of his neck. Ever since he'd raised the idea of them moving down here with him, he'd had to battle this. They'd moved grudgingly, not because they'd wanted a new start, like he had, but because his mum, in the last few weeks of her life, had begged them to look after each other when she was gone.

At the time, he'd genuinely felt moving to the coast would be good for all of them. Now he wondered if it wasn't just a gigantic ego trip; a way to assuage his guilt, while ignoring their needs. Yet again.

His dad walked out of the kitchen and, to Matt's surprise, came back with his coat on. 'You coming, Amy?'

His sister looked over and sighed. 'I guess.'

Matt squashed the urge to jump in the air, raise his fist and yell *Yesssssss*. Instead he gave his dad a small smile. 'Thanks,' he said quietly.

'I'm not doing it for you. I'm doing it because the alternative is making my own tea.'

Matt nodded. 'Understood.'

Yet as he walked a few paces behind the pair of them as they huddled beneath a giant golf umbrella, he felt a small twinge of, if not victory, then hope. This would be the first time the three of them had gone out for a meal together. Briefly he looked up to the sky. *It's a start, Mum*, he whispered. Then hunched his shoulders against the cold as he acknowledged it had come many years too late.

Chapter Three

Lottie drummed her fingers on the café table and again glanced over at Matthew Steele. She could do this, couldn't she?

What was the worst that could happen? He'd say no?

You'll trip up over your feet, fall headlong into him, and find your face pressed against his groin.

Even worse, you'll enjoy it.

Sitting opposite, Sally, her best friend from school, giggled. 'God, I didn't think I'd see the day. Charlotte Watt, bricking herself over talking to a guy.'

'I'm not.' Her eyes skimmed across the Books by the Bay café, only this time she didn't see it as a good place to have a drink while reading a book. This time she saw it as a potential venue for the Beach Reads Book Club.

'Are so.'

Lottie rolled her eyes. 'What are you, ten?'

27

'Hey, I knew you when you were ten, so there's no way you can pull the wool over my eyes. You're shitting kittens.'

'Err, either I'm shitting bricks, or having kittens.'

Sally smiled triumphantly. 'See, I told you.'

Lottie let out a strangled laugh. 'Very funny. I will concede to being a little apprehensive, but only because the last person I asked to host the book club shot me down.'

'Come on, Eve was never going to agree to you using the library for a Beach Reads Book Club.' Sally leant back in her chair, resting her hands over her very round, eight-month-pregnant belly. 'Not only would she see it as a rival to hers, she thinks books like that are only one step away from *Fifty Shades.*'

'So? Look at the sales of *Fifty Shades*. Loads of people enjoyed it, so why shouldn't it be included in a book club? If everyone's willing, obviously.'

Sally winked. 'And they all know the safe word.'

They both erupted in laughter, which drew the attention of the very man Lottie was gearing herself up to approach. Damn, Sally was right. She *was* bricking it.

'So, when are you going to ask him?'

Lottie took a swig of her tea. 'On the way out.'

'Why not now, so I can have fun watching? It's not like he's doing anything, except for looking over here every now and again. I can't work out if it's because we're making too much noise, or he's checking us out.' She sighed dramatically and pointed to her bump. 'Nope, those days are over for me. It has to be you he keeps staring at.'

'Trust me, if he is, it's because I'm being too loud.' Lottie had met plenty of guys who'd flirted with her, checked her out – something about being blonde and driving a van with *Electric Blonde* emblazoned along the side (yeah, not her best idea). Matthew Steele, with his smartly tailored suits and discreetly expensive watch, wasn't one of them.

'How many people have you got signed up for this book club, then?'

'I've not exactly been inundated with requests since putting it on the local Facebook page. In fact, so far it's only Heidi and Gira from the original book club. If it stays that way, we could meet in my van.' Worry niggled and she glanced over at Sally. 'Of course I'm counting on my mate joining.'

Sally raised her eyebrows. 'Err, have you read about what happens to mums with new babies? Sleep deprived, always drinking cold tea because they don't have a chance to sit down. Brain scrambled. I won't be able to manage reading a book, never mind talking intelligently about it. Plus there's the small matter of a tiny, wailing baby.'

Lottie started to laugh. 'Err, first off, did you listen to anything I said about what we'll be reading? Books that are easy to pick up and put down. Perfect to be read on the beach *and* while looking after a new baby. In fact we could have called it the Beach Reads For Everyone Including New Mums Book Club, but it would take up too much space on the flyer I haven't got round to designing yet.' Seeing Sally about to open her mouth, Lottie pressed on. 'My second point is, the book club will be run by me, so why on earth do you think the discussion will be intelligent?'

Sally snorted with laughter. 'Okay, I'll give you that, but it still leaves the wailing baby.'

'Every time he or she wails, I promise to pick them up and do that jigging around on your shoulder thing that always gets them back to sleep, or so I've heard.' As she spoke, the old doubts began to sneak in. 'Oh God, Sally, what was I thinking? I've not done anything like this before. I mouthed off at Eve about the way she ran the library book club, but what if mine is worse? What if nobody else joins, and Gira and Heidi find it boring? What if it ends up with just me sitting here like Lottie No Mates, reading a book by myself?'

'Jeez, Lonely Lottie, I promise to come before the wailing one arrives.' She patted her bump. 'And anyway, the club is going to be a success. You might not have run one before but you're a flipping whizz at talking.' She grinned. 'Even your teachers would have to give you an A-star in it. So why don't you put that talent to good use and ask the dishy guy, who keeps looking over here, if you can use his premises.'

'You think he's attractive?' she blurted, then instantly regretted it.

'Duh, I'm pregnant, not blind.' Sally gave her a sly look. 'Don't you?'

'I haven't really noticed.'

Sally nodded. 'Of course you haven't. I mean, why would you? You're not a fan of green eyes.'

'They're not green. They're a really dark brown. Not Cadbury milk chocolate brown, richer than that, smoother,

30

more expensive. I'm thinking a dark Hotel Chocolat.' Shit, what was she doing, waxing lyrical about the guy's bloody eyes? 'Obviously that's a total guess, because I've not really—'

'Noticed,' Sally filled in, eyes wide and brimming with laughter. 'I can see that.'

Embarrassed, Lottie scrunched up her napkin and threw it at her friend. 'Shut up.'

Sally bit into her lip, hands on her shaking belly. 'I'd ask you to go through the full chocolate range, just to make sure, but I'm going to wet myself if I laugh any more.'

'Okay, so he has nice eyes,' Lottie conceded grumpily. 'All I'm interested in, though, is whether he'll let me hold the book club here.'

'Then go and ask him.' Sally smirked. 'And while you're there, find out for certain if he's a 70 per cent, an 85 per cent or maybe even a 90 per cent cocoa.'

Lottie glared at her. 'You won't be laughing when that medicine ball you're carrying decides to come out.'

'I know.' Sally grinned. 'But when I'm screaming in agony I'm going to wave away the pethidine and picture your flustered expression instead.'

Ignoring her so-called friend, Lottie rose to her feet, pushed back her shoulders and headed over to where Matthew was... God, was he really shuffling the pots of pens round on the counter?

Suddenly the man didn't seem so scary.

Matt glanced up to find the curly-haired blonde he'd been trying not to look at for the last forty minutes walking towards him. And damn, her eyes were on the pots of pens he'd been in the process of rearranging so they were all in height order. Clearly he'd reached a new level of lameness.

Quickly he switched two of the pots round, but when he caught her eye he saw her mouth twitch, confirming his lame status. And doubling it.

Not a problem. He'd brazen it out. It's not like he wasn't used to bluffing, acting confident when inside, his belly was a quivering mass of blancmange. And over far greater stakes than a pot of blasted pens.

'Come for another refund?'

She faltered, and he realised belatedly it had sounded like a dig. If he didn't improve his customer service skills, this venture of his would fail exactly as his dad predicted.

'No refund, but should I bring the cake back up, I'll be sure to let you know.' Immediately she put a hand over her mouth. 'God, that was gross, sorry. Actually I came over to ask you a favour. Not, err, to discuss the challenge of keeping your cake down.'

Her eyes met his and once again he was struck by their clarity. There was no way she could play poker, because those eyes betrayed exactly what she was thinking. She was nervous, which was a shock because so far he'd been the one feeling on the back foot.

'Oh?' It seemed the safest, if also the dullest, response.

'Yes.' She paused and inhaled a lungful of air. 'So, I'm starting a new book club and I asked the library if I could use one of their rooms for a venue, because I know they already run a book club there, as I was a member once, but then you know that, because I told you when I brought the book back, though actually thinking about it, you get loads of customers, so you probably don't remember.'

'I do. Remember, that is.' He wasn't sure who was the more shocked by his admission, him or the blonde.

'Err, okay.' She gave him a hesitant smile. 'So anyway, the library said they wouldn't let me hold it there, so I wondered if the club could meet in your café instead.' A soft light came into her eyes. 'The first book club I joined took place in a coffee shop and I have such really fond memories of it. I'd love this club to be as ... *cosy*, I think, would describe it. Friendly, welcoming. Holding it here would really help with that.'

He wasn't sure if he was required to say anything, so he kept to his default mode and remained quiet.

'We'd come when the shop was closed,' she continued, making him glad he'd kept quiet. 'So maybe there's a day when you stay behind to, I don't know, put out stock, do your ordering. Or whatever it is bookshop owners do.'

'That would be most days.' He'd started to realise owning a bookshop wasn't the doddle some – and yes, he included himself in that – thought it was.

'That's great.' Immediately she'd said it, her smile faltered. 'Oops, that sounded mean. Obviously it's not great for you, having to work late every day, but it's great for me because it gives lots of options. I tell you what, why don't I talk to my club members and I'll email you the most suitable date for us. I'm thinking we could meet at 5.30 p.m. for two hours. We wouldn't expect you to open the café, but maybe we could bring some snacks and drinks?' She smiled properly then, and he felt the warmth, the dazzle of it, like a punch to his gut. 'These things go a lot better when refreshments are involved.'

'I imagine.' But he couldn't, not really, because the idea of discussing something so private as the book he was reading, with virtual strangers, made him shudder. As a kid, reading had been a chance to escape, to get lost in a fantasy for a while. Until he'd been forced to turn his light out, and reality had come crashing back. As an adult, he'd only recently enjoyed returning to the pastime and it had brought back all those feelings from his childhood: comfort, a feeling of security. If he had a book in his hand, he didn't feel lonely.

'Well, that's settled then.' She went to pick up a business card from next to the till and he tried not to wince as she accidentally knocked the stack onto the floor. 'Crap, sorry.'

He shifted to the other side of the counter to help her pick them up, but just as he bent to crouch down, she tried to stand up, and they collided.

'Whoa.' Feeling her stagger backwards, he clutched at her arms to steady her, steady them both. And wow, it was like holding onto a live wire. His body began to react in ways he'd forgotten as his blood pumped faster, hotter.

Abruptly he let go. 'Sorry.' He took a step away, trying to find his equilibrium. Thankfully she didn't seem to notice his mini meltdown. She was too intent on putting the cards back on the counter.

'I, umm, think you'll probably do a better job.'

He glanced behind her to the now haphazardly piled stack. 'Yes. It's on that list of things bookshop owners do.'

Humour lit her eyes. 'Is that before or after rearranging the pen pots?'

He wanted to be offended, but it was hard to be, when her grey eyes twinkled and her flushed face was alive with amusement. 'Before. Neat business cards would seem to be a priority.'

A crack of laughter escaped her. 'Definitely. So, as I was saying before I decided to decimate your display, I'll be in touch with the best date for us and we can take it from there.'

He wasn't sure what he'd just agreed to, but there was only one possible response to a woman who was smiling at him like she was now. 'Yes, fine.'

'Oh, and as we'll be ordering our books from you for future meetings, will it be okay if we don't actually pay for the use of your shop? The club's just starting out and I don't want to put off any would-be members by charging them to come.'

'Understandable.'

'So, we're good?'

He felt dizzy with it all: her use of so many words, the dazzle of her smile, his unexpected reaction to the brush of her body against his. 'I think so.'

'That's great. Thank you.' She waved the business card at him. 'I'll be in touch.'

He watched as she strode back to the café. A mini blonde tornado, dressed in dark jeans and a tomato-red jumper.

It was only later, when he received her email, that he began to wonder what on earth he'd agreed to. Lottie Watt – at least now he knew her name – was bringing her book club to his shop on the last Thursday in every month at 5.30 p.m. For two hours. Starting in two weeks.

Did he want people in his shop after it had closed? Sure, there was plenty he could do, but he enjoyed the peace of being by himself after hours. Sorting stock, updating orders, just him and his books.

That's the old you.

The thought niggled. He'd vowed when he bought the shop that he was going to relax more, to embrace people, let them in a little. Become part of the community. How better to do that, than allow a book club to meet in his shop?

And it was only once a month. Even he could put up with that.

Chapter Four

L ottie parked up outside the house of her next customer and turned off the engine. The temperature dial was up in the red again and she winced. She wasn't sure how much longer the old boy would last, which was a real bugger because money was pretty tight at the moment... For that, read: no bloody way could she afford a new van.

Maybe buying the house had been a bad idea.

With a sigh, she rested her forehead against the steering wheel and took in a few calming breaths. It was fine. She'd manage. If all else failed, she could always take in a lodger. Though quite who would want to live in a crumbling terrace that hadn't been touched since the 1930s, God only knew. She barely did, some nights. Since she'd sorted the central heating system out, it was at least warm, but stained, peeling woodchip wallpaper didn't exactly scream, *Come and live here!* At least the living room was done.

'Only six more rooms to go, eh?' She turned around to look at Chewie, her crazy, gorgeous Labradoodle companion.

He barked and wagged his tail.

'Okay then, Audrey's too old to risk a mutt like you dancing round her ankles, so this time you need to stay put. I won't be long.'

With a kiss to his head, she jumped down from the van. Chewie, used to how this worked, settled back down in his doggie bed to wait for her.

Audrey, just turned eighty but with a brain sharper than most twenty-year-olds, Lottie's included, answered the door.

'One minute I was watching *Loose Women*, the next it was a black screen. Before you ask, the trip switch is down but I can't shove it up again.'

Lottie hoisted her toolbag over her arm and stepped inside. 'Can't have you missing *Loose Women*.'

'Exactly. Used to be three of us watched it together. Me, Maureen and Gladys. Now there's just me.' Sadness crept across her face. 'When you're young, you think your friends will always be there. When you're old, they start dropping like flies.'

Lottie's heart went out to her. She only knew Audrey as a customer she'd visited a few times, once to put in a few extra sockets, once to put some spotlights in her kitchen, because *I can see bugger all with the current lighting.*

'Do you have family nearby?' she asked as she checked the fusebox under the stairs.

'My daughter, Sally, is about an hour or so away. Simon's the other end of the country, but I'm luckier than most. The kids and grandkids all visit when they get the chance.'

Yet Lottie heard what Audrey couldn't, wouldn't say – *It's the other days I'm lonely* – because Audrey was a war child, and they never complained.

As she started to check all the wiring in the front room, Lottie asked, 'Do you read?'

'Course I can bloody read. I've not lost my marbles yet.'

Lottie rolled her eyes. 'Don't I know it! I meant, do you enjoy reading books?'

Audrey cackled. 'Oh, right. Well, sure. The print's a bit small for me these days, but I manage.'

'Have you tried an e-reader? Like a Kindle? You can make the font as big as you like.'

'That's what my daughter said. I told her I didn't want to be holding some slab of new-fangled technology in my hand. A book should have pages. Something reassuring about the feel of the paper in your hands, the action of turning each page bringing you closer to the end. Stubborn woman bought me a ruddy slab of plastic anyway.'

Lottie bit into her cheek to stop from smiling. 'Who's the stubborn one here? The daughter who bought you something she thought would help with your reading, or the mum who refuses to give new-fangled technology a go?' Not finding anything amiss on the left side of the room, Lottie switched to the right and shifted the sofa. 'I'm with you on the real book, though. I use a Kindle for

39

holidays but I still prefer a book in my hand. What books do you like?'

'Me, I love a bit of romance.' She waved a hand up and down. 'The body might be crumbling but the mind's more than willing.'

Lottie was struck by a thought. 'What do you think about joining a book club? I'm just setting one up.'

Audrey grimaced. 'Oh no, I can't be doing with all those highfalutin books. Never had the patience for them.'

'We're going to be reviewing beach reads. Rom coms, easy reads. Books you'd take on holiday with you.'

'Raunchy ones?' Suddenly Audrey's face was alive with interest. 'I read that *Fifty Shades of Grey*, you know. Didn't realise my pulse could go that fast anymore. All the whipping and bondage, him with his big todger. Nearly gave me a heart attack.'

Oh God. Lottie held onto her sides as laughter burst out of her. 'Please tell me you'll come. Our first meeting is next week in Books by the Bay. Do you know it?'

'I was in there the other day. Got a bit of shock when this tall, dark, handsome lad stepped out instead of old Larry. A bit of a Darcy about him, I thought.'

'He's certainly tall and dark.' Nope, she wasn't going to blush. But just in case she did, Lottie busied herself with pulling away the carpet. And immediately found the problem. 'Err, Audrey, have you seen any mice recently?'

'Mice?' Audrey's expression looked horrified. 'Those things you young folk use with a computer, or—'

'The furry things with a long tail, pointed nose and teeth

that gnaw through things, like electricity cables.' She held up the chewed wire for Audrey to see. 'That's why the trip went and you didn't get to see the end of *Loose Women*.'

'Well, I never.'

'I can fix this now, and I'll order you a couple of mousetraps. The humane kind. When you've caught one you just need to put it outside and open the trapdoor,' she added when she saw the blood drain from Audrey's face.

'Thank you, dear.' She grimaced. 'Looks like I've not been as alone as I thought.'

'You'll be even less alone if you join the Beach Reads Book Club.' Hoping to take Audrey's mind off the mice situation, she added, 'We're going to start with *Mount!* by Jilly Cooper. Have you read it?'

'Can't say I have. I liked some of hers though. Especially that Rupert Campbell-Black. I wouldn't kick him out of bed for eating crackers.'

'Well, he's back in *Mount!*, so if you like, I can pick up a copy and drop it off with the mousetraps.'

'Is there rumpy pumpy in it?'

Lottie laughed. 'It's Jilly Cooper, what do you think?'

Audrey gave her a wicked smile. 'I think your book club might have found another member.'

An hour later, Lottie nursed the overheating van on to her next appointment: Victor Wallace, buzzing dimmer switch. He'd be an unlikely recruit for the book club, but it didn't matter. With Audrey, Gira, Heidi and Sally there would now be five of them meeting next week. Five people whose lives she hoped would all be improved, just a little, by the combination of a good book, a mug of tea and the company of like-minded readers. All in a venue that looked out over the Solent, and was jammed to the rafters with books. It even had a broodingly handsome owner.

Not bad, Charlotte Watt. Not bad.

Matt hauled himself out of bed and jammed on his shorts and long-sleeved running top. Some habits from his old life were hard to break. Waking at the crack of dawn and going for a run was one of them. Still, the discipline had probably stopped him from having a total meltdown, so he wasn't going to knock it.

It's just that one day, he'd love to lie in beyond 6 a.m.

Tucking his key into his shorts pocket, he crept down the stairs and out of the house.

'Shit.'

The wind was sharp enough to freeze his balls. February really was the dreariest month of the year. He set off at a canter, heading for the front. It was still dark, but he knew by the time he reached the four-mile point and turned back, the sun would be on the rise and the view across the Solent potentially spectacular. Or potentially a grey version of now, but it was the hope that drove him on…

Grey it was, then.

Yet as Matt headed back along the front, the sight of the waves crashing over the pebbled beach and the smell of the sea were as life-affirming as the run itself. Finally he turned away from the prom ... and nearly fell over his own feet as he caught sight of the young woman heading his way. Dressed in a bright yellow rain jacket and bobble hat, she was being dragged along by a large dog that looked like a Labrador with a heavy-duty perm.

'Oh, hi.' Lottie smiled up at him, a ray of bright yellow sunshine against the dreary grey. 'Going for a run?' Before he could answer, she laughed. 'Duh, why else would you be wearing shorts on a day like today?'

'Because I'm an eternal optimist?' She laughed again, though he wasn't sure if it was at his joke, or the thought of him being an optimist. Either way, he was ridiculously pleased to be the cause.

'Actually, I'm going to revise my earlier statement because from the look of you, you've already been for a run, in which case either your idea of a run is as short as mine, or you were up when normal people are still asleep.'

'I wake early. Force of habit.' He began to feel the bite of the wind, but the lure of a hot shower wasn't enough to make him end the conversation. 'And this is Dougal, I presume?'

She looked confused and he gave himself a mental kick. He wasn't great with people, but usually he was better than this. Wittier, at least. Humour was the one feature even his ex-wife had found redeeming. 'Sorry. Poor joke. I was referring to the dog off *The Magic Roundabout*. The film version,' he added quickly, afraid he might look as old as he sometimes felt.

She smirked. 'The TV series was, what, 1970s?' She gave

him a rather unnerving study. 'By my reckoning, if you'd watched that, you'd be around fifty now.'

'So clearly I didn't?'

His reply elicited another burst of laughter from her, and this time he was pretty certain she was laughing with him. 'I'd put you at early thirties, so either you have a phenomenal skin routine that I need to hear about, or you weren't alive when *The Magic Roundabout* was on the telly.'

'Err, soap and water?'

'Damn, I kind of hoped you'd found the answer to eternal youth.' She glanced down at the now restless bundle of shaggy fur. 'Chewie, meet Matthew. He's letting me use his shop for my book club, so be nice to him.'

'Matt.' A slight flush caught her cheeks, and he wondered if it was the wind, or if she thought asking her to use his shortened name was too familiar. 'So, Chewie after the Wookie from *Star Wars*?'

Amusement sparked in her eyes. 'Interesting that you think there's another option. The gum, maybe?'

He gave himself another kick. Maybe the cold wasn't just tightening his muscles, it was squeezing all sense out of his brain. 'I hear a lot of people name their dogs after chewing gum.'

To call her eyes grey, he realised, was a disservice. They were more silver, especially when she laughed.

'Much as I'm enjoying discussing dog names, I think Chewie's had enough.' As if to emphasise the point, the shaggy mutt let out a bark and tugged again on the lead. 'I'll see you next week for the book club?'

He inclined his head, figuring it was safer than whatever else might come out of his mouth.

When he arrived back, he headed straight for the shower, grateful for the heat as it loosened his muscles. Yet he knew if Lottie hadn't ended their conversation, he'd still be out there, freezing his balls off. It was the first time since his divorce he'd enjoyed talking to a member of the opposite sex. Hell, the first time he'd felt such a powerful connection with a woman who wasn't his wife. He didn't know what to make of it, only that he needed to tread very, very carefully. His old self hadn't been good for Patricia and he wasn't sure if his new self, the one he was trying to invent, would be any better at relationships.

After getting dressed he wandered into the kitchen, only to find his dad already filling the kettle. 'You're up and about early.'

'Noise of the wind woke me up.' His dad busied himself getting out the mugs. 'It was never this windy—'

'Back home,' Matt finished for him. Exhaling, he shoved his hands in his pockets. Should he apologise again for asking him to come? But he'd been through all that. Before coming here they'd had countless discussions about it, how the change wouldn't just do him good but Amy, too. And Amy would settle more if her dad also came.

Of course, during each discussion, Matt had known they were both thinking of his mum's final words, about them looking after each other. It was why he'd always won, though victory felt hollow right now, coming at the cost of his dad's misery. 'Is there anything you actually like about this place?'

His dad grunted as he poured boiling water into the mugs. 'What was that beer we had at the pub the other night?'

'London Pride?'

'Aye. It wasn't Pedigree, but it was drinkable.'

Not exactly fulsome praise, but Matt grabbed onto it like a starving man eyeing up the last burger at a barbecue. 'Maybe we should give it another go. Might taste better the second time.'

'It might.' A mug of tea was thrust into Matt's hands. 'The shop, the pub. I know what you're doing, son.'

'Pardon?'

'You're trying to chivvy me out of my grief. Get the old guy out so he doesn't spend every day moping in his room.'

It wasn't so much his dad's words, but the bitterness of the tone that had Matt looking sharply at him. 'Is that how it feels?'

'At times, yes.'

Heart heavy, guilt and loss tugging hard, Matt put a hand on his dad's arm. 'Then I'm sorry. You're going to grieve, we all are, but you feel her loss more than anyone. I know that.'

The older man nodded, then picked up his mug and headed out towards what Matt referred to as his dad's suite of rooms: a bedroom, bathroom and small living room the builders had created out of the original downstairs dining room and study. Now he wondered if his dad saw it as his own private prison. A place he didn't want to be, but felt locked up in just the same.

Hand on the door to his bedroom, Matt's dad turned. 'About that beer. Tonight?'

Emotion clogged Matt's throat. 'Sounds good.'

When he walked to the shop half an hour later, his step felt a tiny bit lighter. They were all trying, and as long as they kept doing that, surely anything was possible.

Chapter Five

February meeting, nominated book:
Mount! **by Jilly Cooper**

Lottie grabbed Chewie's lead and stared down at him. He looked back up at her with huge, adoring, brown eyes. Crap, she really was a sucker for eyes the colour of chocolate.

'You promise you're going to behave? Because tonight is important for me.'

His long pink tongue licked her hand.

'That's dog-speak for *Yes, Lottie, I promise*, huh?'

She received another lick, and decided it would have to do. Thanks to the inconvenience of her mum and dad going out tonight, the alternative was to leave Chewie home alone. Past experience told her that would end with chewed things she didn't want chewed. And one grumpy dog for the rest of the evening. It was why he went with her to every job. Usually owners were happy for him to come in with her, but on the rare occasions he had to sit outside or stay in the van, Chewie didn't seem to mind because he knew where she was. It was humbling, being adored so much, but at times it was exhausting, too.

'I'm sure Matthew ... Matt...' The shortened name didn't sit quite right on her tongue. Too informal for a man clearly born to wear a suit and tie. Then again, she'd seen another side to him. Windswept, sweaty, his shorts and running top showcasing a long, athletic body she'd tried hard not to stare at. 'I'm sure Matt's not expecting me to bring you, so you need to be perfectly behaved.' As if the word *behaved* was even in Chewie's vocabulary. 'He's going to be mad enough that I'm late.'

When she'd first met Chewie at the rescue centre, he'd been a sad, bedraggled mess. Abandoned to the streets because his owner had found his need for human contact, for company, too much. Lottie gave Chewie a pat. Yeah, she'd take this overly protective, overly affectionate version any day.

Still, she crossed her fingers as she entered the shop. *Please God let Chewie be good today.*

Matthew – damn it, Matt – appeared from behind a set of bookshelves, looking darkly attractive in his habitual suit, tie still straight, collar still done up, even though it was after hours. Immediately his eyes zeroed in on Chewie.

'I'm sorry.'

'For being late, or...' He nodded towards Chewie.

'Both, though they kind of go together. Usually my

parents look after Chewie when I go out, but when I took him round today, they told me they'd had a last-minute invite to dinner with friends.' Crap, nerves must have hit her, because she seemed unable to stop talking. 'Don't worry, I told them how selfish they were being, but apparently they are allowed a life, and I'm the one who decided to have a dog. Though actually I only went to the rescue centre to see my friend Gretchen, but then I saw Chewie, or maybe he saw me first.' She sucked in a deep breath, embarrassed. 'I'm sure you don't want to hear all this. Suffice to say, tonight I'm afraid we come as a pair, but he's promised to be good.'

His dark gaze dropped to Chewie, who was sitting like the most perfectly behaved dog on the planet, and then back up to her. 'Promised?'

'Yep. He crossed his paws and everything.'

'That's a relief.'

Why was it so difficult to tell if he was amused, or laughing at her? She guessed it was that shutter he always pulled over his face.

He waved a hand over to the café where Gira and Heidi were already sitting on a sofa in the large bay window. 'I think you'll find two of your members are already here. Amy arranged some chairs around the coffee table in the window. We weren't sure how many were coming?'

'Four. Plus me,' she added quickly, because four sounded pathetic. 'So there'll be five of us.' She kicked herself. The guy owned an expensive suit, he ran a business. He could bloody add up.

'Thank you for the clarification.'

A blush scorched her face. 'Sorry. I'm weirdly nervous, this being the first meeting.'

His face relaxed and there was a glimmer of sympathy in the small smile he gave her. 'You don't strike me as someone who would accept failure. Not if you want something enough.'

The words were so unexpected, for a few beats Lottie was too stunned to answer. 'Thank you.'

And now he was the one who looked embarrassed. As if he'd overstepped some line he had in his head that stopped him going from polite to personal.

The bell on the door jingled and Lottie turned to find Sally pushing her way in. 'Hi. Sorry I'm late. I had trouble wedging this huge belly into the car.'

Lottie grinned. 'No worries, I've only just got here myself, and I don't have pregnancy as an excuse. Sally, this is Matthew, the bookshop owner.'

'Matt.'

Damn, yes. If he'd only take off his jacket, loosen his tie. Something to make him look more like a Matt.

'Well, hello, Matt.' Sally glanced between the two of them. 'Don't think I'm being rude, but I need to go and park myself and this oversize belly on a chair, or I'll get varicose veins.'

As Sally waddled over to join Gira and Heidi, Lottie turned back to him. 'At least I can cross off one of my nightmare scenarios. I won't be sat here by myself at the first club meeting.'

He cleared his throat. 'Nightmare scenarios?'

'You know, the things that haunt you in the middle of the night when you're worried about something.'

He gave her a pained look. 'Dare I ask what else is on the list?'

'Oh, just the usual. A hurricane, fire sweeping through the building, being attacked by a plague of rats.'

Were those eyes warming, just a little? 'Well, it's good to be forewarned.'

Behind them the door opened again and Audrey barrelled through, bringing with her a blast of cold air. 'I've read the book,' she announced in lieu of a greeting. 'You told me there'd be bonking, but blimey O'Reilly! That Rutshire must have Viagra in the water.'

Lottie's eyes flew to Matt's, and she had to bite the inside of her cheek to stop from howling with laughter at the expression on his face: shock, bewilderment, a dash of embarrassment.

He cleared his throat. 'Right, well. I'll leave you to your … deliberations.'

'Oh, there's no need for you to run off, love.' Audrey gave Lottie an unsubtle wink. 'We can find a chair for him, can't we?'

God, she was so close to losing it. Lottie knew if she took one more glimpse of Matt's face, at the horror he was trying so manfully to mask, she'd end up rolling on the floor with tears streaming down her face. 'Of course Matthew can join us. If he likes.'

'Matt.' She watched his Adam's apple move as he

swallowed. 'And thank you, but I have orders to complete. And paperwork to tie up.'

She couldn't help it. 'Paint to watch dry?'

His eyes sought hers and she could sense his indecision; agree and risk seeming rude, disagree and risk having to join them. Yet just as she was about to give him an out, he did something unusual. He relaxed his features and let out a bark of laughter. 'Was I that obvious?'

And now the joke was on her, because while she could handle handsome but distant Mathew Steele, this man made her belly flip and her brain turn to mush.

'Well, come on, what are we waiting for.' Thank God for Audrey, even though she was now digging into the bag she was carrying and, oh help, producing a huge bottle of gin. 'Matt, was it? Be a good man and bring us some glasses.'

Audrey set off towards the café and Matt's gaze followed her, eyes wide, like a pair of Bournville Giant Buttons. 'Do you think she has tonic?'

Lottie stifled a laugh. 'I think she's happy with it neat.'

'And you?' His gaze slid back to hers. 'Should I ask Amy to get some tonic in for next time? Some limes, perhaps.'

He had the dazed expression of a man who wasn't quite sure what he'd let himself in for. 'You're already providing us with the premises. We'll sort out our refreshments.' She glanced back at Audrey, who was waving the bottle of gin around. 'But those glasses would be good, before she starts swigging it out of the bottle.'

'On it.'

Once again he gave her a smile. For such a hugely

impressive-looking man, it was surprisingly hesitant, shy almost. Yet inside her boots, she felt her toes curl.

He'd finished the orders, sorted out the paperwork. There was no paint to watch dry. Automatically his gaze wandered to the café area. Whatever book they were discussing, the one with the excessive bonking, it was making the five of them laugh.

'I can't work out if you keep looking over at the café because you fancy one of them, and we all know who that would be, or if you wish you could join them.'

He jumped at the sound of his sister's voice. The sister he hadn't even noticed walk towards him because he'd been staring. Damn it. 'Maybe I'm just keeping an eye on them. They are in my shop, drinking gin.'

Amy snorted. 'Because they really look like they're going to trash the place.'

Acutely aware Amy could see more than he wanted her to, Matt changed the subject. 'Are you off now then?'

'Yep.' She gave him a sly smile. 'So you can ogle the blonde as much as you like.'

Heat crept up his neck and Matt was incredibly grateful when his sister turned and headed for the door. He wasn't ogling Lottie, he reassured himself as he took another quick look at the group. He was taking an interest in a club being held under his roof. Still, maybe he'd be better off working at the back of the shop from now on.

Five minutes later, happily unpacking a box of books, he started to whistle, something he hadn't done since he'd been a boy. That's when he heard a shriek.

'Chewie, no! Come back!'

He had a second to realise the dog was heading his way. Another to panic as fifty pounds of curly fur and sharp teeth rounded the corner, knocking over the chair he'd used to set some of the books on, sending them flying. A final second to freeze as the dog came to a juddering stop in front of him, baring his teeth and letting out a growl that was far more fearsome than the teddy-bear picture Chewie presented.

'Chewie, shh!' Lottie appeared, her face flushed to a colour that almost matched her red hoodie. 'That's Matt, he's a good guy.'

Matt swallowed, eyes still on Chewie. It was a bizarre moment to appreciate that finally, she'd got his name right. 'I try.'

'Shit.'

His gaze bounced to Lottie, who was now staring at the floor by Chewie's feet, an appalled expression on her face. Ah. 'Pee, to be more accurate.' He winced as he watched the puddle on the floor expand, creeping towards him. 'Quite a lot of it.'

Lottie sighed, bending to put her arms around Chewie's neck. And now he could see the poor thing was shaking.

'I'm so sorry. He's not done that for ages.'

'Emptied his bladder in a bookshop?'

She rolled her eyes. 'Run off like that, all scared. It was

the whistling, I think.' She rubbed a hand up and down Chewie's back, soothing him. 'I got him from a rescue centre. The staff thought his previous owner had kicked him around. He was found hiding under some bushes in the local park.' She bent to kiss Chewie's head. 'The last time he reacted like this was when he met my cousin. Jack whistled then, too. I reckon Chewie's git of a previous owner was a whistler.'

'I'll make sure never to whistle again.'

'Oh no, it's your shop. You should be able to do what you like. I'll make sure this monster doesn't come here again.' Another sigh, this one from deep inside her. 'Can you point me in the direction of your mop? I'd better get this cleaned up before it stains your lovely wooden floor.'

'I'll do it.' Her wide-eyed expression told him he wasn't the only one shocked by his statement. 'You should get back to your ... discussions.'

'Are you sure?' Her mouth curved in a sly smile. 'You could take my place for a bit. Make Audrey's day.'

'Ah, yes.' He'd worked in a high-pressure environment where confidence was critical, so why did he feel so uncool in front of this woman? 'I'm not sure I'm sufficiently qualified.'

Lottie burst out laughing. 'You mean you don't want to talk about bonking in Rutshire?'

'My taste in books is a little ... different.' Embarrassment meant his comment came out sharper than he'd intended, dismissive almost, and he cringed as he saw the laughter die in her eyes.

'Right, well, if you really don't mind doing the mopping...'

'I don't.' His mind was stuck on how to explain himself. *Ignore me, I'm a prick*, seemed appropriate, but already she was walking away. And he was left staring at a puddle of dog piss.

He'd just wrung the mop out when he heard another shout from the group. This time it was from the hugely pregnant lady – Sally, he thought.

'Oh my flaming God, either I've just peed myself like Chewie, or my waters have broken.'

Matt looked at the mop still in his hand. Could this really be happening?

The group started talking all at once and as he walked back towards the kitchen, he noticed they were hovering over Sally, who was holding her back.

'I think we should time the contractions,' Heidi said, looking concerned.

'And call Paul.' Lottie dug out her phone.

'He'll be on the road, coming back from Birmingham.' Sally was breathing hard, her face pale. 'Tell him to put his bloody foot down or his wife will be having a baby in a frigging bookstore.'

She groaned as another contraction hit and Matt felt his pulse go into overdrive. Dog piss he could handle. Babies were a whole different ball game.

'We're not hanging around here waiting for Paul to come. We need to get you to the hospital.' Lottie dragged a hand over her face. 'Damn, I've been drinking.' She looked aghast as she cast her eyes around the rest of the group. 'We all have.'

Matt shoved the mop into the cupboard and strode towards them. 'I haven't. I can drive Sally. Just let me get the car. I won't be a minute.'

Not waiting for a reply, he sprinted down the road, immediately regretting his decision to come to work in a suit. As sweat beaded down his back, his mind conjured up images of Sally lying along the back seat, screaming that she needed to push. He wasn't a man prone to panic, but the thought of having to stop at the side of the road and help Sally give birth … he shuddered.

A few minutes later he parked outside the back of the shop where they were all waiting for him.

'I'll come with you.' Lottie, thank God, slipped into the back seat next to Sally. But that left a four-legged guy on the pavement, big eyes staring longingly at his owner.

'Oh God, Chewie.'

Matt opened the passenger door and the dog jumped in. 'Hang on.' He scrambled around to turn the airbag off.

'The hospital won't let him come in.' Lottie's expression was a mix of apology and panic.

'He'll be fine with me.' Feeling less confident than his statement suggested, he pasted on a smile. 'I'll be sure not to whistle.'

In the back seat, Sally let out a strangled cry. 'Fuck, how do women have more than one? I'm never doing this again.'

Matt glanced at her in the rear-view mirror. 'It was nine years before my mother had Amy.'

'Nine years to forget the pain? OMG! I did not want to hear that.'

He winced, aware his bid to help her take her mind off things had been less than helpful. 'Sorry.'

His gaze clashed with Lottie's and she gave him a wry smile. 'Hurricanes and rats I'd planned for. Emergency dashes to the hospital, I forgot about.'

A blessedly short while later, he pulled into the hospital and came to a stop outside the maternity entrance. 'Wait here, I'll get someone.'

Within minutes Sally was being pushed into the hospital in a wheelchair.

Standing beside him, Lottie blew out a long, shaky breath. 'Thank God she's in the hands of the professionals now.'

Slowly his heart rate began to return to normal. 'Indeed.'

Lottie jammed her hands into her jacket pockets. 'Right, well, I need to stay with her until Paul gets here, so, well, thanks for taking care of Chewie. And for the pee mopping and taxi service.'

He inclined his head. 'At least we didn't have to add back-of-the-car baby delivery.'

She gave him a small smile, biting into her bottom lip, and for the first time he noticed the freckles dusting across her nose and onto her cheeks. 'I bet you're considering changing your mind about us meeting at the bookshop now.'

Confused, he frowned. 'Why?'

'You thought we were a respectable book club,' she

answered, eyes on Sally, who was still talking to the maternity nurse. 'Not, you know, a bunch of local crazies.'

She walked towards the automatic doors and as they opened for her, Matt called out, 'Give me a call when you're ready to collect Chewie. We'll come and pick you up.'

She looked uncertain. 'I can get a cab.'

'I'm cheaper.'

Her mouth curved. 'You make a persuasive argument. Thanks.'

'Good luck.'

Her gaze darted to the car where Chewie was watching his mistress with worried eyes through the window. 'You too.'

The moment Lottie went out of view, Chewie began pawing at the glass, trying to get out.

'We'll see her soon, big boy,' he told the mutt as he slipped back into the driver's seat. And was surprised to find he was already looking forward to it.

Chapter Six

L ottie's thumb hovered over Matt's number. It felt beyond weird asking him to pick her up from the hospital.

But Paul was with Sally now, and Lottie needed to fetch Chewie and go home. The easiest, quickest way to do that, was to take Matt up on his offer of a lift. And Lottie had always been practical.

Taking a breath, she called his number. He answered on the third ring.

'Hi. Is Sally okay?'

'I'm not sure she'd call it that, considering the *fucking thing still hasn't come out*, but Paul's there now, so I'm off the hook.'

There was a pause on the other end and Lottie wondered if the formal, expensively dressed man didn't like swearing.

'Are you ready to be picked up?' he asked into the silence.

'I'm ready to leave, but like I said before, I can easily grab a cab to yours.'

'It's no problem. I'm leaving now.' Another pause. 'Chewie will be glad to see you.'

Her heart sank at the quietly spoken understatement. 'Oh shit, he's not been a pain, has he?'

'It depends how you define pain.' In the background she could hear rustling, and imagined Matt was on the move, hurrying a confused Chewie into the car. A moment later she didn't have to imagine, as she heard him talking to her dog. *Come on, you hulking mutt. No, this way.* And then an exasperated, *Leave the bloody shoe.* Finally his voice was directly back in her ear: 'I'll be with you in ten minutes.'

He ended the call before she had a chance to thank him. Now she had ten minutes to stew on all the things Chewie could have done, though possibly she only needed a fraction of that time. *Bloody shoe.* It seems the bookshop owner wasn't averse to swearing after all. And her dog had developed a taste for expensive leather.

It should have made her feel guilty, but her first reaction was decidedly less honourable. There was something about the picture she'd conjured – harassed Matthew Steele, hair out of place, tie askew, trying to pull his designer shoe out of Chewie's stubborn jaw – that made her grin. It also made him much more a *Matt*. He'd surprised her this evening, the calm way he'd taken control. She'd expected him to recoil, to distance himself, yet he'd done the exact opposite. He'd stepped up and taken charge with the confidence of a man used to dealing with pressure.

It seems every time she thought she had him nailed, he did something unexpected, forcing her to reconsider. He might have been snotty about joining their book discussion, but he certainly came up trumps in an emergency.

A black SUV came to a halt outside and Lottie immediately noticed Chewie sitting in the passenger seat. The moment he saw her, he started to bark and scramble around, trying to get out.

Matt leapt out and rounded the bonnet. 'I believe he's trying to tell you something.'

'You think?' She stepped forward to open the door but Matt beat her to it. The moment the gap was wide enough, Chewie squirmed his way through and raced up to her, almost knocking her over in his desperation to be hugged.

'You daft boy, I've only been gone two hours.' She raised her eyes to Matt's. 'Not enough time for him to get into too much trouble, I hope.'

She didn't get a chance to see Matt's expression because Chewie's tongue swiped a wet trail across her face.

It took a while to get him back in the car, on the rear seat this time. He refused to sit until he saw her climb into the front. That's when she noticed the muddy paw marks all over the black leather. 'Oh boy, he didn't wipe his feet.' The guilt that had been absent earlier, barrelled through her like a runaway train.

'My fault. I let him out in the garden in case he needed

to … do his business. Couldn't get him in again until he'd chased every bird and squirrel he could hear.'

She pictured the scene. 'And covered himself in mud which he then trailed through the house and into your car.' For the first time that evening, she took note of what they were driving in. 'Your very new, very expensive … wow, is it a Jag? I didn't think they did SUVs. Just low-slung elegant machines driven by CEOs or chauffeurs.'

He glanced sideways at her. 'Should I wear a hat?'

Clearly he meant it as a joke, but once again the guilt gripped her. 'You were meant to be catching up on your shop-owner stuff while we talked about Campbell-Black's exploits with his favourite stud. Instead you get dumped with taxi duty and taking care of a muddy wild beast with a liking for chewing men's shoes.' When he didn't look her way, her stomach dropped. 'Crap, I was hoping I was wrong. Chewie ate one of your shoes, didn't he?'

'I was throwing them out anyway.'

She hiccupped out a laugh. 'Of course you were.'

As he drove through the hospital car park towards the exit, she gave him a few surreptitious looks. He still had on his suit trousers as far as she could make out, though he'd abandoned the jacket and thrown on a black wool jumper. One that looked far too expensive to be worn while looking after a dog. God, he was handsome though. Darkly, strikingly handsome.

He came to a stop at the junction onto the main road. 'Where am I going?'

'I thought you were taking me home?' Then she realised

what he was actually saying. 'Ah, but you don't know where I live. Sorry, I'm on Kings Way.'

'I meant more in terms of right or left?' When his eyes met hers, he gave her a small smile. 'So far I only know the name of the road where I live, the one where the shop is, and Shelby Street, because the Indian there does a great take-out curry.'

'The Spice Garden.' She smiled. 'We can agree on curry, at least.' And oops, she'd not meant to word it quite like that. 'Take a right out of here,' she added quickly. 'Then second exit at the roundabout.'

There was silence as he pulled onto the road. 'At least?' he asked after a while.

Lottie cursed her big mouth. It had a bad habit of opening before her brain had fully worked out what it was about to say. And whether it was a good idea or not. 'I'm sure there are other things we can agree on, too.' Though books definitely weren't on the list. 'You moved here, so you must like the sea.'

'Or I wanted a change.'

She glanced at his profile but it gave nothing away. She'd never met a man so private with his thoughts. It was both frustrating and fascinating. Made her want to keep picking at him until he revealed something. 'Is that why you came here? Not the lure of the sea so much as the lure of something different?'

He was quiet as he indicated to come off the roundabout and Lottie wondered if even her bland question had been too personal for him. 'You need to keep on this road now until we hit the sea,' she said into the silence. 'Though obviously it would be good if you didn't take that statement literally.'

His lips curved, and once again Lottie felt that squirmy sensation in her stomach. It was the first time since Henry had left that she'd felt a spark towards another guy. Totally weird, because the two men couldn't be more different.

Matt focused his eyes on the road. Lottie's question about why he'd moved wasn't a big deal, she was just making conversation. He was the odd one, seemingly incapable of relaxing enough to answer. He just wasn't comfortable talking about himself. He could do polite, he could do general. It was the personal, the stuff that tiptoed around the edges of the line between strangers and friends, he was so appalling at.

It meant he had many acquaintances and very few real friends.

Yet another part of his life that needed changing.

'I used to live in London.' It wasn't an answer, but he hoped she'd see it as a start. An effort on his part to continue the conversation. She would be coming to his shop every month. Her dog had peed on his floor, they'd handled a small emergency together. He had a feeling Lottie could become a friend, if he'd only lower his guard enough to let her.

Plus there was that underlying ... fizz. A sexual tension

he thought she felt, too. He wasn't going to act on it, he wasn't ready for that step, but it didn't mean he couldn't enjoy the prickles of awareness whenever their eyes met.

'I imagine life is a bit quieter here.'

Grateful for her undemanding reply, his hands relaxed on the wheel. 'London can be crazy, but there are places you can go to catch your breath. You just have to know where.'

'I'm sure, but I've lived here all my life so it's hard to imagine not having a prom to walk on to clear my head.' He'd reached the road that ran parallel with the sea and she pointed ahead. 'Not far now. It's the second turn on the left. Just park up next to the rusty old van.' On the back seat, Chewie let out a bark, and Lottie laughed. 'Clever dog, you know we're nearly home, huh?'

He drew to stop outside a small terrace house that, if he was honest, looked like it needed flattening and starting again.

Beside him, Lottie laughed. 'Oh boy, it must look bad, because for once I can read your expression.'

'Not bad,' he corrected, embarrassed he'd been so transparent. 'I'm sure it has the potential to be charming.'

'Very tactful. According to my dad, it also has the potential to be a serious money pit that will take years to make properly habitable.'

'Yet you bought it anyway.'

She grinned. 'I've never been much for taking advice. I'd rather make my own mistakes.'

They had that in common at least, he thought, as he turned off the engine. He was in the process of opening the door when she put a hand on his arm. 'It's okay, you don't need to get out.' She gave him a wry smile. 'I can make it from here.'

'I'm sure you can.' Yet years of having manners drilled into him made remaining in the car impossible, so he climbed out anyway and went to open her door.

On the back seat, Chewie scrambled around, desperate to get out.

'Wait, Chewie.' Lottie climbed out and lunged for the rear door. 'He's probably added scratched leather to the muddy paw prints.' A second later, the dog was out and up on his hind legs, his body plastered against her, his tongue licking her face.

For a fleeting moment, Matt wondered what it would feel like to be pressed against Lottie's trim length. To kiss her, though he hoped his technique was more elegant than Chewie's.

'I know you missed me, but enough.' She patted Chewie's head and the dog settled back onto his four legs. Lottie drew in a deep breath and turned to Matt. 'There are so many apologies I need to make, I don't know where to start. Obviously, I need to pay for your car to be valeted. I know a really good place that's used to removing evidence of Chewie's presence.'

She reached into her handbag and drew out a fuchsia-pink purse. He was starting to realise colour was her thing. 'Please put that away.'

She quirked a blonde brow. 'You have something against pink?'

He smiled. 'I have something against accepting money unless I've earned it.'

'What about if you're owed it, like if something of yours got damaged?' She looked down at Chewie. 'A shoe, for example.'

'I would say accidents happen.'

She exhaled sharply, her exasperation clear. 'You're really not going to help me reduce my guilt levels?'

He studied her face, wondering what attracted him so much. Patricia had been elegant, beautiful, polished. Maybe that's all it was; Lottie, with her freckles, blonde curls, jeans and vivid coloured jumpers, was the total opposite of his ex-wife. 'I let Chewie into my car. I offered to take him home with me.' He stared down at the curly-topped mutt, who was now sitting patiently on the pavement. 'Should the need arise, I'd do the same again. Though perhaps I'd hide my shoes.'

Lottie laughed, and inside he felt a flood of warmth. He'd missed making someone laugh. 'And I'd bring dustsheets for the car.'

'Deal.' Their eyes met and once again he felt that pulse, the zing that had everything inside him sitting up and taking notice.

'Do you want to come in for a drink?' Her smile looked a little awkward. 'The living room is the one part of the house that doesn't have a damp, 1930s vibe.'

Was she asking because she felt the same spark of attraction he did? Or did she feel she had to invite him, hence her need to clarify he'd only be allowed in the living room? Because he didn't know, because even if it *was* the former, he wasn't ready for it, he slid his hands into his pockets and took a mental step back. 'Thanks, but it's getting late.'

'Yes.' Her eyes avoided his so he couldn't see if she was relieved or offended. 'I'd better get this one some food before he eats any more shoes.'

He smiled. 'I'll see you next month?'

'If we've not scared you off.'

'You'll find I don't scare easily.' Though the fact he'd ducked her invite proved he was a coward in some matters. 'Out of interest, you mentioned Campbell-Black and his favourite stud. Which book were you discussing?'

'*Mount!* ... by Jilly Cooper,' she added, no doubt because it was clear he didn't recognise it.

He'd heard of Cooper, though he'd never read any of her books. Amy accused him of being straight-laced, particularly when it came to his reading tastes, but he believed books, like art, were meant to be enjoyed, not endured for the sake of pleasing someone else. One man's Hirst was another man's dead animal. 'And next month?'

She smirked. 'It depends whether Audrey gets her way.'

Did he really want to know? It appeared he did. 'If she does?'

'*The Mister* by E. L. James, the same author who wrote—'

'*Fifty Shades of Grey,*' he supplied, feeling slightly uncomfortable. He couldn't think of the book without thinking of sex. And he didn't want to think of sex while talking to a woman he found attractive, because then he'd start thinking of having sex with her.

Of their own volition his eyes sought hers, and immediately he knew it was too late. The silver/grey twinkled back at him and he inhaled sharply as raw desire throbbed through him. Damn, he needed to push it away, to bury it, but it had been so long since he'd enjoyed the sensation. So long since he'd wanted to have sex.

'So, anyway, thanks for today.' Lottie's voice punctured his haze of lust. 'Unless you come to your senses in the next few weeks, I'll see you in March.'

'Yes.' He swallowed to lubricate his throat. 'And hopefully before that. To buy the book,' he added, so she wouldn't think he was flirting with her. He needed to get his life in a better place, a more settled one, before he could start to think about flirting. About sex.

He watched as she walked up to her front door, trying not to think how deliciously pert her bum looked in the tight jeans she favoured. The unloved-looking house wasn't what he'd pictured for her, he thought as she let herself in. Then again, the tale about rescuing Chewie suggested she had a nurturing heart, so maybe, like Chewie, the place would thrive under her care.

Build the business, mend your relationship with your dad, help Amy find her focus.

Those were his priorities. Not the fantasy of a relationship with a woman who probably only saw him as the stuffy bookshop owner she needed to be nice to.

With a sigh, he climbed back into the car.

Chapter Seven

March meeting, nominated book:
The Mister **by E. L. James**

As Lottie went to push open the door of the bookshop, Sally grabbed at her arm to stop her.

'Are you sure this is a good idea?'

Lottie stared down at the pram Sally was pushing. Little Fredrick's face peeped out from behind the blankets and she felt a surge of what could only be described as warm mush. 'He's so cute, my ovaries are dancing.' Then she looked back at her friend, the pale face, the bags under her eyes. 'Am I sure what is a good idea?'

Sally gave her a tired smile. 'He's cute until he wakes up. Then he'll not only disrupt your meeting, his wailing will piss off the guy you've got a secret crush on, but for some reason won't admit it to your best mate. *That's* why I should turn around.'

'I don't have a crush on him.'

'That would be more believable if you'd look me in the eye. And if you hadn't flushed when I'd asked if you got home okay the night I pushed the medicine ball out.'

Lottie turned to look in the shop, relieved she couldn't see Matt. They'd not bumped into each other since the evening she'd lost her marbles, along with her good sense, and asked him in for a drink. Whether he'd turned her down because he didn't want to risk ruining his designer clothes stepping into her dump of a house, or because he didn't want to spend any more time in her company, she wasn't sure. Just that she'd felt a total fool.

'Do you *want* to join us?'

Sally rolled her eyes. 'Are you kidding? The chance of some vaguely adult conversation? Paul doesn't get back from work until after seven most nights. Freddie's the new love of my life, but right now all he does is sleep, poo and cry.'

'Then you're coming in. So what if Freddie wakes up and screams the place down? We're there to help calm him down. As for the adult conversation, we can definitely do that. Audrey's bound to want to talk about kinky sex.'

Sally shook her head, but her expression was amused. 'I can't believe, ten years after we've left school, you're still making me do things I shouldn't.'

Suddenly the door opened and Lottie found herself staring at a crimson-red tie.

'Ladies.' Matt, wearer of the tie, stepped aside and

waved them both through. 'I wasn't sure if the door was stuck.' His gaze fell on the pram. 'I see you have a new member.'

Sally snorted. 'I tried to tell Lottie I shouldn't bring him but she insisted, so apologies in advance when he starts yelling and remember to blame her, not me.'

Lottie watched as Matt bent to get a closer look at Freddie. 'He doesn't look like trouble.'

'Neither does this one,' Sally said, nudging Lottie. 'But trust me, she is.'

Finally, Matt met Lottie's eyes. 'I believe you.' His gaze was surprisingly warm and a shiver of awareness raced through her. God, she'd forgotten this feeling, the sizzle of attraction, the does-he-like-me tug, warring against the he's-only-being-nice-to-a-customer shove. 'No Chewie today?'

'I promised I wouldn't bring him again.'

'He would be very welcome.'

The sincerity in his expression caused another tug in her chest. 'Thank you, but I thought a crying baby was enough disruption for this evening. Your shoes are safe.'

'Shoes?' Sally screwed up her nose. 'I thought Chewie peed all over the floor.'

'He decided that wasn't enough destruction.'

Sally started to laugh. 'And here's me thinking I was the one having all the fun that night.'

'Not at all.'

Matt's quietly spoken words, the way his eyes remained

riveted on hers... Another shiver rippled through her. But the signals he was sending were confusing. Did he fancy her, or was he just trying to be nice? Though nice wasn't the right word. Far too wishy-washy for someone so striking.

Aware of Sally watching them, Lottie yanked her gaze from his. 'Come on, let's get settled while we wait for the others.'

Sally, clearly trying, though largely failing, not to smirk, started to push the pram towards the café. As Lottie went to follow her, Matt spoke again.

'I see Audrey got her way.'

'How do you know that?' Then the penny dropped. 'Ah, they came in to buy *The Mister*.'

'We had to order in extra copies.' His lips curved in that small smile she was starting to enjoy. 'My father was keen to tell me he'd sold you a copy. I think it made his day.'

Lottie thought back to the chat she'd had with Mr Steele senior. Shorter than his son, his hair now grey, but with the same soulful brown eyes. 'I told him he was welcome to come and join the discussions.'

This time Matt's smile was wider, softening his sharp features. 'He sends his apologies. He wasn't sure his heart was up to it.'

Lottie rolled her eyes. 'There is more to the stories we read than sex, you know.'

His face sobered. 'I'm sure.' It looked like he wanted to say something else, but the door jingled and Audrey burst through it.

'I've brought more gin. Thought we'd need it.' She pulled the bottle out of her bag. 'Where were the spankings? Did I miss them? Can't believe that James woman wrote a whole book without kink. Talk about disappointing.' Lottie watched as Matt's eyes rounded so much, it was almost comical. 'Right, well, I'll go and get the gin poured.'

His eyes tracked Audrey as she marched over to the café. 'There's tonic in the kitchen if you need it.'

Lottie started to laugh. 'Thanks, you're a life-saver. I totally forgot Audrey would be force-feeding us gin again.'

He smiled, this time with his eyes, and as she smiled back the air surrounding them became charged. God, when he let himself relax, he really was incredibly attractive. Her heart gave a little bump.

The moment was broken by the arrival of Heidi and Gira. By the time Lottie had said hello to them, Matt had quietly disappeared.

The group settled into their seats and as Audrey splashed a frightening amount of gin into their glasses, Sally nudged her. 'Don't have a crush on him, my arse. There were so many sex sparks flaring between you two, I had to cover Freddie's innocent little eyes.'

'What's that about Freddie's eyes?' Heidi, who was the other side of Sally, peeked into Freddie's pram. 'Surely it's his ears we should be covering tonight.'

Lottie breathed a sigh of relief that she'd escaped Sally's comment.

Gira smiled. 'True, but this book was no *Fifty Shades*, was it? More of a slow burn. A love story, I thought, rather than a story about sex. To be honest, I wasn't sure I liked it.'

As she spoke her smile faltered and again Lottie was left wondering what was going on in Gira's life that caused the occasional flash of bleakness.

'I thought it was pants,' Sally announced. 'I mean, Maxim was no Christian and Alessia no Anna. To be honest, I skipped right through the first half.'

Audrey barked out a laugh. 'You just wanted to get to the sex, like I did.'

Sally gave her a wan smile. 'You're probably right. I knew with this one I wouldn't have time to read the whole thing properly,' she nodded behind her to the still-sleeping Freddie. 'So I just headed for the good bits. With the way my body feels, and the fact that any moment I know we're going to be interrupted by a yelling baby, I can't see any real sex happening until Freddie's old enough to leave home. Reading about it's all I'll have. And frankly E. L. James really disappointed with this one.'

'Alas, I'm with you in the no-sex club.' Heidi took a sip of her gin, her expression sad. 'I have twin girls, both away at university now. Hard to believe the time has flown that fast. I remember, clear as day, when they were born, how exhausted I felt. How there were days I wanted them to hurry up and grow, at first so they'd sleep through the night, then so they could feed themselves and go to the loo, so I could get rid of nappies. A part of me was even glad when they went to school, as I got some time to myself again.' Tears welled in her eyes. 'Now I'd give anything to have the time back. To slow it all down so I could enjoy them both more.' With a soft laugh, she reached into her handbag and drew out a tissue. 'Oh dear, ignore me, I'm getting all daft and sentimental.'

'There's nothing daft about being sentimental.' Lottie gave Heidi an understanding smile.

'And there's nothing daft about missing your kids,' Gira added. 'My two are still at school, but I dread the day they leave me. I know it's part of growing up, that they need to spread their wings, but I can't imagine looking into their room and finding them not there. You must really miss them.'

'I do. Even though the house has never been tidier.' Heidi's smile turned wobbly. 'Their father and I divorced eight years ago, so for a long while it's just been the three of us. Their first term away wasn't so bad. Maybe it was because it was new, having the place to myself. I had all these great ideas for what I was going to do when I wasn't at work. Then I was made redundant, and now instead of filling a few hours, I have days to fill. And the ideas seem to have stalled.' She shook her head. 'Heavens above, it must be the gin making me maudlin. They're coming home for Easter, so I've plenty to look forward to. Which reminds me.' She bent to retrieve a square tin from the floor. 'I had a baking session and thought a slice of cake might help soak up some of the gin Audrey is so liberal with. This one's coffee and walnut.'

'Oh God, my favourite.' Sally grabbed the first slice the moment it was placed on a napkin. 'You're an angel, Heidi.'

She swallowed down a huge mouthful. 'Wow, that's seriously yummy. Like a slice of heaven on a plate. I heard what you said though,' she continued between swallows. 'And you're right. He'll grow up so fast, I'll try to focus on the joy, not on how knackered I feel.' She licked her fingers and munched another mouthful. 'Before you all judge, I never know when he's going to wake up, so I've learnt to speed eat.'

They all laughed and began to tuck in to the cake Heidi dished out, murmuring words of appreciation.

'So, about this book.' Lottie grinned as everyone turned to look at her. 'We are meant to be a book club, after all. Shall we talk about our favourite parts?'

Audrey plonked her gin down on the table and from the spark in her eyes Lottie knew, without doubt, they were going to be talking sex again. 'My favourite part wasn't in this book at all. It was in *Fifty Shades*, when Christian had her bound in his playroom...'

Standing beside Matt, Amy shook her head.

'God, you should see your expression. You're such a prude.'

They'd just finished tidying up in the café, and the combination of their proximity to their guests and Audrey's overly loud voice meant it was impossible not to hear what Christian liked to do to Anna in the playroom. Though apparently Maxim didn't do it to Alessia, much to Audrey's disappointment.

Did it make him a prude because he'd never read a book that had graphic sex in it? He liked to think he wasn't, that he simply preferred having sex to reading about it.

There's more to the stories than sex. He sighed as he recalled Lottie's words. She clearly thought he was judging, putting them in a box labelled *Shallow*, or *Ignorant*, when in fact he was envious of their group and of the way they'd gelled so easily. He found making friends difficult.

'If being uncomfortable talking about sex with people I don't know makes me a prude, then yes, I suppose I am one.' He glanced again at the group. 'It's not how I imagined a book club to be.'

'What were you expecting then?'

He had a feeling if he wasn't careful, Amy would call him worse words than prude. 'I used to attend a book club many moons ago.' Before work had sucked him in so hard he'd barely had time to sleep, never mind read. 'The discussion was more ... structured.'

Amy raised a brow. 'Is that your way of saying they analysed the book, rather than talking about sex while drinking gin and eating cake?'

He let out a bark of laughter. 'It does sound rather chaotic when you put it like that.'

'I think chaotic sounds fun.'

The wistful note in her voice had him looking sharply over at her. It was the first time she'd showed an interest in anything since they'd moved down here. 'Would you like to join them? I can ask Lottie, I'm sure she'd—'

'No.' Amy glared back at him. 'I don't need my brother talking for me, you know. I'm not ten.'

Damn it. Why did he not have the right words, even when it came to his own sister? 'I know you're not. Sorry. I was just trying to help.'

'I know you were, but guess what, there are some things you can't fix.' She pulled off her apron and shoved it into a bag. 'Me and Dad, we're not your responsibility.' Her eyes snapped to his tie and she gave it a tug. 'Maybe you should start sorting yourself out before you interfere with us. You talk about a fresh start, but you still look and sound like a stuffed shirt. I mean, God, you're so uptight it's ridiculous. You're still dressed like you're going to the flaming office.'

She marched out of the small kitchen and he winced as he stared down at his tie. Christ, she was right. He was in no position to lecture the pair of them. As much as he'd banged on about the fresh start, the new him, all he'd actually done was move to a different place and swop an office for a shop. *He'd* not changed.

With a muted curse, he yanked the tie off and undid the top button of his shirt.

'Oops, sorry.' He jerked his head round to find Lottie standing in the doorway, the amusement in her eyes making them spark like diamonds. 'Is that as far as you're undressing, or should I leave?'

Embarrassment fought with humour. Shrugging away

the former, he forced a smile. 'I think that's enough for now.'

'Audrey's rather lurid descriptions getting you hot under the collar?'

Clearly Amy wasn't the only one who thought he was a prude. 'No.' Her eyes widened and he knew he had to provide a reason he'd taken his tie off, or she'd think him rude as well as a prude. 'My sister informs me I'm too uptight. Apparently I look like a stuffed shirt.'

'Ah.'

'Did my predecessor wear a suit?'

Her brow wrinkled and he wished he could say she looked less attractive when she frowned. Fact was, the moment he'd glanced up to find her in the doorway, the air had hummed with awareness and prickles of attraction had raced across his skin. 'He mainly wore a baggy jumper in an unsuccessful bid to hide his belly.' Her gaze dipped to his waistline. 'You don't have that problem.'

Unconsciously he felt himself straighten – as if to emphasise he was lean and trim? God, he had it bad. 'What do you think I should wear?' And wow, that was not a question he'd ever asked anyone.

Her cheeks flushed and he groaned inwardly. *Way to go, Matt, now you've embarrassed her.* 'Whatever you feel comfortable in. It's your business.'

The awkwardness of the conversation, his total ineptitude when it came to talking to this gorgeous woman... He gave her an embarrassed smile. 'Sorry, that was a totally inappropriate question.' He waved a hand down his body. 'It's just, I actually feel comfortable in a suit. I'm kind of at a loss what to wear otherwise.'

If she had him down as some sort of nutter, it didn't show on her face. Instead she smiled, and God, he could feel the glow from it spread through him, warming everywhere it touched. 'You'll figure it out. Try out some looks and see what sort of feedback you get.' Was that his cue to invite her to drop in and rate his choice next time she was in the vicinity? Before he had a chance to test his theory, to find out if she was, ever so cautiously, flirting with him, she changed the subject. 'I came to get more tonic. Amy said she'd left some on the side.' He shifted out of the way and she grabbed a bottle from behind him. 'Thanks. Audrey has no clue how much gin she's pouring out. Keeps saying she can't see clear liquid with her cataracts, but secretly I think she just wants to get us all plastered.'

Their conversation was interrupted by the sound of crying.

'Oh crap, sounds like Freddie's decided to join the party.'

'All that noise, from someone so small?'

Lottie grinned. 'Hard to imagine, huh? Now you can see why I didn't bring Chewie, too. Sorry, we'll try and keep him as quiet as we can.'

'It's no problem,' he started to say, but she'd already vanished.

An hour later, the book club disbanded and the shop locked up, he let himself into the house. 'Amy, Dad, I'm back.'

The door to his dad's sitting room opened. 'Amy's in her room. Looked a bit upset, so I thought I'd talk to you before going to see her.'

One day, just one day, he'd like to come home to a smiling face. Someone who wanted to see him. He supposed he must have had it with Patricia once, but too many bad memories had erased the good. 'I thought she wanted to join the book club, so I said I'd talk to Lottie for her.'

'But she doesn't want you interfering,' his dad supplied. 'She wants to sort things out herself.'

'Yes.'

His dad gave his face a silent study before letting out a deep sigh. 'It's hard to watch someone you love struggle, but sometimes that's all you can do.'

Matt stared back at him. 'Are we still talking about Amy?'

His dad avoided his gaze. 'Tell me about this book club.'

He could spot evasion when he saw it. 'You don't usually ask about the shop.'

'Aye, but you don't usually have a group meeting up there to discuss erotica.' He waggled his bushy eyebrows.

'It's not erotica,' Matt found himself saying. 'The books are about more than sex.'

'Happen they are, but Amy said they were talking about that *Fifty Shades*. Any salacious details?'

'You should read the book if you're that interested.'

'Maybe I will.'

As they shared the same poker face, it was hard to tell if

his dad was asking to avoid a more difficult conversation, or if he was just trying to connect. Either way, Matt was grateful for the olive branch. 'They did discuss this one scene. It took place in some sort of playroom, though nothing like the playroom we had as kids...'

By the time he'd finished telling the tale, his dad was hooting with laughter. It was only later, when he settled into bed, that Matt realised it was the first time he'd seen the old guy laugh since his mum had died.

Chapter Eight

April meeting, nominated book:
Beautiful Player **by Christina Lauren**

'I thought this book was amazing.' Heidi fanned her face with the book in question. 'The chemistry between Will and Hannah, wow. The words scorched off the page.'

'The sex scenes were really hot too,' Lottie added, then started to laugh. 'How come we always start talking about sex?'

'Maybe because not many of us are getting it.' Sally pointed to herself. 'I know I'm hardly setting any sheets on fire right now. I also know you, Lottie Watt, haven't had any since Henry left, which was, what, two years ago?'

Lottie rolled her eyes. 'Eighteen months, actually, not that any of us, besides you, are counting.'

Audrey huffed. 'That's nothing. It's been so long for me,

I have to read about it to remind myself which bits go where.'

'Me too,' Heidi added wryly. 'Dating after my divorce was such a disaster, I decided it was easier to stay single. Nowadays I bake instead, but good as a chocolate brownie tastes, it's not *that* good.'

'At least you've all got excuses.' Gira's voice came out even more quietly than usual. 'I'm married, with children old enough to know to give their parents privacy. But I've not had sex in three months.'

'Wow, that's worse than me.' Sally, clearly realising she'd been insensitive, gave Gira a sheepish smile. 'Shit, sorry. I wish I could blame post-natal hormones but I've always opened my gob without thinking.'

'She has,' Lottie confirmed, but Gira wasn't looking at them. She was staring down at her hands. Aware she must be at the end of her tether to have admitted something so private, Lottie touched her arm. 'Will it help to talk about it? Or do you want Sally and her big mouth to talk about something else?'

'I don't know.' Gira drew in a deep, shuddering breath. 'I'm not a talker. Maybe we should just keep discussing the book.'

'Okay.' Lottie gave Gira's hand a squeeze. 'So what did we think of Will? He's a player, but so lovely to Hannah.'

'In the beginning I wasn't sure about him, but then he was so sweet to her.' Sally huffed. 'Still, I'm glad Paul never slept around before I met him. I'm not sure I could have trusted him. I mean, once a guy's been used to playing the field so much, is he really going to stay with one woman?'

'Trust is so important.' Gira looked up and there were tears in her eyes. 'I don't know if I can trust Ryan anymore.' She shook her head, reaching across the coffee table for a napkin. 'There I go again. Sorry, I'll be okay in a minute. Let's get back to the book.' She smiled sadly. 'That is what we're all here for.'

'Actually, it's not.' Lottie looked around her, catching everyone's eye in turn. 'As I see it, we're a club first, a book club second. I would like us to build a group that enjoys each other's company. Sure, we all have a common interest in books but that's just a starting point. We're here to have a chat, a laugh. To support each other.'

'This is a safe space, love,' Audrey added. 'Look at me, foolish old woman, talking about kinky sex, but none of you judged me for it.'

'And what about all that moaning I did last month about my empty nest,' Heidi supplied. 'I haven't been booted out. Yet,' she added with a grin at Lottie.

Gira opened her mouth to speak but she was beaten to it by eight-week-old Freddie who started to cry. Sally threw her hands up in the air. 'God, if anyone needs to get booted out, it's me. Look what I subject you guys to every month.' She bent to pick him up and started to pace up and down. 'I'll take him outside. That way you can talk without having to dial your voices up to extra loud.'

'No, it's fine.' Gira looked up at Sally. 'We should just discuss the book.'

Jiggling a fractious Freddie, Sally gave Lottie a despairing glance. They'd been friends so long, Lottie knew exactly what the look said: *I need to take this baby away or Gira won't feel able to talk.*

Behind her, Lottie heard the sound of a male, clearing his throat. She turned to find Matt, and once again did a double take, just as she had when she'd seen him earlier. Black jeans, grey Hugo Boss jumper over a white collared shirt. Clearly, he'd taken his sister's words to heart and this was his version of more casual. *Don't think about how hot he is. Especially don't think about how surprisingly vulnerable he looked when he talked clothes with you at the last meeting.*

'Sorry to interrupt.' His voice, deep yet smooth, sent her belly fluttering. 'I'm popping out to drop off an order. I've got my phone if you need anything.'

Freddie started to cry again and Sally let out a strangled laugh. 'I don't suppose you'd take this wailing baby with you.'

For a brief moment his face betrayed his feelings: surprise, disbelief and a big dollop of wary. Then his usual guard came up. 'I could...' he began cautiously.

Sally leapt at the opening. 'Really? You'd take him out for a bit so we can actually hear each other talk? I mean, you are walking, yes, not taking the car?'

'I am walking,' he confirmed.

Just then his eyes found Lottie's and heat burned through her. *Crap. Don't blush, don't blush.* 'Don't feel you have to. We can take turns walking him up and down.'

'No, it's fine.' His mouth lifted at the corners. 'What could possibly go wrong?'

Such a small smile, yet it did crazy things to her hormones. 'You mean because he's not a dog with a fondness for footwear and a strong dislike of whistling?'

His brown eyes warmed. 'Exactly.'

A few minutes later they watched as Matt pushed the pram past the bay window. It was April but still chilly, so he'd thrown on a charcoal wool jacket. If she'd half-hoped his switch from suit to casual would make him less attractive, she was screwed. He was more dangerous now, because he seemed more approachable. Especially pushing a pram.

More like a guy she could see herself dating.

She turned to find Sally giving her a knowing look. *Bugger.* 'Not now,' she hissed, seeing her friend gearing up to say something she wasn't ready to hear. She glanced sideways at Gira, silently indicating there were more important things to focus on.

Sally nodded, but her responding smirk told Lottie she wouldn't be off the hook for long.

'I know why you asked him to take Freddie out.' Gira looked over at Sally. 'It was nice of you.'

'I pushed my screaming baby onto an unsuspecting guy so we could get some peace. It wasn't *that* nice.' Sally smiled. 'But as we won't be interrupted for a while, why don't you tell us about Ryan. He's your husband, right?'

'Yes.' Gira glanced at each of them in turn. 'I haven't mentioned this to anyone, not even my family.'

'Sometimes it's easier to talk to people who aren't so closely involved.' Lottie nodded down to the glass in Gira's hand. 'It gets even easier when you've had one of Audrey's G&Ts.'

Gira smiled, though it looked tired, as if the weight of what she was carrying around had become too much for her. 'Ryan's out late most nights. He says it's with work but I think he's having an affair.'

Having said the words, she burst into tears.

As Matt pushed the pram back along the seafront towards the shop, he wondered if there was a speed limit which babies in prams weren't supposed to exceed. If there was, it was likely he'd broken it.

Mercifully, Freddie was quiet. Not asleep, though. His bright eyes looked up at Matt, as if to say, *Who the hell are you*? Or possibly, *Why are we going so fast?*

'My experience with babies is from a long time ago,' he told Freddie in answer to the possible question. 'So it's in both our interests to get you back to your mum as soon as possible.'

A few minutes later he breathed a sigh of relief as the shop came into view. But as he passed the bay window, he groaned. Damn, that looked like one heavy conversation. Gira seemed to be crying. Lottie had an arm around her and the others were gazing at her in sympathy, Audrey pouring more gin into Gira's glass.

'Not sure we should go in just yet.' He looked down at the wide-eyed Freddie. 'We'll keep walking for a bit.' He'd been married for six years and gone through a divorce. Seeing a woman cry wasn't new to him, but he didn't think Gira would thank him for bursting in right now.

Just then Lottie caught his eye through the window. She bit into her lip, gaze drifting to Gira, clearly wondering what she should do. He motioned with his hand that he'd carry on walking.

He saw her mouth, 'You okay?'

He nodded and set off again. 'We'll give it another ten minutes.' He eyed little Freddie. 'Don't let me down now. I'd rather like to hand you back as you are now. Happy. Quiet.'

He wondered how much of that desire came from wanting to appear at least slightly competent in front of Lottie.

It turned out the extra ten minutes was eight minutes too long. By the time they reached the bookshop, Freddie was exercising his lungs again. Leaving the pram outside, Matt scooped him into his arms and tried to remember his mum's instructions from twenty-odd years ago. 'Come on, mate, don't make me look like a muppet.'

Mercifully, the boy quietened as Matt stepped back inside.

'There you are.' Sally rose to her feet. 'We were starting to think you might have kidnapped him. At the very least, taken him to the pub for some male bonding.'

'Sorry, I thought…' His gaze flew to Gira, and then to Lottie. *I thought you needed more time.*

Lottie smiled warmly back at him. 'Ignore her, she's got a weird sense of humour. What she meant to say was, we're really grateful to you for taking him out.' Her eyes found his. 'And not rushing back.'

Matt was so trapped in Lottie's clear-eyed gaze, he was barely aware of Sally walking towards him.

'Definitely that, too. You're a bloody marvel.' Sally reached to pick up the tiny bundle, who grumbled as he was removed from Matt's shoulder. 'Hey, come here, little monster. Poor Matt's had enough of you.'

As Sally calmed Freddie down again, Lottie eyed him curiously. 'I didn't have you down as a baby guy.'

'I'm not.'

'Yet you looked perfectly at ease with him. Most non-dads would panic at the first sound of crying.'

'I panicked inside.' The talk of babies made him feel slightly off balance. Or maybe that was down to Lottie, and the expression on her face. Was she interested in him, like he was in her? He swallowed and forced himself to carry on talking, where his usual *modus operandi* would be to shut up. 'I tried to remember how my mum had told me to hold Amy. There's nine years between us.'

'Ah, that explains your proficiency.' She glanced over at Freddie who was now gurgling happily as Gira cooed at him.

'Did you have a useful discussion after I'd gone?' he asked quietly.

When her eyes found his again, he knew she got his meaning. 'I think it was helpful, yes,' she whispered. 'Thank you.'

'Good.' He knew he should walk away and let them get on with it, but somehow he found himself rooted to the spot. 'What was the verdict on The Player?'

'If he really is having an affair, he's a bastard,' Sally answered as she pushed the pram into the corner. 'But we don't yet know for sure.' The whole place went quiet and Sally, who'd been distracted by Freddie, looked up in alarm. 'Oh buggeration, you meant the book, didn't you?'

Christ, his conversation skills were lacking at the best of times. He really couldn't do awkward. 'The book,' he confirmed, deliberately keeping his eyes away from Gira. 'That's what I was referring to. Enjoy the rest of your meeting. I'll be round the back if you need me.'

He walked swiftly to the back office and buried himself in paperwork.

He became so absorbed that he didn't realise Lottie was standing in front of him until she spoke.

'We've finished.'

'Oh.' He glanced at his watch, which confirmed it was already 7.30 p.m. 'That went quickly.'

Her lips curved. 'Probably because you spent a lot of it pushing a pram up and down the seafront.'

'Perhaps.' His eyes swept over her: the purple hoodie, slim-fitting jeans, big yellow coat in her hands. She did casual like she was born to it … He glanced down at his cashmere jumper. He felt he was trying to play the part of chilled shop owner, and mainly failing.

As if she could read his mind, she smiled. 'I'd give the outfit eight out of ten.'

'Only eight?' He frowned, pretending to be upset. 'That won't do. I'm a high achiever.'

'Don't get me wrong, it looks really good on you.' She raised her eyes to the ceiling. 'Oh God, now it sounds like I'm, you know, buttering you up.'

'Are you?'

Her cheeks went pink. 'Not intentionally, but there is a favour I wanted to ask.'

He was surprised how disappointed he was to realise the compliment hadn't been real. 'Ask away.'

'I know you've been kind enough to allow us to bring snacks, and for Audrey to ply us with alcohol, but today we talked about having a pizza or some other take-out delivered. Partly to absorb the alcohol, partly because by the time we get back it's late to start cooking, but mainly because it seems like a nice, social thing to do. We'd make sure to clean up afterwards, but I understand if you think it's shifting the goalposts. I mean, you agreed to a book club, now it's a boozy meal out while we talk about books.' He noticed her hands tighten round the coat she was holding. 'We could always shift the group to someone's house, but I don't want people to feel pressurised to host.' She gave him a weak smile. 'I'd have it at mine, but it's not quite ready for receiving guests, which is a polite way of saying it's as much of a dump on the inside as it is on the outside.'

'I never said it was a dump,' he protested. 'I believe I said it had the potential to be charming.'

'We both know that potential is a long way in the future. Or you would know if you'd come in, which you didn't, though I can't say I blame you.' She drew in a breath. 'Anyway, I'm getting side-tracked here—'

'Whoa, wait a minute.' He studied her face: the cute upturn of her nose, the freckles, the dizzying clarity of her eyes. 'Did you want me to come in for a drink the other night?'

Her brow wrinkled. 'Why else would I ask you?'

'To be polite?'

'So you always turn people down when they invite you into their homes, on the basis you don't think they mean it?'

'No … I mean I can't remember the last time I received such an invitation.' His heart began to beat against his ribs. 'Should I be lucky enough to receive another, I won't make the same mistake.'

A slow smile split her face. 'Okay then.' Silence descended, but it didn't feel awkward. It felt charged, buzzing with unspoken messages. Eventually she glanced towards the door, where he could hear them all helping Sally push the pram out. 'I guess I'll see you next time.'

'Yes. With pizza,' he added, his eyes finding hers.

She smiled right into his, causing everything inside him to sit up and take notice. 'Thank you. We'll save a slice for you.'

As she turned to leave, he couldn't pull his gaze away from her retreating figure, which unnerved him. He'd felt strong attraction before. Hell, he'd married – naively – because of it. Yet he was older and wiser now. He knew the damage that losing his head over a woman could do.

Still, whatever his mind was saying, it appeared his body wasn't prepared to listen.

Chapter Nine

May meeting, nominated book:
The Little Teashop in Tokyo **by Julie Caplin**

'Who doesn't want to go to Tokyo now, having read this?' Heidi sighed wistfully, picking up the book they'd all been avidly reading this month. 'It's given me really itchy feet to go travelling again. Since the girls grew too old to holiday with their old mum, I've not been away. The thought of going by myself just never seemed as exciting.'

Lottie looked over to her. 'You shouldn't let being single stop you. There are so many holiday companies out there who cater for people exactly like you. You'd have a ball, meeting like-minded singles your age. I bet they do a trip to Japan, too.'

'You really think so?'

'Hang on a minute.' Sally's fingers flew over her phone.

'Yep, there you are. This company do a tour of Japan for solo travellers, starting and ending in Tokyo. It says you can linger in the gardens of Kyoto, shoot through the mountain air on a bullet train, and stay in a traditional *ryokan* for the ultimate in Japanese luxury.' She grinned over at Heidi. 'Maybe, like Fiona in the book, you can meet an old crush and fall in love.'

Heidi smiled. 'Julie does write such beautiful romances. Still, I'd be happy if, like Fiona, it helped me, I don't know, find myself again, I guess. Work out what I want to do with this next phase of my life.'

'Shall I book it then?' Sally waggled her eyebrows. 'Just tell me when you want to go, hand over your credit card, and Japan could be yours.'

'Good heavens, you young things are always in such a rush.' Heidi gave a gentle shake of her head. 'It will take me months to make a decision like that.'

Lottie laughed. 'Not with Sally around. She'll hound you, so be warned. I remember once saying I fancied scuba diving. Before I knew it, she'd booked me a week in Croatia.'

'Yeah, and you didn't regret it,' Sally protested. 'That's where you met Henry.'

'Yes.' The reminder sent a dart of melancholy through her. What a holiday that had been. Her first solo venture and she'd not only come back as a certified diver, she'd come back in love with a guy who, amazingly, had been a student at the university not far from where she lived.

Had she been right not to follow him to California? Even

now, eighteen months on, the decision haunted her. Usually late at night, when she missed a pair of arms around her.

'Tell us more about this Henry.' Audrey reached for another slice of pizza. What a genius idea it had been to order in something to soak up the gin, though clearly not enough to keep the eldest member of their club quiet. 'Is he really out of the picture?'

'He is,' Lottie confirmed. She waited for the familiar tight feeling in her chest, but this time it was so slight it was barely there.

'It's high time you moved on from him then.' Audrey took another swig of her second, or was it her third, large gin with a dash of tonic. 'Pretty young thing like you should be having regular sex.'

As Lottie tried to avoid choking on the pizza she'd just swallowed, they were interrupted by a strangled cry coming from the kitchen.

'Stupid machine!'

'Sounds like Amy's having trouble. I'll check on her.' Grateful to get away from a discussion of her sex life, Lottie dashed into the room behind the counter where she found Amy pulling dirty plates out of the dishwasher. 'Hey, anything I can help with?'

Amy shook her head. 'Sorry, I didn't mean to say that so loud.'

'You can say it as loud as you like. We're in your space, not the other way round.'

'Yeah, not really. It's Matt's. I'm just helping out.' She continued to haul items out of the dishwasher.

'This might sound daft, but shouldn't you be putting dirty stuff into the dishwasher, rather than the other way round?'

Amy huffed out a laugh. 'It's not working.'

'Let me take a look.' She flipped the switch to turn it on, and winced. 'That sounds like a blocked pipe. You'll need a plumber. If you don't have one, I can recommend a guy.'

'We don't have one.'

The sound of Matt's voice behind her caused Lottie's heart to jump. 'Hi.'

He slotted his hands into the pockets of a pair of dark blue jeans, and smiled back. 'Hello.'

Her stomach did a somersault and Lottie groaned inwardly. Now she knew why she'd felt a bit, well ... flat this evening. She hadn't wanted to acknowledge it, but there was no escaping the fact. When Amy had greeted them earlier, explaining her brother was out running errands, Lottie had been *disappointed*.

Now she was like a battery that had just received a full charge.

And God, she couldn't stop staring at him. No jumper today, just a slim-fitting blue/grey collared shirt with a discreet pattern. It showcased his broad shoulders and hinted at the curve of his pecs, the trimness of his waist. It made her want to undo the buttons, slip her fingers beneath it and trail them across his skin.

Heat rushed through her and Lottie had to force her gaze away. 'So, my mate Shaun's a plumber.' Her voice didn't sound like her own and she swallowed a few times. 'I'll give him a call if you like.'

'Thanks, yes.'

Amy exhaled sharply and Matt looked pained. 'That's if Amy agrees. The café is hers.'

'Yeah, right. That's why you were phoning new food suppliers yesterday.' She glared at him. 'I heard you.'

Lottie watched as Matt briefly hung his head. 'I suggest we talk about this later.' His gaze locked on Lottie's and beneath the rigidly controlled expression, she saw a glimpse of pain.

Giving her a final, stiff smile, Matt left the room.

'Shit.' Amy wiped her eyes. 'Sorry, that wasn't cool. I'm going to be in trouble now.'

She could see Amy was close to tears and Lottie's heart went out to her. 'I don't know him very well, but your brother looked more upset than angry.'

'Yeah, upset that I embarrassed him in front of you.' Amy wouldn't look her in the eye.

Lottie would like to bet Matt's reaction had been more than embarrassment. 'Shall I call Shaun? He owes me a favour. I might even be able to get him over here tonight.'

'Really?' Amy heaved out a sigh. 'Tomorrow will be mega hard if we don't have a dishwasher.'

A quick call later, and Lottie smiled at Amy. 'He's on his way.'

'Phew, thanks.' She gave an awkward shrug. 'Sorry I made you interrupt your meeting.' She gave Lottie a shy smile. 'That book you were talking about sounded well good.'

'It was.' Sensing Amy's interest, Lottie added, 'I know you said books were more your brother's thing, but if you think you might enjoy it, you're very welcome to come and join us. We'd love more members.'

Amy stared down at the flooded dishwasher. 'I don't know. I mean, I'd like to read more books, sure, but I couldn't talk about them. Not like you guys do.'

Again, Lottie felt her heart go out to her. Amy was only a few years younger than she was, yet that lack of confidence made the gap feel much wider. 'You don't have to talk, not if you don't want to.' She laughed. 'We're not short of people happy to do that. But talking is no good if there isn't anyone prepared to listen.'

The edges of Amy's mouth curved upwards. 'I'm good at that.'

'Then you should join us.' Lottie glanced at the dirty dishes. 'And as you can't do anything about this lot until Shaun arrives, why not come now? Last I heard, Sally was booking Heidi a trip to Japan.'

Amy's eyes widened. 'Seriously?'

'I think she would have done, if Heidi had handed her credit card over. Still, it has got Heidi thinking about planning a holiday.' She gave Amy an encouraging smile. 'You never know, joining the club might spark some ideas for you, too. And I'm not just talking about which book to read next.'

Matt gave Amy half an hour to calm down. And himself half an hour to do the same. Had she been right about him interfering when he shouldn't? Probably, but he was used to being in control of things, or maybe he should say he *liked* to be in control. It wasn't a power kick, it was more about grounding him, keeping him on the level. The shop was his business, so he needed to know what was going on. It was the same reason he meticulously ordered his finances and watched his diet. The same reason he'd got up at the crack of dawn every morning to get into the office in his previous job. And stayed until most people had left.

It cost you your wife, pushed away your family and nearly made you lose your mind. He drew in a deep breath and rose from his chair. Damn it, Amy had been right. He'd put her in charge and then undermined her. He had to learn to let go.

Feeling contrite, he made his way back to the kitchen, only to pull up short when he pushed open the door. Those definitely weren't Amy's legs sticking out from under the sink.

'I take it you're the plumber?'

The body sat up with a start. Early twenties, blond shaggy hair, amused blue eyes. Muscular physique with arms covered in tattoos. 'And if I said no?'

'I'd say you were looking in the wrong place if you're hoping to find a book.'

The guy laughed and jumped to his feet. 'I'm Shaun.' He stuck out his hand for Matt to shake. 'Lottie's friend.'

Matt shook his hand, unnerved by the sudden dart of jealousy. 'It's good of you to come so quickly.'

'Yeah, no worries.' He grinned. 'Lottie's a hard woman to turn down. And that's before I saw the cute café manager.'

Okay, he really wasn't sure how to deal with that comment. He was relieved Lottie and Shaun appeared to be exactly what they'd both said – friends – yet he didn't want to be relieved, because he didn't want it to matter. Then there was the big-brother part of him that was wary about this stranger's interest. 'Amy is my sister.'

'Oh, right.' Shaun clearly heard the warning in Matt's voice. 'Look, I didn't mean anything stalkerish by that. Lottie will vouch for me. I'm a straight-up guy.' He rubbed his hand on his jeans. 'If you were looking for Amy, she's talking books with Lottie and the others.'

'Thanks.' Well, well, had Amy joined the book club? He was about to go and find out when his sister appeared in the kitchen doorway, Lottie behind her.

'Shaun's fixing the dishwasher problem,' Amy announced abruptly, clearly still annoyed with him.

'So I figured.' He caught sight of Lottie over Amy's shoulder and the embarrassment from earlier came crashing back. Bad enough he and his sister were arguing, but to have it witnessed, and by Lottie? 'Thank you for staying behind to sort it.'

'You don't have to thank me for doing my job.'

She looked so disgusted with him, Matt had to turn away, it hurt too much. It seemed that everything he said to Amy upset her.

'You've got yourself a clogged pipe,' Shaun said cheerfully, ignoring the tension. 'I'll have it fixed in no time. Especially if that old bird keeps plying me with gin.'

Lottie groaned. 'Audrey was supposed to be coming to the kitchen to find more tonic.'

'Don't fret, she found it. Not before she'd poured me a stiff drink and invited me back to hers, mind.' Shaun waggled his eyebrows. 'Best offer I've had all week.' His eyes rested on Amy. 'Then again, it's only Thursday. Who knows what the next few days might bring?'

Matt watched as Amy's face turned a deep shade of red. Mortified? Or pleased? He wished he understood her more. Wished he was the sort of big brother she could discuss this stuff with. *Give it time.*

Lottie coughed, drawing his attention. 'Matt, have you got a minute?'

'Sure.'

Her gaze drifted between Amy and Shaun and then back to him. 'Err, maybe we can go to your office?'

And just like that, his mind began to play back images he had no right to be thinking. Her closing the door firmly behind them. Then stalking towards him. Him lifting her onto the desk so he could slide between her thighs. Their mouths crashing onto each other.

As if she could read his mind, her cheeks flushed a little.

'That way we won't interrupt Shaun. He's easily distracted and I know Amy needs this fixed tonight.'

'Of course.' His voice sounded rough to his ears. It didn't help that his gaze fell to her pert backside as she turned and walked out ahead of him.

Stop it. You don't need this, he told himself. *And Lottie definitely doesn't need you.* She was made for fun, laughter. Spontaneity. A guy who wore a pair of jeans like they were second nature. Not a flaming stuffed shirt, as Amy had so aptly pointed out.

The moment they walked into his office, Lottie turned to him. 'I'm sorry about that. It must have sounded like I wanted to get you alone – which I did, but not, you know, for any dodgy reason.'

'Dodgy?' He had to laugh. 'You mean like you want to raid the safe, or...' He let the sentence trail, knowing if he put a voice to the images that had played in his head, she'd be out of the door like a shot.

Her gaze dropped to his mouth. 'I believe it was the *or*.'

Christ. The temperature in his office shot up and Matt didn't know where to look, or what to say. If he didn't feel so scarred by his marriage, so uncertain what he could offer, he'd take a step towards her. Place his hands on her shoulders. Pull her towards him and give her exactly what it looked like she might want. What he definitely wanted.

But he wasn't a guy who had casual sex. And he wasn't sure he could offer Lottie anything else right now.

'So, anyway.' Lottie seemed to shake herself. 'I just wanted to say I've known Shaun a long time. We were at college together. He's a first-rate plumber but also a really good guy.' She looked earnestly at him. 'I know you felt the same sparks between them that I did, and I wanted to ask you not to be put off by Shaun's tattoos and cocky humour. He's a complete softie when it comes to women. Amy would be in good hands if he asked her out.'

Okay, so the wanting to kiss him had clearly all been in his head. 'You think I'm that judgemental?' he asked, stung.

Her cheeks flushed. 'No, that's not what I meant. I just… I could see you getting into big-brother mode and I wanted to reassure you, that's all.'

Great. Now he'd managed to piss her off. He drew in a breath, forced his scattering emotions to calm. 'Sorry.' Rubbing a hand across his face, he gave her a weak smile. 'What you saw was me worrying how to be a big brother. I hadn't got as far as worrying about Shaun.'

'Oh.' She looked confused. 'I assumed you and Amy were close. I mean, she works with you, she lives with you.' She smiled. 'You bicker like siblings.'

He did not want to talk about this. Personal conversation was hard enough, but talking about his mistakes to a woman he liked?

His expression must have given him away because she waved a hand. 'None of which is any of my business. So I'll leave you in peace.'

As she turned to go, Matt felt a tug of acute disappointment. A few minutes ago he'd contemplated kissing her. Now they were back to mere acquaintances. 'We lost touch for a long while.' She halted, a puzzled expression on her face, so he added, 'Amy and I.'

'Ah, I see.' Her feet shifted and she smiled at him. 'In which case I'm sure you'll find that bond again. I mean, you both clearly want it to work, or you wouldn't be living and working together.'

Her words made sense, but Lottie didn't know the whole picture. That Amy was here not through choice, but through lack of choice. 'Maybe trying to do both is part of the problem.' Matt shook the unhelpful thought away. He'd focus on Amy later. For now, he wanted to get back on track with the woman who made him feel, made him want, like he hadn't in a long time. 'You owe me a slice of pizza, by the way.' He didn't usually eat it – too many carbs – but it was worth it for the excuse to have her pop back.

Her eyes flared with surprise. 'So I do. I'll bring one round if there's any left.'

Better, he thought as he watched her leave. Mere acquaintances didn't share pizza. Now, if he could just stop thinking about kissing her, maybe they could move on to being friends.

Chapter Ten

The pizza had been eaten – and yes, she'd given a slice to Matt. The man she'd as good as admitted she wanted to jump half an hour ago.

Lottie cringed at the memory as she helped clear the plates from the coffee table. For a second she'd thought he wanted the same, but then his guard had come up again. All part of the mixed signals he kept giving out.

Time to stop making a twit of herself, she decided. She'd given him two openings now, and he'd turned them both down. Which was actually a good thing, because she was used to easy and straightforward … she *liked* easy and straightforward. Her family, her friends, Henry, they were open books. Matthew Steele had *complicated* written all over his darkly handsome face. Just coming through the other side of a broken heart, she did not need that in her life.

'So Amy, what did you think?' Sally asked as she

bundled a sleepy Freddie into his pram. 'Are you going to join us every month or did Audrey and her gin scare you off?'

Lottie watched as Amy gave Sally a shy smile. 'I enjoyed it. Nearly as much as Heidi's lemon drizzle cake.'

Heidi chuckled. 'Thank you, dear. Baking is keeping me sane. It's just a shame these meetings are only monthly. So many cakes, not enough people to eat them.'

Amy frowned and looked like she was about to say something, but then she shook her head.

'All fixed.' Toolbox in hand, Shaun swaggered into the café in that cocky way he had that made Lottie roll her eyes. People often wondered if the pair of them were more than friends, but she'd never felt the *tingle*. Not like she'd felt with Henry. *Not like you feel with Matt.*

Crap, she really had to stop thinking about him that way.

Speaking of tingles … Shaun looked at Amy, who glanced away, a smile hovering over her lips. 'That's amazing, thanks.'

'Amazing.' He grinned. 'I'll take that.'

Lottie watched as Amy tried to overcome her shyness enough to look Shaun in the eye. 'How much do we owe you?'

'I'll pop in tomorrow with the invoice.' He winked at her. 'Be a good excuse to see you again.'

As Amy blushed all the way to her hairline Matt appeared from around the corner. He slowed his pace when he saw them, clearly not expecting such a crowd still. His gaze latched onto Amy, then Shaun. 'Have you managed to sort the problem?'

'Yep, I've left the dishwasher going through the quick-wash cycle. Reckon it's got about ten minutes left.'

'Great.'

Matt shoved his hands in his pockets, a gesture Lottie was starting to understand meant he felt uncomfortable. It was clear he wanted to ask about the bill but didn't want to step on Amy's toes again.

Amy read her brother's unspoken message. 'He's bringing the bill in tomorrow.'

'Okay, good.'

For a few seconds, there was an awkward silence due to the tension between Amy and Matt, maybe also the *presence* of Matt. He might have discarded the suit, but he still conveyed an air of formality; the boss rather than one of the team.

'Ah, it's the boss man.' Audrey, who'd been chatting away to Gira, either didn't feel the tension, or didn't give two hoots about it. 'Have you changed your mind about coming to our little book club yet?' She glanced around her. 'What do you think, ladies? A male point of view might be interesting.' She winked. 'Especially for the sexy bits.'

Matt's big brown eyes widened and Lottie stifled a grin. Way to clear the atmosphere, Audrey. Bring up sex again.

'I don't believe I would be much help,' Matt said slowly, as if carefully picking out his words. 'I'm more into … doing than talking about it.'

Audrey boomed out a laugh. 'Aren't we all, dear. Even those of us considered well past our sell-by date.'

Matt's discomfort was obvious. It wasn't just the rigid expression, or the stiff set of his shoulders. His whole aura screamed, *Floor, please swallow me up,* yet so far he hadn't made an excuse to leave. Maybe she was wrong, but she sensed, in his own way, he was trying to bond with them, even though he was clearly ill at ease doing it.

'There's no age limit to having sex.' Hands still in his pockets, Matt gave Audrey a small smile. 'It's a question of finding the right partner. As it is for all of us,' he added quietly. Then looked straight at Lottie.

Boom. Her belly swooped and her heart banged against her ribs. Was he thinking, suggesting …? Before she could ask the question of herself, Heidi chipped in with a 'Well said' and Matt averted his eyes, the moment broken.

The next few minutes were a flurry of activity. Chairs were moved back, plates washed, the dishwasher emptied, goodbyes said. Finally, it was just Lottie and Amy left in the café.

'I hope you'll stay and join us next month, too,' Lottie said as she placed the last glass back in the cupboard. 'It's been lovely having another face round the coffee table.'

'Thanks, I'd like that.' Amy started to giggle. 'Audrey's such a hoot. I thought Matt was going to bust a blood vessel when she started talking sex to him. He's like, *so serious* most of the time now. It's weird.'

Suddenly all the lights when out and the café went dark.

A split second later a muffled curse came from the back of the shop where Matt must have disappeared to.

'Oops.' Amy winced. 'He's not going to be happy.'

Lottie stifled a sigh. Typical. She was convinced Amy had been about to tell her a bit more about her brother. 'Probably just a fuse. I'll go and check it out.' She switched on the torch light on her phone and waited as Amy did the same. 'Look, there's no need for you to hang about if you don't want. I'll tell Matt you've gone home.'

'Are you sure? I mean, he is my brother. I should go and help.'

'True.' She winked. 'But I'm an electrician.'

Amy's eyes widened. 'For real?'

'Yep, so off you go. He's in safe hands.'

'Thanks. He's grumpy enough with me. I could do without walking back with him.'

Lottie wanted to tell Amy she believed her brother was annoyed with himself, not her, but it wasn't any of her business.

'Everyone okay?' Matt's voice drifted over as they made their way towards the front door.

His question was followed by a thud and then another curse. Amy looked at her questioningly and Lottie mouthed at her to go.

'It's just me,' she shouted as she closed the door behind Amy. 'I told Amy to go home. Where's your fusebox?'

'That's what I'm trying to find.'

Using her phone-torch, she picked her way through the

deserted shop, trying not to focus on how intimate it felt, just her and Matt. Alone in the dark. As she turned past a bookshelf, suddenly there he was, his face illuminated by his own phone. A slow smile spread across his face when he saw her. 'Hi.'

It was a strange thing to say, considering they'd seen each other several times already this evening, yet maybe he was feeling this intimacy, too. 'Hi back.'

He laughed quietly, dragging a hand down his face. 'Sorry, the dark must be getting to me. No fusebox on the walls. It might be in the office.'

'What were you doing when the lights went off?'

He nodded to the switch on the back wall. 'Turning that off.'

Together they searched the office, finding the fusebox on the wall behind the door. Immediately she scanned the switches. 'This has no place in a business. It should be in a museum. Didn't it come up on the survey when you bought the shop?' She flashed the light in his direction and when she saw him staring at her, she realised he had no clue what she did for a living. 'Ah, you're wondering why I'm slagging off your electrics.'

'I'm curious, yes.'

'I'm a sparky.' When he didn't reply, just kept looking at her, she added, 'You know, an electrician.'

Matt knew he was gawping but he couldn't help it. Lottie had been coming to his place for a few months, yet only now he was finding out she was an electrician? It didn't say much for his vow to immerse himself more in the community when he couldn't even manage basic conversation with the woman who spent several hours a month in his shop.

A woman he found incredibly attractive. One he'd nearly kissed not that long ago.

'You look surprised,' she commented dryly as she fiddled with the switches.

He shook himself. 'Sorry, yes, I suppose I am.'

'I get that all the time.'

There was a slight edge to her voice and he could only imagine how difficult it must be to be a pretty blonde in what many still considered to be a man's world. 'My surprise wasn't so much the job you do,' he clarified. 'More that we've known each other for several months and I'm only now finding it out.'

She glanced sideways at him. 'Neat catch.'

'It's also true.' He perched on the desk, watching as she examined the fusebox. There was something about the dark that made it easier to talk. 'Why an electrician?' She raised an eyebrow and he let out a sharp laugh. 'I guess that's a sexist question, as I probably wouldn't ask it of a man, but I'm fascinated.' *By you,* he could have added, but caution and self-preservation held him back. 'I have no useful skills at all. I can't change a plug.'

'With a surname like mine, what else could I be?'

He tried to recall the email she'd sent. 'Watt?' She nodded, a smile playing around her mouth. 'Very good, but that's your glib answer. I was hoping for the real answer.'

For a moment she looked taken aback and he worried he'd offended her, but then she huffed out a breath. 'Honestly, I'm not sure. I hated school. I was probably a bad student, or so I kept being told, so there was no way I was going to spend any more years being lectured to by teachers who'd basically written me off. And I couldn't stand the idea of being cooped up in an office. I needed something practical where I could be out and about, and where I could meet people because, as you know, I love a good chat. Plus, I was a tomboy, so the idea of doing something that guys usually did was quite a hook.' She paused for what Matt thought was a much-needed breath. 'Mainly though, while I was still deciding what to do, I joined a book club and one of the books we read had a really cool blonde heroine who happened to be an electrician.' A fond smile tilted her mouth at the memory. 'Sure, I was blonde, but I certainly wasn't cool. Still, the group decided that was the job for me.'

'Hence your interest in book clubs.' When she looked confused, he added, 'It helped you find your path.'

'Funny, I'd not thought of it like that. Mainly, I think book clubs are important because they showed me how to enjoy books. I hated reading when I was at school.' She screwed up her face. 'I remember trying to wade through *Of Mice and Men* and totally missing whatever deep meaning the teacher reckoned was behind the words. But then when

I left school I worked in this coffee shop that hosted a monthly book club. I was supposed to be serving customers but when the club met I used to hang around at the back of the café where they sat, pretending to clear tables when actually I was listening in. I couldn't figure out how they could be so excited, just talking about books.'

'Watching you all in action, I would say you know now.'

She laughed. 'Yeah. I found out it was all about finding the *right* book.' The light from her phone bounced round the office as she pushed the fusebox door shut. 'I need to look at that light switch. I don't suppose you've got a screwdriver around here?'

'The guy I bought the shop from—'

'Larry.'

Of course she knew his name. 'Yes, Larry left a few things in the store cupboard. I think there was a toolbox.' He backed up and opened the door opposite the study. Right at the back he found the rusty old toolbox. 'Here… Ooooph.' He hadn't realised she'd followed him. For a few humming seconds they stood nose to nose in the dark. Maybe because he couldn't really see her, just the shadows provided by the light from the phone-torches, suddenly he was acutely aware of how sexy she smelt. A hint of orange and something else, maybe ginger? Whatever it was, it was playing havoc with his system.

Then again, that could be down to the soft press of her breast against his arm.

His body began to kick into life and he stepped back, stunned. No. This was bad timing. Maybe when he was more settled, more certain of what he could offer. And when his dad and Amy were happier. Swallowing hard, he handed her the toolbox. 'Hopefully you'll find what you need in here.'

He wasn't sure whether to be pleased or worried that she looked as unbalanced as he did. 'Thanks.' She settled it on the floor and crouched down to look inside. 'Bingo.' Raising a small screwdriver aloft, she nodded to him. 'Can you shine the light from your phone at the switch?'

He did as instructed and she immediately set about removing the cover from the light switch.

It felt odd, watching her work. The testosterone in him wanted to be the one doing the fixing, yet he was in awe of the deft way she dealt with the wires she revealed, very much aware he wouldn't know where to start.

'Those teachers were wrong.'

She looked up, surprise crossing her face. 'Thanks. I like to think so, but it's too early to say yet.'

He nodded to the wires. 'Not from where I'm standing.' For a few beats there was silence and it surprised him that he was the one to break it. 'So how's the book club coming along?'

She let out a small laugh. 'I guess that depends on your definition of what a good book club should look like. If Eve were to come… She's the woman who runs the library book club—'

'The one you left,' he interrupted. 'If I recall correctly, you went on to accost a poor bookshop owner and demand a refund for an unread book.'

Briefly he shifted the focus of the light from the switch, to her face. His reward was a fully illuminated sight of her laughter. 'True, but I did spend the refund in his shop.'

'Also true.' From that day on, he realised, he'd been entranced by her.

'Anyway, Eve would have a hissy fit at how we're running the club. The booze, the choice of book, the lack of focus.'

'It's not just about the books for you though, is it?'

She turned to look at him and he could sense her surprise at his question. 'What do you mean?'

'I've seen you with the group. You like books, but you also like *people*. And you've a talent for making them feel special, included. Listened to.' He hesitated, but the dark made him bold. 'You appear to have got through to Amy. Something I've failed to do.'

It wasn't so dark that he couldn't make out her frown. 'You know, it's not what people say that gives them away, but what they do. The fact that Amy has agreed to live with you, is willing to work with you … a lot of girls her age wouldn't do that. They'd move in with their mates.'

'Amy couldn't.' He didn't want Lottie to have a false impression so he forced himself to keep talking. 'We lost our mum last year. One of the last things she asked of us was that we looked after each other.' He was really, really glad of the dark now. 'So you see, Amy's not here because she wants to be. She and Dad are here because they made a promise to Mum.'

'Why are *you* here?' she asked quietly.

So much he could say, but despite the cover of dark, he still wasn't that person. The one who could talk openly, freely, about his personal life. 'I thought a move to the sea would do us all good.' It was truthful enough.

'A more relaxed pace, huh?' He caught her wry smile. 'Until you agreed to let a rowdy book club into your shop.'

He found himself smiling. 'Quite.'

She paused a moment and tugged at a wire. 'Well, there's your problem. One of the wires had become loose.' She fiddled and twiddled. 'That should fix it.' With admirable efficiency, she screwed the cover back on the switch. 'I'll go and turn the electrics back on.'

A few seconds later, the bright lights of the shop blinked on again, the intimacy destroyed. He was left wondering how much of himself he'd given away.

'So, that fusebox of yours.' Lottie appeared in front of him and it took him a moment to adjust to seeing her again in the light. Those silver eyes, the bright smile. Gorgeous face. 'I don't want to look like I'm touting for business, but you should really get the wiring looked at and the fusebox changed. When was the last time it was checked? Have you got a certificate?'

He should know, but he didn't. In his unseemly rush to escape the regrets of his old life and get on with starting a new one, the details of the purchase, the nuts and bolts of it all, hadn't seemed important. 'How badly will you think of me if I admit I haven't a clue?'

'Not badly at all if you employ me to look at it.'

He smiled, something he found easier the more time he spent in her company. 'Consider yourself officially hired.'

'Great. I'll take a look at the diary and let you know when I'm free. I'm guessing after hours would be best for you. Less disruption.'

His pulse gave a little jump at the thought of being alone with her again, after the shop had closed. 'That would be helpful, yes.'

They walked together to the front of the shop where she picked up the coat she'd abandoned on the counter. Then surprised him by squeezing his arm. 'Don't worry about Amy. At the moment she thinks you're cross with her because of the ding-dong you had in front of me earlier.'

'Cross? I was in the wrong.'

She smiled straight into his eyes. 'And that's why you guys will work it out.'

Boom, just like that, he felt the zing again. As the warmth from her smile fizzed through him, he wanted to kiss her so much, it hurt. Her mouth was tantalisingly close, his body primed and raring to go and his willpower on a knife edge.

But as he waged an internal war with himself, Lottie stepped away and opened the door. 'Goodnight, Matt. I'll be in touch about your fusebox.'

For a long while after she'd left he stood rooted to the spot, his emotions flip-flopping. It was a good thing he'd not given in, he tried to tell himself. The book club was important to the shop, he could see it growing, giving him the connection to the community he wanted. Amy had just joined it, giving her the chance to develop friends in the area. Doing anything to rock that now would be crazy. Plus he wasn't ready for a relationship, so there was no way he should even be thinking about kissing her.

With a sigh he picked up his jacket, punched the code into the alarm, locked the door and headed home.

Chapter Eleven

Chewie pulled on the lead as Lottie walked up to the bookshop, that now familiar flutter starting in her belly.

'Seems I'm not the only one happy to be coming back here.' Chewie turned and gave her his signature look. The one that said, *I know you're talking to me but I haven't a clue what you're saying.*

It had been two weeks since her last visit to Books by the Bay.

Two weeks since her brush in the dark with Matt.

Heat pooled between her thighs as she remembered the feel of his body when they'd bumped into each other; hard and lean. The fresh, woody scent of his aftershave. Not a brand she recognised, but expensive, she'd like to bet. Like his clothes, his watch. His car. They weren't what she expected from a bookshop owner. Then again, Matt was turning out to be nothing like she'd expected.

It's not just about the books for you though, is it? How did a guy she barely knew see her so well?

And how had she once thought him reserved to the point of cold, when he was clearly tied up in knots over his sister?

Plus there was nothing cold about the way he'd looked at her just before she'd left. His expression had been fierce, his eyes hot. She'd wanted to stay, see if whatever debate he'd been having with himself would end with him kissing her, but at the last minute she'd panicked. She was only just getting over Henry. Starting anything with a man as serious, as intense as Matt Steele didn't seem like a sensible move.

She pushed the door to the shop open and the bell chimed, causing the man at the cash desk to look up and give her a small smile.

'The electrician, I believe.' He glanced down at Chewie. 'And her famous sidekick. I've been warned not to whistle.'

The butterflies in her stomach calmed as she smiled at Matt's father. Maybe Matt wouldn't be here this evening after all. She ignored the kick of disappointment. At least she wouldn't be distracted by the thought of him coming up to her. Lifting her hair and kissing the back of her neck...

'Matt's in his office.' His dad nodded towards the back of the shop. 'He's expecting you.'

The butterflies in her belly set off again. 'Thanks, Mr Steele.'

He waved his hand at her. 'Jim.'

'Right, thanks, Jim.' She grinned. 'I see he's got you working today.'

'Aye.' He looked at his watch. 'But I'm gone in two minutes.'

'Ouch, that bad, huh?'

'I didn't sign up for working here. Told him that when he bought the place.'

Obviously Amy wasn't the only unhappy member of Matt's family. Though if she remembered her last conversation with Matt, Jim was coping not just with a move to a new town but with the loss of his wife, so it was hardly surprising. 'I'm sure he's grateful for your help.' She bent her head closer and whispered, 'Grateful enough to agree to whatever you decide to charge him.'

'Can't do that. He's my son.'

She winked. 'Doesn't have to be money. He could pay you in beer, tickets to whatever you like to watch. Cake.'

'I am partial to a bit of fruit cake. Or carrot cake. Or…' He gave her a sheepish smile that looked incongruous on his otherwise rather dour face. 'Any type of cake.'

She laughed. 'Wow, you're a cheap hire. I might employ you myself.'

He waggled his eyebrows. 'Sparky's mate. I like that. It's got a ring to it.'

'Stealing my staff now, I see.'

Lottie's heart thumped as she glanced up to find Matt watching them. He appeared … pensive, she thought, though his eyes were warm when they met hers. For a second she was tongue-tied, unable to think while he looked at her like that. It was only when she dragged her gaze away that her brain was able to engage. 'Your dad said he'd work for cake. I'd be stupid not to hire him.'

Matt quirked a brow at his father. 'Cake, not beer?'

'Proper cake, mind. Like your mother used to make.'

Lottie watched as Matt's often impassive face betrayed his sadness. 'Her cakes were legendary.'

'They were.' There was a beat of silence, Lottie guessing that both men were lost in their memories. 'She used to make that Oreo cake for you every time you said you were coming round,' Jim added, focus on his son. 'I'd be left eating it for the next week when you didn't.'

Matt drew in a breath. 'I'm sorry.'

'Not me you kept letting down.'

Anguish briefly settled over Matt's face before he seemed to gather his control. 'Can we not have this conversation here?' When his eyes met hers, his guard was firmly up. 'The shop's clear. Let me know when you need to turn the electrics off.'

He turned and walked away, back ramrod stiff.

Jim let out a despondent-sounding sigh. 'Sorry. You shouldn't have had to witness that.'

'It's okay.' Her heart ached for all three of them – Matt, his sister, his father. It was clear they'd lost the one person who'd held them together.

'I shouldn't have said what I did. Raking over old ground. It wasn't helpful. His mother, my wife, we lost her last year.' Jim swallowed, rubbing a hand over his face as she'd seen his son do. 'If she can hear us, she'll be looking daggers at me.'

Lottie smiled. 'Or maybe she'll be doing cartwheels because you were praising her cakes.'

As she'd hoped, he smiled. 'Happen you're right. She was proud of her baking.'

Lottie thought of Heidi, bursting to bake cakes for someone. 'If you're ever around on the last Thursday of the month, you should come to the book club. Not to discuss books,' she added quickly when she saw his look of horror. 'To sample the cake. One of the members loves to bake. We're usually overflowing with cake. And gin.'

'Gin?' His eyebrows flew up. 'I thought book clubs were serious affairs.'

'We are serious. About cake and gin.'

He chuckled, his face turning from dour to attractive. It made her think of Matt, and how stunning he looked when he allowed himself to smile.

'Right, well, I'm off.' He walked to the door and turned the sign from *Open* to *Closed*. 'I'll leave you and your sidekick to it. Don't let my son work you too hard.'

She waved him goodbye and looked down at Chewie who was sniffing at the bottom row of books. 'Come on then, work to be done. At least I have to work. You have to focus on not peeing on the floor and not eating any more shoes.'

They set off towards the back of the shop but she jumped in surprise when Matt appeared from behind one of the bookshelves.

'Crap, you scared me.'

He gave her a quizzical smile. 'You weren't expecting me?'

'No, I mean yes.' She blew out a breath. 'I knew you were here, but I thought you were in the office.'

He nodded to the pile of books on the nearby table. 'Just putting some books back.' She sensed him hesitate. 'I overheard your conversation.'

'The one where I talk to my dog even though he hasn't the foggiest idea what I'm saying?'

'That, too. I was referring to the one with my dad.' His eyes didn't quite meet hers. 'You seem to have a far better effect on my family than I do.'

'That's because I'm a stranger. They have to be polite to me.'

'There are times I feel like a stranger, too.' He shook his head, as if embarrassed he'd let that slip. 'Anyway, I'll just close up and then you're good to start.' He eyed Chewie. 'Is he here to help?'

'I can say with some certainty he won't help. My hope is he won't hinder.' She bent to give the patient Chewie a hug. 'He's here because he hates being on his own.'

'Fair enough. I've bought a few torches and a camping lamp, so we won't be in total darkness when you need to turn the electricity off.'

I liked being in the dark with you. Nope, she wasn't going there. She had a job to do.

Matt watched as Lottie placed her toolbox on the desk in the office and set about checking the connections to the fusebox. The furry mutt gave him a wary look before settling himself down on the floor.

'So, Electric Blonde.' He'd been intrigued by her company name ever since he'd received her email detailing when she could do the work. 'That's what it said on the estimate you sent through.'

Lottie glanced over at him. 'Yep. That's me. A salutary lesson not to register your new company name when you've been playing drinking games.'

Amused, he asked her, 'You don't like it?'

'Let's just say I wouldn't have chosen it, had I been sober.' She shrugged, eyes on what she was doing rather than him. 'I guess I don't hate it enough to bother changing it, though. It raises a few eyebrows, provides a few laughs. People remember me, though it would be nice if that happened because they were thinking, *Let's call Lottie, she does great work.* And not *What about calling that crazy blonde with the funny company name?*'

He sensed something behind her words, a hint she wasn't as confident as she came across. 'You're memorable for more than your name.'

Her eyes found his. 'I'm wondering if that's a compliment or an insult?'

'A compliment.'

'Oh.' He was surprised to see a blush form on her cheeks. 'Thanks.' Her gaze locked on his and he found he couldn't look away. Two weeks ago, he'd wanted to kiss her.

He still wanted to. And it wasn't just because the combination of blonde curls, grey eyes and a killer smile caused his body to react in ways he'd forgotten. He liked her. Funny and chatty, she was so easy to talk to. She'd even got his dad laughing and talking about Mum, something he struggled to do.

Because you're nothing like Lottie. What had Patricia accused him of being in the last throes of their marriage? Too intense, too serious. Emotionally unavailable. *It's like being married to a fucking robot.*

The memory was enough to shake him out of his daze. 'I'm disturbing you.'

'It's fine. One of the advantages of being a female sparky is I can multi-task.'

He thought about the work he could be doing. *Work isn't everything, you fell into that trap last time.* 'Does multi-tasking include being able to drink? I can offer tea and coffee. Perhaps some left-over tonic. No gin, I'm afraid.'

She laughed, and the sound hummed gently through him. 'You don't want me drinking gin while I'm doing your electrics.'

'Good point.'

'Tea would be good, thanks.'

He glanced over to Chewie who cocked his head up. 'And the shoe thief?'

'If you've got a bowl, he'll happily lap up some water, probably spilling most of it on your lovely wooden floor.'

'It's had worse things spilt on it.'

Another laugh. 'Ouch, yes, so it has. I was hoping you'd scrubbed that incident from your memory bank.'

'I do remember scrubbing,' he commented dryly.

She rolled her eyes and he set off to the kitchen feeling lighter somehow, the sharp words from his dad pushed temporarily to the back of his mind.

A short while later the electrics were off and they were in darkness, the only light coming from the camping lamp. As he sat at his desk and watched Lottie work, he felt that intimacy again, just as he had before.

'Last time we were stuck together in the dark we talked a lot about me, but not about you.' She slotted some pliers between her teeth, fiddled … he suspected there was a technical term for it … then grabbed them again. 'Your fault, obviously, because if you ask me a question I'll answer it. Then keep talking until you tell me to stop or you leave the room. Actually, even that doesn't stop me, because I'm so used to talking to Chewie, it doesn't faze me to be gabbling away when I'm the only person left.'

Mesmerised, he stared at her. They couldn't be more different.

'So anyway, to stop that happening I'm going to ask you a question.' She glanced over at him. 'Are you ready for it?'

The private side of him baulked at the idea of answering her. The man in him wanted to stay with her, in the dark, even if it meant talking about his least favourite subject: himself.

'What did you used to do for a living in London?'

'You don't think I ran a bookshop?'

'I think a man who came to work here in a suit is used to working in an office, not a bookshop.'

'Ah, okay.' Feeling faintly embarrassed, he shifted in the chair. In offering her a drink, he'd opened himself up to this conversation. He couldn't now complain he didn't want it. 'You're right. I worked in the city. I was a trader.'

She nodded. 'That makes sense. The smart suit, the expensive watch.' When he raised his eyebrows, she smirked. 'I'm naturally nosy, so I take notice of such details.'

Figuring he didn't need to reply, he waited while she focused on what she was doing for a while, content with the silence. Some people felt the need to fill silences, but the quiet never bothered him. Still, this silence felt friendly, not awkward.

'Am I allowed one more question?'

He swallowed. 'Okay.'

She laughed softly. 'You really don't like talking about yourself, do you?'

'There are more interesting topics.' He smiled. 'Was that the question?'

'Afraid not, so you can wipe the hopeful look off your face.' She eased the old fusebox off the wall and set it on the floor, then took a new box out of the bag she'd brought with her. 'Why did you swop being a trader in the city for a bookshop owner by the sea? It seems quite a dramatic change.'

He picked up the pen on his desk, trailing it between his fingers as he thought how to reply. 'The job was intense, high stress, long hours. It wasn't doing me any good.' He gave her a wry smile. 'This is me learning to relax.'

Her expression looked amused but she didn't comment. As she focused on the fusebox he glanced down at the dog, who cocked his head and gave him a look through his shaggy fur. He found reading humans difficult enough, never mind canines, but if he had to guess, he'd say it was an *I'm watching you* sort of look. Protective.

'Right, that's the hard bit done,' she said a short while later. 'I just need to do some checks.'

Thirty minutes later she declared it in full working order and he walked with her to the door, the dog glued to his owner's side.

'Thanks for fixing it.'

She smiled. 'Thanks for the business.'

He should let her go, yet how could he when she looked at him like that? As if she felt the same chemistry he did. The air crackled, his body pulsed and all sensible, rational thought left his brain. With a groan of surrender, he angled his head towards hers, slow enough that she could back away.

She didn't.

That first press of his lips against hers. He felt the connection in every part of his body, from the curl of his toes to the tightening of his groin and the rush of blood to his head.

What are you doing?

Her mouth opened to let him in and as her tongue tangled with his, he pushed the doubts away, desire surging as he explored the sweet heat of her. The more he plundered her mouth, the tighter he drew her against him, the hotter he felt, his knees starting to buckle as her body melted against his.

He was enjoying himself, relinquishing control. Giving in to pleasure.

But after you've kissed her, what then?

Beside them, Chewie began to growl. With a groan, his breathing sounding ragged in his ears, Matt pulled back.

'Don't apologise.' Her voice was husky, her pupils impossibly large. 'Please.'

'I wasn't going to.'

'Okay, good.' Those beautiful eyes scanned his face. 'But you've got the look of a man who's done something he regretted.'

Damn it, he should have left well alone. He was confusing them both. 'I don't regret it.'

'There's a but coming. I know there's a but.'

He exhaled, rubbing at the back of his neck. 'I'm not sure I'd be good for you. In fact I'm pretty certain I wouldn't be.' *Not yet, at any rate.*

'Shouldn't I be the judge of that?'

Matt glanced down at the dog, who'd stopped growling but was giving him the evil eye again. 'Chewie appears to agree with me.'

'He's not used to seeing me kiss anyone.' Before he could ask why on earth not, she added, 'Looks like he doesn't have to worry about it happening again though, so he'll be happy.'

Her smoky grey eyes were filled with hurt and in that moment there was nothing he wanted more than to pin her against the wall and kiss her again, at least for the next hour. But then he thought of what had happened with Patricia, and took a mental step back.

Lottie opened the door. 'Goodnight, Matt.'

A moment later she was gone, and he was left with the faint citrus smell of her perfume and a feeling he'd let something special slip through his fingers.

Chapter Twelve

June, nominated book:
The Kiss Quotient by Helen Hoang

Lottie looked around the group as they avidly discussed this month's book and felt a burst of pride. It wasn't stilted and awkward like Eve's book club had been. This was fun. Freddie had joined them in a bouncy chair tonight and he looked right at home, watching them while chewing on every toy he could get his hands on. Oh, and eyeing up the mountain of cake Heidi had placed in the middle of the table.

'That line when he first kisses her,' Audrey said excitedly, waving her hand at nobody in particular. 'It was something about sharks.'

'She tells Michael it makes her feel like a shark getting its teeth cleaned by a pilot fish,' Gira quoted.

Audrey hooted with laughter. 'That's it. I spat my tea out laughing at that one.'

'Yet the book was also sexy, and surprisingly romantic,' Heidi added wistfully. '*Pretty Woman* in reverse. Before I started reading I thought I wouldn't like Michael because he was an escort, but I didn't count on him being so patient and caring.'

'And so frigging hot,' Sally added, making Amy giggle. 'Ah, you can laugh,' Sally glanced over at Amy. 'I hear you've found yourself a hot guy to kiss.'

Amy went scarlet, but unlike on previous occasions, she didn't avert her eyes and stare down at the floor. She gave another shy giggle. 'Shaun and me went for a drink on Saturday.'

'And?' Sally prodded. 'Did he kiss you?'

She shook her head, but her eyes smiled. 'He said he wanted to, but he was scared I'd think it was too early, so he'd save it for the second date.'

'Whoop!' Lottie cheered alongside the others, yet she also felt a pang of sadness. She'd found her own hot guy to kiss, but he didn't want a repeat. God, she'd never met anyone so complex. Why had he kissed her, if he'd no intention of doing it again? It was like one big tease. *Here's what you could have had.* And wow, yes, she definitely wanted more. He didn't act like a guy who played fast and loose though, quite the opposite. As for all that stuff about not being good for her … sure, she could see that a guy who'd made such a big shift in his life, who was clearly trying to overcome family issues and grieving for his mum, wasn't the simple, uncomplicated fun she was looking for. Still, the choice was hers to make.

A glance at Gira told her she, too, was having unhappy thoughts. There was no opportunity to ask her how things were at home though, because the very man Lottie had spent the last week obsessing about was walking towards them. Today's outfit, grey polo shirt and the same dark jeans as before, fitted beautifully as usual, outlining a body that looked lean, athletic and sexy as hell. Yet where was the fun, the colour? She'd seen enough snippets of humour to know he wasn't as sombre as the greys and blacks he seemed to favour.

'Sorry to interrupt.' Dark eyes skimmed over them before resting on Lottie, causing her heart to bump against her ribs. 'Dad's just been on the phone. He said something about being promised cake?'

Lottie burst out laughing. 'Cheeky sod.' Matt raised his eyebrow in that expressive way he had that apparently saved him having to talk. 'Tell him the deal was, he gets cake if he's here in person.'

'Ah, okay.' He slid his hands in his pockets. 'As I'm here, do I get a slice?'

Heidi beamed. 'Of course.' She reached down and cut an eye-wateringly large slice of one of the cakes.

Matt's eyes bulged as she handed it to him. 'I'll need to run a few more miles tomorrow morning.'

'Nonsense.' Heidi's gaze dropped to his trim waist. 'It's

carrot cake. Positively good for you. It will help you see in the dark.'

Matt's gaze found Lottie's. 'I like the dark.'

His low tone and the memories it evoked caused a sizzle in her belly, but it was quickly extinguished when she realised they were all staring at her. Groaning inwardly, she slunk into the chair.

What was he doing? She couldn't work the man out.

His eyes left hers and he took a mouthful of cake. 'My compliments, Heidi. This tastes incredible. Do you bake for a living?'

Heidi positively glowed, her cheeks turning pink. 'That's kind of you but no, just for fun.'

Matt glanced over at Amy and the siblings exchanged a look that Lottie couldn't decipher.

'What's today's book?' he asked after he'd taken another mouthful. She had the impression he wanted to retreat to his office but was hovering out of politeness.

'The Kiss Quotient,' she answered.

His eyes widened, gaze once more pressing hers, and she felt a hot flush creep over her face.

'It's about a woman with Asperger's who asks a male prostitute to give her lessons in sex,' Audrey added, thankfully breaking the moment.

Matt was clearly used to them discussing sex now because he hardly flinched. 'Interesting.'

'It is.' Once again, their gazes collided. Once again, Lottie felt that flutter in her stomach.

'Right.' He cleared his throat. 'I'll let you get on. Thanks for the cake.'

The moment he was out of earshot, Lottie steeled herself as the group turned to stare at her.

'He said he likes the dark.' Sally's eyes narrowed on her. 'And you went all … fidgety.'

'I did not,' she protested.

'You blushed when you told him we were discussing *The Kiss Quotient*.' Heidi wagged her finger. 'No denying that one.'

Gira gave Heidi a sly smile. 'I feel it only fair to point out that you blushed when he said he liked your cake.'

Heidi choked on a laugh. 'Okay, I'll admit to getting a bit flustered. In my defence, it's been a long while since I got a compliment from a handsome young man, even if it was just for my baking skills.'

'Your cakes are amazing,' Amy said, glancing shyly at Heidi.

'Thank you, dear.'

Amy opened her mouth as if to say something, then closed it. Picking up a napkin, she started to fold it. Just when Lottie thought she was out of the woods, Amy spoke again. 'The lights went out in the shop the other night.' Her gaze darted round the group. 'I was there with Lottie but she told me to go home, she'd fix them.'

'Are you telling us you left Lottie and Matt alone?' Sally raised her eyebrows suggestively. 'In the dark?'

'I am.' Amy turned to Lottie, her eyes full of questions.

'Well, well.' Sally smirked. 'It seems our leader has been keeping something from us.'

Lottie threw her hands up in the air. 'Flipping heck! A dodgy switch caused the lights to go out. I fixed it and put in a new fusebox last week. End of.'

Audrey looked horrified. 'Lottie Watt, you mean to tell me you were alone in the dark with this town's answer to Mr Darcy, and you *didn't* take advantage of it?'

Everyone laughed and though Amy joined in, Lottie could see she was holding back, quietly watching her.

At the end of the meeting, as everyone began to leave, Lottie touched Amy's arm. 'That was embarrassing. I'm sorry you had to hear it.'

'It's fine. I mean, it was more embarrassing for you, them trying to pair you up when you're not interested.'

Agree and move on. It was the easy option. Lottie liked Amy though, and she didn't feel right lying to her. 'I wouldn't say I'm not interested.' *It's your brother who isn't. At least I didn't think he was.*

Amy's eyebrows shot up. 'You *like* him?'

Lottie felt a dart of hurt on Matt's behalf. 'You don't think your brother is likeable?'

'Well, yeah, sure he is. I just, well…' She twisted her hands. 'You're so nice. Not that he's not nice, obviously. But I wouldn't have put you guys together. He's kind of serious.'

'Who's serious?' Sally piped up, Freddie now settled in his pram.

'My brother.'

Sally laughed. 'Yes, but he's also hot. If anyone can loosen him up, Lottie can.' She grinned at Lottie. 'Make sure to say goodbye to him from me before you leave.'

She wanted to protest that she was leaving now too. After all, there was no need for her to seek Matt out and tell him they'd finished. He knew what time they left.

Yet this was also a perfect opportunity to sort out those mixed messages he was giving.

Matt cursed as he realised he'd put the same order through twice. Now he had a second copy of *Jam Making for Beginners* to find a home for.

All that talk of the dark, of kissing, of sex. He'd not been able to focus.

At the light tap on his door, he turned to find the reason for his distracted state.

Wearing a vivid turquoise top, faded denim jeans and canvas shoes with flamingos on them, she looked vital, radiant. She must have been out in the sun because her skin held the hint of a tan, her freckles more prominent.

'I've come to let you know we've finished.'

'Okay, thanks.' *You don't want her to go, so think of something to say.* 'How were the sex lessons?' He felt his face flush as her eyes widened. Shit, of all the questions he could have asked her. 'I was referring to the book.'

Those beautiful grey eyes sparkled with amusement. 'I know.'

He groaned, leaning back in the chair. 'Then help me out of my misery and tell me what the verdict was on the book.'

She laughed. 'Everyone enjoyed it, me included. One of the best I've read in a while. Funny, but also poignant in places. A real love story.'

Their eyes met and he felt a tingle race down his spine. He could deny it all he liked, but this attraction wasn't going away. It was getting harder to ignore. 'I take it no serial killers were involved?'

She bit into her lip, eyes still dancing, and he felt a burst of pride. *Not so cold now, am I?* Yet he'd made Patricia laugh in the early days, too. By the end, he'd made her cry.

'No serial killers,' she confirmed. 'Just a quirky, intelligent heroine and a gorgeously sweet hero. I haven't picked up a thriller since I bought that book.'

'Bought and then returned.'

She grinned. 'I heard the shop had an excellent refund policy.'

'The book was very entertaining, full of dark humour.' When she raised an eyebrow he shrugged. 'I'd been meaning to read it. You returning it reminded me.'

'It wasn't just so you could rub my nose in it by gloating about how good it was, the next time you saw me?'

He had to laugh, because, okay, he had been that shallow. 'Maybe.' His eyes lifted to hers. 'But it was also so I could have a conversation with you.'

The air hummed: attraction, anticipation, unspoken feelings. 'Why did you say you wouldn't be good for me?'

He might have known she wouldn't leave it alone. But the heated looks he'd given her earlier, his last comment … he hadn't left it alone, either. 'I wasn't good for my wife.'

Lottie paled and took a step back. 'You're married?'

'No. Not anymore.' He dragged in a breath, trying to steady himself. This wasn't him. He didn't talk about personal stuff.

Her stance relaxed a little. 'How long ago did you divorce?' Her face paled again. 'Oh God, please tell me I'm right and you divorced. She didn't…'

'We divorced.'

'Okay, good.' She winced. 'I mean good that she didn't die, not that you divorced, which must be tough to go through.'

'It was.' He was acutely aware he was giving two-word answers.

'I went through a break-up, and even though we weren't married, and it was all amicable, it hurt for a long time afterwards.' Her expression turned unusually serious, her eyes sad. 'It still does.'

How was she able to talk about it so easily, when he could see it was still painful? 'I'm sorry.' There he went again with the two words.

'Thanks, but if it was meant to be, we'd have found a way round it. Henry wouldn't have moved to the US, or I would have followed him. Probably.' She shook her head. 'We'd been going out for four years, practically lived together for most of it, though I was technically still living with my parents at the beginning. I thought we'd get married one day.' Her shoulders lifted as she let out a deep sigh. 'It haunts me sometimes, wondering if I did the right thing staying here. It feels like we gave up on each other.'

He wanted to tell her he was haunted by his divorce, too, though in his case it was by the realisation he'd been the cause. But years of keeping to himself, hiding his emotions, meant he kept the focus on her. 'You didn't try a long-distance relationship?'

'No. A relationship with someone who was hardly ever there didn't seem fair to either of us. What we had was so special, you know? We didn't want it tarnished, our relationship limping along, weighed down by increasing frustration and bitterness until we ended up not even liking each other.'

It sounded so much like the narrative to his marriage, Matt felt it like a physical slap. His expression must have betrayed him because she covered her face with her hands. 'Oh God, that's why you said you weren't good for your wife, isn't it? Your job meant you had to work long hours.'

How easy to blame it all on his job. 'It was part of the problem, yes.' Because he didn't want to discuss his failings with the woman he fancied, a woman who was vibrant, open and so opposite to him, he stood, effectively ending the conversation.

As he walked with her to the door, his body was at war with his mind.

Kiss her, you know you want to.

Don't be so stupid. You'd be giving the wrong message again.

'How long have you had Chewie?'

His question took them both by surprise.

'I took him in about fifteen months ago. Why?'

'Chewie growled when I kissed you. You said he'd not seen you kiss anyone else.' Why had he brought this up? Why hadn't he just waved her goodbye?

'He hasn't. I got him a few months after Henry left. I think we recognised in each other that same feeling of being abandoned. Of needing company.'

He nodded, unsure where he was going with the question, yet stupidly pleased to hear that he'd been the only one to kiss her recently. 'Do you still feel that need? For company,' he clarified.

She shook her head. 'What with Chewie, my family and friends, my job, the book club … I've got all the company I need.'

His heart dropped a little and he regretted asking the question.

But then she smiled. 'Just because I don't *need* it, doesn't mean it wouldn't be fun to hang out some time. If you fancy it.'

Relief whooshed through him, making him light-headed. For one blissful moment he imagined kissing her again, those soft lips against his, but with more urgency this time. He even took a step towards her, his hand reaching to draw her towards him. To feel her body against him, her curves against his hard angles. Her heat against his.

His groin tightened in response, his pulse quickening.

You've agreed to hang out, not to have quick and dirty sex.
And let's face it, quick and dirty was all it would be, it had
been so long. She was worth more than that.

Yet could he give more?

Taking in a breath, he took that step back again. 'I'd like
to hang out.'

She angled her head, considering him. 'Have you been
in the sea yet?'

He barked out a laugh. 'I'm not mad.'

'You live on the coast now, city boy. Going in the sea is
practically compulsory. I don't suppose you've got a wet
suit?'

'Err, no.' His idea of hanging out was to meet for a
drink. Take a walk in the park. Neither required getting cold
and wet.

'Don't worry, I'll ask Shaun.' Her eyes ran up and down
his body, assessing. 'I reckon you're about the same size.'

He thought back to Shaun and decided he'd take the
remark as a compliment. 'Can I ask what you're planning?'

'Nope.' Her expression was one of pure mischief. 'What
are you doing this Sunday?'

'Apparently I'm wearing Shaun's wet suit.'

His answer was met with a burst of laughter. 'Now that I
can't wait to see. Meet me near the beach huts around
midday. We'll do some of that unwinding you've moved
here for.'

He was pretty sure she was kidding about the wet suit –
in nobody's mind could a dunk in the sea ever be termed
relaxing, so he nodded. Whatever she was up to, this was

the reason he'd moved here, to live a different life than the one he'd had before.

To make friends.

Yet as he closed the door behind her, he knew he wanted to be more than friends with Lottie. Whether he was ready for it, whether she was ready for it, whether she even wanted it. They were all unknown.

Chapter Thirteen

Lottie helped Shaun haul his board out of the garage and wedge it into the back of her van, alongside hers. The rigs and harnesses were already in, plus a couple of helmets, buoyancy aids and wet suits, complete with shoes.

Shaun eyed it all up with an amused expression. 'Are you sure he's up for this?'

'Why wouldn't he be?' Inside, Lottie could easily see why taking the formal, serious, Matthew Steele windsurfing might not be one of her brighter ideas.

'Have you met the man? Walks around with a stick up his arse. Can't see him enjoying being tossed in the sea somehow.'

She gave him a sly glance. 'Watch it. That's Amy's brother you're talking about.'

He grinned back. 'Looks like we've both got a thing for the Steeles.'

She elbowed him in the ribs. 'You're the one with the

thing. I'm just using this glorious sunny Sunday to show Matt what seaside living is all about.'

Shaun let out a big booming laugh. 'Tell yourself that all you like. I know you've cooked up this idea so you can see the guy in a wet suit.' He jiggled his eyebrows up and down. 'Then give him the kiss of life when you rescue his sorry arse from the Solent.'

Laughter spluttered out of her. 'Oh God, I'm not sure what it says about me, but you're not wrong.' She imagined Matt's athletic form in a wet suit and heat flooded between her thighs. To distract herself, she turned the conversation back to Shaun. 'How are things going with you and Amy?'

A slow smile spread across his face. 'We passed first and second base on Friday.'

'Please tell me you're not just fooling around with her. I don't want you breaking her heart. She deserves more than that.'

'Chill.' His face sobered. 'I know she's special, so that's how I'll treat her.'

Lottie relaxed again. For all his cocky bluster, Shaun was a decent guy and as she waved him goodbye, she knew he would be careful with Amy. As for her brother, she wasn't so sure what to make of him. It was clear he was still carrying scars from his marriage and if she had to guess, she'd say he was after company, not a passionate affair. A real shame, because a fling was exactly what she needed. She wasn't in a rush for anything deep and heavy, not with her heart still bruised from Henry, but sex...

'God, I really miss it,' she told Chewie as she drove along the seafront.

He glanced over at her, tongue hanging out of his mouth. 'Yeah, you haven't a clue what I'm talking about, have you?' She gave his head a quick pat. 'Maybe it's just as well. Don't want to corrupt your sensitive soul.'

Sex wasn't the right thought to have rolling through her mind as she parked up by the beach huts where she'd agreed to meet Matt, the van doing its usual splutter as she turned it off. The temperature gauge was right over into the red again. Damn it, she'd have to bite the bullet and ask the garage to have a look at it soon, especially now they were going into summer. Maybe it wouldn't be as expensive as it sounded.

At least the money worries had stopped her thinking of sex. But as she jumped down onto the pavement she caught sight of Matt striding towards her, shades hiding his eyes, dark hair blowing in the wind, hands in the pockets of a pair of smart chino shorts that revealed a seriously sexy pair of legs. By the time he reached her, sex was right at the forefront of her mind again.

'Hi.' She had trouble prising her tongue from the roof of her mouth. 'The thought of wearing a wet suit didn't scare you off, then.'

His mouth curved and though the sunglasses gave him a debonair appearance, she missed seeing those dark-chocolate eyes. 'I'm not sure how nervous to be.'

'That depends. How good is your balance?'

His forehead wrinkled as he turned and looked out at the sea. 'There aren't enough waves to surf.'

'True.' She wetted her finger and raised it up to feel the direction of the wind. 'But the weather is perfect for windsurfing.'

'Ah.'

His Adam's apple bobbed and Lottie unconsciously licked her lips. What was wrong with her today? Why did he seem even more attractive? Maybe it was just the sun, the first real hint of summer they'd had. 'Can you translate *ah* for me? You usually give me at least a couple of words to go on.'

His face snapped round to hers, expression pained. 'Am I that bad?'

'You're not bad, at all.' *Right now you seem very tasty.* She hugged the thought to herself. 'You just use words sparingly.' She eyed him thoughtfully. 'Have you got other siblings besides Amy?'

He looked puzzled at her question. 'No, why?'

'I thought it could explain your care with words. You didn't get much chance to talk as a kid, so when you did, you made the words count.'

He shook his head and it looked like he was going to leave it at that, but then he spoke again. 'I went to boarding school.'

She'd not expected that. 'Maybe that's it then. All those other boys yakking away, not letting you get a word in edgeways.'

He smiled, but she didn't need to see his eyes to know it was forced.

Silence settled between them. It wasn't uncomfortable, but the fun from earlier had gone and she needed to get it back. 'Let me have a go. At translating *ah*,' she added when he looked confused. 'It means fan-dabby-dozy, Lottie, I can't freaking wait to squeeze myself into a wet suit and go windsurfing with you.'

Laughter rumbled from his chest and when he lifted his shades to rest them on his head, she could see crinkles around his eyes. It wasn't the sun making him more attractive, she realised. It was the fact that, bar the last few minutes, he was looking more relaxed today. If he ever really let go, she was in trouble.

Those deep-brown eyes – warm, amused but with a hint of something darker – found hers. 'Actually,' he said, 'I was thinking how much I'm looking forward to seeing you squeezed into a wet suit.'

His lips curved upwards and the heat in his gaze caused tingles of awareness across her skin. 'That can be arranged.' She nodded towards the beach huts. 'Mine is the yellow one, second from the left. Let's grab what we need from the van and get this show on the road.'

The smile stayed on his face until she opened the back of the van. Then his face visibly paled.

'Chewie's promised not to laugh.' When he didn't say anything, just kept staring at the boards, she winced. 'You thought I was kidding about the windsurfing, didn't you?

That this was just you and me, prancing about on the beach, paddling.'

'No, no.' He ran a hand over his meticulously clean-shaven chin then glanced sideways at her. 'I didn't put you down as a prancer.'

'But you did put me down as a hoaxer.'

'Maybe?' He looked back into the van. 'I'm not sure what I thought. Only that it didn't involve me getting on something that looks like that.'

He didn't look terrified, she thought. Nervous, yes, but she could handle that. 'Can you swim?'

'If I say no, can I sit on the beach and watch you?'

He gave her one of his slow, devastating smiles and Lottie felt something inside her chest shift, like her body was a flower, starting to bloom. This man, with his serious good looks, his quiet ways and careful use of words, was really starting to grow on her.

Mesmerised, Matt sat on the beach next to Chewie and watched Lottie race across the sea on her board. It made his attempts to windsurf look pitiful. Shaun's wet suit had certainly been put to good use.

'She's pretty great, isn't she?'

The dog ignored him, eyes on his owner. He'd noticed Chewie was more wary around him now, as if he sensed he had a rival.

Twenty minutes later she waded out, dragging the board

up the beach. He marched down to help her, eyes greedily raking over her curves in that tight, tight wet suit. Her blonde curls were plastered against her face, her cheeks pink and her eyes brimming with life.

Sexy didn't begin to describe her. She made other women seem two-dimensional in comparison.

'You were incredible.' He knew she'd take the words to mean her ability to windsurf, though actually he meant it more literally.

'Thanks, but I've had years of practice.' Seawater droplets fell from her hair and ran down her cheeks as she bent to fuss over Chewie. 'You weren't bad for your first session. By the tenth I'll get you surfing all along the bay.'

He baulked. 'Tenth? I was hoping my next venture to the beach would be a little less … wet.'

She shook her head as she laughed, the movement shaking a few drops of water onto him. 'We can do less wet.' Her eyes darted towards his. 'That is, if you want to hang out again.'

'I'd like that.' The surprise wasn't that he wanted to, but how much he wanted it. 'Maybe we can try this again next Sunday. Without the windsurfing.'

Her teeth nibbled at the bottom of her lip as she looked up at him, and he felt an answering throb in his groin. He wasn't a man driven by lust, but right now all he wanted to do was follow her into that beach hut and have fast, heart-pounding sex.

'If you agree to give windsurfing another try some time, it's a deal.'

It was a measure of how full of sex his head was that he readily agreed. 'Deal.'

She put out her hand and though his fingers happily curled round hers, it felt inadequate. 'We could kiss,' he found himself murmuring. 'To seal the deal.'

Grey eyes rounded, wet lashes glistening in the sunlight. 'We could.'

His mouth hovered over hers. Hadn't he done this before, and decided not to repeat it? But his body pulsed with desire, his blood was running hot and Matt didn't want to be that guy he'd always been: cautious, circumspect. For once in his life he wanted to be reckless. To not think about consequences, to be ruled by his body, not his head. 'Fuck.'

A smile tugged at her lips. 'Maybe we should try kissing first.'

Horrified he'd said the word out loud, he lurched backwards. 'Sorry, I didn't mean... It was a curse, not a suggestion... Shit.' He heaved in a breath, told his rapidly beating heart to calm. 'I want to kiss you, but I don't want to confuse either of us. I'm not sure I'm ready...' Unbalanced, he dragged a hand through his hair. 'Hell, I'm making a huge assumption here. You're probably not, either.'

'Stop over-thinking,' she said softly. 'It's just a kiss.'

She was right, of course she was. What sort of guy has a gorgeous woman in front of him, willing to kiss him, and doesn't make the most of the opportunity? *A fucking robot.*

He shoved Patricia's damning assessment to the back of

his mind and focused instead on the naked pink lips in front of him. Cupping her face, he bent to touch his mouth to hers. Immediately he felt a zap, like an electric bolt, that sent sparks shooting through him. It emptied his head of everything but her, allowing his body to do what it wanted. Unerringly his tongue slipped through her lips, finding her heat, revelling in her taste. She smelt like the ocean, with a hint of coconut.

But he was on a public beach and Chewie was making that low growling noise again in the back of his throat. With a sigh Matt forced his mouth away, and dropped his hands to his sides, when what he really wanted to do was run them all over the wet suit that moulded to her body. Then unzip it and run them over her skin.

'Well.'

He didn't know what to say, his mind too tangled. 'Well indeed.'

'I'll consider the deal well and truly sealed.' She gave him a shaky smile before walking back to the beach hut to change, her trusty companion lolloping beside her. Every now and again Chewie turned to look at him, as if to say, *Loser, I'm the one going home with her.* He wanted to reassure the dog he had no plans to do the same, but it felt like a lie just now.

When she returned, hair a tangle, legs looking amazing under her brief denim shorts, she was unusually quiet. Had he upset her? he worried as they worked together to haul the equipment back into the van. Was his kissing technique so rusty, she was wondering how to turn him down next

Sunday? Maybe she'd made allowances for him for their first kiss back at the shop, but after this one she'd realised it wasn't for her? Yet he'd been blown away by them both. Surely she must have felt *some* of what he had?

She slammed the rear doors to the van shut and turned to face him. 'See you same time next week then?'

Relief flowed through him. She might not let him kiss her again, but at least he'd get to see her. 'Unless you need to make an urgent book purchase in the meantime.'

'Nice try, but I bought July's book from you last week.'

'So you did. Sue Moorcroft. *Summer on a Sunny Island*.'

'Yep. I can't afford to go on holiday, so I'm going to let Sue take me to Malta.' She winked as she jumped up into the passenger seat. 'She's got a gorgeous guy lined up for me, too.'

He didn't know what to say to that. He'd never been great at flirting – God knows how he'd ever managed to attract Patricia – and his dubious skills had felt even more shaky since the divorce. So he simply smiled as she lifted her hand in a little goodbye wave.

Thankfully the walk home was so short he didn't have any time to agonise over what the hell he was doing.

There he found Amy in the kitchen, biting into an apple.

'You look nice,' he commented as he took in Amy's flowery top and cropped white jeans. 'Off out somewhere?'

'I'm seeing a friend for a drink.'

Her eyes avoided his and he sighed. Would they ever achieve that level of closeness where they could talk about things outside work?

'Well, I'm sure he'll appreciate it.'

'Who said it was a guy?'

You, he wanted to say, by the very fact she was hiding it from him. 'Sorry, I just assumed.'

'Girls get dressed up to meet other girls too, you know.'

He decided the best way to avoid rubbing her up the wrong way was to nod and remove himself upstairs.

He was nearly at the doorway when she spoke again. 'I want to ask Heidi to make cakes for the café.'

Okay, so they were back to work talk again. Still, as he swivelled round to face her, he consoled himself with the thought that at least this time she'd instigated it. 'That's a great idea. I thought the same when I ate the carrot cake the other day. I tried to catch your eye to tell you.' He was careful about what he ate – low fat, no processed meats – but cake was his one downfall. Perhaps because their mum had been such a fan.

'I thought of it before that.'

The defensive tone was back. 'Have you asked her?'

Amy's face reddened. 'Like I could do that without checking with you first.'

'Amy.' He thrust a hand through his hair, frustrated with the situation, with himself. This was his sister. Why couldn't he get her to see how much he loved her? Wanted to *help* her? 'I'm sorry if you've felt I've been interfering. I put you in charge of the café. You have the authority to make decisions, you don't need to check with me. Not unless you want to.'

'Right.' She looked down at the floor, hands twisting in that familiar way.

'Is there anything else?'

Her shoulders lifted and she let out a deep breath. 'I don't know how to ask.' Her face reddened again and when she finally looked at him, his heart lurched as tears welled in her eyes. 'I started to, then I got cold feet. I mean, Heidi's part of the book club. What if she's offended? And even if she wants to do it, how do we sort it out? How many would she want to make? How much do I pay her?' She wiped her cheeks with her hands. 'I feel so stupid.'

'Hey.' Walking up to her, Matt brushed away the tears with his thumb. 'Those are all good questions. The type a smart, sensitive person would ask.' He smiled. 'Truth is, I don't know the answers. I've never run a shop before, either.'

'Yeah, but you're clever. You got a degree, earned lots of money.'

'Money and a degree doesn't make you clever.' His heart ached for her, she looked so lost. When their mum had first fallen ill Amy had ducked out of uni to be with her. She'd bounced from job to job ever since. 'Why don't we put a plan of action together tomorrow after work?'

She nodded and as he strode up the stairs to his room to shower off the sea, he felt he'd made another tiny step in the right direction.

Chapter Fourteen

Lottie opened the van door for Chewie who jumped up and went to sit in his basket behind the passenger seat.

'That's us finished for the day.' She glanced at the clock on the dashboard – six o'clock. Gira would be back from work. She'd been on her mind since the last book club. Though she'd joined in, smiled, her eyes had looked horribly sad. 'Shall we see if Gira's in?'

Chewie woofed in agreement.

'This is the quiet lady,' she reminded him as she pulled into the road. 'Not the one who makes cakes.'

Chewie wagged his tail, probably because he understood the word *cake*. She'd like to bet he wouldn't wag it if they were calling on Matt, instead.

Her mind flashed through images of last Sunday and she pressed a hand to her chest where she felt her heart jump. Matt's face as he'd seen the windsurf board in the van. His awkwardness as he'd walked out of the hut in his wet suit. Yeah, his body in that wet suit. Lean, muscular, with a bum she really, really wanted to get her hands on. She hadn't realised bums were her thing, until then.

Matt laughing as he'd hauled himself back onto the board, having fallen in for the umpteenth time. Her heart skipped a beat. That had been the best sight of the day. She'd been right, Shaun had been wrong. After his initial wariness, Matt had been game. More than that, he'd proven he didn't take himself seriously. When he'd been focused on staying on the board, unable to think about anything else, he'd been fun.

Matt's expression when he realised he'd said *fuck* out loud. God, he'd looked so vulnerable, she'd melted.

Matt's eyes, hot and intense, just before they'd kissed. 'He wanted me then, didn't he, Chew?'

Later though? *Well indeed.* Who says that after such a mind-blowing kiss? *A guy who didn't enjoy it as much as you.* 'Do you think that's why he was so withdrawn afterwards? He didn't enjoy it?' Chewie remained silent. A great companion, but not a great Agony Aunt. 'And what was with the jealous growl, anyway?' she asked him as she parked outside Gira's. 'You're the only dog in my life, but I have to be allowed to kiss non-canines occasionally.'

He woofed and clambered over the seat to lick her face. 'Okay, okay, I'll make sure to kiss you more.' The way things were going there didn't seem to be much danger of her breaking her promise.

Gira looked surprised when she opened the door to them and, Lottie thought sadly, disappointed. 'Crap, you thought I was Ryan back early, didn't you?'

She gave Lottie a wan smile as she waved them in. 'For a brief moment, yes. But then he'd use his key, so it was a stupid notion.'

'There's nothing stupid about being hopeful.'

'Maybe. But putting my head in the sand, hoping everything will be okay, isn't going to solve anything.' She put a hand to her face, her expression troubled. 'Listen to me, you've barely stepped through the door and I'm moaning. Sorry, Lottie, it's lovely to see you.' Chewie barked and Gira gave him a tired smile. 'And you, Chewie.'

'Is now okay for a chat? I don't want to butt in if you're busy.'

Gira waved her in. 'Now is perfect. The kids are both out, apparently doing homework with their friends, at least that's what they tell me.'

Lottie accepted a cup of tea and as they went to sit in the living room she looked around the neat, uncluttered room with envy. 'You've got a real eye for décor.'

'Thanks. Ryan pretty much let me choose what I wanted.' She waved at the inky blue walls. 'I worried it would be too dark, but I think it works.'

'It definitely does. And now you've mentioned Ryan's name, I can seamlessly move on to the topic and ask how are things? It doesn't sound like there's been an improvement.'

'Things are worse, if anything.' She placed the mug on

the glass coffee table and looked at Lottie with dark, sorrowful eyes. 'I had it out with him, asked if he was having an affair. He didn't just vehemently deny it, he took umbrage and accused me of not trusting him. Now we're not even talking.'

'Do you still think he's seeing someone else?'

She raised her hands in the air. 'I don't know what to think. If you'd asked me two years ago I'd have said no way, he wasn't the sort. But if he's not out with another woman, he's still not here, at home, with me. I spoke to his secretary the other day. She let slip she saw him in the bar round the corner from their offices the other night.' Tears welled in her eyes and she squeezed them shut. When she opened them again, she looked defiant. 'Enough. I spend too much time thinking about him, wondering what he's doing. Take my mind off it all and tell me what's happening with you.' She angled her head. 'You look like you've caught the sun. Did you get out at the weekend?'

'Actually, I did.' She paused, knowing she was in for a barrage of questions but recognising that Gira needed the distraction. 'I took Matt windsurfing yesterday.'

Gira looked momentarily shocked. Then a slow smile spread across her face and she rose to her feet. 'This calls for another cup of tea.'

Matt sat at the dining-room table next to Amy, copies of the café's contracts with vendors stacked neatly between them.

When he'd bought the place, he'd kept with the existing vendors, figuring it was easiest.

But Heidi's cakes were worth making a change for. As was the opportunity to sit down with his sister and work together on something.

'We're doing all this and she might not even want to supply us,' Amy grumbled.

'True, but at some point we're going to want to review all the contracts anyway, so the time isn't wasted. And if she does say yes, you're going to look very professional.'

Amy glanced at him. 'I'll be the one talking to her?'

'I hope so, yes.' *She needs more than that.* Matt searched for the words that would give her confidence and not undermine the fragile truce. 'For as long as you want it, the café is yours. I wouldn't say that if I didn't feel you could run it.'

'Okay.' She drew in a breath, nodded. 'I can do this.'

'I know you can.'

It was the perfect moment to hug her, kiss her cheek, do something other than smile, but he was too scared she'd back away, so like a coward he stood up. 'Right, I'd better see how Dad's getting on in the kitchen.'

'He's not happy. When I went to the loo I heard him muttering that if he was cooking, he wanted to choose what to make.'

'Thanks for the warning.' They'd agreed to spread the chores out between them and today should have been his turn making dinner, but he'd wanted to catch Amy while she was still keen.

He entered the kitchen warily and found his dad hacking at a chicken breast.

'What's wrong with a whole chicken?' he grumbled without looking up.

'It doesn't cook well in a wok.'

His dad grimaced. 'Why do we need to eat foreign food when this country of ours created the roast? Sausage and mash. Steak and kidney pie. Fish and chips.'

Matt smiled and gently pushed his dad to the side. 'Because it's nice to have a change. And because some foreign food, as you put it, is healthier and quicker to make.'

They worked in silence for a while, him chopping, his dad getting out the bowls and cutlery.

'What about this Shaun fella Amy's seeing?'

Matt looked up with a start, feeling an irrational burst of jealousy that Amy had confided in her dad, but not him. 'He's a friend of Lottie's. A plumber. They met when he came to fix an issue in the café.'

'Is he okay?'

'Lottie says he's a good guy.'

'She does, huh.' Silence again and Matt held his breath while he turned the chicken in the wok, braced for the inevitable. 'You seem to get on with her.'

'You've met her,' he countered. 'It would be hard not to.'

'Pretty girl.'

Okay, he was really going there. 'I think most men would agree with that statement.'

His dad let out a sharp laugh. 'Bloody hell, son, stop sitting on the damn fence. You like her, admit it.'

Matt pushed down his irritation. A moment ago he'd been annoyed that Amy hadn't told him about Shaun, yet here he was, keeping his own feelings deeply hidden. It's how he'd learnt to cope and breaking the habit wasn't just hard, it felt terrifying. 'Of course I like her. I can't imagine anyone not liking her.' Having had enough of the interrogation, he turned the conversation round. 'Are you going to come to the next book club for your cake, then?'

His dad looked over from where he'd been setting the table. 'Is this a ruse to get me to work in the shop?'

Keep calm. Matt carefully slid the chopped peppers into the pan with the now sizzling chicken. 'No. It's simply a question.'

'I might, if I'm free.'

'And what else might you be doing?'

'Playing bowls.'

The answer caught Matt off balance. 'You've joined the bowls club?'

'No.' He gave Matt a sly smile. 'But I might.'

Matt started to laugh. 'Well, I hope you do. And if they don't play on Thursdays, I hope you'll come to the shop.' His dad opened his mouth to speak, but Matt got in first. 'You don't have to work. I've registered your views on that.' His dad looked away quickly and busied himself wiping down the worktop that Matt had wiped five minutes ago. 'Dad?'

'I heard you.'

There was something else going on that the old man wasn't telling him. Matt smiled at the irony and sent Patricia a silent apology. If he was as annoying as his father, no wonder he'd been hell to live with. No wonder she gave up on him.

'You can tell Amy dinner will be ready in a few minutes.'

His dad nodded. 'She still working on stuff for the café?'

'Yes. She's going to ask Heidi, who makes the cakes Lottie was talking about, if she wants to supply the café.'

'That good, are they?'

Matt smiled. 'You can find out if you turn up to the next book club meeting.'

His dad swore. 'Think you're clever, don't you?'

Matt's smile slipped. 'No, I don't.' If he was that much of a genius, he wouldn't be divorced and all but burned out at the ripe old age of thirty-three.

Whatever his dad saw on Matt's face, made his expression soften. 'Well you are, son. You managed to put a spark back on young Amy's face.' His voice turned gruff. 'It's been a long while since I saw it.'

As he left to find Amy, Matt swallowed down the lump that had slid into the back of his throat.

This, he thought with a flare of hope, was why they'd moved. He had a feeling Shaun was the reason for Amy's spark, not him or the café, but he'd take the small win. It wasn't just Amy who seemed happier, either. It might only be Monday but already he was looking forward to Sunday, and spending the afternoon with Lottie. Jammed into a wet suit, being thrown into the sea, glared at by Chewie ... he didn't care. Only that he'd have the chance to see her wide smile again, gaze into those smoke-grey eyes.

And with a bit of luck, ogle her legs.

Chapter Fifteen

How lucky that it was another glorious Sunday, Lottie thought as she tucked *Summer on a Sunny Island* into her beach bag along with her towel and sun cream. Chewie was guarding the cool bag, which was crammed full of picnic goodies ... sausage rolls, pork pies, cheese, ham, pickle, crusty bread. Tomatoes and melon for health. Crisps and cake for joy.

As she opened the door to leave she glanced down at her phone and saw Matt had replied to her text telling him to bring something to read, something to sit on and something to drink.

Book, check. Towel, check. Drink ... water or wine?

She smiled as she tapped out her reply.

Your choice L x

Henry wouldn't have asked, he'd have just loaded a cool box full of beer.

A second later came another text.

Are you drinking it too?

He was so meticulous, careful. She wondered if he'd ever done anything spontaneous. Like get rip-roaring drunk on the beach on a Sunday afternoon.

Yes. So choose wisely L x

Another buzz, and she laughed out loud.

Too much pressure. Maybe we should go windsurfing instead?

'Why did I ever think he was serious?' she asked Chewie as she lifted the cool bag over one shoulder and the beach bag over the other. 'He's funny.' It wasn't the lazy, laid-back humour of Henry and Shaun. Matt's wit was sharper, drier.

She was starting to enjoy it as much as she was starting to enjoy him.

It was about a mile's walk to the beach but Lottie didn't mind it. Chewie was happy, sniffing every bin and lamp post along the prom, and she enjoyed being out in the sun. The anticipation of the afternoon ahead.

They were first to arrive and she opened up the beach hut – it belonged to her parents but they all had a key. After dragging out the blanket, she filled Chewie's bowl with water. 'Let's hope you're the only one drinking that.'

He looked up, water dripping from his mouth, his eyes adoring. Briefly she wondered what it would feel like to see that look in another pair of deep brown eyes. Then laughed at how ridiculous she was being.

You're going daft. It must be the sun.

Or maybe it's him, she thought as she looked up to find Matt making his way towards them. Same smart shorts, same shades. And her body responded with the same answering sizzle in the pit of her stomach.

He was carrying a smart, grey, *expensive* Yeti drink cooler. She knew it was expensive because she'd admired one in a shop, then baulked at the price and put it down.

As he neared her, he shifted his glasses onto his head and gave an exaggerated look to the left and right. 'No boards?'

She shook her head. 'No boards. Just you, me and a picnic blanket.'

'I like the sound of that.'

God, that slow burn of a smile did it for her every time. 'Good.'

As if aware he was being left out, Chewie barked and she went to hug him. 'Sorry – you, me and Chewie.'

'Your canine chaperone,' he murmured, giving her a small smile and Chewie a wary glance.

'You don't have to worry, you know. He's a big softie.'

'I thought so too, until recently. Now I think I'm under surveillance.'

Chewie let out another woof, which made her laugh. 'You know, if you want to distract him, you only have to let him have one of your shoes.'

Matt's eyes settled on hers, amused, yes, but with enough heat to make her toes curl. 'It seems a small price to pay.'

Her skin prickled and suddenly the day felt too hot, her bikini top too tight. 'What did you choose?' she asked, nodding to the cooler, her mouth so dry, she had difficulty forming the words. Whatever it was, she needed a big glass of it.

He dropped the cooler onto the blanket and opened it up. Nestled inside she saw a bottle of fizz, a bottle of white and two large bottles of water. 'Ah, so you didn't choose.'

'I wasn't sure what activity was planned, so it seemed wise to cover all bases.'

She laughed. 'I can't argue with that. The only activity I have planned is to eat, read and relax.'

'Relax.' He glanced down at the heavy-duty blanket she'd spread out over the pebbles – no soft sand on this beach. 'On that?'

'Which part are you not comfortable with – the relax bit, or the sitting down on a bed of hard, round stones?'

His smile caused the corner of his eyes to crinkle. 'I'm sure I can manage both.'

It was only when they shifted onto the rug that Lottie realised she wasn't quite ready to strip off to her bikini. Growing up by the beach, she was used to swimming and sunbathing with her friends, male and female. Sitting next to Matt felt different, though. Not a friend she felt comfortable with, but a man she was acutely aware of.

'Are you ready to eat?'

He nodded, reaching into the drink cooler to retrieve two plastic wine glasses. 'Wine, water or champagne?'

'*Champagne?*' When she hung out with her friends they had cans of lager, or occasionally someone would bring a box of wine.

He stared at her blankly. 'Is that a question or an answer?'

Grabbing a glass, she held it out to him. 'It's both. Fill it up please, and while we munch through the pork pies – which, by the way, if I'd known you were bringing champagne, I'd have swopped for smoked salmon – you can tell me which book you've brought to read.'

He handled the bottle with the deft ease of a man used to opening champagne, and in seconds her glass was filled with bubbles. With the sun shining down, the gentle waves lapping up the shore, the occasional squawk of the seagulls, it felt like more than a Sunday afternoon on the local beach. It felt special. Something she knew had more to do with the man sitting next to her than the drink in her hand.

'Richard Osman's *The Thursday Murder Club*,' he answered. 'As the title suggests, it's not a romance.' His lips twitched. 'And so far I've not come across any sex.'

'How disappointing.'

'Perhaps not in this case. The main protagonists are all pushing eighty.'

'I plan to still be having sex when I'm eighty.' *Still?*

You're not even having it now. Unconsciously her eyes skated over to Matt, who sat cross-legged next to her, smiling in that cautious way he had. It was different to the smiles he'd given her last Sunday when he'd not had time to think too hard, too busy falling off the board.

'It's a nice thought. To grow old with the person you love.' The smile disappeared and she knew he was thinking of his ex-wife.

'Can I ask what happened with your marriage, or is that too nosey?'

'It's fair. You told me about Henry.' He swallowed down some champagne. 'I let her down. The hours I worked, it wasn't fair on her. In the end she'd had enough and found someone else who could give her the attention I'd failed to give.'

'She had an affair?' Lottie felt outraged for him. However upset his wife had been, surely there was no excuse for going behind someone's back and seeing someone else. 'What happened to honesty, to trust?'

Matt realised he'd never seen Lottie angry, until now. And it wasn't even for herself, it was for him.

'I don't blame her.' He gazed down at the picnic food she'd laid out, but didn't feel hungry. Usually he'd have deflected the question about his marriage, but Lottie had been so open about her relationship with Henry. He knew if he wanted to keep seeing her, on whatever level, he had to try and be open, too. 'I wasn't a nice person to live with.'

She picked up a slice of pork pie and munched on it

with an apparent total disregard for the dubious, fat-laden contents.

'What do you mean? I can't see you losing control and getting angry. Throwing plates and the like. I picture you straightening them in the cupboard. Once you've put them in height order.'

'Ouch.' He tried to laugh, but he felt only intense embarrassment at the image she must have of him.

Her hand touched his arm, fingers tightening briefly around it before she pulled back, leaving his skin tingling. 'Sorry, that was meant to be funny but it came off as bitchy.'

Talk to her. He drew in a breath, gaze looking out to sea, because that was easier than watching the pity on her face. 'The pen-arranging is a hangover from my childhood.' He shifted to hug his knees, the champagne forgotten. 'Life was … tough in boarding school. I found straightening the pencils and pens on my desk, or tidying my drawers, would calm me down. Helped me feel in control again.'

'You missed your parents.'

It was a statement, not a question, and Matt knew he could agree and let the matter slide, but that was the old him. The one who'd caused his wife to leave him. He wanted to do better. Be better. 'I did, but that wasn't the tough part.' He rubbed at the back of his neck, feeling the tension. 'I was bullied. Poor kid on a scholarship, surrounded by a school full of rich ones.'

'Crap.'

At the soft tone of her voice he turned to look at her, and

was nearly undone by the sympathy that shone from her eyes. 'That sums it up nicely.'

'Surely they weren't all toffee-nosed bastards?'

'No.' The smile on his face felt incongruous with the memories in his head, yet that seemed to be one of Lottie's superpowers. An ability to banish dark thoughts, at least temporarily. 'But boys seen talking to me were ostracised too, so it was easier to keep myself to myself.' Needing something to do, he picked up the glass, horrified to find his hands were trembling. 'The experience left me very comfortable in my own company, but not so good in other people's.'

Lottie screwed up her face. 'Your wife clearly fell for you, so you can't have been that bad.'

'I think she liked the *dark mysterious* side of me, as she called it.' His jaw tightened as flashbacks of arguments looped through his head. 'But then work became more intense, the hours brutal.' He hung his head and stared down at the pebbles, the bleak thoughts sending a chill through him despite the beauty of the day. 'When I said I wasn't nice to live with, it was more than not being there for her physically. I became withdrawn, so focused on work, I was useless to Patricia. She was different to me, a real extrovert. She liked to be around people, to talk things through, so she found someone else to do that with.' Bitterness coiled in his gut. 'They just didn't stop at talking.'

'I'm sorry.' Lottie gave him a wry smile. 'Call me biased but I still think she's a bitch. It's not like you were off enjoying yourself. You were working.'

'True, but what sort of man puts his work before his wife?'

Her eyes narrowed on his. 'Why did you decide to work in the City in the first place?'

He let out a huff of laughter. 'The money. My parents struggled, and I didn't want that for myself. Not the arguments about which debt to pay off first, the choice between food or heating.' Embarrassment caused warmth to crawl up his neck. 'Plus I wanted to show those bastards at school.' He'd thought he was winning, proving something as the six-figure, sometimes seven-figure bonuses had rolled in. In reality he'd lost: his marriage over, his family estranged, his mental health struggling. 'It seems the height of stupidity now.'

'I think you've beaten yourself up enough over it.' Lottie's expression held no reproach, no disgust. There was nothing but understanding in her eyes. 'It takes two to make a relationship work. Carry your share of the blame for the breakdown, sure, but it's not fair on you to carry the whole burden.' She glanced down at the food she'd spread out, and his barely touched glass. 'Right, we have to make some serious effort on this picnic now, because I'm not taking any of it home.' Her head turned towards Chewie who lay at her feet, eyes fixed on the sausage rolls. 'Chewie only has so much willpower and I really don't think processed meat is good for him. Or for us, for that matter.' She picked up a sausage roll and grinned. 'But it is bloody tasty.'

He eyed what she'd brought, not quite as convinced.

Did she have any clue what was in the stuff she was eating? He reached for the cheese and placed it on his paper plate along with a hunk of bread, some tomatoes and two slices of melon.

They ate in silence for a few minutes, Lottie laughing as Chewie watched every mouthful they took, eyes full of longing. 'You'll get your treat at the end,' she told him, wriggling her bare toes against his side. The action drew Matt's attention to her feet, and then again to her legs.

He wondered if his eyes were now showing a similar longing. One that involved reaching out to run his hands over the smooth skin and up, beneath her short white skirt.

Arousal arrowed through him and he had to look away before his lustful thoughts became evident.

'So, after we've eaten.' He coughed to rid the husk from his voice. 'We read?'

'Yep. We clear away the food, roll out the towels, lie down and shove our noses in our books.' She eyed him thoughtfully. 'When was the last time you spent a Sunday afternoon doing nothing but read?'

'Never?'

'Exactly. It'll be good for you. Help reduce your blood pressure.'

He eyed the red ties of her bikini, showing at the back of her T-shirt. 'I'm not so sure.'

Her gaze followed his and she smirked, clearly aware of how his thoughts were going. 'I don't have to take the T-shirt off.'

Deliberately he ran his eyes up her legs, over her body and up to her face. 'I hope you do.'

With a small, mischievous smile, she tugged at the hem of her shirt and pulled it over her head. A bolt of lust ran through him as his gaze landed on the two triangles covering her breasts. Christ. He shifted, his boxers feeling way too tight. It wasn't an overtly sexy bikini, the material safely covering her, but now he could see the curve of her cleavage, the weight of her breasts. Now he could imagine how they would feel in his hands.

She grinned at his expression and he had to consciously check that his tongue wasn't hanging out of his mouth. 'I'm supposed to focus on reading?'

Laughter bubbled out of her and the sound warmed him far more than the sun currently beating down. 'I'm hoping this isn't a one-way street.' She waved towards his polo shirt, her eyes daring him. 'You look awfully hot.'

He was a runner. He knew he looked okay, so he quickly shrugged the shirt off, enjoying the way her bold gaze ran over his bare chest.

After swallowing down the rest of her champagne, she handed her glass to him. 'You top us up, I'll clear away. Oh and by the way.' Her smile was an intriguing combination of sensual and mischievous. 'You look even hotter now.'

He hadn't received a compliment for a long time so instead of responding like a normal guy with a charming/cheeky/sexy/witty/playful remark of his own, he just smiled awkwardly.

As they settled onto the blanket, noses in their books, he found it hard to focus.

Not just because she was lying next to him, tempting him in that red bikini.

Not just because instead of wanting to read, he wanted to kiss every inch of the glorious body on view.

He was tortured by his thoughts. His initial intention to keep away until he was ready was the right one. He couldn't bear to fail again, to hurt someone else. Yet the more time he spent in Lottie's company, the more the decision seemed increasingly impossible to live with.

Chapter Sixteen

July, nominated book:
Summer on a Sunny Island **by Sue Moorcroft**

Lottie declared it was too glorious an evening to be inside so they carried the chairs out of the café and onto the beach. She spread her trusty blanket in the middle of them and Sally put Freddie down on it. Immediately he started rolling around, his chubby hands grabbing at the toys Sally placed near him. With the evening sun, the lapping waves, it was a fitting setting for a book set on the holiday island of Malta.

It was also sufficiently relaxing to take her mind off the fact that the van had overheated so much this afternoon, steam had hissed out of the engine. But it had been hot, she reasoned. If she could limp through summer, she might get away with not having to spend money on it until next year.

As the conversation flowed around her, a tiny bit of

Lottie knew that by sitting outside, she was also avoiding Matt. After she'd effectively told him he was hot the other Sunday on the beach, he'd withdrawn from her. They'd read in companionable silence for a while, then taken Chewie for a stroll along the beach, but though Matt had smiled, replied in all the right places, he'd put up a wall between them.

When it had been time to go, he'd done the gentlemanly thing and walked her home, even insisted on carrying everything, but instead of the hot make-out session she'd been hoping for, she'd received a distracted kiss on the cheek.

So much for her powers of seduction.

Either he preferred to do the flirting and chasing, or she'd imagined the heat in his eyes when she'd revealed her bikini. Or maybe he did fancy her, but not enough.

'Earth calling Lottie.' Yanked out of her thoughts, she turned to find Sally watching her with an amused expression. 'Where did you go? Because it certainly wasn't to a sunny island. Not with that look on your face.'

'Sorry. Got lost in my thoughts.' She shook herself, reaching for her glass – Audrey's gin and tonic tasted extra special in the evening sun. 'What were you saying?'

'If you want the quick summary, I said it was a bloody good book and everyone agreed.' Sally smirked. 'Now tell us where you went in your head.'

'I didn't go anywhere interesting.'

Audrey huffed and held out her hand. 'Give me your glass.' She proceeded to glug an obscene amount of gin into it. 'You know it's coming to this club that keeps me going. And I don't mean the book talk, good as it is. I mean the *other* talk. When you get to my age and spend most of your days sat by yourself in your front room, you have to live your life vicariously. Just a bugger we only do this once a month.'

Lottie glanced at them all. 'Well, if Matt and Amy are willing, there's no reason we can't meet every fortnight, if we're all up for it.'

'Whoopee, I second that.' Heidi raised her glass, and everyone voiced their agreement.

'Don't worry about my brother.' Amy gave her a determined look. 'I'll make sure he's okay with it.'

'Well then, drink up everyone,' Audrey announced. 'Especially Lottie, so we can interrogate her.' She cackled. 'Never understood why special forces don't use gin to extract information.'

Lottie eyed her glass warily. 'If I drink all that you'll never get anything out of me. I'll be in a coma.'

'But you'll also have improved digestion, healthier-looking skin and live ten years longer.' Gira smiled. 'I read about it in *The Times*. Juniper berries are like a super-fruit.'

'We'd best all have a refill then.' Audrey began to lurch unsteadily to her feet but Amy, bless her, beat her to it.

'I'll serve.' She let out a shy laugh. 'It's my job, after all.'

Before Audrey could get round to the interrogation, Lottie heard a scrunch of feet on pebbles. Heart pounding, she turned, only to find it was the older Steele coming towards them.

'Hi, Jim.' She hoped to God her disappointment didn't show in her face. 'Come for your slice of cake?'

His eyes darted towards the shop. 'I have, but Matt doesn't know I'm here.'

'He's banned you from joining us?'

He screwed up his face, looking faintly embarrassed. 'Well, no. But I told him I couldn't work this afternoon because I was playing bowls.'

Amy giggled. 'Dad, you lied to Matt?'

'White lie,' he hurriedly told his daughter. 'I'm saving a row. Can't tell him I don't want to work in his ruddy shop.' His gaze dropped down to the gooey chocolate fudge cake, eyes devouring it.

'Here.' Lottie handed him a serviette. 'Better wipe your chin, you're drooling.'

He rubbed it and Heidi started to laugh. 'She's teasing you.' While Jim shot Lottie a baleful look, Heidi cut him a huge slice. Chewie, lying on the blanket by Lottie's feet, watched Heidi's every move. 'Here you go. Enjoy.'

'I suppose I should take care of the oldies.' Amy stood and went to sit on the blanket. 'Have my seat, Dad.'

'Hey, less of the cheek.'

Audrey chuckled. 'Jim's not old, love. He's in his prime, like me. We just need to convince you young folk to see that and not treat us like we've reached our expiry date. There's plenty we can still do, given the chance.'

'Exactly. As long as it doesn't involve new-fangled technology.' He slunk into the chair. 'Or standing, because my knees aren't what they used to be.'

Everyone laughed and Jim started to chomp on the cake.

Lottie rolled her eyes as Chewie eyed up the plate. 'Chewie.' He raised his head to look at her. 'Stop staring at Jim's cake. You're not getting any.' If dogs could pout, she was certain he'd be doing it right now.

'Are we serving this in the café yet?' Jim mumbled between mouthfuls, then paused, his face paling. 'Bugger, Matt told me not to say anything.'

Amy's face turned scarlet as they all looked at her, confused. 'Err, I was going to ask Heidi after we'd finished.'

'Ask me what, dear?'

'If you wanted … no.' Clearly agitated, she drew in a breath. 'Whether you'd be interested in supplying us. You know, with your cakes.'

Lottie watched as surprise filtered across Heidi's face. 'You want to sell my cakes. Here. In the café?'

Amy nodded. 'I mean, we'd pay you. I have all the stuff I'm meant to talk to you about written down, but it's in my bag back in the shop.' Her cheeks coloured again. 'Sorry, I'm supposed to do this in private. Matt's going to be well cross with me.'

They were all so focused on Amy, they didn't hear the scrunch of footsteps until it was too late. 'Why am I going to be cross?'

The sound of the familiar smooth, deep voice caused Lottie to look over with a start. Matt's eyes met hers briefly, his expression unreadable, before he looked at his sister.

'It's my fault.' Jim wiped his chocolate-coated mouth with the serviette she'd given him and gave his son a brief rundown of what had happened. 'I blame the cake, loosening my tongue. Mighty fine it is. Mighty fine.'

'I thought you were playing bowls?'

'Ah, yes.' Jim scrunched up the napkin, eyes avoiding his son. 'Decided not to go. Lure of the cake and all that.'

Matt's jaw tightened. Lottie didn't fully understand the undercurrents between them all, only that father and daughter clearly carried some resentment towards Matt. And that Matt was hurting because of it.

There was a moment of strained silence, broken by Heidi. 'I'd be delighted to make cakes for the café.'

Amy stared at her. 'You would?'

'Good heavens, of course.' She gave Amy a beaming smile. 'I can't imagine any better way to fill my days than baking for someone who actually wants my cakes. Thank you both.'

'It was Amy's idea,' Matt said quietly. His gaze swept round the group and Lottie became acutely aware of how it looked, Amy and his dad sitting with them. Matt on the outside. 'Sorry for the interruption. I actually came to scrounge a slice of the soon-to-be legendary cake.'

While Heidi fussed over cutting him a slice, Lottie watched him, a strange ache in her chest. A complex man. Totally unsuitable for the fun fling she felt ready for. Yet while logic said she should avoid him, she'd always been ruled by her heart, not her head.

As he sat in his office, Matt contemplated the half-eaten cake on his desk. He'd given up trying to tally up his accounts. That was for another day, when his mind was able to focus. He couldn't explain how mixed up he'd felt seeing the group on the beach when he'd stepped outside. From a distance he'd watched Amy giggle, seen his father join the circle, chatting away as if he'd known them for years. The dog, the baby, the entire generation span enjoying the evening sun.

But while he was happy to see his dad and sister joining in, and pleased to see Lottie's book club gelling, he'd also felt an acute sense of isolation. He'd come here to make a fresh start, yet once again he was the loner. Sitting in his office.

His gut twisted and he pushed the cake out of sight. He had no one to blame but himself. He was the one falling into the same bad habits. Keeping people at arm's length. *Like Lottie.*

There was a tap on his door and he glanced up to find the object of his thoughts standing in the doorway. Cropped jeans and a shirt that tied around her waist, giving him a glimpse of the soft curve of her stomach.

Immediately all his blood rushed south.

'Amy said to tell you everything is back in place in the café and ready for tomorrow.'

He sighed, failure clawing at him again. 'Thanks. I hoped I'd already made it clear that I trust her to run the café. That it's hers.' He swallowed, shaking his head. 'Obviously I've more work to do.'

KATHRYN FREEMAN

'It's not just on you.' Lottie stepped further into the office. 'Amy's still finding her feet. Until she's confident, she'll keep deferring to you.' Her eyes met his. 'You shouldn't see it as a bad thing. She wants to please you.'

He took a breath, thought through what she'd said. 'She shouldn't feel she's let me down. That stuff about me being cross.' He exhaled sharply, frustration bubbling. 'I hate that she thinks that. I'm the one who let her down. I let them both down.'

Lottie shifted so she was perched on the edge of his desk, her eyes so full of sympathy, he couldn't hold her gaze. 'Whatever you did, I'm certain you've beaten yourself up enough about it.'

He smiled, his mouth tight. 'Sorry. You shouldn't be such a good listener. It makes people want to talk to you.' *Even tight-lipped, insular bastards like me.*

'Hey, I do more than enough talking of my own. It's only fair I listen now and again.'

She got up to go and he realised if he didn't say something now, it could be another month before he saw her again.

'Come to dinner with me,' he blurted.

She froze, grey eyes showing both confusion and surprise. 'You mean now? Because you're hungry and don't want to eat by yourself—'

'I'm asking you out on a date.' He slumped back on his chair and rubbed a hand down his face. 'Though I seem to have lost all my social skills, which doesn't bode well.' Amusement flickered on her face and he relaxed enough to

196

try again. 'Please would you let me take you to dinner tomorrow. Or Saturday. Or any day you're free. If you'd like that.'

The silence that followed his second, only marginally better, attempt seemed to stretch for hours, though he suspected it was only a few seconds.

'What happened to you not being good for me?'

His stomach fell, the doubts, the fears, resurfacing. 'I'm still not.' He wanted to leave it at that, but he'd blown hot and cold enough with Lottie. It was time to be straight. 'Honestly, I'm not a good bet. "Emotionally unavailable" is how my ex-wife described me. But I'm trying to be better.' His gaze locked with hers. 'Despite appearances to the contrary, this is me making an effort to lighten up. To talk about myself more and let people in.' He gave her a wry smile. 'I'm still a work in progress but I figure you're level-headed enough, open enough, to tell me where to go when I cock up.'

A smile tugged at her mouth. 'You can count on that. Where are you planning on taking me?'

'Ah. I haven't thought about it yet.' It was telling that he'd been here six months and only eaten out at the pub down the road. 'Is your answer dependent on the venue?'

Her warm, unrestrained laughter filled his office. 'It might be, but not in the way you think. I'm not a candlelight and get dressed-up kind of girl, so it doesn't need to be fancy. But if my parents can't look after Chewie, it will have to be dog-friendly.'

He thought of how he wanted to spend the evening, the

ways he wanted to touch her afterwards, God and Lottie willing. None of it included being watched by an over-protective canine. 'I'm a candlelight and get dressed-up kind of guy.' He found her eyes. 'And you deserve fancy, so let me take you out properly. Please.'

She gave him her big, sunny smile. 'Well, when you put it like that, how can I say no?'

'I'd hoped you wouldn't. Let me know what day works after you've checked with your parents.'

'Okay.' She considered him. 'Is that your roundabout way of saying you plan on kissing me and don't want Chewie in the way?'

'No. It's my way of telling you I'd like to wine and dine you, Lottie Watt.' His eyes fell on her mouth, on the naked pink lips he couldn't stop thinking about. The lips he wanted to caress, to savour. To feast on. 'But I do plan on kissing you again.'

She let out a breathy sound that he hoped meant she was as aroused as he at the idea. 'Definitely no Chewie then.' She pretended to fan herself but from where he was sitting the heat felt very real. Then she gave him a sidelong glance, teeth nibbling at her lower lip. 'Do you think we should have another go now? Get in some practice?'

He recalled his earlier fears about being rusty. Christ, maybe this was her way of saying he was. It was hard to tell, because he wasn't used to forward women. Then again, he wasn't used to women, full stop. Patricia. One girlfriend before her when he'd been a student, drowning in hormones. A shameful one-night stand after her, when he'd been at a low ebb, drowning in self-pity.

Heart hammering, he rose to his feet and walked round the desk to stand in front of her. Her eyes were luminous, her breath choppy. 'I definitely need practice.' He placed a hand on her face, feeling the connection all the way to his groin. His heart was so loud in his ears, he wondered if she could hear it. Then he bent his head to capture her mouth. And stopped thinking.

Time and again his tongue explored her sweet depths, at times teasing, others devouring. The more he tasted, the more he wanted. Shifting them, he pressed her curvy body against the desk, aligning it to the hard planes of his, heat against heat…

'Lottie, are you coming?' Sally's voice echoed through the shop and they sprang apart, their breath sounding hot and heavy in the small space of the office. 'Freddie's started to get fractious – for that, read he's bawling his eyes out – and Chewie's pining for you. For that, read he's straining at the lead, desperate to come and find you.'

'Shit.' Lottie gazed up at him, her mouth swollen, her cheeks flushed. 'I'm a terrible dog mum. I forgot I'd left him with Sally.'

Matt drew in a breath, trying to get his heart to calm, his mind to de-fog. 'Thank God he's on a lead or I'd be dead.'

She hiccupped out a laugh. 'He's not that bad.'

'You haven't seen the death stares he's been giving me.'

She rolled her eyes. 'It would be death by slobbering.'

'Whatever you're up to,' Sally continued, 'I'll send Chewie in to break it up if you don't get out here now.'

Lottie started to laugh. 'Oh God. I'd better go before she sets the hound on us.' He started to walk out with her but she put a hand on his arm. 'Sally will embarrass the hell out of us if you come out with me.'

'I'm not afraid of your friend.'

She arched a brow. 'Or my big furry dog?'

He paused. 'Maybe I'll say goodbye here.' She started laughing again and that's when he knew he was in trouble because he got such a kick from seeing her giggle, even though it was at his expense. 'Let me know when I can pick you up.'

'I will. Oh, and Matt,' she added just before she turned the corner. 'You didn't actually need the practice.'

From the back of the shop, out of view thanks to the giant bookshelves, he heard Chewie bark and Lottie fuss over him. Heard, too, Sally's barrage of questions: 'What were you two doing? Why are your eyes sparkling, your mouth like it's been stung by a hive of irritated bees? ... I know you've been snogging my mate!' she shouted.

He shook his head, smiling to himself as Lottie squealed and tried to shush her friend.

'You'd better treat her right or you'll have me to contend with,' he heard Sally yell, just before the door slammed shut.

Slowly the smile left his face. Was he right to be doing this? He'd made Patricia's life miserable. He couldn't bear the thought of doing the same to someone as vital, as kind-hearted, as sunny-natured as Lottie.

Her earlier words from when they'd kissed on the beach floated back at him: *Stop over-thinking. It's just a kiss.*

This was just a date.

Besides, Lottie, for all her warmth, had a backbone of steel. She was entirely capable of taking care of herself. It was more likely he'd be the one left bruised after she'd had enough of him. In the meantime though, perhaps they could have some fun.

Finally he was going to start this new life he'd promised himself.

Chapter Seventeen

Saturday evening, and Lottie stared again at the clothes she'd laid out on the bed, then down at Chewie. 'What do you think?'

She picked up the green dress she'd bought for her friend Michele's wedding. Slim-fitting with three-quarter sleeves and a narrow silver belt, it had looked good for a spring wedding, but for a summer dinner date? 'Too formal?'

He wagged his tail, which could mean anything. 'You know you're not going with me, right?' She picked up the next option, a flowery summer dress she'd worn to see Henry's parents for the first time. Bought by him, chosen by him.

'You've got a sleepover with Grandma and Grandad,' she told Chewie as she held the dress against her in the mirror. 'No way am I going to let a jealous dog interrupt our next kiss.' Or whatever would, maybe, hopefully, happen afterwards.

'Shit, I can't wear something chosen by my ex to a first date, can I?' That left the white trousers and slinky, off-the-shoulder yellow top. One of her favourites, but... 'Is he expecting me to wear a dress?'

With a sigh, she reached for her phone and quickly typed out a message to Matt.

How dressed up do I have to be? L x

She glanced at the time. Half an hour before he picked her up. 'I'll give him five minutes, then I need to make a decision.'

Chewie lay back down on the carpet, his doggy eyes looking up at her as if he was listening to every word. Her phone buzzed, then again, and again. And again.

You don't have to be anything.

I'll be wearing a suit.

But I'm a stuffed shirt.

I guarantee you'll look better than me, whatever you choose.

Smiling, she picked up the trousers.
At seven sharp, Matt knocked on the door.

Lottie looked down at the brown paw print she'd been trying to rub off and cursed. Typical of the man that he was fastidiously on time. Abandoning the idea of drying the damp patch with a hair dryer, she went to greet him.

Her heart did a swoop when she took in his light grey suit and white, open-collared shirt. Then somersaulted when she caught sight of the bunch of yellow roses in his hand.

'Wow. Thank you.' She reached for them, inhaling their scent. She wasn't a flowers girl, just as she wasn't the candlelit restaurant sort, yet she couldn't explain how giddy she felt right now.

His eyes took in her top. 'You seem to like yellow.'

'I do.' There was an intensity to him, a focus, that made her stomach flutter. 'Apparently I also like roses, though I didn't realise until now.'

His dark brows shot up. 'Henry didn't buy them for you?'

She laughed. 'We were both students when we started going out, he was studying journalism at uni and I was doing an electrician course at the local college. Our idea of a date was fish and chips on the beach with a can of lager. To spend money on flowers would have seemed like a waste.' He blinked and looked away. It was only then she realised how ungrateful she sounded. 'I didn't mean... These aren't a waste. They're lovely.'

'As are you.'

She appreciated the sentiment but his words sounded too polite, his manner too stiff. She didn't want polite words, she wanted heartfelt ones. Was he regretting asking her already? 'Thank you. Do you want to come in? I'll just put these in water.'

He exhaled heavily as he stepped into the hallway. 'That sounded cheesy, didn't it?'

It was only when she saw his weak smile that she realised what was wrong. He was *nervous*. 'Not cheesy, no. Just a bit formal.'

He groaned. 'Sorry.' Raking a hand through his hair, he gave her a wry glance. 'Hard to imagine, but I did have some moves, once upon a time.'

'Umm.' She glanced flirtatiously up at him from beneath her lashes. 'Would you like to show me one?'

His eyes flared and he took a step towards her. 'First,' he said, his expression serious as he reached for the roses and put them on the small table in the hall, 'I'd remove any objects with sharp thorns.'

Laughter bubbled. 'I'm not sure about smooth, but that's definitely sensible.'

'Don't worry, smooth is coming.' He swallowed, his Adam's apple doing a sexy rise and fall above the collar of his shirt. 'I hope.'

She touched a hand to his freshly shaven cheek. 'I won't care if it doesn't.' Smiling, she glanced down at her trousers. 'I'm standing here in my pokey, damp hallway. My trousers have a muddy paw print on them I was trying to wash out before you came. I'm not a girl who needs smooth.'

'No.' His fingers touched lightly at her curls, his dark eyes skimming over her face. 'But I don't want to fail with you, Lottie. Ditch me because I'm boring, because I have an odd compulsion to straighten pens. Because your dog hates me. But not because I failed to treat you right. Failed to *appreciate* you.'

The earnestness of his words caused a shift in her chest. They were a reminder that Matt was different to other men she'd known. Deeper, his character shaped by a lonely childhood, his confidence scarred by a painful divorce. This, whatever it was between them, wouldn't be simple, or easy. 'We haven't been on one date yet and already you're talking about splitting up?'

A slight curve of the lips she wanted to kiss, despite the worries that niggled. 'I'm making a hash of this, aren't I?'

'No, but this is heavy talk and, if I'm honest, I'm after something light.' She hesitated, searching his eyes, which flickered with an emotion she couldn't put her finger on. 'I think that's what you need, too.'

His smile appeared forced. 'In case you haven't noticed, light isn't my forte.'

'In case you haven't noticed, it is mine.' There was a beat of silence and then he laughed, the tension easing from his face. It relaxed her enough to risk teasing him. 'So, those moves you bragged about earlier. Still want to show me one?'

This time his smile was wider, his eyes joining in. 'Okay.' He straightened his shoulders and turned to look around them. 'Second, I look for prowling predators. Lions, wolves. Dogs.'

She chewed at her lip, fighting the urge to giggle. 'Chewie's at my parents'.'

'Then we can go straight to move three.'

Her pulse rocketed as his smile turned sensual, his eyes hot, any hint of nerves vanished. The man who pressed his lips to hers, who teased them open with his tongue while his hands slid down her back, bristled with male confidence. The more he took from her, the more he pulled her tight against his rapidly hardening groin, the more his mouth devoured hers, the more her head spun.

She moaned when he drew away, keeping her arms around his neck partly for balance – her knees seemed to have disappeared – and partly because she enjoyed the feel of his body against hers; the power in his chest, the tension in his tight muscles. 'I'm a fan of move three.'

Laughter rumbled through him and he pressed his forehead to hers, his breath sounding as fast and uneven as hers. 'Maybe I can show you more moves after dinner?'

The mix of authority with vulnerability; sexy with sweet. He was dangerous, but she was unable, and unwilling, to heed the warning. 'Maybe you can.'

He was a lucky bastard, he decided, as he watched Lottie walk back towards him after her trip to the ladies'. The eyes of every male watching her. She looked stunning, blonde curls bouncing, the yellow of her top lighting up her gorgeous face, the cut of it revealing a sexy tanned shoulder he itched to kiss. To think, he'd almost blown it before he'd even got her to the restaurant.

She wanted light, and he'd shown her the uptight, insecure part of him he was trying to bury.

'The loos are to die for,' she said as she slipped back into the seat opposite him. 'There's even a plush velvet sofa you can sit on, though why you'd want to sit in the ladies', I don't know. Unless you're hiding from your date.'

He smiled and took a sip of water. 'I'm grateful to see you back.'

She smirked. 'On balance I figured I'd have a better time with you.'

He knew she was joking but he couldn't help but wonder if she was, actually, enjoying herself. She seemed a little … restrained. As if she was holding some of herself back. 'Have you not been here before?'

'God, no.' He winced at the incredulous tone and though he'd had a lifetime of hiding his feelings, clearly Lottie had superpowers because she reached a hand across the table to touch his. 'That came out wrong. I haven't been here because Henry and I didn't do posh restaurants, as you know, and it isn't the kind of place a bunch of mates hang out in, is it? It's more the place you come to impress your clients, or your date.'

'I admit that was my plan.'

'Then consider me impressed.' She frowned, twirling the stem of her wine glass with her fingers. 'But I would have enjoyed anywhere you'd taken me, because I was looking forward to spending time with you.'

He swallowed, his throat tightening. Patricia, Amy, his dad … it had been a while since anyone had wanted his company. 'Ditto.' *Seriously, Steele? She pays you a compliment like that, and all you can manage is 'Ditto'?* He shifted uncomfortably on his chair. 'Do you and Henry keep in touch?' And yep, he wasn't sure he wanted to know the answer.

'I guess, sort of. We update each other on our families, the people we know, that sort of thing.' She smiled, but it held a hint of sadness. Perhaps even regret. 'Are we really doing this, discussing our exes?'

'No.' He realised he didn't want to know any more about the man she'd loved. The one she clearly still had feelings for.

'Good, because there's something else I wanted to discuss with you.' Lottie gave him a sweet smile. 'If you're feeling mellow after your meal, maybe now is a good time.'

Thanks to Amy, he thought he knew what Lottie wanted. 'The answer is yes.'

'That's a pretty bold reply, considering you don't know what I'm about to ask.'

'I'm pretty sure yes would always be the answer.' Her cheeks flushed a little and he smiled, enjoying seeing her unbalanced. 'But in this case Amy has already put in the request on your behalf. The book club is welcome every other week. Or every week, for that matter. Now, would you like to see the dessert menu?'

Her face took on a mischievous look. 'Do you even have dessert? You chose the low-calorie fish with steamed veggies while I binged on the steak-and-ale pie. That's not a man who finishes his meal with a pudding.'

'True.' His discipline about what he ate, and about exercise, had come on gradually; the more work had sucked him in, the more rigid he'd become. He could only guess it was because so much else in his life had seemed out of his control. 'But I'm happy to watch you eat one.' It was almost erotic, seeing the enjoyment she got out of food.

'Well, it kind of depends on whether you have anything to offer back at your place that can beat sticky toffee pudding laden with cream.'

The husky tone, the promise behind her words … it all sent a bolt of arousal humming through him. 'I can try.' Immediately he signalled for the bill, making her laugh.

It was only when the waiter returned with it that his blood-deprived brain remembered why going back to his wasn't such a good idea. 'Amy, my dad. You might bump into them.'

'I don't mind if you don't.'

His erection pushed painfully against his zipper. 'Will it offend you if I admit that right now all I really mind about is getting you into my bed as fast as humanly possible?'

A smile split her face. 'It would offend me more if you didn't.'

He quickly settled the bill – she tried to pay but he waved her effort away. 'I invited you.'

Moments later they were in the car, his hand resting on her thigh as he manoeuvred out of the car park. Beneath the thin layer of cotton, her skin felt hot and the ache between his legs grew sharper. It had been nearly a year since he'd last had sex, and that had been a very forgettable experience, his mind still mired in guilt and grief over his divorce.

The guilt was still present, but the grief had gone. Tonight, for the first time in years, he felt hopeful for the future. He still had a way to go in repairing his relationship with his dad and Amy but he was enjoying the shop, the slower pace. Being his own boss. He glanced sideways at the woman next to him and acknowledged she had a lot to do with his current, unusual state of optimism.

'What are you thinking?'

He slowed at the traffic light and turned to face her. 'I'm thinking how lucky I am to have met you.'

Her eyes widened and for a moment he wondered if he'd cocked up again, said too much when what she wanted was fun. But then she smiled, her cheeks dimpling in a way he'd not fully appreciated until now. 'If you carrying on saying things like that, you'll get even luckier.'

For the rest of the short journey they were quiet, though the electricity pinging between them crackled loudly in his ears, sending shivers of anticipation through him. As he pulled into the drive he wondered if she felt the same nervous energy, the raw heat of lust.

He managed to get round to her side of the car just in time to help her out. She smiled as she took his hand. 'Thank you, but I'm a modern woman. I don't expect you to open my door.'

He raised her hand to his lips and pressed a kiss on her

knuckles. 'I'm an old-fashioned guy, Lottie. I *want* to open doors for you, buy you dinner, carry your bags, bring you flowers.'

She nibbled at her bottom lip. 'Does that mean you won't sleep with me on our first date?'

Bringing his hands to her hips, he drew her against him before bending to whisper in her ear, 'Not a cat in hell's chance.'

Then, the sound of his pounding heart drowned by the sound of her laughter, he clasped her hand and led her towards the house.

Chapter Eighteen

Prickles of excitement raced across her skin as Lottie followed Matt up the stairs. *Note to self, tell him how amazing his house is when you come up for air.*

For now, she needed all the oxygen just to keep one foot in front of the other. God, she could never remember feeling like this. Even the giddy first few dates with Henry hadn't felt so intense. They'd been like slipping into a deep, hot bath. Right now she felt like she was about to plunge into a mountain pool; invigorated, thrilled, yet a little scared because she couldn't see the bottom. Didn't know how deep she was about to fall.

They reached the top of the stairs and he paused to run a finger down her cheek. Already racing, her heart missed a beat at the tender gesture, so at odds with the heat in his smouldering brown eyes. 'We can take a left to my bedroom, or go back downstairs to my car.'

His statement surprised her. Surely he could see there

was no decision to be made? It was true she'd been out of
her comfort zone for most of the evening; the posh
restaurant, the at times heavy conversation. His clearly
worth-a-shit-tonne-of-money house. Yet she'd also never
felt so energised. Excited to keep going and see what more
this journey would bring.

'You promised me moves.'

His smile reached his eyes. 'I did.'

He tugged on her hand and they walked the last few
steps along the corridor, stopping before the door at the
end. 'Just so you know, Amy sleeps at the other end of the
house and Dad's rooms are downstairs.'

'So I can be as loud as I like?'

He let out a soft huff of laughter. 'Christ, Lottie.'

Crap, he wasn't Henry. He was a guy who went to fancy
restaurants and felt at home in a suit. 'Too crass?'

'No, God no.' Eyes blazing, he pulled her into his arms,
his hands sliding down her back. 'You're … unexpected.'

'Unexpected bad, or unexpected—'

'Perfect.' He drew in a ragged breath. 'You're perfect.'

Relief rushed through her and she gave him a brief,
fierce kiss. 'Then what are you waiting for?'

She squealed as he lifted her into his arms and carried
her into his bedroom to lay her on the bed. As he shrugged
off his jacket she had a brief moment to take in the dark
blue walls, the solid oak furniture. Then he was kissing her,
his hands busy removing her clothes.

'It's like I've been given a gift,' he whispered, breath hot
against her skin as his fingers slipped beneath her top. 'I

desperately want to rip at the packaging to get inside, yet it would be a tragedy not to savour the beauty of the wrapping.'

Breath caught in her throat and she stared up at him. 'Who are you?'

'Sorry?'

'You're using words, Matt.' Words that made her heart somersault. 'The Matt Steele I know doesn't say any more than he has to.'

He smiled and tugged gently at the silk of her top, easing it over her head. His gaze landed on her strapless bra and he groaned, pressing a kiss in the valley between her breasts before tracing a finger over the lace. 'Can I?'

He's a gentleman, she realised belatedly. Old-fashioned, he'd called himself, but really it was manners to ask, where others would have just assumed. 'Of course. It's part of the gift wrapping.'

Reverently he ran his hands over her stomach and across her bra before easing her on her side to get at the clasp. For a few seconds he struggled and she was about to help when it finally gave way.

'Sorry,' he rasped, eyes settling back on hers. 'Out of practice.'

There was that vulnerability again. Her heart squeezed and she knew she'd been right to be scared earlier. This man wasn't a fun affair, to be enjoyed and easily forgotten. He was a man a woman fell for.

'You're stunning.' Suddenly she was the one unable to talk and he was the one filling the silence as he pulled off the bra and cupped his hands over her breasts. 'Breath-taking.' He bent to kiss her left nipple, flicking his tongue across it and watching as it puckered. Then he breathed on it, causing shivers of arousal to course through her.

'The other one,' she gasped, aching, wanting. 'It's feeling left out.'

Immediately his head dipped to her right breast, giving it the same thorough attention. Producing the same delicious response. Then his mouth trailed down to her stomach, his fingers undoing her trousers and sliding them down her legs while his lips continued their tantalising path across her skin.

'I ... Oh, God,' she croaked as his hand slipped beneath her underwear to find her drenched core.

He cursed softly, fingers exploring, eyes on hers, watching her reaction to his movements with a quiet intensity. 'You like that?'

'No, not like.' She arched her back, arousal burning across her nerve endings. 'Too wishy-washy.'

His mouth followed where his hands had been and she couldn't talk, couldn't think as his tongue worked its magic, bringing her to a shattering climax in an embarrassingly short amount of time.

'Oh my frigging God.' She collapsed back against the mattress, boneless, head spinning. She'd expected caution, care. A silent, earnest round of thoroughly nice sex. She'd not expected to be feel cherished, adored. Or to lose her mind and explode so dramatically under such a confident, masterful touch.

She looked up to find his mouth glistening, his gaze so hot she could practically see the flames in his eyes. 'You're incredible.' He ran his hand tenderly down her face. 'So responsive.'

'Yeah, because you have a magic mouth.' She blew out a breath and waved at his fully clothed body. 'How come I'm naked and you're not?'

He smiled. 'Because I was in a rush to unwrap you.'

'Well, I want my turn now.' She wriggled her toes. 'Just give me another minute to get the feeling back in my legs.'

'There's no hurry.' Again his hands swept over her skin, as if he couldn't stop touching her. 'I'm hoping you'll stay the night.'

There'd be no awkward moment once they'd had sex, she thought blissfully. Just the chance to snuggle in his big wooden bed. And with a bit of luck, do it all again because if that was the starter, she couldn't wait for the main course.

Matt trailed his fingers across Lottie's flushed skin. He'd forgotten how glorious, how extraordinary sex could be.

His groin throbbed, pressing insistently against his fly, but despite the ache he was enjoying simply watching her. Never had he seen a woman give herself over to pleasure in such an uninhibited way. It made him feel like a king, when for years he'd felt uncertain of his ability to make a woman happy in that most fundamental of ways.

He was dragged out of his head when a pair of deft

fingers began to undo the buttons of his shirt. The occasional touch of skin on skin, the look of concentration on her face, the jiggle of her glorious breasts as she worked. It was all too much for his poor, agonisingly hard groin.

'I can't...' He grabbed hold of her hands, stopping her. 'You'll unman me,' he whispered as she gave him a confused look. 'Next time. Right now I just need to be inside you.'

He pushed himself off the bed and stripped off quickly, his movements efficient, not sexy. *That's just the way you are. You can't blame the three hours of foreplay.* He pushed the unhelpful realisation aside, finding it surprisingly easy once he glanced back on the bed.

'I was right.' She gave him a smug smile, gaze running greedily over his naked body. 'Even before you took your shirt off on the beach, I knew you were packing a smoking hot body beneath the swanky clothes.' Her eyes zeroed in on the part of him that throbbed, desperate for her touch. 'I just didn't realise how hot, or how *impressive*, until now.'

He let out a strangled laugh, turned on even more by the appreciation in her eyes. 'Says the sex goddess lying on my bed.' With hands that weren't quite steady he reached into his bedside drawer for the condoms, all fingers and thumbs as he wrestled to open the packet.

'Let me.' As she took over the job, she glanced sideways at him. 'A new packet, huh?'

Only now did he realise how that might look. 'I bought them after my divorce. Not for tonight. I hoped, yes, but—'

'Relax. I'm teasing you.' With a foil packet now in her

hand, she glanced up at him. 'This is exactly where I wanted the evening to end, so if you had bought them for tonight, I would have given you full marks for forward planning.'

He gazed at her in wonder. She was so open with her thoughts, her feelings. 'Lottie, I...' He trailed off, unsure how to put into words how he felt. Much as he enjoyed her, admired her, he was terrified he was wrong for her.

Grey eyes searched his and she must have seen his confusion because she placed a finger on his lips. 'Shh, it's okay. I'm a lot to take in, I know. I talk too much and it's not always cool. Especially when I'm naked on your bed with a condom in my hand.'

He shook his head, trailing a hand down her cheek. 'You take my breath away.'

She nibbled her lip. 'Do you mean that in a good way, or a *what is this weird woman doing on my bed* sort of way?'

'The first. Definitely the first.' He didn't have her words, so he bent to kiss her, hoping he could tell her with his mouth, his hands, what he couldn't articulate out loud.

When he drew back for air, she waved the condom in the air and grinned, cheeks rosy pink. 'I think we need to put this on.' He reached for it but she pushed him away. 'No way. Why should you have all the fun?'

Of course she didn't just slip it on quickly, as he would have done. First she teased with her hands, with her mouth, until in the end the sensations became too much. 'Enough.'

Taking over from her, he secured it in place before leaning over her and aligning himself with her core. As he pressed inside he kept his eyes on hers, watching them widen, then flutter closed.

'God, Matt, you feel frigging huge.'

He laughed, raining kisses over her face as he began to move. He wasn't used to talking during sex but if she kept saying things like that, he was fully on board with the idea. 'You feel amazing.'

Her lips curved. 'Yeah?'

In answer he thrust deeper, manoeuvring slightly so he could capture a nipple with his mouth, grazing it with his teeth.

She let out a strangled moan, arching up to meet him. 'More,' she panted. 'The thing with the teeth, and, you know, your hips.'

'Like this.' He shifted, the new angle meaning he could go deeper. He knew he'd found the perfect position when she swore.

'OMG, yes, exactly like that.' Head pressed back against the pillow, pleasure racing across her face, she gripped at his buttocks. 'That's soooo good. Keep going, don't ever stop.'

He kept going for as long as he could but the way her heat gripped him, the sounds she made, the bounce of her beautiful breasts … it was all too much. 'I can't hold off—'

He didn't finish his sentence because suddenly she was coming, crying out his name, her exuberant response tipping him right over the edge with her.

He came back to earth to find he was sprawled over her, his body wrecked. 'Sorry,' he managed, hauling himself off and onto his back. 'For crushing you,' he clarified quickly, reaching for her hand. 'Not for...' Again he trailed off, this time because he wasn't sure how to put into words what they'd just experienced.

'The stupendous sex.'

He paused a moment, letting the words flow happily through him. Then, his ego swelling, he wound his arm around her and drew her against his side. 'Exactly.' On a tidal wave of tenderness, he kissed the top of her curly blonde head.

'I hope I didn't wake the house up.' Her fingers traced a line down his chest. 'Now you know I wasn't joking about being loud.'

'I don't care if you did.' He grasped her fingers with his free hand and raised them to his lips, kissing them before settling her hand back on his stomach. 'I've discovered I'm a huge fan of sex talk.'

She leant up on her elbow, smoky eyes on his. 'You know I'm bursting with questions now, don't you?'

He laughed, hugging her closer, making himself say the next words out loud because if he was to have a chance with her, he had to learn to voice his feelings. 'I was never sure if Patricia enjoyed it.' His mind skipped involuntarily back to those dark days before they separated. 'The fact she went elsewhere strongly suggests she didn't.'

'Bollocks.' Lottie sat bolt upright. 'She had an affair because you weren't paying her attention, though in my opinion there's no excuse for going behind your back like she did. Talk to you, have it out with you. Sneaking around isn't just a betrayal, it's cowardly.'

He appreciated her words, but in his heart he knew he'd let Patricia down, though perhaps now he could see there was fault on both sides.

In a flash Lottie was straddling him, her breasts jiggling in front of his eyes. She caught the direction of his gaze and smirked. 'I thought that might be an effective distraction from whatever dark thoughts you're having.'

He reached to cup her and immediately his mind was full of Lottie. Only Lottie. She must have felt the direction of his thoughts because she moved on top of him, rubbing against his rapidly growing erection. 'You're far more than a distraction,' he murmured, pulling her towards him so he could nuzzle her breasts.

She smiled down at him, though something flashed across her face, a flicker of emotion that for once, he couldn't identify. But then she lifted herself over him, and onto him, and he was lost to the thrill of her body, her loud, lusty words, all over again.

Chapter Nineteen

Lottie lay in Matt's bed, the lingering smell of his aftershave surrounding her as she listened to the sound of the shower coming from the ensuite.

Her body felt utterly relaxed, sated from round... Wow, she'd actually lost count. But though the sex had been off the charts, her mind refused to chill like her body had. Last night was meant to have been all about fun. A nice meal, laughter (God, she loved his sharp sense of humour), followed by some much-needed sex, which she'd missed like crazy.

Instead, she was worried it had changed everything. This morning, when she'd sleepily watched him dress for his morning run, she hadn't seen a handsome man who needed lightening up at bit. She'd seen a man she could fall for. *You're more than a distraction.* And crap, yes, perhaps also a man who could fall for her.

Was a serious relationship really what she wanted? And

with Matt? He'd said he wasn't good for his wife, and though she knew he was a good man, did they make any sense as a couple?

From its place in her jeans pocket she heard her phone buzz. Welcoming the distraction, she hopped out of bed and grabbed it before diving back under the duvet.

Expecting Sally, her stomach dropped when she saw who it was.

Hey, Goldilocks. How's things? H x

Clutching the phone to her chest, she stared up at the ceiling, trying to picture Henry's face. But in place of vivid blue eyes was a pair of chocolate brown ones, instead of a wide, grinning mouth she could only see a sensual curve. There was no dirty-blonde hair, just thick nearly black hair.

A lump jumped into her throat. This was bad. One night with Matt and already she'd forgotten what Henry looked like?

'Everything okay?'

Matt stepped back into the bedroom, a navy towel around his waist, rivulets of water running down his chest, through the dusting of dark hair on his pecs, over the ripples of his abs and down to the arrow of his groin.

'Lottie?'

With a shake of her head she looked up into his handsome face with its strong profile and sharp cheekbones. 'It's fine. Just … Henry, saying hi.' It felt wrong, saying his name out loud in the bedroom of a man she'd spent the night having sex with.

The muscle in Matt's jaw twitched. 'Does he text often?'

'No.' She made sure to catch Matt's eye. 'What we had is in the past. Now we're just friends who message from time to time.'

It was good she no longer held a vivid image of Henry in her mind, she knew that, yet it was terrifying how quickly Matt seemed to have replaced him.

Matt inclined his head in a brief nod before stepping into black boxers followed by dark jeans and a grey T-shirt in quick, economical movements. She liked how unshowy he was, as if he had no clue how attractive he was.

'If you want to take a shower,' he said, doing up the button on his jeans, 'I'll make us breakfast.'

Her eyes were drawn to his still bare feet. 'Is that cereal and toast or a full English?'

He rubbed at his hair with the towel. 'If I say cereal?'

She forced her gaze away from the sexy feet and onto his equally sexy face. 'I'll pretend to be happy but secretly I'll be worried you're a health freak.'

He winced. 'I'm not sure I like the term "freak".'

She remembered back to the picnic, and how she'd plied him with fatty, processed meat. 'God, you hated my picnic, didn't you?'

'No.' He gave her a wry smile. 'I enjoyed the cheese. And the fruit.'

Lottie started to laugh. 'Oh boy, we really aren't compatible food-wise, are we?'

He stilled. 'What I eat is not that important to me.'

She thought it was pretty important, but the fact he didn't want to make an issue over it said volumes about the kind of guy he was. And perhaps how he felt about her.

'We could compromise. You can do scrambled eggs, yes? That's pretty healthy.'

His expression relaxed. 'I can even add mushrooms. And tomatoes. Do you want me to bring it up to you?'

'I'm sure I can find my way to the kitchen.' A horrid thought occurred. Was he embarrassed she was here? 'Unless you'd rather I kept out of the way.'

'Good God, no.' He gave her an incredulous look. 'I thought you might be uncomfortable. Dad's sure to be up, though Amy is unlikely to surface till lunchtime.'

'I like your dad. He's all grumpy on the outside and marshmallow on the inside.'

Matt gave her a wry smile. 'He is for you.'

'Things aren't getting any easier between you?'

Matt averted his eyes, hand rubbing across his chin in that way he had when he was thinking, very carefully, what to say. 'We're doing okay.'

She let out an exasperated breath. 'Nope, that's not going to do.' She met his startled gaze. 'I know you don't like talking about yourself, but you told me you were trying to be better at it. And honestly, if this is going to happen, if we're going to keep sleeping together, I need you to open up to me now and again.'

He was silent for a moment and she held her breath, wondering if he was going to call it quits. Sex with her wasn't worth the aggro. But then he sighed and went to sit on the end of the bed. 'You're right. Sorry.' Elbows on his thighs, hands clasped, he glanced sideways at her. 'I've spent so much of my life keeping my feelings to myself.'

She remembered his comment about being bullied at boarding school and wondered if he wasn't reserved by choice, but by circumstance. Having spent his childhood mainly in his own company, it was hardly surprising he'd withdrawn into himself. 'I don't expect you to change overnight, to suddenly want to sit me down and tell me your full life history.' She drew her legs up, resting her head on her knees as she looked at him. 'And I don't want this between us to get too heavy,' she added, more as a reminder to herself. 'I don't think either of us are ready for that. I would like to think we're friends though, and friends share their feelings. They talk to each other.'

He nodded, shifting his gaze to stare down at his hands. 'It wasn't just my ex-wife I let down,' he said quietly after a long pause. 'In the pursuit of my career I had no time for my family, either. By the time I realised how ill Mum really was, it was too late.' When he turned to face her, his eyes were filled with so much misery, it hurt to see it. 'I'd broken so many promises to come and visit, wasted all those opportunities to spend time with her. And to help Amy and Dad.' His voice choked on his words and he drew in a shuddery breath. 'I saw her twice in the last six months of her life. *Twice.* And one of those times was the week before she died.'

Lottie's heart filled and she leant across to put her arms

around him, hugging him tight. It was easy to blame him, to say work should never come before family, yet that overlooked the reason for his obsession with it. It wasn't money, or power, but a determination to show the bully boys what he was capable of.

Besides, this complicated, serious yet ultimately kind-hearted man had already beaten himself up enough over it.

Matt felt the back of his eyes prick as Lottie's arms wrapped around him. If he'd been asked, he'd have said he wasn't a hugger. A childhood spent mainly away from home, a wife who wasn't very tactile... Hugging wasn't something he was used to, but by God it felt good.

'I'm sure your mum understood.'

Lottie's voice, full of sympathy, reminded him what they'd been discussing and he carefully extracted himself from her embrace. 'She deserved more from her only son. As did Dad and Amy.' The fact he'd been so blinkered, selfishly focused on his career to the detriment of those he loved, would haunt him for the rest of his life.

'We all do things we regret. It's how we make amends that counts.' She reached for his hand, holding it between hers. 'You moved your dad and sister down here to start a new life together. That's important.'

He wanted to think so but he wasn't yet convinced, though at least Amy seemed happier. Raising his eyes from their entwined hands, he opened his mouth to thank her, but the words died on his tongue when he realised she was still naked, her breasts hanging gloriously free.

'Ah.' She caught the direction of his gaze and pulled the duvet around her.

Shaking his head, he pulled it back down. 'They're too beautiful to keep hidden.'

She narrowed her eyes in a way that made him feel she could see straight through him. 'You're only saying that because you want the distraction.'

He gave her a sheepish smile. 'Maybe it's both.'

'Well, thank you for opening up to me.' He placed his hand on her right breast, and she smiled. 'When you said you and your dad were doing okay, what you actually meant was okay, *considering*.'

He barked out a laugh. 'You mean I could have left it at that?'

'You could. But I'm glad you didn't.'

Their gaze collided. She didn't want heavy and yes, he wasn't ready for that either. But as he sat beside her, one lush breast in his hand, an understanding, an acceptance he'd not felt before written across her beautiful face, his heart opened up in his chest.

Clearing his throat, he bent to kiss her breast before rising to his feet. 'I promised you scrambled eggs.'

'You did.' She smirked. 'And a chat with your dad.'

'Good luck with that.' He walked towards the door but paused before opening it, his mind going back to the last book club meeting. 'Any idea why he's avoiding the shop? It's like he doesn't want to work, which surprises me because he's been a grafter all his life.' He hesitated. 'Unless he doesn't want to work for me.'

'I don't think that's the problem.' Her smile had a touch of secrecy about it. 'But leave it with me. I have ways of making people talk.'

'Don't I know it.' His gaze fell to her breasts. 'But don't show him those. They're only for me to see.'

He wasn't sure where the possessive tone came from. Only that he couldn't bear the thought of anyone else touching where he'd touched. His mind flashed to earlier, and her text from Henry. It was clear her ex was the reason she didn't want another serious relationship. Obviously they still shared something, a bond that time had failed to break.

The realisation settled heavily over him. If he wasn't careful, if he didn't guard his heart, he would find himself in another world of hurt.

'I have no intention of showing my boobs to your dad, or any other man for that matter. Not while I'm seeing you.' She laughed as she climbed out of his bed, all curves and glorious nakedness. 'And the same rules apply to you. No flashing your impressively manly parts to anyone else while you're sharing them with me.'

'Impressively manly, huh?' A flush crept up his neck and he felt like a teenager being complimented by the coolest girl at the party.

'You know, with anyone else, I'd think they were fishing for more compliments, but with you…' She shook her head as she strolled up to him and ran a hand down his chest, causing his *impressively manly* parts to sit up and take notice. 'I really believe you don't know how gorgeous you are, so here goes. You, Matt Steele, are an honest-to-God hunk.' She patted his face. 'Now go and take that smoking-hot body of yours downstairs and make me the breakfast you promised.'

He watched her walk naked to the ensuite, her hips swaying; whether consciously or unconsciously, he didn't know and didn't care. By the time she closed the door behind her, a broad grin had settled across his face. When he reached the kitchen, he realised he was whistling.

'Must have been one hell of a night.'

The sound of his dad's voice behind him made Matt jump. 'Morning. I'm making scrambled eggs. You fancy some?'

'Am I still breathing?' He lifted himself onto the barstool. 'She still here then? The woman who's put that smile on your face.'

It wasn't just Lottie he needed to start talking to more, he realised. 'Lottie is taking a shower. She'll be down in a minute.'

'Lottie, eh?'

He was acutely aware of his dad watching him as he cracked the eggs and placed the tomatoes and mushrooms into the grill pan. 'Yes.'

'You've got good taste.'

Matt smiled to himself. He knew his dad had a soft spot for her. 'I think so.'

'Just make sure you don't cock this one up.'

Okay then. He gritted his teeth and vented his frustration on the eggs, whisking them to within an inch of their life. When he was sure he had his emotions under control, he turned to face his dad. 'I have no intention of cocking anything up.'

'Bet you said that about Pat, but look how that turned out.'

He wanted to argue that he hadn't been the one who had an affair, but what was the point? He was the evil one in his father's eyes. The bad son who neglected his wife, his mother and his sister.

Thankfully Lottie chose that moment to walk in on them. Her hair still damp, the curls more contained than usual, she had the same clothes on as yesterday, only without the makeup. And still she looked gorgeous enough to make his breath catch in his throat.

'Morning, Jim.' Her eyes sought Matt's and from the sympathy he saw in them, he knew she'd heard at least some of the conversation. 'This is a lovely place you've got here. Any chance of a tour while Matt cooks us breakfast?'

His dad immediately shuffled off the stool and Matt shot her a grateful glance as she followed him out of the kitchen.

Baby steps, he reminded himself as he checked on the mushrooms under the grill. The relationship with his dad would take time; he had a lot of trust to rebuild. At least the man seemed happy showing Lottie around the house he'd not wanted to move to, though he suspected that had more to do with the woman he was talking to than any excitement about the house.

Chapter Twenty

Early August, nominated book:
The Truest Thing **by Samantha Young**

T*his will be fine,* Lottie told herself as she pushed open
the door to the bookshop. She was perfectly capable
of talking to Matt without being reduced to such a puddle
of hormones that everyone guessed they'd been seeing each
other.

Having sex with each other.

Okay, there was that. They'd managed two further dates
since that first one ... and it had resulted in two further
nights of phenomenal sex back at his place.

The bell did its usual jingle and immediately Matt
looked up from his position behind the counter. Their eyes
met and everything around her seemed to fade into the
background. God, he was handsome. Especially when he

gave her the small smile he was giving her now, the one that was more with his eyes than his mouth.

The one she was pretty sure he only reserved for her.

'Hi.' Way to go, girl. An excellent start.

'Hi back.' He smiled, eyes crinkled at the corners. 'Good timing, the last customer has just left.' His eyes flickered behind her. 'No Chewie today?'

Was he asking to protect his shoes/floor, or was he asking because…? His eyes flared, amusement and heat, and now she knew. 'No Chewie,' she confirmed.

He stepped out from behind the counter and walked towards her, gaze zeroing in on her mouth, which tingled with anticipation. But just as he got close enough to do something about the simmering heat that pinged between them, he halted. 'Do the others know about us?'

'I don't think so. I mean, your dad does, and Amy, but I wasn't planning on making some big announcement.'

He clasped her hand and led her round the corner. 'Then let me do this here.' His mouth swooped on hers, greedily, hungrily. As his hands slipped straight under her T-shirt he pushed her against the bookshelves, pressing his erection against her stomach. It sent her arousal state from medium to off the scale in record time. Utterly turned on, she kissed him back. 'More.'

He lifted her right leg around his hips, seating himself more firmly between her thighs, bending so his hardness found her core. His hips began to thrust, his tongue keeping rhythm, his fingers squeezing her nipples. 'Oh God.' She was going to detonate, right here in his shop, without removing any clothes and with minimal foreplay. 'Yes, there, just there.'

She was dimly aware of the bell ringing, of Audrey's voice. Of chatter. The babble of Freddie, Sally laughing.

But then his thrusting hips found exactly the right spot and suddenly she was climaxing, pleasure rushing through her as she gasped and clung to his shoulders.

'Shit,' she panted, her legs like jelly. 'That was some kiss. Thank God you brought me back here.'

He laughed softly, resting his forehead against hers. 'Wish I'd locked the damn door.' He drew back, eyes hot as they skimmed over what she was sure was her flushed face. 'I will when they leave.'

She swallowed, her face growing redder. 'Why Mr Steele, are you planning on seducing me in your bookshop?'

'Definitely.'

He took a step back and she patted her hair. 'How do I look?'

His smile held a hint of smug. 'Like you've been ravished against a bookshelf.'

'Great. Audrey will be wanting full details.' She drew in a breath, narrowed her eyes at him. 'This is your fault. You should come and face the music with me.'

He grinned, looking down at the clear bulge in his trousers. 'I don't want to give Audrey a heart attack.'

It was only when she'd walked round the corner that Lottie realised she'd just seen a new side to him, *playful* Matt. She liked it. Liked him. A lot. Careful, a voice niggled but she pushed it away. Where was the harm? She was enjoying herself and he looked… Yes, she was going to blow her own trumpet. He looked *happy*.

'Well, well, here she is.'

As she stepped into the café they all turned to face her and Lottie felt like a zoo exhibit. 'I was just with Matt, checking the fusebox I put in.' She felt the lie creep across her face and wondered why she'd bothered. She'd never been any good at it.

'Is that what you call it?' Audrey's canny gaze settled on Lottie. 'In my day, we called it snogging.'

She supposed it served her right for acting like some horny teenager, yet as she faced the hyper-inquisitive group, Lottie couldn't be sorry. Making out with Matt was worth a few seconds of embarrassment. 'There may have been some snogging going on.'

The second she admitted it, Sally shrieked, alarming Freddie, who began to cry, drowning out the barrage of questions Heidi and Audrey were firing at her.

She put up her hands. 'Flipping heck, quiet, please! This is a respectable book club.'

As everyone laughed, Gira's face turned from smiling to horror.

Lottie froze. 'What is it?'

'We have a visitor,' she whispered, eyes focused behind Lottie's shoulder.

Lottie turned to see and her jaw dropped. 'Eve?' Bloody hell, could this get any more surreal? 'What brings you here?'

Eve hesitated, her sharp features wary as she took in the

scene in the café. Sally, trying to hush Freddie, Gira looking as if she'd seen a ghost, Amy and Heidi still chuckling. Audrey pulling a gin bottle out of her handbag. 'I'm here for the respectable book club.'

'You … what?'

Eve straightened the pearls around her neck. 'I heard you were running a book club from here and,' she paused, straightening her shoulders, 'I came to see if it was true.'

'It is. This is the Beach Reads Book Club. We focus on feel-good stories.'

Eve's gaze skimmed over them. 'Yet you don't seem to be discussing a book.'

Audrey hooted with laughter. 'Why would we when we've got our own live romantic saga going on in front of our eyes?' She waved the gin bottle at Eve. 'If you're coming in, park your bum and grab a glass. We're about to grill Lottie on her sex life.'

Okay, so she'd gone from not announcing her *thing* with Matt, to… She'd give it maybe a day before Eve had everyone in town knowing about it.

'Thank you, but no.' Eve gave Audrey a cool smile.

'Your loss.' Heidi held her glass out to Audrey, but her eyes remained on Eve's. 'You'd enjoy it if you did. Lottie runs a really fun club.'

'We've had some amazingly good reads so far this year,' Gira added. 'We're reading one of Samantha Young's at the moment. Have you read her?'

Eve looked taken aback. 'No.'

'You should. She writes deeply emotional love stories.'

'With plenty of cracking sex scenes,' Audrey added helpfully. 'Might get the stick out of your arse if you did read her. Or Jilly Cooper. Or how about a bit of *Fifty Shades*? That'll really loosen you up.'

Eve's eyes widened and her lips thinned. 'I bid you good evening.'

'Well.' As the door banged closed behind Eve, Lottie staggered to the nearest chair and launched herself into it. 'I need one of Audrey's gins.'

'Coming up.' Audrey paused mid-pour. 'And don't think that uppity woman's untimely interruption has got you out of the interrogation, missy. We want every detail, in full technicolour. Including the sex.'

Lottie let out a strangled laugh. 'You're incorrigible. Who says we've even had sex?'

She winked. 'You're a smart woman, Lottie Watt. No way you'd not have sex with that man-hunk if the opportunity arose.'

'Okay, okay, I'll share a few details. Of our *dates*,' she added as Audrey's eyes lit up. 'But only if everyone else updates on what they've been doing over the last few weeks.' Her gaze fell on Audrey. 'And if Audrey promises to do something for me.'

'If it's got anything to do with the man-hunk, count me in,' she chortled, knocking back another mouthful of gin.

'Actually,' Lottie smiled, 'it has.'

Matt had been in his office for an hour. Long enough for his hard-on to subside, but not long enough to get the taste of Lottie out of his mouth, the smell of her out of his nostrils.

He was starting to become obsessed. Sex-obsessed and, well, just straight obsessed with her.

If he listened hard enough he could hear her laughter. Whatever they were discussing, he didn't think it was a book. Then again, the sort of books they read, maybe it was. Whisper it, but he'd started to read *The Kiss Quotient* and was actually enjoying it. A few smiles, moments when he'd felt a tug of emotion. He didn't find it as engrossing as his usual reads, but after a period of heavy, it was a refreshing change to have some light.

Maybe he was more like Lottie than he thought.

Smiling, he rose to his feet. He'd done retreating into his office. Last month, on the beach, he'd felt left out. Tonight he was going to join them.

His bravado slipped when he saw that whatever they were discussing now, the humour had gone.

It slipped even further when they stopped to stare at him. Hell, what was he doing? He might have managed to convince Lottie he wasn't always an uptight arse incapable of decent conversation, but it didn't mean he'd totally left that side of him behind. 'Sorry, I—'

'Come for your cake?' Lottie flashed him a warm smile, which loosened some of his tension. 'Or we also have pizza tonight.'

Okay, too late to bail. 'Cake would be great.'

Audrey waved towards the window. 'Why don't you fetch one of those chairs and join us?'

His eyes met those of his sister and she shrugged. It wasn't exactly *Yay, my big brother's here*, but it wasn't a no, either. 'Thanks, if you're sure?'

Sally picked up Freddie's hand and waved it at him. 'Freddie says he could do with some male company.'

He smiled and pulled up a chair. 'Whatever you were discussing, don't change on my account.'

Lottie glanced at Gira, who nodded. 'Actually, we've been plotting. I'll talk to you about it after we've finished here, as we'd like your help.'

Sally started to laugh. 'Watch it, Matt, the moment we're gone she'll have you pinned against the bookcase again. Or was it you pinning her?' She gave him a wicked smile. 'We weren't quite sure from the noises which way round it was.'

'Definitely the latter.' It was only when he heard a loud bark of laughter from Audrey, and saw embarrassment flood Amy's face, that he realised he'd just verbalised that out loud. He caught Lottie's eye, giving her a dry smile, and she bit into her lip, clearly trying not to laugh.

This wasn't him, he thought, discussing his love life with a group of virtual strangers. With his sister. And yet he couldn't stop smiling.

He stayed for the rest of their meeting, not really interested in the book he hadn't read, but happy to watch their interactions. Gira was quietly spoken and to the point, Amy surprisingly vocal about what she enjoyed. Heidi smiled a lot, agreeing with everyone. Sally was loud, saying what she thought without filter, and Audrey had a wit that left him chuckling more than once to himself. Throughout there was Lottie, encouraging, making sure they all had their say, passionate when it came to giving her own views. Damn funny when she verbally sparred with Sally and Audrey.

The more he watched her, the more she fascinated him. She was bright, bubbly, extrovert yet also a nurturer. Much like she'd taken Chewie in, she'd taken this group under her wing.

Finally it came to an end and he began to move the chairs back into position as the group straggled out.

'Don't you young things do anything I wouldn't do,' Audrey shouted over her shoulder as she left.

Lottie, who was clearing the table, looked at him and grinned. 'I guess that leaves a lot of scope for whatever you had planned.'

'I—' He was about to say something crude along the lines of finishing what they'd started by the bookshelf, then moving to his office for round two, when he realised Amy was watching them from the counter. 'I think we can manage from here, Amy.'

She huffed. 'I'm not a baby, you know. I can talk about sex, I even have sex. But fine, I'll leave you to clear up the rest. I'll probably see Shaun tonight. Don't wait up.'

With that she picked up her bag and flounced out.

He heaved out a sigh but before he could say anything, Lottie kissed him lightly on the mouth. 'This is on me, not you. I didn't realise she was there. She's not upset, she's embarrassed, probably even more so than you. It's kind of yukky thinking about your sibling having sex.'

He shook his head. 'Yeah. I definitely don't want to think about what she might be getting up to with Shaun.'

'She's twenty-four. Old enough to do what she likes without you making her feel bad. It's your job to be there when she wants to talk, or if things don't work out.'

'Okay. I can do that.' He gazed down at Lottie. 'You're really good at this. Putting yourself in others' shoes. Looking out for them. Makes me wonder why you didn't go into a people-focused profession – doctor, nurse, psychologist.'

Her eyes darted away from his. 'Electricians work with people.'

'They do,' he agreed. But they didn't need to understand what made their customers tick, he wanted to add. It was something this otherwise remarkably open woman didn't want to talk about though, so he changed the subject. 'You mentioned you needed my help for something?'

Immediately her body lost its tension. 'Ah, yes.' She gave him a playful push onto a chair and straddled his lap, eyes now bright and clear. 'How do you feel about taking Gira out on a date?'

As he struggled to get his brain around the concept, she leant forward and pressed her lips to his. Bold, confident, she kissed him until he couldn't think about anything but the way her breasts felt against his chest, the rhythm of her hips as they writhed in his lap.

'We need to take this round the back,' he rasped when

she let them up for air. 'Before our window display takes on a whole new meaning.'

She giggled, easing back, and he groaned as her heat left him.

'What about Gira?'

He shook his head, dazzled by her. 'I don't know what you're cooking up, but you can guarantee I'll agree to anything you want right now.'

Laughing, she jumped to her feet. 'Excellent.'

Suddenly he found himself grabbing her hand and running, yes *running*, through his shop. He barely had the foresight to make sure the door was locked and they were out of sight before he was tugging off her T-shirt and making short work of removing her bra.

'I can't get enough of you,' he murmured as he dipped his head to her breasts, kissing, sucking, overwhelmed with a need to bury himself inside her.

'Good,' she whispered, arching her back to help his access. 'Because I haven't nearly finished with you yet.'

As he pulled down her jeans, yanked at his own, as he slipped on a condom and thrust greedily, hungrily, joyfully inside her, he wondered if he could ever see a time when *he* would be finished with *her*. She was changing him. Since meeting her he felt less uptight, happier. More the man he wanted to be. The man he felt she was looking for.

He could only hope he'd changed enough.

Chapter Twenty-One

Lottie ended the call from the garage and slipped her phone back in her pocket. She wanted to cry, which was utterly pathetic. It was just a van, and it was only money. She'd manage. If she cut back on anything that wasn't essential and chased those customers who hadn't paid her yet, it would all work out.

A wet tongue licked her hand and she glanced at Chewie, who was sat next to her on the sofa, 'It's okay, buddy. I won't skimp on your food.' Okay, wobble time was over. She needed to pull herself together. 'Come on, we're due at Gira's in half an hour.'

She'd promised Gira she'd help her choose something to wear for tonight's 'date' with Matt, though really Lottie knew Gira just wanted some moral support. It had the potential to be a big night for her... Maybe she'd find out if there was anything left of her marriage.

Chewie leapt off the sofa the moment she reached for his

lead, and started wagging his tail. 'Yeah, yeah. I know someone who'd rather walk than take the van.' But she couldn't walk to all her customers, and she needed the van to carry her tools. The garage had told her the head gasket could blow any time and she really needed to get it fixed now before it did any further damage. Not in a month or so when she'd maybe scraped enough money together, but now.

Worrying as it was though, at least she didn't have a husband who might be cheating on her, she reminded herself as she shut the front door behind her. In fact, she had a man in her life who was proving, well… Images of what had happened in the bookshop last week flashed through her mind and she stumbled, nearly tripping over the doorstep. He was proving more passionate, and far more distracting, than she'd anticipated.

Distracting as in she couldn't stop thinking about him.

Distracting as in her pulse kicked up a gear and her belly fluttered with a thousand butterflies as she anticipated seeing him tonight.

Gira looked tense as she opened the door. 'This is madness. Remind me again why I'm doing it?'

'Because you want to see what Ryan does instead of coming home? And because now, thanks to his secretary, we know the bar near his office seems a good place to start?'

'Yes, yes.' Gira wrung her hands as she stepped back to let Lottie in. 'But I should go there by myself. I don't need to put you and Matt out.'

'First, you're not putting us out. We're happy to do

this. Second, if Ryan is there, what would make him realise he's being stupid more: seeing you by yourself, come to snoop on him/to nag him, take your pick; or seeing you saunter in there on the arms of a handsome guy?'

Gira gave her a wobbly smile. 'My fake date is certainly that. I knew there was a reason I agreed to option 2.'

Seeing her look so sad, so worried, Lottie wrapped her up in a hug. 'You don't have to do anything, you know,' she said as she eased away. 'You could stay at home and curl up with a good book.'

'I know, but I've gone to the effort of taking the kids to my parents and besides, if I chicken out I'll still be in limbo-land. At least when I know what he's up to, I can start to move on.' She straightened her shoulders. 'Enough wallowing. Come and tell me what I should wear to remind him what he's throwing away.'

As Lottie followed Gira up the stairs her phone buzzed. When she took it out to check the messages, she laughed. Gira gave her a questioning look over her shoulder. 'I don't know whether this is good news or not, but Heidi's just messaged. She wants to join us and apparently Audrey has insisted on coming too, so can we pick them up on the way?'

Gira smiled. 'That's sweet of them.'

'You might not be saying that when Audrey's chatted up half the bar staff, danced on the tables and given your Ryan a piece of her mind.'

Gira shrugged, but the misery in her eyes, the tightness

of her expression, were anything but casual. 'It might take my mind off the end of my marriage.'

When the doorbell sounded an hour later, they'd whittled the choice down to a sexy red dress that was maybe too much for a casual drink but looked fabulous against Gira's dark skin, or a pair of wide, flowing, black trousers and a slinky top. Chewie, who'd been waiting patiently downstairs, started to bark.

'Okay, okay.' Lottie glanced at her watch. 'That'll be Matt, bang on time as usual. I'll get it while you make a decision. For what it's worth, I think you're a knock-out in either, but the red dress has real wow factor.'

'Maybe I should let Matt decide? He is my date, after all.'

He didn't seem to be the sort of guy who'd have much to say about female fashion. Then again, she hadn't thought he was the type to have sex against the shelves in his bookshop, either. Lottie smiled. 'Maybe you should.'

The butterflies started up as she raced downstairs and flung the door open. Belatedly she thought she should have shown some decorum, perhaps not made it quite so obvious she was excited to see him. But as he saw it was her, the smile he gave her was so wide, so warm, she didn't care.

'I'm not sure of the etiquette of greeting the woman I'm dating, when she's opened the door for the woman I've come to take out for a drink.'

Lottie's eyes rested on the two bunches of roses he was carrying, one yellow, one red, and her heart melted. 'I'd say if you've bought us both flowers, you can make up your own rules.'

'Good.' He cupped her face with his free hand and bent to kiss her.

Immediately Chewie began to growl, but this time Matt didn't pull away. He kept right on kissing her until she felt the heat from it invade every cell in her body. When he pulled back he stared down at Chewie. 'You're going to have to get used to this, because I plan on kissing your mistress as many times as she'll let me.'

Chewie cocked his head, eyes not leaving Matt's. Then he sat down, which Lottie supposed was some sort of truce.

As Matt bent to pat Chewie, she took a moment to appreciate the man who was doing them a big favour. He was dressed in a brown/grey linen jacket, striped collared shirt and smart cream chinos, the combination highlighting the deep brown of his eyes, the light tan of his face. With his dark good looks and the expensive tailoring, he was like an advert for Armani. Add to that the heady smell of his aftershave and she felt a sudden pang for what she was about to miss out on.

'Gira's upstairs, getting ready.' She nudged him. 'You look awesome, by the way. Wish I was spending the evening with you.'

He smiled and dropped a soft kiss on her lips. 'I'd rather hoped you'll spend the night with me.'

The smooth tone, the hint of low husk, sent her pulse racing. 'That's an offer I hate to turn down.' She nodded to the mountain of fur now lying on the floor, looking up at them. 'But I have Chewie tonight.'

'That's okay. I think the big guy and I have come to an understanding.'

It wasn't what she meant but she was saved explaining because at that moment Gira appeared at the top of the stairs, looking fabulous in the red dress as she walked hesitantly down towards them.

In a gentlemanly gesture that made Lottie's heart squeeze, Matt bent to kiss her on the cheek as she reached the bottom step. 'Hello, Gira.' He stood back, eyes skimming over her. 'You look lovely.'

'It's this or black trousers.' She ran her hand down the dress. 'I'm not sure if it's too much.'

'It's perfect,' Matt answered, giving Gira a reassuring smile. 'How are you feeling?'

'Terrified.'

He winced. 'Oh dear. I'll try not to make it too awful.'

She groaned and put a hand over her mouth. 'I didn't mean it like that. You're being so kind. I'm just... I'm scared of what I might find when we get there. If he's with another woman, that's one thing. Even if he's not...' – she twisted her hands – 'he's with people whose company he prefers to mine.'

As Lottie put her arms around Gira and gave her a hug, Matt shook his head, his expression pained.

'I don't think you can come to that conclusion yet. Work can suck you in.' He gave Gira a sad smile. 'Ask my ex-wife.'

In that moment Lottie realised she'd been so focused on helping Gira, she'd forgotten Matt had once been in Ryan's shoes, the bad guy staying out late every night. Now she was making him relive it all, only from the woman's side.

No doubt he'd spend the evening beating himself up all over again.

Crap.

Stupidly, Matt realised he hadn't prepared himself for this. Taking a woman out for a drink, he could handle, but going back through his failure again? Talking about that shameful, miserable part of his life out loud with people he wanted to make a fresh impression with? Unconsciously he glanced over at Lottie and she mouthed *I'm sorry*.

'You used to work late every night?' Gira looked surprised.

His stomach knotted and he pushed a hand in his trouser pocket. 'I did.'

'Do you mind me asking, how did your wife deal with it?'

Swallowing hard, he met Gira's eyes. 'She had an affair.'

'Oh no.' Gira's brown eyes filled with sympathy. 'I'm sorry. That's, well, that's not nice.'

His gut twisted as he remembered the day he'd found boxers he didn't own, under his bed. 'Maybe I deserved it.'

'No.' Gira lifted her chin. 'I don't know your circumstances, but I do know that no matter how angry I feel at Ryan, I couldn't contemplate seeing someone else just to spite him. I love him too much.'

Maybe that was his answer. He hadn't loved Patricia enough to haul himself out of his work spiral, and she hadn't loved him enough to want to fight for him, like Gira was doing now.

Drawing in a breath, he pushed the past aside and held out his arm. 'Then let's show your husband what he risks losing if he doesn't change his ways.'

With a determined look on her face, Gira slipped her arm through his. 'Yes, thank you. I'm ready.'

It was only when he opened the passenger car door for her that he considered what he was actually doing. Taking another man's wife out. 'How tall is he, by the way?' he asked casually.

Obviously it wasn't as casual as he'd hoped because as Lottie climbed into the back seat, having settled Chewie in the boot, she started to laugh. 'Are you worried he'll beat you up?'

'I can handle myself.' He sent up a silent prayer that Gira's husband wasn't six foot eight and build like a tank.

He felt like a taxi driver as he picked up first Heidi, then Audrey. Make that a school bus driver, because the non-stop chatter, the flow of laughter, interspersed by occasional giggles, was more like a school trip. He guessed they were trying to distract Gira, which seemed to be working from what he could see in his occasional glances in her direction.

'You'll all be sitting outside?' he confirmed with Lottie as he parked the SUV in the wine-bar car park.

'Yep. They won't let Chewie in but we'll be at one of the tables on the terrace, sending good luck vibes.' Ready to console Gira, if needed. She didn't add the words, but Matt knew that was why they'd come, and felt a burst of admiration for the little book club Lottie had set up all those months ago. These women hadn't stopped at sharing their joy of books, they'd begun to share their lives. They looked out for each other.

'Let us know if there's any aggro with that husband of hers.' Audrey waved her hefty bag in the air as they all climbed out. 'It won't be the first time I'll have clocked someone with my handbag.'

He caught Gira's eye and she smiled. Then she took a deep breath and reached for his arm.

Just as he was about to step forward, Lottie touched his other arm, stopping him. Then she whispered in his ear, 'You're a good man, Matthew Steele.'

The words seeped through him as he led Gira inside. Two years ago, a year ago, he'd have said he definitely wasn't a good man. Blinded by a desire to succeed financially, to stick two fingers up at bullies who'd belittled him, he'd made terrible, selfish mistakes. Maybe that was all behind him now, though. Maybe this fresh start, the new him, the *real* him, was at last taking shape.

'He's not with a woman.'

Gira's quiet words refocused him and he followed her gaze over to a table of five guys, all in suits, though their jackets were off, their top buttons undone. Ties loosened.

'That looks like drinks after work,' he replied, pulling

out a bar stool for her. 'Let's sit here, in their eye-line.' He gave Gira an encouraging smile. 'I guarantee he'll notice you in a few minutes.'

He ordered her a glass of white wine, and himself a sparkling water, as he was driving. Around them the bar hummed with chatter. Next to him, Gira sipped quietly at her drink, her posture stiff. In an attempt to relax her, he tried making small talk.

After ten painful minutes, he put down his water and bent to whisper in her ear. 'We should look like we're enjoying ourselves.'

'Sorry. I'm not much of an actress, am I?' She screwed up her face in apology. 'And now I've insulted you.'

'I'm not insulted.' Christ, he was no good at this. Gira needed a confident, outgoing guy to take her out of her head. Instead she'd got lumbered with someone as reserved and awkward as she clearly felt. 'How about I tell you a bar joke? Try and make you laugh?'

'Do you know one?'

He gave her a mock insulted look. 'I know several.' They were jokes he'd stored for moments when he'd felt out of his depth socially, times he'd needed to convince clients and work colleagues he was funny and easy-going, when he knew he wasn't either. 'A lizard walks into a bar pushing a baby in a stroller. *What's your kid's name?* asks the bartender. *Tiny,* answers the lizard, *because he's my newt.*'

'Oh dear, that's awful.'

Buoyed by the fact she was smiling, he tried another. 'Okay. How about this one. An amnesiac walks into a bar, goes up to a beautiful blonde and says, *So, do I come here often?*'

She let out a strangled-sounding laugh. 'I think that's worse.'

Matt caught movement out of the corner of his eye and glanced up to see a guy walking towards them, eyes focused on Gira. 'Luckily for you, I think your husband's spotted you and is coming over.'

Gira swung round, her expression hardening as the man came to a stop next to them.

'What are you doing here?' he demanded, hands in pockets. Then his gaze swung to Matt. 'And who the hell is he?'

Matt slipped off the stool so he was at his full height. Thankfully a few inches more than Ryan. 'I'm Matt.' He held out his hand. 'Pleased to meet you.'

Ryan clearly didn't want to shake it, but politeness won over.

'Matt's a friend,' Gira said. 'He offered to take me for a drink, as you always seem to have better things to do.'

Ryan's jaw tensed. 'I told you, I'm out with work.' He nodded over to where the other guys were sitting.

Matt shifted on his feet, feeling uncomfortable. He didn't want to be the cause of a row, he wanted Ryan to see how lonely Gira was. To understand how precarious his marriage was if he didn't change his ways. Automatically he looked out of the window, his eyes seeking Lottie. She would know how to handle this.

'You're always out with work and I'm fed up with

sitting on my own at home.' Gira surprised Matt by standing and threading her hand through his arm. 'If you want to talk, we'll be sitting outside.'

Taking her lead, Matt walked with Gira out to the terrace. The others all looked up.

'Well?' Audrey glanced from one to the other. 'Do you need my handbag?'

Gira smiled, but it was a small, tight effort. 'I'm not sure.'

Lottie looked over her shoulder. 'You need to make a quick decision because he's followed you out.'

They all turned to see Ryan standing by the door. The anger had drained from his face and he looked lost. More than that, Matt realised with shock. He looked distraught.

'What should I do?' Gira stared at her husband, her expression betraying her mixed emotions: fear, anger, upset. Hope.

'It looks like he wants to talk.' Lottie gave Gira's arm a squeeze. 'That's good, isn't it?'

To his surprise, Gira looked at Matt. 'What do you think?'

His instinct was to shrug his shoulders, to say he didn't know, but he realised she was asking because he'd been in Ryan's situation. 'You should hear him out. Sometimes work is like a hamster wheel, it's hard to get off. My bet is, he's only now realising what he could lose.'

As he watched Gira walk towards her husband, Matt wondered where he would be now if Patricia had done what Gira had and confronted him, instead of giving up on him and going behind his back.

Then he looked at Lottie, her eyes welling with emotion as she watched Ryan fall to his knees in front of Gira, and realised he didn't want his old life back. He wanted the one he was starting to carve out here, by the sea, with his sister, his dad. And the Electric Blonde who was rapidly stealing his heart.

Chapter Twenty-Two

Lottie wiped her eyes as she watched Gira and Ryan hug. They would have some hard conversations ahead, but it was clear Ryan still loved his wife dearly.

'I do love a happy ending.' Heidi pulled a tissue out of her handbag and blew her nose.

Audrey chuckled. 'I suspect our Gira will be ending her sex drought tonight.'

'Audrey!' Heidi looked reprovingly at the older woman.

'I think what Audrey meant is, it will be lovely to see a real smile back on Gira's face next time we see her.' Lottie's gaze shifted to Matt, who was still watching Gira and Ryan. Was he wondering about his own marriage? Wishing he'd done something about his own late-night working so he and his wife could still be together?

The thought caused a sharp wrench inside her chest. Did it make her a bad person that she was glad he hadn't?

At that moment his gaze shifted, those dark-chocolate

eyes finding hers, and his mouth curved in a slow smile that sent tingles down her spine. Maybe he wasn't thinking about his ex-wife at all.

'Who's for another drink?' Audrey waved her empty glass. 'It's not every night this old dear gets to go to a bar. I need to make the most of it.'

Ah. Lottie watched as disappointment flashed across Matt's face. He'd been on a promise of sex, now he was faced with a night of making conversation with an increasingly intoxicated octogenarian. 'Matt probably needs to get home. Unlike us, he's got work tomorrow.'

Just as Audrey's face started to fall, Matt squared his shoulders and picked up her glass. 'We've plenty of time. Another gin and tonic?'

Audrey beamed. 'Make sure to ask for the tonic in a separate bottle. Don't want them drowning the gin.'

To his credit, Matt's smile looked genuine. 'Understood. Heidi, same for you?'

'Well, it is Friday night.'

He turned to Lottie, but she waved him away. 'I'll come with you.'

The moment they were out of earshot, she groaned. 'God, I'm so sorry.'

'What on earth for?'

'Lumbering you with a Friday night out with half my book club. The older half, at that.'

His eyes skimmed her face until they landed on hers. 'But I'm also spending it with you.'

Her heart gave a long, slow flip. 'Wow, you can be quite

the charmer when you want to be. What with bringing Gira flowers, settling her nerves, making a fuss of her. Then buying Audrey gin even though you know it's going to loosen her tongue even more.'

He smiled. 'I like her. She's … entertaining.'

Lottie studied him, wondering if now was a good moment to discuss what she'd tentatively broached with Audrey the other day. She wasn't sure her Big Idea would come to fruition, but she did know Audrey needed to do something besides watch *Loose Women*. 'She's in her element tonight. She's so bored at home.' Figuring it wouldn't harm to sow the seed, she added, 'I'm thinking of a way to get her out more, meeting people. It's what she thrives on.'

His eyes found hers and she saw something shift in them. Then he shocked her by bending to place a kiss on her temple, the gesture so tender, her knees buckled. 'What was that for?'

'You're always thinking of other people, working out how you can help them.' Admiration shone from his eyes. 'It's a lesson I'm trying to learn.'

She wanted to argue that his concern for his family, the way he'd helped Gira tonight, were proof he'd already learnt, but the bartender was hovering in front of them. Leaving Matt to put in their orders, she glanced over to where Gira and Ryan were sitting, still talking. The way he held her hand, the way Gira leant towards him, Lottie knew the couple would be able to work through their differences.

When they got back to the table Audrey immediately thrust out her hand. 'Thank you, young man.' After taking a swig she studied him over the top of her glass. 'So, has Lottie talked to you about me working in your shop yet?'

As Heidi inhaled sharply, Matt blinked and for a split second he looked like a trapped deer, all big, brown, terrified eyes. 'Sorry?'

Damn it. She'd not been wrong about the gin loosening Audrey's tongue. 'Err, actually I was going to mention it to him next week.' She shot Matt a quick, apologetic look, but his gaze was on Audrey.

'Oh.' The old woman looked upset, her light dimmed in a way that tugged at Lottie's heart. 'Probably a foolish idea anyway.'

'What was foolish?' Matt asked, his hands toying with his glass of water – clearly his self-discipline didn't allow for an additive-loaded Pepsi.

'Old woman like me, working again.' She gave her head an abrupt shake. 'Heavens, I have enough trouble keeping up with those daft women on the TV.'

'I'm sure I can put you to good use.'

Matt's quietly spoken words caused Lottie to glance over at him. When he caught her eye his mouth curved just enough for her to know he'd surprised himself.

Immediately the light came back into Audrey's eyes. 'Well then, young man, you won't be sorry. I promise you there's plenty of life in this old dog yet.' She patted her hair. 'My Harold used to say I was a born saleswoman.'

'Is that what you used to do?' Lottie asked, both intrigued and thankful. Maybe this didn't have LOTTIE'S BAD IDEA written all over it, after all.

'Harold was a butcher. He had his own shop.' Audrey's chest puffed out with pride. 'I helped him out, when the kids were at school.'

'Then you already have experience.' Matt's relief was clear. 'You'll be teaching me.'

'I'm not sure, love. I spent most of my time round the back, making sausages.'

Heidi immediately started to giggle and the combination of her mirth and Matt's horrified expression was too much for Lottie. She started to giggle too. Audrey soon followed, her cackle loud enough to draw the attention of the tables either side of them.

'Making sausages.' Heidi took in a breath, clearly struggling to contain her glee. 'Maybe we can do a double act. Cake and sausages.' She wiped her eyes. 'Oh, Audrey, you're priceless.'

'I'm still partial to a sausage.' Audrey took a slurp of her gin. 'None of those tiny little chipolatas, mind. They're no good to anyone. I like a big, fat sausage. One I can get my chops round.'

The twinkle in Audrey's eyes was Lottie's final undoing. She threw her head back and howled with laughter, which of course set Heidi and Audrey off again. Matt seemed utterly bemused. When his gaze slid to Lottie's though, his face was relaxed, his eyes warm, and she knew that while he didn't totally get their childish sense of humour, he enjoyed watching them.

'I can't offer sausages,' he told Audrey when they finally quietened. 'I can offer books. Perhaps books on sausages.'

She waggled her eyebrows. 'It's your sausage I wouldn't mind handling.'

It set them all giggling again. Clearly it didn't help that they'd all been drinking and Matt was sober.

'Thank you,' Matt replied, his eyes darting briefly to Lottie's before focusing back on Audrey. 'But I'm afraid my sausage is taken.'

They all erupted again, only this time, when she reached to squeeze his hand, Matt brought hers to his lips, kissed her knuckles. And started to laugh along with them.

Matt breathed a sigh of relief as he jumped back into his SUV, having made sure Audrey was safely in her house.

It wasn't that he'd had a bad evening. In fact he would go as far as to say it had been fun, even knowing he'd gained an octogenarian assistant partial to gin, sausages and ribald humour. But having spent so much of the evening sitting next to Lottie, his thigh brushing hers, his eyes transfixed by her animated face, he was desperate to get her alone.

He glanced behind at Chewie, who was watching him warily from the back seat. Okay, alone*ish*.

'One more stop,' he said as he re-started the engine. Immediately her head turned to stare out of the passenger window and a niggle of worry wormed through him. Had she changed her mind about spending the night with him? He tried to recall their conversation ... something about her having Chewie. Maybe she'd never actually agreed to him staying over?

'It was kind of you to take on Audrey,' she said into the silence. 'She was made up.'

His anxiety increased when she didn't meet his eyes. 'It was a business decision. She might help attract more young-at-hearts into the shop.'

Lottie slipped him a smile, but it seemed strained. 'We both know that's not why you agreed to hire her.'

She was quiet for the rest of the short journey.

'No van?' he asked as he pulled up into the place in front of her house where she usually parked it.

'No. It's poorly. It's in the garage.'

'Damn. Can they fix it by Monday morning for you?'

She twisted her hands in her lap, another indication that something was up. 'Mum said I can borrow her car, so I'll be okay.'

He wasn't sure if it was the van, or him, but one of them was upsetting her. 'What's wrong with it?'

Lottie sighed. 'It needs a new head gasket.'

'Ouch.' He whistled. 'That's expensive.'

'Exactly.' She gave a quick shrug of her shoulders. 'So I need to scrape together some funds before I get the garage to repair it.'

He watched her carefully. 'Is your mum's car big enough to carry your tools? And, of course, your helpful canine assistant?'

Lottie huffed out a laugh. 'It's a Mini.' She turned to face him. 'Just in case you were going to offer the loan of this ridiculously snazzy car, the answer is no. I'd be terrified to drive it and besides, the customers would think I'm ripping them off if I turn up in a Jag.'

He could see her point, just as he could see borrowing her mum's car wasn't a great solution either. But if he offered to lend her the money to fix the van, she'd not only turn him down flat, she'd be embarrassed. 'What if I told you I had a van I could lend you?'

Her eyes rounded in surprise. 'I'd say either you were playing a trick on me, which I'd have to immediately discount because you're not that mean, or you're suffering some weird memory lapse, because no way does Matthew Steele own a van.'

'That's where you're wrong.' Or she would be, by Monday morning. 'I bought one to help with the move here,' he bluffed. 'And to set up the shop. I kept it on to help me with large deliveries.' Ironically, if he had done, it would have been bloody useful – more so than the F-Pace. Still, in his book, luxury would always win over practicality, though he suspected the opposite was true for Lottie.

'Are you being serious?' She looked like she was scared to believe him.

Years of working in the city had taught him to bullshit with confidence. 'Absolutely. It's yours for as long as you want it.'

'But won't you need it? You know, for the deliveries.'

Ah yes, the phantom huge deliveries. 'I'm sure I can manage with this *ridiculously snazzy* car for the time being.'

'Wow, well, that's great.' A smile split her face, and she looked more like the Lottie he knew. 'Thank you.'

For a few beats silence echoed round the car and it was then Matt realised she wasn't going to invite him in. He tried to rein in his disappointment. Maybe she was just tired. *Maybe she's just not that interested in you.*

'Look, I—'

'Perhaps I should—'

She bit into her lip. 'You were going to suggest you went home.'

'I thought that was what you wanted,' he answered carefully.

'It's not.' She looked back up at him. 'God, look at you, all debonair and gorgeous, and that's even without factoring in what you've just done for Gira and Audrey. Of course I don't want our night to end yet, it's just...' She sighed and nodded over to her house. 'My place is an embarrassment, Matt. I've managed to sort the living room so I can just about invite people in for a drink without cringing, but as for the rest of the house, including my bedroom...' She groaned and briefly buried her head in her hands. 'It looks like something out of a 1930s time warp. The wallpaper is peeling, the carpets are brown and probably growing fungus in places. The bathroom has cracked tiles, the shower should be renamed dribble because that's all it does, and then there's the mould, which I've tried to remove but remains stubbornly of the won't-budge-despite-what-you-squirt-on-it variety. The place isn't fit for overnight visitors, especially the type who drive ridiculously snazzy cars.'

He stared at her, bemused. 'You think I care about any of that?' He cupped her face in his hands. 'Do you honestly believe I'll see anything but you?'

Her eyes blinked, and when they looked back at him they glistened. 'Crap, now you're making me cry.'

He trailed his thumb under her lashes, capturing the tears. 'You can come back to mine, you and Chewie, if that's what you'd prefer. Or I'm happy, make that very happy, to take my life in my hands and stay with the mushrooms and unkillable mould.'

Her smile wobbled. 'Okay. But don't say I didn't warn you when you try and take a dribble shower tomorrow morning and a tile falls on your head. Then you slip on the mould.'

He bent to kiss her, finding her lips soft and welcoming beneath his. 'I'll take it as a win if you and Chewie allow me to stay the night.'

Chewie barked, clearly hearing his name, and Lottie went to pat his head. 'Matt is going to stay over,' she told him. 'So no funny business.'

Matt glanced down at his shoes and sent up a silent prayer that his brogues would survive the night.

As she gave him a brief tour a few minutes later, Matt realised she hadn't been exaggerating. The house had bags of potential but was currently quite a way off realising it. Yet as he followed her up the rickety stairs, all he could see was the way her buttocks glided beneath her short summer skirt. The shapely legs.

When she opened the door to her bedroom, he couldn't have told anyone what state the carpet was, or how busy the wallpaper. He could only gaze into her eyes and feel his heart go into freefall.

Hands moved to undress, to touch, to glide across heated skin, and as he eased her back onto the bed, as he sank into her, he knew this was no longer a bit of light fun, not for him.

'Thank you for tonight,' she said softly a long while later, her head on his chest, his arms wrapped tightly around her.

He smiled against her hair. 'You don't have to thank me for taking you to bed.'

She elbowed his ribs. 'I didn't mean for the sex, though okay, that was pretty stellar.'

'Only *pretty* stellar?'

'Fine, it was unbelievably stellar.'

He chuckled, mollified. 'Better.'

She shifted to lie on her front, eyes looking up at him. 'I'm trying to be serious here. Thank you for what you did for Gira. The flowers, how you treated her. You gave Gira her dignity back.'

The shame he'd tried to push away all evening slithered back into his gut. Had Patricia been as twisted up over his late nights as Gira? Had she agonised over whether he was cheating on her? Had she discussed him with her friends?

Soft lips pressed against his chest. 'Stop torturing

yourself. You made mistakes, but you weren't the only one. Gira chose to fight for Ryan. Patricia chose to betray you.'

Some of the weight lifted from his shoulders at her words. He would always carry guilt for the break-up of his marriage, but perhaps Lottie was right. Perhaps not all of the burden was his to bear.

His gaze found Lottie's and as he saw her compassion, her fierce determination to defend him, he felt his chest swell.

'I wasn't expecting to find this, to find you,' he whispered through the tightness of his throat.

Her expression softened and she leant up to kiss him. 'Me neither.'

Once more he lost himself to the heat of her mouth, the lush plumpness of her lips. His last remaining thought was how he could stop himself falling in love with her.

And whether it was already too late.

Chapter Twenty-Three

M onday morning, and Lottie stood back and let Chewie jump into the back of Matt's Ford transit. Only one year old, complete with Sat-Nav, it was like driving a Rolls-Royce compared to her bone-shaker.

She'd really got lucky. And she wasn't only talking about the van.

'Even you're starting to like him, huh?' Chewie stared at her from beneath his shaggy fringe and wagged his tail. 'He kind of grows on you, doesn't he?'

He was certainly growing on her. She'd bragged that she was an expert at light, yet her feelings felt anything but light as she recalled the weekend. What had he said? *I wasn't expecting to find this, to find you.*

He'd taken the words right out of her mouth.

How wrong she'd been to worry about him seeing her house, to assume a man who wore a Rolex and Ralph Lauren polo shirts would turn his nose up at damp walls and mildew. She was used to men being straightforward; what you see is what you get. Matt, though, continued to surprise her. And God, to *delight* her.

She grinned as she recalled Saturday morning and his face when he'd seen her cooking bacon.

'When was the last time you had a bacon butty?' she'd asked as she'd pushed the plate towards him.

He'd stared down at the white-bread sandwich, grease dripping onto the plate. A healthy eater's nightmare. 'School.'

'Okay.' She'd shrugged and grabbed an apple from the bowl. 'If you'd rather have this, go ahead. Your loss.'

He'd squared his shoulders, like he was about to tackle something horrendously difficult. 'You made it for me. It would only be polite to eat it.'

She'd struggled to contain her laughter as she'd watched him stoically make his way through the butty. When he'd finished it and she'd asked him what he thought, he'd smiled. 'I'm happy to eat bacon sandwiches every morning if it means eating with you.'

Her heart had gone into total freefall.

Then there had been Sunday morning when she'd felt the bed dip and Matt had slid in beside her, smelling of shower gel, his hair damp. 'You've been for a run,' she'd guessed. He'd murmured yes, then spooned against her, letting out a deep, contented sigh. When she'd asked why he was getting back into bed, she'd felt his smile against her nape. 'I didn't want to miss waking up with you.'

'He's such a charmer,' she murmured to Chewie. 'I don't know how to defend myself against him.'

She was about to start the engine when her phone rang. Hoping it was Matt, she lunged for it, only to let it slip through her fingers when she saw who was calling.

'Shit.' He *never* phoned, only ever emailed or messaged. After scrabbling around on the floor, she snatched at the phone. 'Henry?'

'Hey, Goldilocks. How's things?'

Emotion washed through her at the sound of his lazy drawl. 'Good, thanks. Is everything okay?'

'Everything is hunky dory.' He paused and she could imagine him sitting back on his sofa, one leg crossed casually across his thigh, mouth smiling. 'Have you got time to catch up with an old friend who happens to find himself back in England?'

'Oh wow, of course.' She wasn't sure how she felt; excited, shocked. Numb. 'Are you over here to see your parents?'

'Well sure, I'm going to visit them but actually, I'm back for good.' Lottie's hand tightened on the phone as she tried to absorb his words. 'I've got a job in London, working for *The Times*.'

'That's amazing. Congratulations.' She remembered the young journalist who'd started life on the local gazette before heading off to LA where connections had secured him a job on the *Daily News*. This was yet another step up and she felt genuinely delighted for him.

'Thanks, I'm pretty chuffed.' He paused again, and this time his voice was softer. 'I really want to see you, Lottie.'

Dazed, *that's* how she felt, as if someone had knocked her on the head. Henry was in her past. She'd spent the last eighteen months coming to terms with that and was only now coming out the other side, enjoying life again. Enjoying it with Matt. She didn't want all the old feelings for Henry stirred up again, complicating things. She'd moved on.

Yet this was *Henry*. A man she'd once loved. 'I'd like to see you too.'

She heard his long exhalation over the phone. 'Thank God for that. I was half afraid you'd say no. That you'd found someone else.'

An image of Matt's face hovered in her mind and her heart twisted viciously. 'I am seeing someone.'

'Oh.' She could hear both disappointment and … was it surprise? 'How long has that been going on?'

Was it *judgement*? 'It was your choice to move abroad,' she reminded him tartly. 'You left me.'

'Yes, yes, I know. Shit, Lot, I didn't mean you should still be pining away for me.' He drew in a breath. 'I guess I'm just gutted. And jealous as hell.' There was a beat of silence. 'Is it serious with this guy?'

It was the million-dollar question. 'I don't know.'

Another breath, followed by a rustle of clothing as she imagined him sitting up straighter, phone clamped to his ear. 'Okay, I'm driving down to you today. We'll grab dinner tonight. I'll sleep on your couch.'

'Whoa, hang on a minute.' She felt like she was on a

merry-go-round that was going faster and faster. She wanted to jump off, but was too disorientated to work out how. 'Yes to dinner, but no to the couch.'

'Come on, Lot, you're not going to make me stay in a hotel, are you? We're mates. Your boyfriend will just have to understand. Message me your address and I'll be there around 6 p.m.'

He ended the call before she had a chance to disagree, or to tell him six o'clock might not be convenient.

He's anxious to see you.

More confused than ever, Lottie pressed *Call* on the one number she knew she could rely on for honest, no-holds-barred advice.

'A Monday morning call?' Sally's voice came on the phone. 'That means either your weekend went spectacularly well, or spectacularly badly.'

Lottie leant forward, head resting on the steering wheel of the van she was borrowing from the guy she'd started to fall for. 'It isn't about the weekend.' She went on to tell Sally about the call from the man she'd once been head over heels in love with.

'Oh shitting heck.' Lottie heard a shuffling sound in the background. 'Hang on a minute, I need to get Freddie in his playpen so I can focus.' There was a pause, then the cute sound of baby babble. 'Okay, I'm sitting down now. Wow.' She blew out a breath. 'It's raining men, huh?'

'God, Sally, what do I do?'

'Duh, you see Henry. Sounds like you won't get much choice in the matter anyway. Typical of the guy,' she added under her breath. Sally and Henry had got on, but there had always been an underlying niggle between them. 'I presume you do actually want to see him?'

'Of course I do.' Henry had once been the most important person in her universe. 'It's just these last few months, spending time with Matt...' She closed her eyes, picturing his face, those earnest brown eyes. 'I can't remember a time when I've been happier. I think ... crap, Sally, I think I'm falling for him.'

Sally's tone softened. 'That's not crap, Lottie, it's *good*. I like him.'

'But what about Henry? What if when I see him, all those feelings come back?'

'Then maybe you'll have a choice to make. But that's a way down the road yet. All you're doing tonight is having dinner with an old friend.'

'You're right.' Lottie sat back up, feeling calmer. The call from Henry had blindsided her, but there was no reason to get all weird about it. It had been two years since Henry had left, it would be good to see him.

Once again she pictured Matt's face and her chest tightened. The light, casual affair she'd wanted had felt like it had taken a different, deeper turn last weekend, for both of them. Their feelings were still so new though, and largely unspoken, the relationship in its infancy. She couldn't help but wonder if Henry's arrival was the worst possible timing for them.

Matt watched Amy fill up the sugar pourers as he helped her get the café ready for opening. Mondays were slow, but while nobody was in a big rush to buy books, there were a few elderly prom walkers who liked to dive into the café for a pot of tea after their stroll.

'Is everything okay?' he asked after she'd sworn for the third time, once again spilling sugar over the table.

'Sure.'

He sighed heavily and went to stand next to her, putting his hands on her shoulders. 'Talk to me,' he said softly. 'Please. You never know, your big brother might be able to help.'

She snorted. 'Right.'

He swallowed his hurt as she turned away and went to unscrew the lid of the next sugar pourer. That's when he saw her hands shake. Silently he took the container from her and placed it on the table. 'Is it Shaun?' he asked quietly.

She gave him a teary-eyed glance. 'How did you guess?'

'I figured it was either him or me who'd upset you.' He gave her a wry smile. 'Selfishly I hoped it was Shaun.'

Her breath hitched and she sat down on the nearest chair. 'He wouldn't let me come back with him on Saturday night after the pub. Some excuse about having to get up early on Sunday. Then he never phoned and when I called him, it went to voicemail.'

As he studied his sister's tear-stained face his heart twisted in sympathy. Relationships. So bloody difficult because neither partner knew exactly what the other was thinking. Patricia had probably contemplated having an affair long before she'd begun one, yet she'd not warned Matt their marriage was on the rocks. Ryan had felt pressured to drink with his work mates in order to get on at work, but he'd not voiced his worries to Gira. *You're falling in love with Lottie, but you haven't told her.*

He pushed the thought away and focused on Amy. 'He might have had a tough weekend. He'll probably phone you today and explain everything.'

'I called him already.' Amy stared down at her hands. 'He said he was working.'

This was why I moved. He wasn't sure if he could help, or even whether she would appreciate it, but at least now he was part of her life, he could try.

'He probably *was* working.' He paused, trying to put himself in Shaun's shoes. 'Men are good at compartmentalising their feelings, especially when it comes to work.' He gave her another wry smile. 'I should know. When he's done whatever it is he needs to do, I'm sure he'll be back in touch.'

'Maybe. Doesn't explain why he didn't want to see me at the weekend, though.'

Matt thought of Lottie, and how he'd misinterpreted her reluctance to allow him back to her place on Friday. 'When emotions are involved, not everything is as straightforward as it appears. They make us afraid, unsure. Vulnerable.' He squeezed her hand. 'There's likely another explanation to the one you've got in your head.'

Her smile wobbled. 'I hope so. Otherwise I'm going to have to rip some cow's eyes out.'

Matt laughed, but inside he felt a surge of protectiveness. 'If Shaun is doing anything to hurt you, he's the one who'll have to answer for it.'

'You're going to beat him up, huh?'

He'd never hit anyone outside a ring, but it didn't mean he wasn't prepared to, in order to protect those he loved. 'I boxed as a kid,' he reminded Amy, recalling the gym at boarding school. The bullies had hurt with words, but he'd made sure they couldn't harm him physically. As Amy started to look alarmed, he gave her a reassuring smile. 'It won't come to that. Lottie said Shaun's a solid guy and I trust her judgement.' He made sure to catch Amy's eye. 'If what you have with Shaun is real, you need to trust him, too.'

She nodded, and he was pleased to say she looked brighter as she stood and went back to filling up the sugar.

'You and Lottie then,' she asked a few moments later. 'Is that the real deal?'

He slid the chair he'd been straightening under the table. He didn't talk about his feelings, found it hard enough to admit them to himself, never mind anyone else. Yet his sister had been brave enough, open enough, to admit hers to him. 'Yes, I think it is.'

'Yay.' For the first time that morning, Amy gave him a proper smile. 'She's so cool. If you get married we'd be like, sisters.'

'Whoa, wait a minute.' A fission of something ran down

his spine. Fear, shock, *excitement*? 'I tried that once already and look how well it turned out.' Going through it all again was not on his radar.

And yet...

It took no effort at all to imagine a future where he went to bed with Lottie every night. Woke up with her every morning. Walked Chewie together along the seafront before coming back to eat her beloved – and, he had to admit, extremely tasty – bacon butties.

'Aw, look at your face.' Amy's voice knocked him out of his daydream and he found her smirking at him. 'You're well and truly hooked, big brother. Watching this play out is going to be so much fun.'

He smiled, surprised to find he was unfazed by the discussion of his private feelings or the gentle ribbing. It was a small price to pay for a relationship with the sister he once feared he'd lost.

The morning passed quickly and before he knew it, he was gearing up mentally for the arrival of his two o'clock appointment.

He didn't have long to wait before the door chime jingled.

'Good God, that ruddy bell's going to give me a heart attack.'

He smiled at the visitor. 'Afternoon, Audrey.'

'Boss.' She turned back to look at the door. 'First thing we need to do is stop the door making that noise every time someone comes in. Otherwise you'll find me in a heap on the floor, clutching my chest.'

His lips twitched, even as the voice in his head screamed *What have you done?* 'I'll see what I can do.'

'Now then.' She rolled up her sleeves. Literally rolled them up. 'I know you wanted to show me around before I start, but I figured first things first. How are things going between you and our Lottie?'

The voice in his head screamed louder. 'Perhaps we should do the training part first?' he suggested mildly. 'It is rather important.'

She tutted at him. 'I told you, my Harold said I was a natural. Customers come in, I talk to them. Nothing to it.'

He didn't know whether to be awed, or terrified by her confidence. 'And if they ask if we have a certain book in?'

'I'll tell them to look on the shelf.' She winked. 'Or find you.'

He couldn't help but laugh. 'And if by some miracle they want to buy a book?'

She glanced at the till. The one he'd spent weeks mastering. The one his dad refused to go anywhere near. 'I suppose you'd better show me how to use that thing.' She sniffed. 'It's not on that interweb, is it? My daughter keeps telling me I need to get on it but I told her, that's all very well, but where's the instruction book?'

Matt took a breath, reminded himself this was only a shop. The worst Audrey could do was lose him money and customers. 'Why don't I start by showing you where the fiction and non-fiction shelves are?'

'You could.' She looked up at him, all five foot nothing

of her. Silver hair, a twinkle in her faded blue eyes. 'After you've told me what was bothering our Lottie on Friday.'

It was a mistake, he realised, to assume the woman who liked to joke, who was always so full of talk, didn't also pay attention. 'Her van needs a new head gasket. I think…' He trailed off, unsure how to phrase it. He didn't want to speculate about Lottie's finances. It felt like a betrayal. 'It's expensive to repair,' he settled with.

'How's she managing without it?'

'I've loaned her mine for as long as she needs it.'

Audrey narrowed her eyes. '*You* had a spare van?'

Matt could feel himself flush. Hell, the woman was too astute. 'I do now.'

The old lady started to chuckle, reaching out to pat his arm. 'Oh my, you're like my favourite chocolate in the selection box. Dark shell, soft gooey centre. Now show me where these ruddy books are. Then remind me I need to arrange an extraordinary general meeting of the book club, without Lottie.'

'Now wait a minute.' He felt a flicker of panic. 'She's fiercely independent. She won't want any handouts.'

'Trust me, dear, we'll be as discreet as a politician's mistress.'

Chapter Twenty-Four

Lottie had a break before her next customer so she drove to the seafront. Chewie needed the walk, and she needed a dose of fresh air to clear her mind.

The call from Henry weighed heavily on her as she threw Chewie a ball to fetch. She knew part of that was because she needed to tell Matt. And she would, just as soon as she'd found her balance. She wasn't used to feeling like this, so … adrift, as if she'd been knocked off course. She wanted to find her way back to the weekend, to Matt's softly spoken, heartfelt words, to the way he'd spooned against her in bed, arms wrapped tightly around her.

How would she feel if he announced he was having dinner with his ex? Her stomach churned, giving her the answer: sick, riddled with jealousy. Maybe add in angry too.

She groaned and looked down at Chewie. 'What am I doing? This isn't me. I'm not complicated. I don't fall in and out of love easily, don't have two men on the go at the same time.'

You're having dinner with an old friend.

She felt some of the tension leave her. Sally was right, she was getting in a stew about nothing.

'Come on, Chewie. Let's find Matt.'

They scrunched the short way across the pebbles to the shop. When she reached the window she stopped for a moment to stare through it. Matt, wearing a collared shirt, sleeves rolled up to reveal his tanned forearms, was clearly trying to show Audrey how to use the till. From the look on her face, she was utterly lost, yet enjoying every second.

And who wouldn't, being the sole focus of those expressive brown eyes. That darkly handsome face.

Feeling a flutter deep in her belly, she pushed the door open.

'Err, hello?' she called out, surprised not to hear the usual loud chime.

They both looked up and gave her a smile.

'He's been showing me what to do with this infernal machine,' Audrey announced. 'I told him, there's too many buttons. He needs one of those good old-fashioned tills like my Harold used to have. Damn cash drawer kept getting stuck, mind.'

Lottie glanced at Matt, whose amused eyes twinkled deliciously back at her. 'Is she proving to be a star employee?'

He let out a low laugh. 'She doesn't like the door chimes so we've had to take the battery out. She doesn't like the shop layout, too much bending down. Oh, and she's not going to use the till, too complicated, so she's going to write everything down.' His gaze fell on Audrey and Lottie's heart melted at the affectionate look he gave the older lady. 'She's not short of good ideas, though.'

Audrey positively glowed, looking a decade younger. 'I told you I was born to do this.'

Lottie laughed. 'You told us you used to make sausages.'

'Excuse me?' They all turned towards the voice, which belonged to a middle-aged man who was holding out a book. 'Can I buy this?'

'Certainly.' As Matt stretched out his hand to take the book, Audrey grabbed hold of it and studied the cover.

'It's not one of his best.'

Matt's eyebrows shot up and Lottie had to smother a laugh as the customer looked warily at Audrey. 'Oh? Which book would you recommend, then?'

'Come with me, young man. I'll find you a better one. Or how about you buy both and we'll cut you a deal.'

Audrey set off with the bemused customer and Lottie tried to stifle her laughter. 'Did you tell her she could cut deals?'

'No.' Slowly he slipped his hands into his pockets. Then he darted her a dry smile. 'To be honest, I'm no longer sure who's in charge.'

Oh God, this man she'd thought so serious, so reserved, was utterly adorable. She wanted to throw her arms around his neck and kiss his sensuously curved lips. To push him onto the nearest chair and snuggle into his lap.

But the call from Henry hung over her and suddenly all of that seemed terrifyingly out of reach.

Feeling suddenly nervous, she bit into her bottom lip. 'Can we have a quick chat in private?'

Surprise flickered and his eyes searched hers. Whatever he saw made him frown. 'Should I be worried?'

'No.' The last thing she wanted to do was make this into something bigger than it was. 'It can wait until the customer's gone.'

He clasped her hand, the warmth causing a flutter deep in her belly. 'I'm sure Audrey has it under control.'

So many jokes she could make, but they died on her tongue as she stepped into his office. While Chewie circled, finding a place to lie down, the butterflies in her stomach twitched nervously and Lottie had to remind herself this was not a big deal.

You wouldn't be saying that if he told you he was seeing Patricia.

'Hey.' His fingers were gentle on her chin as he lifted it so he could look into her eyes. 'You really are worrying me now. You've gone quiet.'

She tried to smile, but it was hard when what she was doing suddenly felt so wrong. A few months ago seeing Henry again would have put a spring in her step, joy in her heart. Now she wasn't sure she wanted to go through with it.

'I'm seeing Henry tonight.'

For a split second shock crossed his handsome features, but then a guard came up. The one he'd worn so frequently when she'd first met him. 'Okay.' His jaw tightened fractionally. 'Is he over here on business?'

'No.' Damn it. No matter how she worded this, she knew if she were in his place, she'd be hurt by what she was about to say. 'He's actually over here for good now.'

The muscle in his jaw jumped. 'I see.'

What did he see, exactly? She wanted to reassure him Henry was in her past, yet she wasn't one hundred per cent certain she could say that. Not until she'd met him. 'He's got a job in London, working for *The Times* newspaper. He's a journalist, and that's a really good step up for him. He's really excited.' Okay, Matt probably didn't want to hear about the promotion of the guy she'd once been in love with. The one who was taking her out to dinner tonight. 'I think he just wants to touch base now he's back. You know, meet up with his friends before he starts his new job.'

Matt exhaled heavily, running a hand through his short, dark hair. 'I'm not sure what you want me to say. Of course you're going to see him. I respect that.'

She couldn't get a read on him; his thoughts were locked up tight. Was she overreacting, putting her emotions into the situation when actually his didn't run that deeply? Maybe he wasn't that bothered she was seeing Henry. 'Okay. I just wanted you to know. I mean, we haven't put a label on us, or what we're doing, but I wouldn't want you hearing from someone else that I was in a restaurant with another guy.'

'Lottie.' Her name seemed forced out of him. Stepping towards her, he put his hands on her shoulders, twin dark eyes insisting she made him her whole focus. 'I don't know what label you want, but I do know I wish it was me taking you to dinner tonight.'

She swallowed, throat feeling horribly tight. 'Me, too.'

'Maybe you'll let me take you out tomorrow?'

Slowly she shook her head, but as his face fell, she reached up to whisper in his ear, 'I'd prefer it if you came to mine. Take-out, TV, bed.'

Heat flashed in his eyes, and the tension eased from his face. 'Yes to the last two, but I'll cook.'

'You're doing that health freak thing again, aren't you?'

He smiled, eyes skimming her face in that sexy way he had that made her feel admired, cherished. 'I'm looking after our arteries.'

'I'm not going to say no to a handsome man volunteering to cook for me.' His smile turned strained and she played back the words in her head. 'Let me rephrase. I'd love it if *you* cooked for me.' So he was in no doubt how she felt, she rose up on her toes and kissed him. Immediately his arms wrapped around her and he kissed her back, taking control, deepening it. In a flash, he'd lifted her onto his desk and stepped between her thighs. As he pressed against her core, heat flashed through her.

But then Chewie started to bark. Much as she wanted to ignore him, to keep Matt where he was, *doing* what he was, Chewie was too loud, the noise too distracting.

With a sigh she drew back. 'Come on, buddy. I thought we'd got over this.'

Matt looked at Chewie and shook his head. 'I don't

think he's barking at us. I think he heard something in the shop.'

They raced out to find the central book display on a heap on the floor, Audrey on her hands and knees, skirt around her thighs, picking up the scattered paperbacks. She looked cross. 'Which plonker put a display together that's so easy to knock over? I'm telling you, it's a good job you've got me working here. This place needs a lot of sorting out.'

Lottie glanced sideways at Matt, who ran a hand down his face and heaved in a breath. 'I'll pick those up, Audrey. Why don't you take a break? Put your feet up and get Amy to make you a drink.'

'Good idea.' As she started to lurch to her feet Matt dashed over to help her up. After dusting herself down, Audrey turned towards the café. 'Is it too early for gin?'

Matt gave his new employee a tolerant smile. 'The way today is going, I'd say gin was entirely appropriate.'

Matt was restless. He kept looking at his watch, wondering what Lottie was doing. Correction: what Lottie *and Henry* were doing.

His stomach knotted and he jumped off the sofa, shoving the book he'd been trying to read onto the coffee table. As a child, books had been his safe space, a world he could retreat into when the real one became too upsetting. Now he couldn't focus, though. Instead of words he saw Lottie's face, smiling into the eyes of a guy who wasn't him. It didn't help that he was still reading *The Kiss Quotient*.

Annoyed with himself, he marched off to the kitchen. Audrey preferred gin, but whisky was his go-to. He'd just dragged the bottle out of the cabinet when his dad appeared, his gaze falling on the bottle in Matt's hand.

'Must have been a tough day.'

He wasn't ready to talk about Lottie, or about Henry's arrival, not until he'd got a better handle on his raging jealousy. 'Audrey started work with us.'

His dad's bushy eyebrows flew up to his hairline. 'You've got her working in the shop?'

Matt shrugged, his mind still elsewhere. 'Lottie's idea. Apparently Audrey is bored at home. Do you want a glass?' When he glanced at his dad for an answer, he found he was staring at him. 'Dad?' He waved the bottle at him. 'Do you want to join me?'

His dad shook himself. 'Aye, pour me one.'

Silence descended as Matt took out the glasses and poured two healthy measures. When he handed one to his dad, he realised the man hadn't moved from his current spot. 'Are you okay, Dad?'

He blinked a few times, then reached for the glass and took the sort of swallow Matt felt *he* needed. He followed suit, welcoming the burn and the distraction. Maybe now he could get back into his book. As he set off to the living room though, his dad spoke again.

'Suppose you don't need my help anymore.'

Matt halted. Was the man upset Audrey was working there? 'I've always needed your help. Still do.' He paused, pushing himself to say the words he should have said right at the start of this project. 'I wanted this to be a family shop. You, me, Amy, all working together.' His throat felt tight, the words not coming easily, yet Matt knew if his relationship with his dad was going to move on, to grow, it was important he said them. 'I know it's not what either of you chose, and I understand if you're not interested, but there's nothing I'd like more than to build this business together.' He swallowed. 'There's nobody I'd trust more to help me than you.'

His dad took another swig from his glass. When he finally looked at him, Matt was shocked by the shame in his eyes. 'I can't use the flaming till.'

'*That's* the reason you don't want to work in the shop?'

His dad shuffled his feet. 'It's a bloody good reason. The thing terrifies me. No point having someone help who can't take the money.'

Matt would have laughed, but he could see how embarrassed his dad was. 'There are ways round that, if you're interested,' he said carefully. 'I didn't show you properly in the first place because I was still getting to grips with it myself. Six months on and I think I've mastered it, so if you want me to show you again, I'll be a better teacher. Or we can just replace the damn thing with something simpler.' He smiled at his dad. 'Or there's always Audrey's solution – you can write everything down for me to enter later.'

His dad barked out a laugh. 'That's how the old dear is playing it, eh?'

'Apparently the old ways are the best ways.'

'She's not wrong.' Now when his dad's eyes met his, Matt saw humour and mischief. 'How helpful was she?'

'She made up her own sales deals, knocked over the display I'd spent the morning setting up, forced me to remove the battery from the door chime, so I didn't know when the customers came in.' He smiled. 'Aside from that, I think she'll be an asset.'

His dad chuckled. 'Sounds about right.' He looked again at Matt's glass, his eyes narrowing. 'So it wasn't Audrey's arrival that drove you to drink. Which begs the question, why are we drinking whisky?'

Matt could fob him off, say he just fancied a drink, or that Audrey's 'help' meant he'd have a lot of catching up to do tomorrow. But if his proud dad could lower his defences enough to admit he was scared of the till, Matt could surely admit to his own fears.

'Probably a conversation best had sitting down. For me, anyway.'

They walked towards the sitting room and as he sat down opposite his dad, Matt perched forward, the tension back in his gut.

His dad sat back, observing him. 'Is this about Lottie?'

Matt swirled the whisky around in his glass. 'How did you guess?'

'Because only a woman can screw with a man's head enough that he resorts to the hard stuff on a Monday.'

Matt half smiled. Placing the glass down on the coffee table, he rested his arms on his thighs and tried to give voice to the emotions running rampant in his head.

'You don't have to tell me,' his dad interrupted, misreading his silence. 'You never did like talking about yourself. You'd tell us how the football team had done, what the teachers were like. What grades you got. But never how you felt.'

Because I was miserable. How could a child tell his parents that, when they'd been so proud he'd earnt a scholarship to go to the school? He couldn't turn the clock back, but he could try and build bridges now. 'Lottie is out with her ex tonight.' Inhaling a deep breath, he looked over at his dad. 'I'm terrified she'll want to go back to him.'

Surprise flickered across his dad's face. 'This is serious then, you and her?'

Matt reached for his glass again, needing something to do with his hands. 'It wasn't, or at least it wasn't supposed to be.' He took a sip, trying to work through his feelings. 'She wanted fun and I … I couldn't resist her. She's light to my dark, laughter to my serious, open to my closed. Warm to my cold.' Emotion surged through him, pricking at his eyes, tightening his throat. 'I'm not right for her, wasn't ready for her.' The lump in his throat felt like a boulder. 'But I fell for her anyway.'

'You're not cold, son. You keep your feelings hidden, like me. Used to drive your mum mad,' he added with a sad smile. 'Doesn't mean you're not capable of loving deeply, but it does mean Lottie won't know how you feel unless you tell her.'

Matt knew his dad was right, but would it make any difference? She'd loved Henry once, would still be with him now if the man hadn't moved away. It was hard to see a scenario where seeing him again wouldn't bring those feelings flooding back. Where Henry wasn't currently holding her hand, looking deep into her sparkly grey eyes. Where she wasn't falling for him all over again.

His gut churned and Matt swigged back the rest of his whisky, hoping to quell the rising nausea.

It didn't help.

Chapter Twenty-Five

As Lottie walked along the seafront with Henry, she looked down at the hand that had just clasped hers. It felt both familiar, and wrong.

Much like the evening.

It was still warm so they'd opted not to go out for a meal, but to eat fish and chips on the beach like they used to. It had meant she hadn't needed to push Chewie on her parents again, though the poor guy looked confused to see her with a man who wasn't Matt.

He wasn't the only one confused. Even as they'd laughed, drinking lager and chatting about old times with all the familiar ease, Lottie had thought of Matt, and how he would have been horrified. No dressing up, no smart restaurant. Greasy food.

'You've gone quiet.' Henry gave her hand a tug. 'Talk to me, Goldilocks.'

Henry flashed his wide, easy smile and something in her

chest shifted. A memory, maybe. Or something real. It *was* good to see him. He looked better than ever, his blue eyes bright against his tanned face, fair hair bleached by the Californian sun. 'I'm thinking I shouldn't be holding hands with you.'

She pulled her hand away and hurt came and went in his eyes. 'Worried the boyfriend will see you? Friends can hold hands, you know.'

'I'm not worried about Matt. It just doesn't feel right.' She glanced into his handsome face. 'You must have dated since you left here. How would you have felt holding my hand if I'd come out to see you?'

His gaze held hers. 'I would have gripped it tight and never let you go.'

She sucked in a breath as she felt a dart of pain in her chest. 'You can't say that. You're the one who left me.'

'And I've regretted it every day we've been apart.' He halted, turning to face her. 'Lottie, I'm still madly in love with you. Yes, I dated out there, but none of it was serious, none of it meant anything. You were always in my heart.'

Oh God. He'd always been so good at this, she realised. Telling her how he felt, making her feel special. She'd known, absolutely, where she stood with him.

But then he'd left.

'You put your career before me, Henry.' She pushed her hands in her pockets so neither would be tempted to hold hands again. 'I don't blame you for it, I get that it was important for you to do that, but it changed everything between us and our lives moved on. We can't just go back to the way things were.'

He exhaled in frustration. 'I'm not asking for that.'

'Then what are you asking for?'

His eyes searched hers, and she still felt their pull. They were the first things she'd noticed about him: so pretty, so eloquent. But now she'd experienced deep and mysterious.

'I'm asking you to give us another chance. I'm not starting work for two weeks. Let me stay with you until then. Prove to you what we had is still there, still worth fighting for.'

Memories of their years together hovered, pushing into her consciousness, reminding her of the laughter, the fun they'd had. Dating Henry had been like dating her best friend: easy, stress-free, mellow. They had shared interests, knew what each other was thinking. With Matt everything felt sharper, more electric. High definition rather than soft focus. And no, they hadn't had a chance yet to label what they had, but it didn't mean it was any less real. 'I have a boyfriend, Henry. You can't stay with me.'

He nodded, a determined set to his jaw. 'Okay, fine. I'll stay in a hotel. But I want to see you, spend time with you.'

Irritation pricked. 'I work. I can't just take two weeks off on a whim.'

He looked like she'd kicked him. 'But you work for yourself. I'm sure you could jiggle customers around and find some time for us, if you really wanted to.'

She had a van that needed a new head gasket. A house that needed both money and attention. Yet she could never refuse those blue eyes. 'I'll try and make time to see you for lunch.'

'Okay, lunch is good. I can work with lunch.' He smirked. 'Now we've just got to agree weekends and evenings.'

She blew out a breath. 'Henry, I'm seeing—'

'Someone, I know.' He gave her his wide charm of a smile. 'But I've only got two weeks to persuade you. I need as much of your free time as I can get.'

He was exasperating, yet he was also the Henry she'd fallen for. The one who used his considerable charm to bulldoze through her objections until she'd end up wondering why she'd ever objected in the first place. 'I'll think about it.'

He grinned. 'Thank you.'

They carried on walking, Chewie doing his usual sniff and wander, while always keeping an eye on where she was.

'When was the last time you windsurfed?' he asked as they strolled past the sailing school where boards and sails were neatly stacked.

'A few weeks ago actually. I took Matt.'

'Was he any good?'

Lottie smiled as she remembered the day. It had been the first time she'd seen the lighter, relaxed side of him. 'It was his first time. He spent most of it in the water.'

'Maybe we can all go on Saturday.'

Lottie glanced at Henry. 'You just want to show off in front of him.'

Henry laughed. 'Busted, but hey, it would be good to get back in the sea. California is great and all that, but you can't beat the murky English Channel.'

'At least the Channel doesn't have sharks,' she countered. 'We can't do Saturday, Matt has to work.'

'Even better.' She elbowed him and he laughed. 'Okay, okay, we could make it Sunday instead.' He kicked at a ball hidden in the scrub, then picked it up and threw it for Chewie, who raced along, ears flapping.

Another point to Henry, she guessed. Chewie seemed to have taken an instant liking to him, unlike the tentative truce he had with Matt.

'So what does he do for a living, this Matt?' Henry asked, pushing his hands into the pockets of his faded jeans as they stood and watched Chewie. With a rip at the knee, and worn patches on the bum, they were the type of jeans Matt wouldn't be seen dead in, she thought with a wry smile.

'He took over the bookshop on the front. You know, Books by the Bay.'

'Bookshop owner, huh? Aren't they usually crusty old guys? Bookworms whose own lives are so dull, they have to resort to a fantasy land to spice it up.'

She halted, staring at him. 'Is that what you think of me? That I read because my life is dull?'

'Of course not. You're not a bookworm.' He flashed her a grin. 'More a book butterfly. Sure, you like to read, but you don't spend all day in the dark, burrowed in books. You flutter between books and real life.'

'That's true of all people who love books.' She paused as he picked up the soggy ball Chewie had dumped at his feet and threw it back onto the beach. 'I started up a book club.'

'For real? Is it full of worms or butterflies?'

'Come along next Thursday evening and find out for yourself.'

He smiled, eyes glinting. 'Now you're getting the hang of this. What are we going to do for the other thirteen evenings?'

She rolled her eyes, but as he walked her back to her place, she wondered what exactly she was going to do while he was here. On the one hand, she really enjoyed seeing Henry again. America hadn't changed him. He was still easy, laid back. Fun. But that feeling when her stomach dipped and she thought her heart was going to burst out of her chest ... she didn't get that when she looked at him. Maybe she'd never had it.

Yet she felt it the moment she thought of Matt.

Tuesday morning, and Matt had been up since the crack of dawn, run eight miles along the seafront and was now pushing his cereal bowl into the dishwasher, ready to walk to work.

He felt shattered, thanks to a night tossing and turning. His heart knew Lottie wasn't Patricia, she wouldn't sleep with Henry behind his back, but it didn't stop his tortured, sleep-deprived mind from making up gut-wrenching scenarios.

It didn't help knowing that this wasn't a one-off. Lottie would want to keep seeing Henry. Even as he'd pounded the pavements, his feverish brain had refused to shut up. It had imagined the phone call he was going to get from her today, cancelling their night out, because why would she want to see him, when the love of her life was back in the country? It wouldn't be long before she'd come to the shop to tell him in person it was over...

'OMG Matt, are you okay? You look awful.' Amy gawked at him from the kitchen doorway.

'Thanks.'

'No, seriously, what's wrong? Have you and Lottie had a fight?'

He clenched his jaw, took his time carefully closing the dishwasher. This was why he liked to keep his private life exactly that, private. It stopped questions, however well meaning, that he didn't know how to answer. 'No, we've not had a fight.' He couldn't imagine ever *fighting* with her. Arguing, disagreeing, sure, but she wasn't volatile or high maintenance like Patricia had been. Because he was an expert at deflecting, he asked a question of his own. 'How are you and Shaun? Have you spoken to him?'

She avoided his eyes and went to sit on one of the bar stools. 'Yes. He phoned me last night, like you said he would.'

'And?' he pressed, no longer just asking to take the heat off himself.

'He got all embarrassed. Eventually he admitted he'd had to leave his flat because he couldn't pay the rent, so he'd spent the weekend packing up his stuff.' Finally she met his gaze. 'That's why he couldn't ask me back. He's kipping on a mate's floor.'

The big brother in him wanted to tell her it was time to stop seeing him. Let Shaun sort himself out, prove he was a man to be trusted. But Amy had come out of her shell since she'd met him, and he knew she'd developed real feelings for the guy. 'Did he say why he couldn't pay his rent? Is his plumbing business not doing well?'

'Something about a bad loan he took out to get the business going, that he wanted to pay off. He kept saying not to worry, it was temporary. He'd find somewhere else.'

He made a mental note to phone Shaun when he had a few spare minutes. 'How do you feel now you know all this?'

Her back straightened, her eyes flashed. 'I'm not going to dump him just 'cos he's got no money, if that's what you mean.'

He hung his head, a little ashamed, as it was exactly what he'd meant. 'Sorry. Of course you're not. I just...' *Say the words*. He wondered if this sort of conversation would ever come easily to him. 'I've not been a good big brother, missed too many years, but I want to be a better one for you now.'

She seemed to consider his words, her expression cautious. 'Then will you not tell Dad? Please. He'll be like you and assume Shaun's not good enough for me, or some crap like that, and it's not true. He's kind and funny and I really like him.'

He walked over and kissed the top of her head. 'Deal. I won't tell Dad, but I will have a chat with Shaun.' She stiffened and he sighed. 'I just want to find out if there's any way I can help.'

She looked up, and it was only then he realised how like their mum she was. Hazel eyes, straight brown hair, stubborn attitude, soft heart. 'That's all? You won't give him shit?'

'I promise not to give him shit.' He touched her cheek, love swelling inside him. 'I've done plenty wrong myself, Amy. I'm hardly in a position to throw stones.'

'Okay.' She pushed herself off the stool. 'I'd better get to work. Don't want to piss off the boss.'

He hesitated, then voiced an idea he'd been turning around in his head. 'What would you say to having a stake in the shop? That way you wouldn't just manage the café, you'd effectively own it?'

Her eyes widened. 'Seriously?'

'It's purely selfish on my part. I like working with my sister.' He smiled, feeling that tug of emotion again. 'I'd like to encourage her to stick around.'

Amy shocked him by throwing her arms around his waist. 'I like working with you, too. Plus the café is way better than I thought it would be. I get to meet people, be my own boss, and when it's quiet I can look out at the sea.' Her head moved against his chest. 'God, I was such a bitch when we first moved down, but now I get why you brought us here.' She wiped her eyes. 'Shit, now I have to sort out my face.'

'You look beautiful, Amy.' He brushed the tears from her eyes. 'You're so like Mum.'

He watched the emotion pass across her face before she gave him a playful shove. 'Stop it, go to work before you make me cry even more.'

The first hour in the shop was quiet and he used the time to phone Shaun, arranging for the guy to meet him at the house at six. He figured it would still give him enough time to get to Lottie's for seven.

If she still wanted to see him.

A steady stream of customers kept him occupied until lunch when Audrey arrived, bringing her usual combination of chaos, humour and much-needed distraction.

Every hour that went by that Lottie hadn't phoned was a good sign, Matt told himself. Tonight was still on.

At 3.30 Audrey announced she had to leave early, she was having a new television delivered. 'Now I can watch those loose women in this thing called high definition,' she'd announced. 'The man in the shop says I'll see all their wrinkles.'

At 3.55 – just as he'd been gearing up to mentally cheer the passing of another hour – his phone rang. And his heart lodged into the back of his throat when he saw who was calling.

Clearing his throat, he answered. 'Hi.'

'It's me, Lottie.' As if he didn't immediately recognise

her voice ... or already have her saved as a contact. 'I'm phoning about tonight.'

His heart slithered all the way down to his brogues. 'I understand.'

There was a pause and he heard some barking in the background. 'Yes, yes, I'm pleased to see you, too.' A breathless laugh. 'Sorry, I'm just climbing back in the van, *your* van, and Chewie's expressing his delight at seeing me, even though I was only gone a few minutes. Hang on a sec.' He imagined her putting down her toolbox. Maybe encouraging Chewie to take his paws off her. 'Okay, now then, what do you understand?'

He took a breath and started to reorganise the pens. 'That you want to cancel tonight.'

'Well, I'm glad you understand, because I don't. Why do I want to cancel?'

Because Henry's back in your life. He couldn't say the words, knew they'd make him sound like an insecure prick. And she didn't sound like she was cancelling, so maybe he was making too much up in his head. 'Sorry, I just assumed that was why you'd phoned.'

'Nope, I wanted to check what time you were coming over, so I can make sure I'm back. Okay, confession time, also so I can make sure I've cleaned up by then. Obviously the mould and damp will still be there, just to set your expectations.'

He wondered if she'd cleaned up for Henry, or if she was so relaxed around her former lover, she didn't feel she had to. 'I'm coming to see *you*, Lottie, not your house. I want to cook for you, talk to you. Take you to bed and make love to you.'

He was pleased to hear her breath hitch. 'You don't care if the sheets are due for changing, the sofa's full of dog hair and the kitchen bins are overflowing?'

'No.' Unconsciously he started reorganising the pens again. 'How was Henry?'

'On good form.' She paused, and he hated how his heart thumped. 'He's down here for two weeks, so you'll get to meet him.'

Briefly he shut his eyes, trying to find his calm. He felt adrift, a dinghy cut loose in a turbulent sea. All he kept thinking was, if only he'd had more time with her before Henry had come back into her life. 'I'll look forward to it.'

She laughed softly. 'You might not when I tell you his first idea was that we all go windsurfing on Saturday.'

He didn't need to ask if the guy was any good at it. What better way to show Lottie what she'd been missing? 'I hope the second idea is better.'

'The second idea is we go on Sunday instead.'

He winced, aware he was going to have to give the guy his moment. At least he'd be with Lottie, which had to be better than imagining what they were doing. 'I'm starting to see a pattern.' Just then the bell in the shop rang – he'd snuck the chime back as Audrey had left – and he looked up to see his dad walk in. 'Sorry, I've got to go. I have an unexpected visitor.'

'Julia Roberts? You know, from *Notting Hill*? Hugh Grant

plays a bookshop owner and... Oh boy, you probably haven't watched it, have you?'

'Just because I don't read romantic comedies doesn't mean I haven't watched the classics.' He waved at his dad. 'But actually, the visitor is Dad.'

There was a beat of silence, and when Lottie spoke again, he knew, just knew, she wasn't as surprised as he was. 'Well, you'd better see what he wants. I'll see you later, with or without clean sheets and a tidy house.'

Smiling, he ended the call and turned to his dad. 'This is a nice surprise.'

His dad shifted on his feet, looking ... embarrassed? 'Thought it was about time I helped out. Keep an eye on Audrey for you.' He glanced around. 'Is she here today?'

Suddenly the pieces slipped into place. Lottie insisting he take Audrey on, Lottie saying she didn't think his dad's issue with the shop was working for him. She'd *planned* this. Realised the old man wasn't work shy, he was lacking confidence. Then shown him, through Audrey, that there was nothing to fear.

Silently he sent Lottie a prayer of thanks.

And slipped even further into love with her.

Chapter Twenty-Six

I t was Sunday, the sun was out and Lottie was on the
beach with three of her favourite males, yet she
couldn't, in all truth, say she was enjoying herself.

First there was Matt, who smiled in all the right places,
listened, asked polite questions, but was back to the stilted,
reserved Matt she'd first met. Not the caring, funny one
she'd got to know. The one who'd turned up on Tuesday to
cook for her with his ingredients in neat plastic pots.
Salmon burgers with sweet-potato fries.

'Proof that healthy doesn't have to be boring,' he'd said,
his lips curving into a captivating smile.

Then there was Henry, who was his usual, chatty,
charming self and yet … Lottie could feel the testosterone
bouncing off him. It was competitive Henry who'd come
out today, the one who saw Matt as a rival. Three times he'd
asked Matt if he was sure he didn't want to windsurf. Three

times Matt had said he was happy watching and looking after Chewie.

Finally there was Chewie, who kept watching Matt, but seemed happy enough to chase balls thrown by Henry. It was as if he was telling her he liked Henry best, though Lottie thought it went deeper than that. He saw Matt as a threat to his position as top dog, but not Henry.

'He's nearly as good as you,' Matt remarked as they watched Henry out on the water.

Lottie laughed. 'Clearly you know nothing about windsurfing. He's far better than me. California has been good for him.'

She was aware of Matt giving her a quiet study. 'Do you ever regret not following him out there?'

'What, to improve my windsurfing technique?' He smiled, but she knew he saw behind her glib reply. 'Regrets aren't useful or healthy. Sure, at times I wobbled and wondered if I'd done the right thing but I refused to keep rehashing it. I made the decision and moved forward.'

'I admire that.' His gaze shifted out to sea. 'Before I moved here my life was a long series of regrets. Things I wish I'd done differently.'

Her heart ached and she reached for his hand. 'I told you before, you torture yourself too much. Amy's so much happier now and I can see your dad's started to come out of his grief. Much of that is down to you and your brave decision to move here.'

He gave her a sidelong glance. 'It's also thanks to you.

You teased Amy out of her shell, and Shaun's been good for her.'

'Is this the same Shaun who suddenly finds himself with a month of solid work in your house, just when he needs to find a deposit for a flat?'

Matt avoided her eyes. 'Amy needs an ensuite, I promised her one before we moved. And Dad needs a wet room so there's nothing to trip over.'

She nudged at his shoulder. 'And you've got a big heart, Matt Steele.'

He shook his head. 'I'm getting work done for a reasonable rate by a guy I trust who makes my sister happy.' He paused as they watched Henry turn smoothly back to shore. 'Speaking of Dad, he's helped out in the shop every afternoon this week.'

Lottie smiled. 'That's good, isn't it?'

'Oh yes. Gives me some time off, gives him a focus.' He slid her a look, and her heart beat faster at the emotion in his eyes. 'I have a feeling I've got you to thank.'

'I only suggested Audrey work for you. Something you might not be thanking me for soon.'

His gaze wouldn't leave hers, and she couldn't explain how one simple look, one simple *adoring* look, could make her feel so dizzy, so choked. 'To you it's not a big deal. Another person you've helped, but to those you listen to, pay attention to, it can be a life changer,' he said quietly. 'I will always be grateful you came into our lives.'

Tears pricked and she struggled with how to respond. It was like he saw more in her than anyone else ever had.

'Whoa, things look a bit serious here.'

She looked up with a start, unsure whether to be relieved or annoyed at the interruption. Henry was staring down at them, beads of water running down his face, eyes blue as the sky, his muscular frame outlined by the wet suit. He was like an advert for the Californian dream and yet ... her skin didn't shiver, her heart didn't yearn. Her blood didn't heat.

She thought it had once, but the memory had faded. All she knew for certain was that it didn't now.

He peeled off the wet suit and rubbed himself down with the towel. He was more muscled than Matt; a gym body, not a runner's body. 'What's with the serious faces?'

For once she was the one who didn't know what to say, and Matt the one who found the words. 'I was thanking Lottie for her help with my dad.'

'Yeah?' Henry plonked himself down on the picnic blanket opposite her. 'She's always been one to take care of the waifs and strays.'

The dismissive way he said it set Lottie's teeth on edge. 'Matt's dad is hardly a waif or a stray.'

Henry laughed, running a hand through his wet hair as he turned to Matt. 'Oops, sorry, buddy, didn't mean that to come out like it did. I'm sure your dad's a stand-up bloke. I just meant that Lottie's always been soft-hearted.'

'Generous-hearted.' Matt kept his gaze steady on Henry. 'She's no pushover.'

Matt looked almost angry and she wanted to reassure

him that Henry didn't mean any slight, but Henry was talking again, clearly not put out by Matt's quiet rebuke.

'You'll get no arguments from me on that score. I remember this one time...' Henry started telling a tale from a few years ago, one of her first customers who'd ignored three reminders to pay his invoice. He'd been a shopkeeper and Lottie had gone to his shop, piled the most expensive items into her basket and started walking out without paying.

'Lottie can tell it better than me.' Henry grinned at her. 'Go on, tell Matt what you said when the dude got all arsey about you pinching his stock.'

'I said it's not nice when someone tries to wriggle out of paying, is it?'

Henry chuckled. 'Makes me laugh now, but I wasn't laughing when she told me.'

The memories flooded back. 'You were livid I'd gone to face him on my own.'

'Too right I was. You're five foot and a bit, he was well over six foot. I made you promise that next time you'd let me deal with it.'

'I didn't promise that,' she reminded him. 'I agreed to tell you what I was doing, so you could be there for backup if needed.'

'Yeah, yeah, always so independent.' He rolled his eyes. 'Drove me nuts.'

'I needed to prove I could run the business on my own.' She wondered how many years it would be before she could stare at her image in the mirror and say, *You did it, girl. You showed them. You're a success.* Living in a dump, having to borrow a van off Matt, it didn't say *Be proud.* But she was working on it.

'Prove to who?' Matt asked, though she suspected from the way he looked at her that he already knew the answer.

'Myself, mainly, but now I think about it, I'd be really happy to get a call from some of my old teachers, especially old Dragon Lady or Mr Zit. Show them I did make something of myself.'

'Zit?' Henry asked.

'Real name was Mr Whitehead.'

He laughed. 'Good one.'

But when she glanced at Matt, he was quietly appraising her. *He understands,* she realised, thinking back to what he'd told her of his own schooldays and the bullies he'd felt the need to prove something to.

'God, I'm starving.' Henry jumped to his feet. 'I could murder a sausage roll. Does that greasy spoon café still do them?'

'It does.' She shot Matt a look of apology. 'But it also does non-artery-clogging alternatives.'

Matt wanted to dislike Henry, but it was hard to when the guy was like a male version of Lottie – easy-going, likeable. Except he didn't have Lottie's empathy, her ability to read people, because if he did he would have understood why her business was so important to her. And if he had, he'd also have understood why she couldn't follow him to America, and would surely have waited for a job opportunity closer to home.

'You're one of those healthy-eating types?'

Matt glanced up to find Henry staring at the grilled chicken wrap on his plate. 'I'm not sure we're a type.'

He eyed the half-eaten sausage roll on Henry's plate, and on Lottie's. He didn't feel envious because he wanted to eat one. He felt envious because it emphasised how similar Lottie and Henry were.

And how different he was.

'Matt likes to look after his arteries,' Lottie supplied, smiling at him with, he thought, fondness. 'We should probably do the same.'

Henry laughed. 'I know, but can you imagine not eating fish and chips?' Matt watched as Henry's face sobered. 'Some of my best times have been you and me on this beach, eating fish and chips.'

Matt couldn't take any more. The shared memories, the expression of adoration on Henry's face as he looked at Lottie. He stood abruptly. 'Sorry, I just need to … make a call.'

He strode away from the picnic bench they'd been sitting on and set off down the prom, acutely aware they were both watching him. Lottie was probably confused, Henry probably thinking, *Yeah, nothing to fear here. Lottie will soon realise the guy's a nut job.*

Belatedly he realised he was meant to be phoning, but his damn phone was in his jacket pocket, on the bench. Still, he couldn't stomach the idea of going back yet. Not to listen to Henry relate one more anecdote from their past. Nor to see how good they were together, how well matched. How much Henry still cared for her, though he didn't fully appreciate her, which angered Matt. She deserved someone who saw her for everything she was, not just the gorgeous blonde, or the fun girl who made everyone laugh, or the businesswoman equally at ease with a toolbox or a windsurf board. There was a special side to her, the one who'd created a real support group from a simple book club. Who'd saved Gira's marriage, welcomed Amy into the fold, helped make Audrey feel useful again. Given his dad the subtle push he'd needed.

He was so lost in his thoughts that he wasn't aware Lottie had followed him. Not until he felt her arms circle his waist from behind.

'Hey.' His heart thumped against his ribs as she looked up at him, eyes full of concern. 'What's wrong?'

'Nothing.' He forced a smile. 'Needed to check on Dad, that's all.'

'What, by mental telepathy? Because I know you keep your phone in the inside pocket of your jacket. Which is still with Henry and Chewie.' She grasped his hand and tugged him to the nearby bench. 'Talk to me, Matt.'

One of the hardest things anyone could ever ask of him. 'He wants you back, doesn't he?'

Lottie drew in a breath, then let it out slowly, her hand still clasped around his. 'He says he wants a second chance, yes.'

Even though he'd known, Matt felt the bottom fall out of his stomach. 'He still loves you.' He said it as a fact, because it was obvious, but Lottie answered anyway.

'So he says, yes.'

His throat was tight, his chest tighter. Matt knew he had to ask the question, even though the answer terrified him. 'Do you still love him?'

Her hand slipped from his and she drew her feet up on the bench, hugging her knees. 'I still have feelings for him, yes.'

Suddenly his heart felt heavy in his chest, dragged down by a sense of inevitability. 'When does he start his new job?'

'He's here until next Sunday. I've invited him to the book club.' She smiled. 'I can't wait to see what he makes of Audrey.'

'From what I've seen, he'll charm her.' Jealousy bit. It had taken him six months to feel comfortable with the group, yet he already knew Henry would fit in easily. That Audrey would love him.

Silence descended and they both stared out at the horizon, watching the small waves churn up the beach, dragging the pebbles into the sea. He sensed she was thinking carefully about what to say next, how to avoid upsetting him. 'I'm busy next week.' Her head jerked to look at him and he knew his bald statement had come out too strong, too blunt. 'Stock taking,' he added, doing his best to give her a wry smile. 'Not my favourite job.' Nor one that needed doing for several months, but it was good to get a head start on it.

As he watched her eyes scan his face, the clear grey against her blonde hair made his breath catch, as it did every time he looked at her. 'I could help. I'm a whizz at counting.'

His chest ached as he imagined them doing the task together. How much fun she'd make it. *She won't still be with you by then.* 'Thanks, but it's a specialist job.' He smiled to show he was joking, then reached for her hand, raising it to his lips for a brief kiss before settling it on his thigh. 'I think you need to spend the time with Henry,' he added quietly.

She bit into her lip, eyes looking huge in her face. 'It feels like you're pushing me away.'

His heart stuttered and unconsciously his hand gripped tighter to hers. 'No, not at all.' How to explain that he'd fallen in love with her, without her feeling pressured? Plus he'd already lost one woman to another man. He knew how much it hurt. He couldn't bear the thought of her leaving him for Henry further down the road. 'You owe it to yourself, to both of you, to take the time to get to know each other again.' Each word felt like a knife through his chest. 'See if you still feel the same as you did two years ago.'

Her eyes glistened and she looked out to sea. 'And you and me?'

'We take a step back. A pause.' He told himself it could only be for a week, yet in his heart he knew there was a good chance it would be for ever.

Her eyes searched his. 'You're not going to do a Ross on me?'

'Sorry?'

'From *Friends*? You know, when Rachel and he were on a break? He slept with someone else because he argued they'd broken up, but for her it was just a pause.' She closed her eyes, shaking her head, and he didn't know whether she was amused, or exasperated. 'I can't believe I'm explaining *Friends* to you. I thought everyone watched it.'

'I rarely watch TV.' Another thing they didn't have in common. Reason 1,072 for her to choose Henry over him.

'Seriously? You've got something against sitting on your bum, relaxing?'

With the healthy eating, now the TV, she must have him down as some smug, ultra-virtuous freak. 'At school it meant going in the common room.' He'd never felt more alone than sitting in a room of boys who studiously avoided talking to him. 'Then, with work, there was never the time.'

She nodded. 'I guess you don't miss what you've never had.'

Silence again, a thick, heavy quiet that pulled at his heart. *Tell her how you feel. That you can't contemplate the thought of being with anyone else.* Would it be fair, though? He didn't want her to stick with him because she felt she ought to, because he was the one she was seeing. *That's just an excuse.* Maybe it was, but this surely wasn't the time to bare his soul, to leave himself open and vulnerable. Not for her sake or his own.

But he could say something.

He squeezed her hand. 'I've had you, Lottie. And I'll miss you terribly.' He tried to smile. 'I promise I won't do a Ross. He sounds like a prick.'

Lottie laughed, as he'd hoped, and though it was quieter, less carefree than usual, it at least dispelled some of the heavy emotion. 'He was a bit. Joey was always my favourite.' She nudged him. 'Maybe we'll sit down one Sunday and binge watch the first few series.'

His throat tightened, emotion bubbling so close to the surface, he was terrified it might boil over. 'I'd like that.' Because he couldn't afford the hope that tried to wriggle into his heart, he rose to his feet. 'We'd best be getting back. Chewie will wonder where you are.'

'He's okay. He's taken a liking to Henry.'

Even her dog thought she should choose Henry, he thought glumly as they walked back. Reason 1,073.

The wriggling hope died.

Chapter Twenty-Seven

I t was Wednesday evening and Lottie was with Shaun, Henry and Amy in the pub. Shaun and Henry were reminiscing about when they'd gone around in a gang. Shaun had been dating Madeline then, and there had also been another couple who'd since moved away. The six of them had had some wild times: camping holidays, festivals, pub crawls, BBQs on the beach into the small hours.

Happy days, yet they seemed to belong to another life. One when she'd had no mortgage, no business. When things had been simple and she'd been carefree. Inevitably it brought her mind back to Matt. She wondered if he'd ever had a time in his life when he'd felt that way. When he'd not been head down, insular, driven.

'Another drink?' Henry shook his beer bottle in front of her face, jerking her out of her thoughts.

'Sorry, yes, please.' She'd avoided Henry on Monday, claiming she was too busy when really she just needed some space to work through her thoughts. Yesterday she'd met him for lunch, and though it had been pleasant, she'd felt annoyed at being pushed into it, both by Henry and by Matt.

Henry because he expected her to make time for him, even though it was his choice to remain down here. Matt because despite his denial, it felt like he was shoving her into Henry's arms.

'Hey, it's my round. I'll get them.' Shaun eased off the bar stool but Henry waved him off.

'No way, I invited you guys, remember? Plus I'm not here for long. Let me treat you so you don't forget me too fast when I'm not around.'

His eyes rested on Lottie and she knew he was thinking what she was. The book club was tomorrow, then they only had Friday and Saturday before he went back to London.

'London's hardly California,' Shaun pointed out. 'You'll be back.'

Henry kept his gaze on her. 'Depends what there is to come back for.'

Lottie was very aware of Amy and Shaun watching them intently.

'Well, let me at least help you carry the drinks,' Shaun offered and followed Henry to the bar, leaving Lottie and, she knew, a very confused Amy.

'Are you seeing Henry again?' Amy asked, then glanced away. 'Not that it's my business, it's just, well…' Her gaze found Lottie's again and this time she jutted out her chin. 'Matt's my brother.'

Lottie gave a silent cheer. Her relationship with Matt might be going backwards but at least he'd achieved what he'd desperately wanted. A close relationship with his sister. 'I've been catching up with Henry while he's been down here, but only as a friend.' She put her hands on the table and leant forward. 'Matt broke things off between us, Amy. He said' – she swallowed, hard, remembering that awful conversation at the beach – 'He said he wanted me to spend time with Henry. See if what we had was still there.'

Amy stared down at her drink. 'Is it a real break, or a pause? You know, like Ross and Rachel had in *Friends*?'

Lottie couldn't help but smile. 'It's a pause.'

'Okay, good. That means you'll get back together again.' She picked at the label on her beer bottle. 'He's been proper happy since he started going out with you.'

Then why is he pushing me away? Lottie didn't understand. Surely if he really wanted her, now would be the time to keep her close, not drive her into the arms of her ex? 'I've been happy since I started dating him, too.' Determined to keep the conversation light, Lottie turned the tables on Amy. 'Speaking of happy, you and Shaun look like the poster couple for happiness.'

Amy giggled. 'He's well nice. I mean, when I first met him I thought he was fit, but knew it. A bit cocky, you know? But now...' She let out a dreamy-sounding sigh. 'I reckon I might be falling in love with him.'

Lottie reached across the table to touch her hand. 'I'm so pleased for you, Amy, and for him. I think you're really good for each other.'

'Yeah?' She blushed. 'I didn't think I stood a chance with him. He's so good-looking, so confident and outgoing. I'm like the total opposite.'

Lottie thought of her and Matt, and then her and Henry. 'Finding the perfect partner doesn't necessarily mean finding your mirror image. I think it's more about balance. You ground him, Amy.'

'And you loosen Matt up, make him, I don't know, more chilled. It's like he was all buttoned up tight and you undid some of those buttons.'

Lottie smiled fondly. 'I did, didn't I?' He hadn't been the only one who'd benefited these last few months, though. She'd always been the chatty blonde, one of the lads. To Matt, she'd been so much more: the electrician he admired, the woman he brought flowers, the person he actually believed could have been a doctor. She'd not been able to look him in the eye when he'd said that, too embarrassed. Yet the very fact that he thought she – the tomboy who'd left school with so little in terms of academic grades – was capable of it had surely proved he'd not just liked her, he'd *respected* her.

So why had he let Henry come between them?

Shaun and Henry arrived back, clearly still in the middle of a heated debate about cars. 'I'm telling you, if I didn't need the space, I'd be driving a Maserati.' Shaun mimicked putting one hand on a steering wheel, his arm nonchalantly resting on an imaginary open window. 'Can you imagine the looks on the faces of the customers when I rolled up to fix their blocked bogs?'

Henry threw back his head and laughed. 'Yeah, really you need an old banger, something that says I'm poor because I don't fleece my customers.' He elbowed Lottie. 'You need to change your van, Lot, it's too fancy.'

'It's not my van. Mine is an old banger. It's stuck in the garage, waiting for when I can afford to pay for a new head gasket.'

'You lease the one you're using now, then? Because that's got to be a waste of money. I can always loan you—'

'No, I'm fine.' Did he not realise how small that made her feel, that he could easily afford to lend her the money, when she was desperately saving up? 'Anyway, I'm not leasing it. The van belongs to Matt.'

Amy snorted. 'Matt's never had a van.'

Lottie carefully put the bottle she'd been about to take a swig out of back down on the table. 'It's the one he used to help you guys move.'

'We came down in his F-Pace. The removal company took all our stuff in their lorry.' She paled and put a hand over her face. 'Oh shit. Now I remember. I wasn't supposed to say anything.'

Lottie felt numb, her brain a mess of mismatching neurones as she tried to make sense of what Amy had let slip.

'Sounds like the good bookshop owner has been telling porkie pies,' Henry drawled.

A chill ran down her spine. So much for respecting her. Matt had lied to her. He'd clearly felt so sorry for her, he'd hired a bloody van. She didn't know whether to be angry, or mortified. Or both.

Clutching her handbag, she jumped to her feet. 'Sorry to bail on you, but I need to get back. My parents have got Chewie and they don't like it when I'm too late.'

Ignoring Henry's protests that it was still early, she strode out of the pub, her mind a hot mess.

'Lottie.' She turned to see Amy had followed her. 'Please don't be cross with him.'

'I'm not – well, not as much as I'm … disappointed.' Disappointed that he'd lied, and that he'd felt the need to lie. 'Also embarrassed.' How much was this blasted van costing him?

Amy pulled at her ponytail. 'He'll have some sappy reason for not wanting you to know.' She looked pleadingly at Lottie. 'He really likes you.'

'Thanks, Amy.' Lottie believed her, but *like* wasn't enough. Not when she'd gone and fallen in love.

Matt was trying to get into his new book – he'd abandoned *The Kiss Quotient*, not wanting to read about someone else's romantic life when his own was in tatters.

A thriller had seemed a better choice, but as good as Louise Candlish's writing was, *The Other Passenger* just wasn't doing it for him right now. He was starting to think dating Lottie had not just ruined him for other women. It had ruined his powers of concentration, too.

The ring on the doorbell was a welcome distraction, and when he saw who it was, his sad heart jumped right into his throat.

'Lottie, this is a surprise. A good surprise,' he qualified, aware the last time he'd spoken to her, she'd accused him of pushing her away. 'Stupendous surprise.' Automatically he reached to cup her face, his need to kiss her a fierce burning in his chest. But then he noticed her eyes were flat, her expression closed off. 'What's wrong?'

'Why did you lie to me about the van?'

Damn it. Heaving out a sigh, he glanced behind her into the road. 'Are you on your own? Where's Amy? I thought you guys were meeting up.'

'We were, until the van came up in conversation. Amy said she didn't realise you had one.'

For a split second he considered lying again, telling her Amy must not have been around when he drove it down, but lies of any sort, even lies intended to protect, to help – like his lie about the van – sounded like a betrayal when they were found out. He couldn't blame Lottie for being mad at him.

He opened the door further. 'Let's not talk about this on the doorstep.'

She was clearly torn, reluctant to come in, but finally she stepped inside, though he could feel the tension vibrating through her body. The same body he yearned to pull into his arms. Given how angry she looked, it was a distinct possibility he'd never be given that honour again.

'Can I get you anything to drink?' he asked as she

perched on the edge of the sofa. Like she was ready to leave the moment she had what she came for.

'I just want an answer, Matt.'

'Yes, of course.' Figuring if he sat next to her she'd jump up, he chose the armchair, lowering himself slowly to give himself time to think. 'I wanted to help.'

'So why lie? Why not be up front with your offer?'

'Because I knew you wouldn't take it.'

'And you'd be right, which only makes what you did feel worse. You knew I wanted to stand on my own two feet, yet you deliberately arranged things so I wouldn't.' She looked away from him, her expression tight. 'It was hard accepting the loan of your van, but I figured as you weren't using it, I wasn't taking too much. Nothing I couldn't compensate you for with a bottle of whisky. But now...' Her voice trailed off and her gaze found his. 'Are you hiring it or...' Her face paled. 'Oh God, did you *buy* it for me?'

He'd thought he was doing the right thing, so why did he suddenly feel so stupid? 'Not directly. I bought it so you could use it.'

She swore. 'Come on, that's the same thing.'

'No, it isn't. When your own van is up and running again, I figured I might keep it for deliveries, like I said.'

She gave a sharp shake of her head, as if she didn't believe him. 'I thought you understood me,' she said quietly, the disappointment in her voice causing a painful twist in his chest. 'I thought you respected me.'

It felt like a weight had landed on him. 'Christ, Lottie. I do respect you.'

'Then why go to these lengths to deceive me? Just because I don't have a degree, didn't leave school with a stack of A Levels and GCSEs, doesn't mean I'm not capable. I don't need handouts.' She drew her hand over her eyes, her voice shaking. 'You've made me feel like a charity case.'

Matt felt sick. How had he managed to cock this up so badly? 'You think I don't know how capable you are? You do things with wires I couldn't begin to attempt, you own your own business and your own home, run a club that has changed the lives of the people who attend it.' He leant forward, arms on his knees, eyes pleading with her to understand. 'You're always helping everyone else. I wanted to do something for you.'

He wanted to do more. Hell, if it was his choice he'd *give* her the van, but he knew her pride wouldn't allow it. He'd hoped this way he could help her while letting her keep her dignity. And he'd failed spectacularly.

'I know your heart was in the right place, but right now I wish I hadn't accepted the offer to borrow it.' Her expression hardened. 'I'll be sure to pay you back what it would have cost me to hire one.'

He exhaled sharply, fighting to control his exasperation. 'Come on, Lottie. Don't be like this. I've got money, not a crazy amount, but enough that I don't need to worry about spending it.'

She smiled sadly. 'But I do.' She rose to her feet. 'No need to show me out. I remember the way.'

His heart plummeted. He was losing her, and maybe not even to Henry. 'Lottie, please.' He reached for her arm and clearly his body didn't realise how precarious their relationship was, because it reacted in all the usual places when his hand touched her skin. 'I can't regret wanting to take some of the stress away from you, but I can regret, deeply, that in doing so I made you feel less about yourself.' Risking a slap, he touched a hand to her face, trailing his finger down her cheek. 'You are so much better, so much more than you give yourself credit for. I see it, my family sees it. Your book club sees it. Your customers must see it.' He smiled though his face felt tight. 'And if your teachers could see you now, they would see it, too.'

Tears streamed down her face and she blinked furiously, pushing his hand away. He wanted to think it was just so she could wipe her wet cheeks, but he couldn't be sure. 'Bugger it, you've turned me into a blubbering mess.'

He allowed his gaze to roam her face, the glistening eyes, wet cheeks, soft lips. 'You're a beautiful blubbering mess.'

'You're lying to me again.'

And though she smiled, he felt the sting of her words and dropped his hand, slipping it into his pocket so he wouldn't be tempted to touch her again. 'Enjoy the rest of your week with Henry.'

'Thanks. I'll see you tomorrow.' He must have looked confused because she added, 'The book club.'

'Yes, of course.' Usually he looked forward to it, sneaking kisses with Lottie before the gang arrived, thinking of ways he could entertain her, entertain them both, when the meeting had finished. But tomorrow she'd be with Henry, and he would have to sit and watch as the man charmed both the club and its leader.

It was an hour later when Amy tapped gently on his bedroom door. He was sat on the bed, nose back in the thriller, head miles away.

'I screwed up, didn't I?' Amy's face was full of apology.

He leapt off the bed and wrapped his arms around his sister. 'No. I was the one who screwed up.'

Amy sighed against him. 'She seemed pretty mad.'

'I'm not sure mad is the right word.' He pictured Lottie's face, and his heart lurched. 'Disappointed. In me.'

'But you were only trying to help her.' Amy looked up at him. 'I mean, buying a van for her, that's proper nice. She can see that, right?'

'I hope she will. In time.' He smiled at his sister with more confidence than he felt.

Later, as he gave up trying to sleep, he stared up at the ceiling and pondered the whole sorry mess. On the surface Lottie was so straightforward compared to him. His miserable time at boarding school, stress from his job, guilt over his marriage and his mum – it had turned him into an insular mess. A man who found it hard to open up to others. Yet he'd forgotten that beneath the surface, Lottie suffered insecurities too. And in forgetting, he'd trampled right over them.

Chapter Twenty-Eight

End-of-August meeting, nominated book:
The Love Square **by Laura Jane Williams**

H er last job had overrun so Lottie was running late. Only half an hour before she was due at the book club, and it took at least twenty minutes to walk there. As she rushed about, dropping food into Chewie's bowl, trying to find her keys, Henry sat on the sofa with his feet on the coffee table.

'Tell me again why we have to go to this book club thing?'

She was losing patience with both the men in her life. She cast a glance over at Chewie, who was wolfing his tea down. Okay, two of the three men in her life.

'Because I run it. Because people depend on me being there.' She spotted the keys on the draining board and snatched them before turning to Henry. 'Because this club is important to me.'

'Okay, okay, message received.' He eased off the sofa. 'It's just we've only got a few nights left. I kind of hoped we'd spend them together.'

'We will be together.' She looked at him pointedly. 'And you'll be meeting my friends. I thought you might want that.'

'Of course I do.' He hesitated. 'But you can meet new friends, set up a new club, if you move to London.'

She looked at him sharply. 'Why would I move?'

He gave her a sheepish grin. 'To be closer to me? Maybe move in with me, if you want.' Before Lottie could say anything – and her brain had just frozen so she wasn't sure what would come out – he strode up to her and gripped her shoulders. 'I know this is too quick. I didn't intend talking about it until Sunday, and I was going to do a way better job than I've just done.' He breathed out, resting his forehead against hers. 'But the fact is, I would love you to move to London, for us to be a couple again. So please, just think about it, yes?'

'What about my business, Henry?'

She felt they'd come full circle. Here they were again, with the same issue.

Except she knew it wasn't just her business that was making her pause.

'I know this might sound totally out there, but London needs electricians too.'

Once again she was the one having to make the sacrifice.

Perhaps that was unfair, because he couldn't be the journalist he wanted to be down here. *He could commute, he could at least try and find a way around the problem without assuming you'll be the one to follow him.*

It wasn't the time for this conversation though, so Lottie rolled her eyes, like he expected, and went to fetch Chewie's lead. 'Come on, we need to get moving.'

'Will Matt be there?' Henry asked as they walked briskly towards the seafront, Chewie almost pulling her along, he was so excited to be out.

'I suspect so.' Why was it her heart always gave a little bump when his name was mentioned? 'He does own the shop.'

'And will you be talking to him?'

'What do you mean?'

'Last night in the pub, you were pissed off with him for lying to you.'

She still was, but the sharpness had worn off. It had the moment he'd made her cry with his kind, insightful words. Now she just longed to go back to the days before Henry's arrival when she and Matt had been so *happy*. He'd never said it out loud, but at times she'd thought he was falling for her, as she was for him. A look from his velvet-brown eyes, a touch, a secret smile meant only for her. More than just a simple *like*, she'd thought. Now she wasn't sure where they stood. He'd insisted he wasn't pushing her away, but she couldn't get past the fact that if it had been his ex back on the scene, she'd have fought tooth and nail for him.

Not taken a step back.

And then there was the matter of the van, of him lying to her. She knew she was being unreasonably sensitive, letting the crap from school still affect her, but how could she be in a relationship with someone where she wasn't considered an equal?

She glanced at Henry, and it was like the final piece of the puzzle suddenly slotted into place. That was why she'd not followed him to the States. He'd loved her, yes, but not as his equal. His career, his needs would always come first.

'Hey, Goldilocks.' His shoulder nudged hers. 'Where did you go?'

'Sorry.' She pushed the thoughts away for another time. 'I was thinking about your question. I'm not angry with Matt, and yes, of course I'll talk to him if he's around.'

'You've not seen him much since I came down.' His blue eyes fixed on hers. 'I hope I've not made things awkward between you.'

Lottie barked out a laugh. 'Come on, be honest. You're really hoping the opposite.'

He grinned. 'Okay, you've got me there.'

They walked in a comfortable silence the rest of the way. When they reached the shop, Lottie was about to push open the door but Henry held her back, reaching for her hand and holding it to his chest. 'About what I said earlier. You need to know what I really want is for you to be happy.' He flashed a smile. 'Obviously I think I'm the best person to help you do that, but if you don't, if you believe Matt or anyone else could make you happier...' His face grew serious, his eyes holding hers. 'That's good with me.'

Her heart tugged and she leant into him. 'Thank you.'

When she turned to open the door, she caught sight of Matt standing by the till. He gave them both a tight smile as they entered. Tight enough for her to know he'd been watching them. 'Welcome. You're the first to arrive.'

Henry sauntered in, eyes skimming round the front of the shop. 'Quaint place you have here.'

'Thanks.'

There was a beat of silence – an uncomfortable beat, at least from Lottie's perspective, though Henry acted as if he wasn't aware of it. 'Must be cool, running your own shop.' He shot Matt an easy smile but she didn't think either man was fooled into thinking they could be friends.

'It has its moments.'

Anxious to get away from the tension, Lottie nodded towards the café. 'We'll get out of your hair.'

'Afternoon, Lottie.' As they reached the café area Jim strolled out from the kitchen. His smile faltered as he noticed the man standing next to her. 'I see you've roped in a new club member.'

By the time she'd made the introductions, Sally had appeared, pushing Freddie in his pram. She was followed by Gira and Heidi, and as Lottie introduced Henry, Audrey entered, puffing her way through the shop to join them.

'Thought I was going to be late. The new bus driver's yet to be persuaded to drop me off where I ask. Says he's not a taxi...' She trailed off as her eyes fell on Henry. 'Well, what do we have here? Another member for the club?' She peered harder. 'Wait, you're not one of those stripagrams, are you? Whose birthday is it?'

Henry laughed, flexing his muscles, which made Audrey cackle with delight.

'This is Henry, Audrey. He's here until the end of the week when he goes back to London.'

'Henry? That fella you used to go out with before our Matt?'

'Yes.' Lottie could feel her cheeks turning red. Trust Audrey to say the words out loud, where the others had simply given her the *we know who Henry is* look. 'He wanted to see the book club in action.'

'Well there's no shortage of action in this club.' Audrey waggled her eyebrows comically.

Henry smiled. 'That's what I heard, hence my request to come and see for myself. Plus she told me I'd be surrounded by beautiful women.' He winked at Audrey. 'Clearly she wasn't wrong.' As Audrey glowed at the compliment, he turned to Lottie. 'By the way, which book are you guys discussing today?'

Unconsciously Lottie glanced over at Matt, who was doing something to the till, possibly because he needed to. Possibly because he was trying to look like he wasn't listening. '*The Love Square*.'

Matt's head shot up, but the moment his eyes found hers, he looked away.

It was Henry who spoke. 'Wow, I've heard of a love triangle, but a square? Is that what I think it is, a woman with three blokes to choose from?'

The Beach Reads Book Club

'Yes.'

Lottie was painfully aware of everyone's gaze ping-ponging between her and Matt, who was now diligently organising the pens on the front desk.

The familiar action made her heart ache.

'Well, this should be fun.' Henry grinned and rubbed his hands together. 'I can't wait to see who she picks.'

'So that's him.'

Matt had been staring so hard at the group in the café, he hadn't realised his dad had come to stand beside him.

'That's who?'

'The famous ex. The reason you've been a right grump this last week.'

Matt forced out a laugh. '*You're* talking to *me* about being grumpy?'

'Less of the cheek.' He stepped forward, eyes not leaving Matt's. 'Why aren't you out there, reminding her she has a choice?'

Matt couldn't hold his gaze. 'Because she loved Henry once.'

'She's not Patricia,' his dad pointed out quietly, and Matt's chest clenched.

True, but who was to say it wouldn't end the same way?

'You're taller than him.'

This time Matt's laugh was more spontaneous. 'Well, that's something.'

'It's a start.' His dad put his hands in his pockets and Matt tensed, familiar with the gesture, as he did the same when he was about to talk about something he found difficult. 'I also know you'll be better for her than him.' His eyes sought Matt's. 'You've got a huge heart, son. You deserve someone special, like Lottie. I'm sure she'll realise that.'

Matt felt a burn at the back of his eyes. 'I don't know how you can say that, not after…' He had to swallow, hard, before he could carry on. 'Not after the way I let Mum down. Let you all down.'

His dad grasped Matt's shoulder. 'I should never have been so hard on you. You had a tough job, stressful. Instead of shaming you for not making it home, I should have thanked you for all the money you sent us over the years.'

Matt glanced away, shame coiling in him. 'I sent money, but that wasn't what you wanted, was it?'

His dad sighed, releasing his grip on Matt's shoulder. 'It wasn't as important to us as it seemed to you, no. But you had your reasons for that, so don't be too tough on yourself.' The words, the look he gave Matt, made him wonder if his dad knew about the bullying. Then he didn't have to wonder, because his dad gave him a wry smile. 'You think we couldn't guess what happened at that school, a boy like you mixing with all those rich kids? Me and your mother, we were so pleased when you got that scholarship. Thought we were doing right, sending you there. Figured it would give you the start in life we never had.'

'It did.'

'Aye, happen it did. But at a cost.' His face softened. 'You should know your mother never complained. Not once. She was just grateful to see you when she did.' His throat tightened and Matt felt his eyes well. But his dad hadn't finished. 'She'd be damn proud of how you've helped your sister, and me, this past year or so.'

That was it. He couldn't carry on this conversation, not without sobbing his heart out, and there was no way he was doing that in the shop. Not with Henry liable to see him.

Turning away from his dad, Matt rubbed his eyes with the heel of his hand.

'You keep any alcohol in that office of yours?'

Matt let out a strangled laugh, grateful for the change in topic. 'I've an eighteen-year-old Macallan, if that's any good.'

'It'll do.' His dad chuckled. 'Beats Audrey's gin.'

They headed to the back of the shop and sat in an amicable silence for a while, knocking back the whisky – well, his dad did the knocking back. Matt savoured the drink, as the distiller intended. That was twice already this week the whisky had come out. Henry's arrival was turning him into an alcoholic.

Just as he was about to pour another glass, he heard a howl.

His dad winced. 'Something's upset Chewie.'

Matt listened harder. 'I've not heard him make a noise like that since the time I whistled.' Immediately he jumped up from his chair. 'Sorry, I—'

His dad waved him away. 'Go. Don't worry about me.'

He reached for the bottle and poured another measure into his glass.

'It's not you I'm worried about. It's the £200 it'll cost me to replace the bottle.'

His dad spluttered, as Matt had known he would, and as he walked away he could hear him muttering, *Bloody ridiculous* followed by *A man could buy thirty bottles of Bell's for that.*

When he made it to the café, he found Lottie trying to calm a trembling Chewie, and Sally trying to soothe a clearly distressed Freddie.

It was Amy, dashing back from the kitchen with a mop in her hand, who spoke to him. 'We were talking about best love-triangle books and then Henry started whistling the theme tune to *The Notebook*.'

'Didn't realise it would set the dude off.' Henry shuddered as he watched Amy wield the mop over the puddle of pee. 'Lottie says the same thing happened to you.'

His gaze caught hers over the top of Chewie. She looked harassed, but also *upset*, just as she had when she'd entered the shop. He'd figured it was because he'd caught her and Henry clearly having a moment – and yes, what a heart crusher that had been to witness – but now he wondered if she just wished he wasn't there at all.

All this talk of love triangles must be mortifying for her.

'Yes, I had the misfortune to whistle in Chewie's presence,' he confirmed, aware Henry was still waiting for an answer. Then he glanced round the group, his eyes resting finally on Lottie's again. 'Is there anything I can do to help?'

Lottie shook her head and once again he had that gut-wrenching feeling that he was in the way. The guy who'd embarrassed her with his over-the-top van purchase, then lied about it. The guy she'd slept with for a while until her real love had come back.

'You could weave your magic with Freddie.' Sally, hugging a still fretting Freddie, smiled in his direction and he could have sworn she knew exactly how unwelcome he felt. 'I'm sure he'll settle if you could push him in his buggy along the prom.' She glanced at Chewie. 'I suspect Chewie would appreciate getting out for a bit, too.'

'Sure.' He glanced at Lottie. Old Lottie, the one before the van saga, before Henry, would have beamed at him in gratitude. This Lottie could only manage a stiff smile.

'That might help, if you don't mind.' She stood and reached for Chewie's lead, waving it at him. 'Walk with Matt?'

Chewie stopped shaking and gave a rather lacklustre wag of his tail.

Freddie bawled his eyes out when Sally strapped him into his buggy.

Looked like both Matt's charges were as happy as he was.

When Lottie handed him Chewie's lead, her eyes didn't quite meet his. 'Don't force it. Come back if he's dragging on the lead.'

'Of course.' He obviously wasn't as good as he'd

thought at hiding his irritation, because she flinched.

The weight already pushing down his shoulders, intensified.

Anxious to get out of the shop, away from the tension, the speculative glances, Matt set off towards the door.

'Wait, I'll walk out with you.' Sally's voice forced him to slow, to remember belatedly that he was meant to be taking Freddie, too.

When they were outside, Sally studied him. 'What's happened between you and Lottie? And I don't mean Henry's arrival, though I imagine that's been hard on you. There's something else, a reason she's looking so sad today.'

Weighed down by misery, he stared out at the sea. 'Amy let slip about the van.'

'Crap. I can imagine how well that went down, she's so damn prickly about receiving help. Wants to do everything herself.'

He turned to look at her. 'She needs to prove she can,' he countered.

Suddenly Sally's face softened and she patted his cheek. 'And that's why I'm on team Matt. You appreciate her, but more than that, you *get* her. Henry never did.' She nodded down to Freddie. 'You sort my son out and I'll regain you a few Brownie points.'

Matt couldn't see how that was possible, but he smiled anyway, appreciating the gesture. 'Thanks, I need all the points I can get.'

She touched his hand. 'Don't you worry. The Beach Reads Book Club has your back.'

Chapter Twenty-Nine

Back at the café, Lottie slumped onto her chair, exhausted. The tension with Matt, trying to keep a smile on her face despite the ache in her heart, then Chewie getting upset. This was one book club meeting she actually wanted to forget.

'So, memo to self, don't whistle in front of Chewie.' Henry chuckled into the silence that followed Sally walking out with Matt.

'Yes, sorry, I forgot to warn you.' Amy wandered back from the kitchen and Lottie gave her an apologetic smile. 'And really sorry you got stuck with mopping it up, Amy.'

The last time it had happened, Matt had offered to mop, she remembered.

'It's fine.' Amy slipped back onto her seat, but like everyone tonight, she, too, seemed on edge.

Lottie wondered if it was because Henry was here, or if they'd picked up on her own tension. 'Let's get back to the book, shall we? What did you think of Penny's love choices?'

'I liked Francesco.' Gira sipped at her gin. 'Thomas was too glib for me, all style over substance.'

Was it her imagination or had Gira just aimed a pointed look in Henry's direction?

Henry, clearly oblivious, was rummaging around in his pocket. 'Sorry, I've got a buzzing in my trousers.' He flashed a grin as he pulled his phone out and looked at the screen. 'Ah, my new boss. Better take this.'

He loped off, phone to his ear, and almost collided with Sally in the doorway as he headed out while she was coming in.

Lottie knew it wasn't her imagination as she felt the tension in the room ebb away. 'Well, now he's out of earshot...' Audrey turned to her. 'Time to tell us why you and our Matt can barely look at each other.'

Since when had he become *our* Matt, she wondered? 'I don't know what you're talking about,' she started to argue, but was cut off by Sally.

'I do.' Sally came to sit back on her chair. 'Aside from the obvious which-guy-will-she-pick thing going on, Lottie's got the hump with Matt because he lent her his van.'

'Now hang on, that's not fair.' Lottie looked daggers at her friend. 'Matt told me he had a van he could lend me.'

'Which was true, wasn't it?'

She didn't like the way her supposed friend was turning this round. 'He didn't have a van when he promised it,' she said tightly. 'He lied to me.'

'But only so he could help. So we could all help,' Heidi added, glancing round the group until she stopped at Audrey. 'Maybe Audrey should explain. She was the one who called the Beach Reads Book Club extraordinary general meeting.'

Lottie's jaw fell open. 'You had a meeting without me?'

'Now don't get your knickers in another twist.' Audrey, who was sitting next to her, patted Lottie's hand. 'We wanted to do something to make your life better, just as you've done for every one of us.' She narrowed her eyes at Lottie. 'Matt wanted to give the van to you, but he knew you wouldn't accept it, so while you were borrowing it, we all did a bit of fundraising so you could get your old van fixed.'

'I baked cakes which Amy sold through the shop.' Heidi smiled at her. 'Trust me, it wasn't a hardship.'

'The shop raffled off tickets for a social media consult with me,' Gira added. 'It worked out really well because I ended up getting calls from people who hadn't won, but wanted to use me anyway.'

'Shaun auctioned a morning of his time,' Amy piped up, then smiled shyly. 'And I offered to help him hold his toolbox.'

'That's not what they called it back in my day.' Audrey chuckled. 'Now where were we? Oh yes, Sally, you sold off some of Freddie's old baby outfits, if this old brain of mine remembers correctly.'

'And I helped put some of your ... what's a polite word for old junk?' Sally winked at Audrey. 'Let's call it clutter, shall we?' She turned to Lottie. 'You'd be amazed what people paid for it on eBay.'

'I ... I don't know what to say.' Lottie's mind raced, stuck between embarrassment that they'd had to do this for her, and wonder that they'd pulled it off behind her back.

'Before you grumble, it's not charity,' Audrey added. 'It's a thank-you for being the heart of our club.'

Oh God. She felt traitorous tears start to spill down her cheeks. Already on an emotional precipice, she was embarrassingly close to blubbing in front of them all. 'I'm speechless.' She fumbled around for a tissue, then gave Audrey a wobbly smile as the older woman thrust a napkin under her nose.

'That'll be a first.' Sally grinned at her. 'If only it had happened at school, we might have escaped all those hours in detention.'

'I want to be cross with you all for plotting behind my back.' Lottie wiped her eyes. 'And I'm definitely embarrassed you had to do all that, just so I could pay a bill.'

'We didn't *have* to do anything.' Audrey fixed her with a steely stare. 'Everyone needs help in life from time to time. I was lonely.' She paused and looked at Gira.

'I was losing my husband.'

Heidi smiled. 'I didn't have a purpose.'

'I would have gone nuts with just me and Freddie all day, every day,' Sally added.

'I was so shy I could barely talk to any of you.' A flush

bloomed on Amy's cheeks. 'Plus, you introduced me to Shaun.'

'And now we can't shut her up talking about him,' Audrey added dryly, though she shot Amy a look full of fondness. 'So young Lottie, are you saying we should be embarrassed that you helped us?' Audrey didn't give her the chance to reply. 'Of course we shouldn't. We're bloody grateful, that's what, so just you be bloody grateful back, and we're all quits.'

Lottie's chest felt tight, her throat chock-full of emotion. 'Okay, okay.' She gazed round at the group. More than a book club, they'd become a support group ... no, more than that, even. They'd become firm friends. 'I *am* bloody grateful, and not just for the money.' She patted her eyes again. 'I'm grateful to have friends that look out for me.' For a moment her mind flashed to Matt, the person who'd started all this. The one who'd only lied to her because he'd known she wouldn't accept the help otherwise.

'Hear, hear.' Audrey raised her glass, then realised it was empty, so she snatched up the bottle and slopped a measure into each of their glasses. 'To the Beach Reads Book Club and all who join it.' There was a murmur of agreement, a clinking of glasses.

'I see Audrey's got the gin out again.'

Lottie looked over Amy's shoulder to find Jim smiling at them.

He shook his head when Heidi offered him a glass. 'I'm full of ridiculously expensive Macallan.'

His eyes rested on Lottie and she tried to read what he

was thinking, but like his son, Jim didn't give much away. 'If you're looking for Matt, he's taken Chewie and Freddie out for a walk.'

'Right, thanks. Tell him I headed off home.'

As she watched him walk towards the door, she knew she couldn't leave it at that. 'Jim, wait.' Excusing herself from the group, she dashed over to him. 'Are you upset with me?'

He frowned. 'Why on earth would I be?'

'Matt tried to help me, and I was ungrateful.' She glanced out of the window, watching the seagulls fighting over somebody's discarded chips. 'I thought he might have said something.'

'He didn't.' Jim hesitated. 'I only know he was happy a few weeks ago. Now he's not.'

Lottie drew in a breath as pain arrowed through her. 'Nothing feels right between us anymore. That guard he always wore, the one I managed to push down. It's shot back up again.'

Jim shoved his hands in his pockets. 'Did he tell you his wife had an affair?'

'Yes. I'm not sleeping with Henry, if that's what you're getting at,' she added quickly, annoyed he would think that. 'He's just a friend.'

Jim made a dismissive noise. 'That's none of my business.'

Lottie followed the direction of his gaze and saw that he was watching Henry slip his phone back in his pocket and start to walk back towards the shop.

'If you want to know why my son's guard is back, ask him who his ex-wife had the affair with.'

———————————————

Matt halted a few yards away from the shop and peered over the top of the buggy, expecting to find Freddie asleep, he'd been so quiet. But no, he was wide awake, taking in the world around him.

'Well, he seems to have forgotten all about the scary dog barking.' Matt glanced down at Chewie, who stared back up at him with his expressive brown eyes. 'How about you? Forgotten about the scary man whistling?' Chewie barked, and Matt nodded. 'Okay, point taken, you don't find him scary. Must just be me.'

Henry frightened him because he threatened to come between him and the woman he'd fallen head over heels in love with. Matt didn't know how he could dust himself off and carry on if Lottie went back to her ex.

Yet, in an act of extreme cowardice, he'd not even told her how he felt. She'd never know she'd broken his heart.

Maybe that was just as well. He knew how guilt could weigh a person down, squeeze the joy out of life. He didn't want that happening to Lottie. Didn't want her light dimming because she felt bad about hurting him.

He stared into the café as he walked past, and jealousy bit as he saw Henry holding court. Whatever tale he was telling, it had everyone listening and laughing.

He'd never been that guy, the one who could tell

amusing anecdotes, who could sit easily in a group of people he'd never met before.

Yet Lottie had dated him anyway, he reminded himself as he wedged the door open so he could manoeuvre the buggy inside.

'Wow, you handle that like a pro.' Sally dashed towards him, arms outstretched as she bent to release Freddie from his straps. 'And you've quietened this little monster.'

Matt glanced over his shoulder at the group, who were talking amongst themselves. 'Are we still trying for the Brownie points? Because extolling my childminding skills feels like scraping the bottom of the barrel. And nobody appears to be listening.'

Sally burst out laughing. 'The Brownie points are in the bag, mister. I've thrown the childminding thing in free of charge.'

'What Brownie points?'

They both turned to find Lottie walking towards them.

'I told Matt I'd try and get him back into your good books and I did, didn't I? You've forgiven him for the van thing.' She looked between them. 'Okay, so this is my cue to leave you both to it. I'll wind the meeting up while you guys kiss and make up.'

He watched Sally carry Freddie back to the café, nerves making knots in his stomach. Then he turned back to Lottie, swallowing as he slid his hands into his pockets. 'So.'

A glimmer of a smile tugged at her mouth. 'So.'

God, he wanted to hold her so much, he ached. 'Sally thinks we should kiss.'

The smile broke out in full. 'Sally was always a bad influence.'

Their gazes collided and there was more than amusement in hers. There was a spark, a light that caused hope to seep into his chest. Dangerous, yet desperately needed. 'Are we okay?'

She nodded, and the hope expanded. 'I'm sorry I was such a prickly cow.'

His lips twitched. 'I believe that's the remit of hedgehogs, or porcupines. Not bovines.'

'I can be pricklier than both when it comes to receiving help.' Her eyes fluttered closed for a second, and when she opened them again, they stared straight into his. 'Thank you for caring enough to buy the van so you could lend it to me.'

'Always.' He reached for her hand and squeezed it between his, hoping she could feel the strength of his love through his fingers. 'I will always be here for you.' Her eyes glistened, and his own started to prick. Christ, that was twice in an hour he'd almost cried. 'There are things I need to say,' he added quietly, the weight of his unspoken feelings pressing heavily on his chest.

She stared down at their entwined hands. 'Henry goes back on Sunday.'

Though it hurt him to say it, Matt knew he had no choice. He'd pushed her into Henry's arms. Now he had to face the consequences. 'Next week then.'

She released her hands and gave him a tremulous smile. 'Yes.'

Over her shoulder he saw everyone get to their feet. Amy gathered the glasses to take through to the kitchen. Heidi and Gira pushed the chairs back to where they belonged. Audrey put the gin bottle back in her bag.

Henry strode towards them.

'You ready to head off?' he asked Lottie.

Matt flinched as Henry placed an arm around her shoulders. Would he ever have another chance to put *his* arms around her?, he thought, the panic returning. Or would everything he had to say, be too late?

'Thank you for taking Chewie out,' Lottie said softly.

Belatedly he glanced down to find Chewie sitting placidly next to him. He'd not growled when he'd held Lottie's hand, Matt realised. Was that a good sign? 'No problem. I think he's getting used to me.'

'Old Chewie been causing you problems, has he?' Henry ruffled Chewie's ears. 'Funny, he's always been fine with me.'

Okay, so the swords were coming out. 'Maybe he doesn't see you as a threat.'

The remark bounced off Henry. 'Nah, I think he just likes me best.'

Matt had to hand it to the guy, his self-confidence was impressive. 'It's what Lottie thinks that I'm more interested in.'

When he risked a glance at her he saw she was staring at him wide-eyed, a flush on her cheek. One look over her shoulder and he could see why. He and Henry weren't just posturing in front of her. They were doing it front of everyone.

'Right, well, we should go.' She turned, presenting her back to him, and he didn't know whether it was a deliberate slight, or a way to say goodbye to the others.

It seems he was destined to keep cocking up his relationship with her.

As they filed out, Gira and Heidi gave him a sympathetic smile and Sally touched his arm in a sweet gesture. When Audrey reached him, she rose up on tiptoes and gave him a smacker of a kiss on his cheek. 'Don't let the bugger win,' she whispered into his ear, though of course this was Audrey, so it was loud enough for Amy, who was standing next to her, to hear. And snigger.

'I'll try not to.'

'Audrey's just saying that because she likes working here,' Amy remarked, smirking.

'There is that.' Audrey patted his cheek. 'But this old woman would choose tall, dark, brooding and sincere every time.'

When they'd all gone, Matt closed the door and leant against it, tiredness seeping all the way to his bones.

In an act of sibling solidarity, Amy moved to stand next to him, mirroring his stance. 'It'll work out okay. Lottie's smart, she'll see through Henry.'

'See through him? Don't you like him?'

'Nah. I mean, he's okay, but he's all about himself.' She nudged him with her elbow. 'You're so much nicer, it's not even a competition.'

Touched, he kissed the top of her head. 'Dad says I'm taller.'

Amy giggled. 'Yeah, that, too.'

And though his heart still ached, his chest felt a little less tight at the sound of his sister's laughter.

Chapter Thirty

It was Friday afternoon and Lottie had finished her last job early. As she climbed back in the van – the one Matt had bought for her but knew she'd be too proud to accept – she made sure Chewie was settled before reaching for her phone. She needed to clear her muddled head.

Sally answered on the first ring.

'Wow, usually I have to wait for ever for you to pick up.'

'Yeah, well, usually I'm mid nappy change, or sponging pureed food off my shirt, or trying to tiptoe out of Freddie's room without him waking up.' There was the sound of movement, followed by a squeak and a gorgeous baby giggle. 'Today you caught me on a rare occasion when Freddie's happy playing with his baby gym, and I was about to do some online window shopping for clothes I don't need, but believe I deserve because I'm finally back to my pre-Freddie weight.'

'You totally deserve them.' Lottie fiddled with the bottle of water she kept in the drinks holder. 'Have you time for a quick visit, or will that interrupt the shopping splurge?'

'I always have time for visitors. I'll splurge later when Freddie's in bed and Paul's watching TV. He'll think I'm trawling through Facebook.'

Five minutes later Lottie was sat on Sally's cream leather sofa – cream because Sally had wanted class, apparently. Leather so she could easily wipe off baby goo.

'Is this an I've-finished-early-and-fancy-a-chat visit,' Sally asked as she handed her a mug of tea, 'or is it a counselling session? And FYI, I'm hoping it's the latter because this love triangle you've got going on is way more exciting than anything on the TV right now.'

Lottie wanted to laugh, but everything felt too much, her emotions too heavy. Whatever Sally saw in her face made her sit down next to her and reach for her hand. 'Damn, it never was a real love triangle, was it?'

Lottie shook her head, aware tears were creeping down her face.

Sensing her unhappiness, Chewie shoved his wet nose into her hands. Lottie dropped a grateful kiss on his head. 'Life would be simpler if it was just you and me, huh?'

'But there's the dog-breath problem when you kiss,' Sally remarked dryly. Then she sighed. 'Yesterday was a bit awkward, wasn't it? In hindsight, *The Love Square* wasn't the best choice.'

'No.' She rubbed Chewie's ears. 'It was a good book though.'

'And it had a lovely ending,' Sally reminded her. 'So maybe we should focus on that. Henry's here for a few more days, yes?'

'That's the plan. I've promised to make him lasagne tonight.' She reached for a tissue from the coffee table and wiped her cheeks. 'It's always been a bit of a joke between us, because I make it too sloppy. He calls it my lasagne soup.'

'Don't tell Gordon Ramsay, he'll put it on his menu.' Sally studied her, eyes brimming with sympathy. 'How can I help?'

'I don't know. I guess I just wanted to talk to someone. My brain feels so ... overloaded somehow. I'm scared I'm not thinking clearly.'

'That's because the brain shouldn't be involved when it comes to falling in love.'

'I know, but God, Sally, this is Henry, the guy I loved for years, the one I thought I was going to marry. And he loves me. He wants me to go to London with him, and I know if I do I'll be okay, because I was happy before with him, so I can be again.' She drew a breath, let all her jumbled thoughts flood out. 'But it's also Matt, the too-serious, way-too-complicated man I met only a few months ago, and, hell, I didn't even like him at first.' She dabbed at her eyes and looked sadly at her friend. 'I don't know what he wants from me, though actually it's worse than that. It's likely I'll never know because he doesn't talk about his feelings like Henry does.'

Sally smiled. 'He is dark and mysterious, isn't he?'

'Apparently that's what his ex-wife thought, but there are reasons he's like that, good reasons that help explain him, and when you know, you fall for him that little bit more.' She scrunched up the tissue, smiling briefly when Chewie tried to lick her face. 'But now he's shut me out and I don't know if he even wants to let me back in.'

'When you say shut you out, what do you mean?'

'I mean he's put us on pause, insisting I spend time with Henry. Something about owing it to myself to get to know Henry again. See if we still have feelings for each other. But who does that to someone they're supposed to be in a relationship with?'

'Maybe he was trying to be honourable?'

'It felt like he couldn't be bothered fighting for me.'

Sally shook her head. 'The man I saw having a ding-dong with Henry yesterday was definitely fighting. Just without the blood and fisticuffs.'

Lottie groaned and put her head in her hands. 'God, that was *so* embarrassing. I didn't know where to look.'

'Yeah, but come on, it was also a bit funny, wasn't it? Henry sort of suggesting he was the best choice because Chewie thought so, and Matt all steely-eyed and tight-jawed, declaring it was what you thought that mattered.'

'He's really good at that,' Lottie admitted. 'Making sure to ask me what I think. Not assuming anything.' Suddenly she remembered something else from yesterday. 'Jim said a funny thing to me just before that whole the-dog-prefers-me exchange. He said if I wanted to know why Matt had been so distant, I should ask him who his ex-wife had an affair with.'

Sally screwed up her face. 'That's weird. Why would it matter? It's not like you knew them back then.'

'That's what I thought.' Suddenly Lottie noticed the time. 'Shit, I need to get moving. I've got a house to tidy, myself to clean and a ruddy meal to make.'

'You forgot the bit about putting clean sheets on the bed.' Sally smirked. 'Or do you like things dirty these days, now you're juggling various men?'

Lottie did what only best friends could do without offence: she gave Sally the middle finger. Then she darted out of the house, Chewie loping after her.

'Call me,' Sally yelled after her. 'I want to know how the love triangle ends.'

'There is no flaming triangle,' Lottie muttered as she climbed into the van with Chewie. But as she thought of tonight, of the conversation she was going to have with Henry, butterflies started to flap in her belly. There might not be a triangle, but there were three humans, which meant three sets of complicated feelings to take into account.

Matt had just locked up and was about to sort out the tills when he heard a knock on the window.

He turned to find Gira indicating for him to let her in.

'Sorry I'm so late,' she said once he'd opened the door. 'I'd hoped to get here before closing, but life got in the way.'

'No problem. Books by the Bay is always open to our favourite customers.'

She eyed him from beneath her dark lashes. 'That's a charming thing to say.'

'Is it?'

She nodded, smiling. 'Owning this shop is starting to suit you.'

He winced. 'Does that mean I was awful before?'

'Not awful, no, but, well, the jacket and ties were a bit much.'

He glanced down at his shirt and dark blue jeans. 'Lottie and Amy gave me stick about them.'

'You seem more relaxed now. Like you've grown into the job.'

He considered her words. 'I've not really thought about it, but you're right. Standing here doesn't feel new anymore. It feels right.'

'My friend at the school says you're working with them on a project trying to get teenagers to read more.'

He rocked back on his heels. 'I am.'

Gira laughed. 'You look surprised. Obviously you've not rid yourself of all your big-city mentality. People in small towns talk. They know your business.'

'I'm forewarned, thank you. Speaking of business, how can I help?'

She averted her eyes, and for a split second looked uncomfortable. 'Um, I came to buy the book for the next meeting. The Suzanne Brockmann one, *Gone Too Far*.'

'Yes, of course.' He turned to take one from the pile he'd ordered the moment Lottie had messaged him with the next book club title. 'I was surprised by this, as it's been out for a while now. You usually choose more current titles.'

'Lottie requested we read this one. It's a favourite of hers, from *The Troubleshooters* series.' Gira paused, taking the book he handed over. 'It's about a couple who share an intense relationship, but things don't go smoothly for them. Lottie says she loves it because the hero, Sam, has a really sharp wit, and the heroine, Alyssa, is ... how does Lottie put it? ... kick-ass strong.' Gira looked up at him. 'The thing Lottie says she loves most about the book is that despite everything that is thrown at them, they manage to find their way back to each other.'

Was Gira trying to give him a message? 'It sounds like a good read. Hopeful.'

'Yes. I'm looking forward to diving into it.'

Again she hesitated, and because he sensed a similar, introverted, private soul, Matt suddenly realised she'd come to see him, not really to pick up the book.

'Was there anything else? You and Ryan...' He trailed off, wondering how on earth to ask the personal question. 'Is everything okay?'

Gira's face relaxed. 'You look about as uncomfortable as I've just been feeling. Everything is good, thank you. Really good. Ryan admitted he was trying so hard to be one of the guys at work, to fit in, he lost sight of what was important. Now he's working on a better balance.' Silence. While Matt struggled to find something to say, Gira broke it with a huff of soft laughter. 'And now you're wondering what I'm doing, still standing here instead of slipping off, now I've got my book.' She glanced down at it and gave him an ironic smile. 'That same book we both know you would have popped through my letter box, as usual.' For the last few months, he'd been delivering the book club's books, as everyone lived locally.

'I confess, I am curious, yes.' A knot formed in his stomach as he saw the indecision on her face. 'Whatever you have to say to me, it might be easier on us both if you do it quickly.'

'Like ripping off a Band-Aid?' She smoothed a strand of her long dark hair back behind her ear. 'Sorry, I'm clearly making this worse by not just coming out and saying it, but the truth is, I've been in two minds whether to interfere. Your relationship with Lottie is your business. Then again, my marriage was my business, but if it hadn't been for the interference of Lottie, the book club, of *you*, it might still be on the rocks.'

Automatically he took a mental step back. It had been hard enough talking to Amy, to his dad. He couldn't do this with Gira. 'Look, I appreciate you coming, but...' He trailed off, not wanting to sound rude.

'Butt out?'

'I was trying for something more polite.'

'I know.' She smiled. 'You and I, we're similar. We don't open up easily, don't make friends easily. But I took that risk with Lottie, with the rest of the book club, and I don't regret it for a moment. I'd like to include you in that circle of friends.' Her dark eyes held his. 'As your friend, I thank you for helping me fight for my love. And I urge you to fight for yours.'

As he absorbed the words, he had an immediate urge to defend himself, to argue that Lottie wasn't his to fight over. Whether she wanted him, or Henry, or neither of them, it was her choice. And yet … could she make that choice if she didn't have all the facts? If she didn't know how he felt? Maybe it wouldn't make any difference, but Gira was right, if he didn't at least try, if he didn't take that risk and open up to her, was he even worthy of her in the first place?

'I can see I've made you think, which is all I wanted to achieve.' She lifted up the book. 'Thank you for this, and for listening. I hope everything works out for you, as it did for me.'

In a daze, he unlocked the door and watched her slip out. She was nearly round the corner when he managed to shake himself out of his stupor for long enough to shout out her name. When she turned, he nodded. 'Thank you.'

She smiled. 'Good luck.'

He was going to need every damn ounce of it, he realised as he slid the locks back into place. With Patricia, he'd never had that heads up, never realised his relationship was in danger until it was too late. With Lottie, he'd known Henry was coming, yet he'd pulled away when he should have been holding on tight.

Damn it, he should have told her how much she meant to him.

Instead, he'd made her feel unwanted. He'd like to bet Henry was, right now, not being stupid enough, or cowardly enough, to make such a colossal mistake.

Chapter Thirty-One

The following morning, for the first time since he'd taken over Books by the Bay, Matt didn't want to be there. He was in the stockroom, sorting through the latest delivery, but his thoughts, his mind, his heart, were all with Lottie.

He'd made his mind up last night. As soon as the shop closed, he was going round to see her. He knew it was her last evening with Henry, but telling her how he felt before Henry went back now seemed hugely important.

Acutely aware he'd waited too long, he was finally going to come out fighting.

'Oh, fudging, fiddling … fiddlesticks.'

He was so lost in his head, the words made him jump. Smiling, he put down the books. Having Audrey in the shop meant he was never bored.

He found her on her knees by the till, surrounded by pens that had scattered across the floor. 'Which colour was it you wanted again?' She picked up a pen and waved it at a bemused young man. 'Green?'

'Err, black, actually.' The customer hunkered down and began to help her put the pens back into the pot. At which point Audrey grasped the counter and hauled herself upright.

'Right, when you find a black one, give it to me and I'll pop it in a bag.' Matt didn't know whether to laugh or cry when she added, 'And while you're down there, be a love and see if there are any stray rubbers lying about. I knocked them over last week.' She let out one of her lusty chuckles. 'And by "rubbers" I don't mean the things you young folk buy from vending machines in gents' toilets.'

The customer gave her a shocked look, but just as Matt felt he ought to step in and prevent any further embarrassment, the man laughed. 'Sure. Anything for you, Aud.'

Matt watched, mesmerised, as the young guy slotted all the pens back into the holder, placed a couple of errant rubbers on the counter, and gave Audrey a huge hug before walking out clutching a small paper bag.

'He's my friend's grandson.' When Audrey turned to face Matt, he was surprised to find her eyes had misted over. 'The lad's so like her, it's uncanny. Same green eyes, same naughty laugh.' She sighed. 'I miss the old dear something rotten, but it's nice to see her family are still around.' She shuffled back to perch on the stool he'd placed for her behind the counter. "Course, I wouldn't have seen him if I hadn't been working here, so I've you to thank for that.'

He smiled. 'And I've you to thank for—'

'Knocking the pens over. Losing the rubbers.' She groaned. 'Blimey O'Reilly, I forgot to get the scallywag to pay for the ruddy pen, so you can add that to the list.'

'Actually, I was going to say I've you to thank for brightening my day.'

It might have been his imagination, but he thought her eyes misted over again.

Just then, the door clattered open.

'I'm glad I've found you both.' Heidi breezed into the shop carrying two bags loaded with cakes for the café. 'Have either of you spoken to Lottie today? I phoned on the way here to let her know I'd heard from Eve, and I thought Lottie sounded upset. She denied it, said she was fine, but I just had this feeling everything wasn't as okay as she said it was. Then again, it may have been the shock of what I had to say. I mean, Eve wanting to join our next book club meeting? That's enough to throw anyone off their game.'

Matt didn't hear any of the words Heidi said after the words *Lottie* and *upset*.

The urge to run out and keep on running until he made it to her house was so powerful, he took a step towards the door. But then he found his control. He couldn't just leave Audrey in the lurch.

'Go.' Audrey was watching him, her cloudy blue eyes seeing far more than people half her age did. 'We'll rope Jim in. Heidi can help me and Amy hold the fort until he gets here.'

Heidi nodded. 'Absolutely.'

For a split second he simply stood and stared at them. To support him against Henry was one thing, but this felt deeper. As with Gira yesterday, and Sally the day before, it felt like they weren't just doing this for Lottie, they were doing this for *him*. That, for the first time in his life, he belonged to a gang. 'Are you sure?'

'We're sure,' they both spoke at once.

He didn't ask again. Didn't even check to make sure Audrey knew his dad's number. He ran.

Ten minutes later, he arrived on Lottie's doorstep and rang the bell. His heart hammered away in his chest but it had nothing to do with the short run. Was Henry there now? Was he upsetting Lottie?

Unconsciously his hands balled into fists.

He heard Chewie bark, then a moment later Lottie opened the door. His chest twisted as he saw the red of her eyes, the damp on her cheeks. 'What is it? What's wrong?'

She shook her head. 'Nothing, not really.' Dragging a tissue from her pocket, she wiped her eyes. 'Henry's just left.'

His fists tightened. 'Is that why you're crying? Did he say something?'

'What?' His face must have betrayed his thoughts because she raised her eyes to the ceiling. 'God, Matt, you're being ridiculous. Henry didn't cause this meltdown, at least not intentionally. I'm upset because he left to go back to London.'

He reared back, feeling as if he'd been sucker punched, the blood, the life, draining from him. 'I see.'

And he did. He saw his chance at happiness, true, real happiness, slip from his grasp. He saw a lifetime of regret, of loneliness. Of never finding anyone who would come close to giving him what Lottie had: joy, laughter, warmth. Compassion, understanding and wild, hot sex.

Fuck.

His chest crumpled, his knees buckled and he had a feeling he would have sagged to the ground had Chewie not chosen that moment to come up to him and lick his hand.

'Hey.' Now the mutt chose to like him.

'I've just realised, you should be in the shop.' Lottie peered at him closely. 'What are you doing here?'

'Heidi said you sounded upset on the phone.' It didn't explain why he'd legged it there like a madman. *Tell her,* he told himself. *Even though it's too late, BLOODY TELL HER!*

'And you came running, thinking Henry had, what? Hurt me? Had a row with me?' She let out a strangled laugh. 'Oh God, Heidi must have got her wires crossed. I'm sorry it's been a wasted journey.'

'It hasn't.' He allowed his eyes to drink her in. The familiar blonde curls, the freckles, the beauty of her grey eyes. 'How could it be, when I got to see you?'

Lottie's heart began to pound as she became the focus of Matt's deep-brown gaze. What was he doing here? And how could she stop this awful hope now stirring in her chest?

Slowly she became aware that he was still standing on her doorstep. 'Do you want to come in?'

'Please.'

There was silence as she led him into her lounge. Silence as he sat on the sofa, not sprawled and laid back like Henry but upright, arms resting on his thighs. Tense.

He coughed, and the sound ricocheted around the silent room. 'I thought Henry wasn't going back until tomorrow.'

'He wasn't. But then he changed his mind.' She'd known, after the conversation last night, that Henry wouldn't stick around for another day. Not when he'd heard what she had to say.

Matt swallowed and looked down at his hands, jaw muscle jumping. 'When will you see him again?'

'I ... I don't know.' She thought they both needed some space. Last night had been hard, she'd hated hurting him, but the reality was, though she did love Henry, she was no longer *in love* with him. Her heart had belonged to Matt the moment he'd stood on her doorstep with yellow roses in his hand. Or maybe even before that, when he'd eaten her unhealthy picnic without complaint. Or when she'd taken the mickey about his pen arranging and he'd quietly explained he'd done it ever since he'd been bullied as a child. Actually, maybe even before that, on the beach after the windsurfing, when he'd looked so appalled at having said 'Fuck' out loud, then kissed her with an intensity that had astonished her.

So many facets, so many parts of him she could find to love. If only he'd let her.

Matt drew in a breath, the cotton of his shirt tightening across his chest, outlining his pecs. *Ogling him now is not appropriate.*

'I'm terrified I might be too late, but there are things I need to say.' His gaze pressed hers, dark, intense. Impossible to look away from. 'I know he saw you first. I know you loved him. But he let you go.' Matt shifted to face her fully. 'If I was lucky enough to have you, I'd never let you go.'

She stared back at him, confused. 'But that's exactly what you did.'

He hung his head. 'I thought I was doing the right thing. I wanted you to be sure. I *needed* you to be sure about your feelings for Henry.' When he looked up at her again, she saw his expression tighten. 'I didn't want to go through what I did with Patricia.'

Lottie remembered Jim's words. 'This is about the affair she had, isn't it?'

Pain was etched across his face. 'Tom was her first love. The guy she was dating when I first met her. Then Tom moved away, and she was devastated. Gradually we became friends, then lovers. Finally man and wife.' His eyes darted away from hers. 'Tom came back into her life a few years later. I knew she was catching up with him when I worked late. What I didn't know was the extent to which they'd slipped back into their old relationship.'

Lottie rubbed her chest, just above her heart, as everything started to make sense. He hadn't been pushing her away. He'd been protecting himself. 'Oh, Matt, I'm sorry you had to live through that.'

This time when he looked at her, his expression was fierce. 'I'd live through it again, as long as it brought me to you.'

Her heart flipped, and hope began to stir again, pushing against the sadness. 'What are you saying?'

He gave her a wry smile. 'I thought I'd been clear, that you understood how I felt, but then I realised I'd not actually said the words.' His face sobered, eyes finding hers. 'I need to get better at that, at talking about my feelings, but you need to know I love you. And I won't ever stop.' Joy spread, warming her from the inside, but he gave her no time to react. 'I understand if you decide to go back to Henry,' he continued, expression so earnest it nearly burst her swelling heart. 'But I couldn't let you do that without telling you how much you mean to me. How just the honour of knowing you has changed my life, changed *me*. These last few months have been incredible—'

She crushed his mouth with hers. 'God, will you just stop talking for a moment,' she told him between kisses, half laughing, half crying.

He pulled back, eyes clouded with confusion. 'Sorry.'

'No.' She put a hand on either side of his handsome face. 'Don't ever be sorry. I love listening to you, but this time I have something I need to tell you.' She smiled right into his eyes. 'I love you, too.'

Emotion burned through his gaze. 'You do?'

'I do.' She kissed him lightly, a promise of more. 'I enjoyed seeing Henry again, and he will always be dear to me, but I told him last night that my heart is yours, and has been for some time.'

Matt looked like he couldn't believe what was happening. 'That's why he went back early?'

'Yes. He called round this morning and said staying would be too hard.' Her smile wobbled, just a little, as she recalled the sadness on Henry's face. 'He told me to tell you Chewie clearly has more taste than I do.'

Matt briefly shut his eyes. 'He's probably right.'

She laughed, pressing her forehead to his, breathing him in. 'Chewie was jealous of you. Now he knows there's room for both of you in my heart, he's cool.'

Matt smiled. 'That dog is not cool.'

It didn't matter what he was saying, because Lottie could see right into Matt's eyes, and they were worshipping her. 'Are we really doing this then? You and me? A grown-up, serious relationship?'

'I warned you I didn't do light.' His mouth found hers, pressing soft, tender kisses. 'I don't just want next month or next year, Lottie. I want forever with you.'

Just when she thought her heart couldn't feel any fuller. 'Even if I tell you I need to expand the book club because I've got another interested member?'

His adoring smile didn't dim, his eyes didn't waver. 'Even then.'

'Even if I decide to run a second one? I'm thinking bonkbusters for the over-eighties. Find Audrey some like-minded friends.'

He paled, just a little, but his eyes never left hers. 'You can run a Fifty Shades Book Club and I'll still love you.' He dipped his head to kiss her. 'Though maybe we could find another venue for it?'

She started to laugh, but then he captured her mouth again, and this time there was no gentle, no light. This time the passion that lay tightly coiled beneath his cool, reserved surface broke free and swept them both away.

Chapter Thirty-Two

November meeting, nominated book:
Happy Ever After **by Nora Roberts**

Matt sipped at his gin as he looked around the animated group. Some things about the Beach Reads Book Club had changed in the last few months, but many had stayed the same.

Audrey still brought gin, still filled their glasses so full, the tonic barely had a chance to squeeze its way in. And she still brought sex into the conversation as often as she could.

Heidi still brought a cake, and it still tasted like the best cake you'd ever eaten.

Gira still had the most insightful comments.

Chewie still eyed up his shoes when he thought nobody was looking.

Sally still said exactly what she thought, without applying a filter.

Amy was still the quietest.

Lottie was still the inspiration, the one who coaxed more than just a book discussion from them all. She was still the one that lit up the room, though he had to concede he was a tiny bit biased.

'Matt, what did you think?' Lottie looked over at him, a smirk on her gorgeous face. She knew damn well he hadn't been listening.

'I thought the ending was very … apt.' One thing he'd learnt about the books the club read, they always had tidy, uplifting endings.

'Umm.' She shook her head, eyes dancing. 'Clever. Or it would have been if we hadn't been discussing what it is about Nora Roberts' writing that makes her such a superstar.'

He gave Lottie his best winning smile. The one she'd admitted made her belly flutter and her hormones swarm. 'She writes such apt endings?'

He still felt that little burst of pride when he made the group laugh. No longer did he stay in his office on a Thursday. Now he joined them – mark that down in the things-that-had-changed box. He couldn't say he read the books as voraciously as the others or – whisper it – that he always read them to the end, but he did enjoy the meetings. The way the discussion pinged easily from topic to topic, sometimes about the book, sometimes about life, always entertaining.

'She has an effortless, flowing style of writing.' Eve's voice cut across the laughter. The club's new member.

Which brought him to some of the other things that had changed.

He wasn't sure what to make of Eve. She'd declared she wanted to try the club out before committing to it, but this was now the third meeting she'd been to. She didn't fit easily with the others, at least not yet, though Lottie was drawing her out, chipping off her sharp edges.

'Ga.' A thump, followed by a delightful baby gurgle. 'Bababa.'

Freddie was now nine months old, and a proper club member. His highchair was part of their expanding circle and while his comments weren't erudite, his giggles never failed to raise a smile.

Even from Eve, Matt noticed, as a crack appeared in her usually austere face. 'I think he agrees with me.'

Audrey knocked back the rest of her glass. 'Maybe, love. Or maybe he's saying she writes good sex scenes. Not hot, mind, more … classy.'

Eve's eyes bulged and Matt worried he was seconds away from having to get down on his hands and knees and look for them when they popped out. 'Audrey, do you have to bring sex into every discussion?'

'Well, it does make the conversation more interesting,' Audrey countered. Then winked at Eve. 'Makes a book more interesting, too.'

Matt did a double take. Was Eve *blushing*? And while he was too polite to say anything, others weren't.

'OMG Eve, you're going red.' Sally giggled in a way that wasn't too dissimilar from that of her son, only hers had a naughty edge. 'I think you secretly like reading about sex.'

Matt held his breath as Eve slowly looked round the group. Was she ready to walk out? He noticed her halt at Lottie. Noticed too, Lottie giving her a wide, encouraging smile.

'I did read that *Fifty Shades* book you mentioned,' she said finally, turning back to Audrey. 'I can't say I enjoyed it that much.' She cleared her throat. 'Though it did do wonders for my sex life.'

The group burst out laughing, nobody more than Audrey. 'You devil, Eve. I always say, it's us quiet ones that you have to look out for.'

That sent another wave of laughter through everyone, including Eve this time.

'Is that why you joined us?' Sally smirked over at Eve. 'You wanted to read more books about sex?'

'You'll have to excuse Sally,' Lottie interrupted as Eve froze. 'We'd like to tape her mouth up sometimes, but it moves so much we can't manage it.'

Eve relaxed and Sally gave her an apologetic look. 'Lottie's right, my mouth moves before my brain engages. I meant it as a joke. None of us are shy about enjoying a well-written sex scene, but what we really want is a stonking good story with real, vivid characters.' Her eyes fell on Matt's. 'Romance before sex. Wouldn't you agree, Matt?'

Something else that had changed. His ability to take their teasing in his stride, even when it was about sex. He looked over at Lottie and felt the familiar heat, the rush of blood. The pull on his heart. 'Romance with sex is even better.'

Lottie rolled her eyes, a blush on her cheeks. But the smile she shot him was full of promise, and sent another bolt of arousal shooting through him.

Another thing that had changed – an important, miraculous change. Lottie and he now slept in the same bed every night. Sometimes it was at hers, more usually at his. Always, they were together.

The chairs were returned to their usual positions, the glasses taken to the kitchen. Freddie's highchair wiped down.

The end of another book club meeting. As requested, Lottie slipped the last slice of Heidi's sticky ginger cake into a bag for Jim. He was a frequent visitor to the club, but tonight he'd stayed at home to make dinner.

Home.

She'd started to think of Matt's place as home, she'd spent so much time there recently. Her house was practically uninhabitable since she'd begun stripping off the grotty wallpaper and Shaun, bless him, had started on the bathrooms. He would often join her on a Saturday while Matt and Amy were working in the shop. Sundays were her favourite days, though. That's when Matt – him of the designer clothes and healthy bank account – rolled up the sleeves of his Ralph Lauren denim shirt and joined her.

She'd discovered there was nothing sexier than the sight of Matt Steele with bits of paper in his hair, posh jeans splattered with woodchip, biceps bulging as he scraped off eighty-year-old wallpaper.

The sound of a throat being cleared interrupted her daydream and she turned to find Eve.

'Did you enjoy today's meeting?'

'Yes, thank you.' Eve fiddled with the strap of her handbag. 'You run it very differently to how I run mine.'

Lottie laughed. 'I suspect the gin makes a big difference. Loosens everyone's tongues.'

'Perhaps.' For the first time since she'd known her, Eve looked unsure. Vulnerable almost.

'You know, I don't believe there's a right or wrong way to run a book club.' Lottie made sure to catch Eve's eye. 'It just needs to be right for the people you're running it for.'

Eve glanced towards the rest of the group. 'I can see my club wouldn't be right for Audrey.'

'No. But this club wouldn't be right for people who want an in-depth discussion, who prefer more literary books.' She smiled. 'It isn't a competition, it's about bringing the joy of books to all readers, no matter what their tastes.' She thought of Jim, of what they were going to discuss tonight. 'In fact I think the more book clubs, the better. Let's get everyone reading and enjoying books as much as we do.'

'Yes, you're right.' Eve looked like she was about to go, but then spoke again. 'If people enjoy a wide range of genres, they could belong to more than one club.'

'Of course.'

She gave a sharp nod of her head. 'Then I look forward to seeing you here again for the December meeting.'

As she watched her stride off, Lottie felt a warm hand clasp hers. 'Everything okay?'

She leant into Matt, her heart feeling full. 'Everything is perfect. I think Eve and I have just come to an understanding.'

'Good.' His lips found her temple and he gave her one of his tender, heart-melting kisses. Always discreet, but letting her know she was cherished.

Slowly everyone drifted away and Matt locked up. They found Shaun hovering outside, clearly waiting for Amy.

'Are you joining us tonight?' Matt asked when he spotted him.

Shaun shook his head, grinning as he wrapped his arm around Amy. 'No way. Your dad's cooking. I'm not that brave.'

Amy giggled. 'That's mean.'

Matt laughed. 'But accurate. Have a good night, the pair of you.'

Lottie sighed with contentment as she watched them head off, hand in hand, back to Shaun's new flat. 'Young love. Isn't it sweet?'

Suddenly she was pinned against the shop, Matt's smiling mouth inches from hers. 'What do you call our love?'

She bit into her lip, laughter brimming. 'Nearly middle-aged love?'

He shook his head. 'You can do better than that.'

'Passionate love?'

His gaze heated and he kissed her, long and deep. 'Close.'

Her eyes drank him in. 'True love.'

He kissed her again, gentler this time. 'Amen to that.'

When they arrived back at the house, Jim greeted them with his oven gloves on. 'There you are. Chewie and I were about to send out a search party.'

'We're hardly late,' Matt countered mildly, taking her coat and hanging it up neatly on the peg along with his own.

'Maybe not, but your young lady and I have got a lot to talk about. We need to crack on.' With that he bustled back into the kitchen.

A frown creased Matt's brow as he looked down at her. 'Are you aware of this?'

'Of course.'

He looked put out. 'Why am I not involved?'

'Because you don't have the necessary expertise,' she teased.

He raised his eyebrows. 'I think you'll find I've got plenty of expertise where it matters.'

'I agree, but your dad needs a more cerebral expertise.'

Before Matt could put voice to the question he was clearly dying to ask, Jim shouted from the kitchen, 'Shift your backsides in here before it gets cold!'

'What are we eating?' Matt asked as they sat down at the kitchen island.

'What does it look like?' his dad replied crossly.

Matt's gaze drifted over to her, amusement flickering across a face that was far more relaxed, far more open than it used to be. And even more handsome for it. 'I'm not sure.'

'Cheeky sod.' Jim spooned a healthy amount of … something onto their plates. 'It's cottage pie, only I forgot the carrots, so I've just shoved them in with the potato.'

'There's a reason I'm in charge of cooking round here,' Matt murmured.

'Aye, well, me and Lottie have more important things to focus on.' Jim shovelled a mouthful onto his fork. 'So, this book club lark. How do I start setting it up?'

Matt spluttered, putting down his fork. 'What?'

Jim gave Matt a bland look. 'I'm going to run a book club. Lottie's helping me.' He pushed more of the pie onto his fork. 'We're going to focus on murder mysteries.'

'You, running a book club?' Matt said slowly.

'And why not? For the past year you've done nothing but bleat on about me getting out more. Well, now I will.'

Lottie had to fight not to laugh. It was a measure of how far their relationship had moved forward that father and son could now take the piss out of each without either taking offence.

'Don't get me wrong, I think it's a great idea,' Matt countered. 'I'm just wondering where you're planning on holding this new club of yours.'

Jim gave his son a sly grin. 'Where else? Just got to think of a name.' He reached for the bottle of wine he'd put on the table. 'And stock the café up with a booze that isn't gin.'

As the pair of them began to reel off suggested names – Murder Reads Book Club, Who Dun It Club – Lottie felt a sense of *déjà vu*. It hadn't even been a year since she'd sat in the bookshop with Gira and Heidi, deciding on the name for the Beach Reads Book Club.

Yet how different her life felt now.

The club had given her a fresh purpose, and a group of staunch, loyal friends.

It had made her realise that being able to talk to people was a strength. An attribute she should be proud of, though okay, maybe she shouldn't have done it quite so much at school during class.

Her gaze lingered on Matt and a deep, satisfying warmth filled her chest. The book club had also brought her love.

Just then he glanced up, his eyes meeting hers. 'You're unusually quiet.'

'I can't get a word in edgeways.' She smiled. 'You're such a chatterbox, Matt Steele.'

Acknowledgments

My first big thank you is to my amazing publisher One More Chapter. It's a real pleasure to work for such a professional, energetic, positive publisher. And speaking of professional, energetic and positive, a massive thank you to my editor, Charlotte Ledger, for being so supportive, so inspiring and for providing yet another fabulous book idea. When she suggested the title, *The Beach Reads Book Club*, I immediately had this picture in my head of an eclectic group of friends, chatting about everything and nothing (oh, and occasionally books) while swigging gin and tonics on the beach. Perhaps not everyone's idea of a book club, but thankfully Charlotte gave me free rein to let my imagination run riot and form a book club I'd love to be part of. Thank you also to the lovely Bethan Morgan for being my go-to for any and all questions, and to Lucy Bennett for providing yet another gorgeous book cover.

The character I had most fun writing has to be Audrey,

and I'm so sad that the inspiration behind her, my own Aunt Audrey, is no longer with us. Hopefully her daughter, Shelley, and her granddaughters, Kirsty and Karley, will read this and see some of their wonderful Mum and Nan (though Aud's love of talking about sex is purely fiction!). I have such fond memories of her holding court while my mum and dad, Aunt Shirley and Uncle Bob all chuckled. And while Audrey's husband, my Uncle Harold, rolled his eyes, wondering no doubt what on earth she was going to say next.

I had a great time putting together the 'play' list of books for each meeting. I wanted them to help drive the story, but I also wanted to include those I'd loved reading. It meant some were chosen for their titles (*The Love Square*) and others snuck in just because I couldn't not include them (*Gone Too Far*, *The Truest Thing*). All but one were books I really enjoyed (my thoughts on that one were in line with Gira's!).

Thank you once again to all my friends and family still gamely showing an interest in my writing; my Mum and Dad 2 (Anne and Keith), cousins Shelley, Karley, Kath, Kirsty and Hayley, my sis-in-law Jayne, friends Laura, Sonia, Jane, Carol, Tara and Priti (yep, you keep reading them, I'll keep writing them). And of course thank you and a huge hug to my own very special octogenarian, my lovely Mum – here's another one for you, you'll have to read quicker!

To my husband, who gritted his teeth and ploughed his way through an earlier version of this so he could spot any howlers for me, I promise I won't make you read another romcom … until the next time!

Finally, a massive thanks to you, the reader, for buying *The Beach Reads Book Club*. I sincerely hope it brought you a little sunshine.